RED GRANITE
The Grains of Truth
Beneath the Sands of Egypt

ALEXANDER RETROV

IV

SAQQARA - ABUSIR

RED GRANITE

The Grains of Truth Beneath the Sands of Egypt
IV
Saqqara - Abusir

Alexander Retrov

Editor: Alexander Retrov
Graphic Design: Goran Djcinovic
Publisher: Renaissance Entertainment Pty Ltd
Printer: Amazon books

This work is 90% fact and 10% fiction.
It's up to you to determine which is which.

To see the truth for yourself and join Krystal or Alex
on one of the Red Granite or Goddess Reawakening Tours
go to the website for more details on the next tour.

www.alexanderretrov.com

© 2018 Renaissance Entertainment Ltd Pty
Second edition
First edition printed in Australia by Eureka Printing
ISBN: 978-0-9943146-6-6

www.alexanderretrov.com

RED GRANITE

The Grains of Truth
Beneath the Sands of Egypt

IV

Saqqara - Abusir

ACKNOWLEDGEMENTS

My deep gratitude goes to Krystal,
without whose support and patience
this book would never have been written.

I also want to acknowledge Source
for choosing me as the conduit for this work

To my brother in Egypt, Abdou Ashour

This book is dedicated to the truth.

CHAPTER 28 – ONE STEP AT A TIME

I knew this tunnel; I'd been in it before, the tension, the excitement, the danger. But this time it was different; I was deep within it, deep within the earth, deep in trouble. This time it was crunch time, something was about to happen, *had* to happen. We hit a T-intersection and went to head left. Saeed grabbed me by the strap of my backpack and pulled me back.

'No, not that way, Dummy, it leads straight to the Embassy?'

'But isn't that where we want to go?'

'It is if you want to walk into a trap; there is a hidden shaft of deadly cobras guarding the entrance. This way!'

Saeed took off to the right and, after briefly hesitating, I quickly followed. However, moments later we turned the next corner and found ourselves at a dead end. I groped around the walls searching for some hidden lever or trigger that would open a secret door.

'Nothing. Brilliant!'

I heard the shrieking caws of vultures and spun around to look back down the tunnel just as a torrent of water surged around the corner, Amun Priests morphed as crocodiles and Secret Police as spitting cobras riding the turgid waves on surfboards of sarcophagus lids.

Turning back to face the end of the corridor, I frantically fumbled the wall, feeling the arrows of venom being shot out by the cobras fizzing into the centre of my backpack.

'Fuck, where the hell is the release?'

'Feel the stone.'

The voice was coming from the shadows beside us.

'I *am* feeling the stone.'

'No, you're touching the stone. *Feel* the stone.'

With the cacophony of sound rapidly approaching, I placed my hands gingerly on the end wall, closed my eyes and tried to tune in. At first there was nothing, but then I heard, or rather *felt*, a faint low hum; what did it mean, what do I do now? I started humming along with it and instantly felt the stone start to groan and rumble.

'Saeed, put your hands on the wall and do as I do.'

'What?'

'Just do it.'

He placed his hands on the wall and I changed from humming to toning "Ah". The minute Saeed joined in, the wall shuddered and started sliding into the side wall of the corridor. On the other side of the doorway stood Crystal, dressed as an Egyptian High Priestess, behind her a large open chamber with ornate columns.

'Hurry up, we're nearly there.'

There? Where? I didn't think we were going anywhere in particular, I thought Saeed and I were trying to escape *from* somewhere. Never-the-less, Saeed and I quickly scrambled through, the cascading waters advancing rapidly down the corridor.

Then I saw, ahead of our adversaries, Nemo, frantically flipping and flopping, dolphining through the bow-wave, dodging the snapping jaws of the crocodiles and lighting strikes of the cobras. He was struggling, clearly tired, but determined to stay ahead of the marauding menace that was bearing down on him.

'Come on, Nemo, you can make it.'

The sliding door started closing, the gap decreasing; this was not a good sign. Three feet, two feet, it was going to be touch and go whether Nemo would make it or not. The gap was down to about six inches and Nemo still had about six feet to go. At the same time, the crocodiles and cobras were zeroing in on him.

'Just a little further, you can do it!'

The opening was down to three inches, barely enough for Nemo to squeeze through, but he was within reach. In one last ditched effort, a huge cobra lunged towards him and …

…an alarm went off behind me in the chamber, pulling my attention away from the outcome. By the time I'd regained my senses, I was lying in bed in my hotel room. Did the door slam shut and did Nemo make it through before it did, or did the cobra clasp him tightly in its fangs?

I turned my alarm off, dragged myself out of bed into the shower as was dressed by the time there was a knock at the door.

'Mr. Alex, breakfast.'

'Thanks; I'll be right out. I'll have it in the lounge.'

'Very good.'

I picked up my iphone and laptop and headed off to the lounge, where Abdo had set up breakfast and was sitting working on his laptop.

'Abdo! Good to see you.'

He stood to greet me with a huge embrace.

'Mr. Alex, good morning, how are you my friend? You are sleeping well?'

'Like a baby.'

'Oh, I am sorry, you have spat it your dummy and wet the bed.'

Clearly Abdo had not only picked up some Australian colloquial sayings from other Aussie travellers, but some of their sense of humour as well. I decided to let it go through to the keeper.

'Can you put my notebook in the safe please?'

'Certainly.'

'While you're there, can you do me a favour?'

'Yes, of course.'

With Saeed back in Luxor, and Mohammed in Hawarra, there became a point when I had to trust someone else local, someone other than Mark and Frank, if I was going to escape Egypt alive *and* with Kareem's papers. I figured Abdo was the likely candidate.

'There's a pile of papers in a folio I left in the safe earlier. If you have time this morning, could you do me a huge favour and scan them for me, as jpegs or pdfs?'

'But of course.'

'Thanks. They're…ah.. rather sensitive, so *please* don't let anyone else read, or even *see* them, OK?'

'Not a problem, it will be fine. You have it the USB stick?'

'No, do you?'

'Not here, no, but I will go and buy it one for you.'

'Thanks, just let me know how much it costs.'

I took the opportunity over breakfast to flick through the files on my iphone to see if I had anything on Abu Raoush. There wasn't much, but fortunately I had at least a page about it.

"Called 'Djedefre's Starry Sky', the pyramid of Abu Raoush belongs to Djedefre, son of Khufu, and the third ruler of the 4th Dynasty."

Well, I didn't believe that for starters. If Djedefre was Khufu, who was Imhotep, or at the very least the son of Imhotep, then, according to my reading of the evidence from this and other pyramids, Djedefre was at best responsible for repairing Abu Raoush. However I would reserve judgment until not only reading the rest of my notes, but, more importantly, seeing the pyramid with my own eyes.

"Part of the very northern part of the necropolis of the ancient Egyptian capital of Memphis, the pyramid is Egypt's most northerly pyramid, located near the village of Abu Raoush on the plateau of Gaa, about eight kilometres north of the Giza pyramids and about fifteen kilometres west of Cairo. It sits atop Gebel Abu Raoush, at an elevation of about 150 metres above the Giza Plateau, in the continuation of the Gebel el-Ghigiga on the western fringe of the Nile Valley, and is bounded to the north by the depression of Wadi Qarun and the south by Wadi el-Hassanah."

I wasn't so much interested in its geography, more in its geology.

"For unknown reasons, Djedefre abandoned the necropolis at Giza and built his pyramid at Abu Raoush. The move to this location is an odd but interesting choice, and it is often suggested that Djedefre had some sort of falling out with his family, or at least his brothers, as his successor, Khafre, immediately returned to Giza. However, this conflict with his family is far from certain, and more recent evidence suggests that there were in fact no problems at all."

Well of course it's uncertain, especially if Djedefre was Imhotep and the pyramid at Abu Raoush wasn't build during the 4th Dynasty at all, but thousands of years earlier. The paragraph was a perfect example of the dangers of 'presumptive speculation' and of future generations just accepting that speculation to be fact. Rather than just say, "we don't know", the early Egyptologists ascribed ownership to structures based on the flimsiest of evidence and subsequent generations of archaeologists have just accepted those ascriptions as true, then invented 'conflicts' and other fictitious storylines to support their misconceptions and false premises.

"Although briefly investigated by Lepsius, then Perring, and later by Petrie in the 1880s, the earliest excavations and first systematic investigation of the ruins didn't occur until the beginning of the 20th Century, when, between 1900 and 1902, Emile Chassinat of the French Institute of Oriental Archaeology in Cairo, discovered the remains of a funerary settlement, a boat pit, and numerous statuary fragments that had the name of Didoufri (an early reading of Djedefre), which allowed for the identification of the tomb owner."

That contained so many stabs in the dark it was like a blindfolded Jack the Ripper let loose in the deepest underground chamber at midnight. It would be like me finding the head of a Barbie-doll in the garbage of the White House and deducing that the President of the United States was a nine-year old girl.

"Although much of the destruction of the site had previously been attributed to the 4th Dynasty, recent discoveries have indicated that the complex began to deteriorate at the beginning of the Roman period, when the Romans maintained a sizable force in this location due to its tactical elevation, and it served as a quarry. The stone continued to be quarried into modern times, and in fact, the site was in much better condition in 1839 when Perring and Vyse visited it, than it is today."

Miffed at the range of 'fictions' I was having to endure, I scanned through the next paragraph that detailed numerous other investigations and regions in the necropolis including; a Coptic monastery, crocodile burials from the Late Period, a Thinite necropolis, a Middle Kingdom fortress, mastaba tombs from the 5th and 6th Dynasties, graves from the 3rd and 4th Dynasties, and a necropolis of the Early Dynastic Period.

If there were so many archaeological sites there then why was the area designated a military zone? Simple, there was clearly a lot of 'stuff' being discovered beneath the surface that the Egyptian Authorities were keeping for themselves and not telling the world about. Military Zone? Fuck off, that was just a modern name for 'Treasure hunt'. Despite all that, without any notable discoveries to go by, I felt the key to my theories, as it had been at the other sites, was the pyramid itself, around which everything else was centred.

However, two choice tit-bits caught my attention. The first, was that several objects bearing the names of the 1st Dynasty pharaohs, Aha and Den, were found near the pyramid, and the second, was that part of a statue of Queen Arsinoe II, the sister and wife of Ptolemy II Philadelphus, the second ruler of Egypt's Greek Period, was discovered in the nearby Wadi. That meant the area covered almost the entire span of the dynastic history of ancient Egypt, and to me that meant it had some special significance. What exactly that significance was, I had no idea. Hopefully I would find out when I got there.

There were a few more paragraphs dealing with actual details about the pyramid and its surrounds, but, as it was 5:59, I figured they could wait until I arrived on site, so I finished up my juice and headed out the door.

'I'm not sure when I'll be back, but it should sometime around lunch.'

'Do you need it a taxi?'

'No thanks, Abdo, I'm being picked up downstairs.'

'Very good, enjoy your day.'

Frank and Mark were waiting downstairs, the streets waking to the calls of the day. As I climbed into the back seat, I paused to watch a young teen on a bike balancing a massive sheet of wood on his head that must have had a thousand freshly-baked buns stacked high on it. As he slalomed down the road navigating his way around cars, horses and pedestrians, for a split second I contemplated our two lives. His seemed so simple, so predictable, and yet there he was exhibiting a feat of skill that was astonishing to behold. And my life? Mine was growing more complex with every day, and the only skill that seemed to be prevailing was the ability to unearth hidden-secret after hidden-secret about the true history of ancient Egypt, and dig myself deeper and deeper into a hole in the process.

Getting underway, Mark was quick to cut to the chase.

'Slight change of plan, we're going to Zawiyet el-Aryan first, then to Abu Raoush, and we'll leave the Embassy 'til last.'

'How come?'

'After we dropped you off last night, Frank and I got talking about all the possible outcomes of you going to the Embassy; we think you need a safeguard, just in case.'

I didn't tell them about my dream that night, but expressed my concerns.

'Me too, I've been thinking about what Saeed said; maybe it's not such a good idea, what if the Secret Police are expecting me?'

'I'm pretty sure they will be; if the Secret Police are smart, and in this case we do know they're on to you, then they'll most likely have the airport covered, and they'll know you need a new passport. They'll know you have to go to the Embassy, but they won't want you to get inside and hand over the documents. Once you're inside, it'll be too late, so Frank and I think they'll be waiting for you outside the Embassy, ambush you, and arrest you before you get through the gates.'

'Great! So why would I go, I don't have a death wish?'

As pragmatic as ever, Frank chose his words succinctly.

'Because there's also a chance they may *not* be there; the country is so fractionalised at the moment, disorganized, distrustful, everyone is looking out for themselves, the sites are being looted by the very people charged to protect them, and communications between factions of the police departments and the military may not be as harmonious and affable as we might be led to believe.'

Mark took over.

'At the very least, the Embassy needs to know about your circumstances, *and* about the papers. If you don't contact them, and you don't make it to your boat in Alexandria, or out of the country, then there's little Frank and I can do to help, and the papers are probably lost forever.'

'Did you get my email?'

'Yeah, that's good thinking, and, as soon as you get the scans, send me the copies. And that'll be great, that protects the papers, but it doesn't cover your ass in case anything goes wrong.'

'So what do you suggest?'

'You and I are about the same age and appearance, so my guess is that if the Secret Police *are* there, they'll easily mistake me for you; I doubt there's many Aussies in Egypt at the moment....'

He held up an A4 envelope.

'...So I'll go in first, carrying an envelope containing some innocuous legal papers. If I'm not stopped, you'll know the coast is clear and can follow me in.'

'What if they are there, what if they *do* stop you?'

'Then you and Frank will know they're there and you can make your escape while I delay them. I'll just play it dumb, show them my passport, tell them I'm a lawyer here on official Embassy business, even create a bit of a scene if necessary. They've got nothing on me, and no one can connect us.'

'What about the Colonel at Hawarra, and the Antiquities Police at Meidum and Dahshur?'

'I wouldn't be worried about them; if they knew anything about you, they would have done something at the time. Besides, to them, you were just another university professor joining us to check out the sites.'

5

'I suppose it's Ok. But how is that a better option than me just not going?'

'Because if the police *are* there, once they realize they've got the wrong person and let me go, I'll go inside and tell the Embassy officials all about you and the papers, give them a heads-up, so that if you *are* captured they'll know exactly what's been going on.'

I wasn't too happy with Mark putting himself on the line for me, but, as he said, they actually didn't have anything on him, so maybe it would be OK.

'I guess so. So, where are we heading first again?'

'Zawiyet el-Aryan...'

As Mark filled me in I pulled out my iphone and flicked through my Egypt file for any reference to it.

'...It's four kilometres south of Giza, on the west bank of the Nile almost opposite Memphis, on a slightly elevated area just on the edge of the desert, and just before Abu Ghurab. It's a relatively unknown area that contains two unfinished pyramids and supposedly nothing else.'

'Maybe they haven't dug deep enough?'

'You may be right, but I doubt it.'

'Why?'

'Because Zawiyet el-Aryan is another military zone.'

'Shit!'

At first I was a little shocked, because I thought we were headed back into danger, but then I figured, that like at Meidum and Dahshur, they wouldn't be expecting me, so I got a tad excited, because to me "military zone" sounded like another neon sign that there was "stuff" to be discovered below the surface.

Zawiyet el-Aryan

As we hit the outskirts of the city, I couldn't help but notice the roadblock was still in place on the other side of the road, the path in to town. It seems they didn't anticipate me *leaving* the city. Hopefully that was also the case heading north to Alexandria.

Turning back to my iphone, I found a few notes and several photos about Zawiyet el-Aryan.

"Dating to the 3rd Dynasty, the older, and most advanced, of the two pyramids at Zawiyet el-Aryan is called the Layered Pyramid by Egyptologists, and Haram el-Meduwara, or the 'Round Pyramid', by locals. If it had been completed, it would have been a Step Pyramid, and it's layer structure is still quite evident despite the fact it appears as a pile of rubble 16m high.

In 1896 Jacques de Morgan discovered the descending entrance passageway, but its subterranean corridors were not explored until the Italian archaeologist Alessandro Barsanti excavated in 1900. However, most of the pyramid has still never really been investigated.'

'It says here the Layered Pyramid at Zawiyet el-Aryan has never really been investigated.'

From the front seat, Frank scoffed.

'Well, that's what they tell us, but I for one don't believe it for a minute. What are they going to say, "we've just started digging and already we've found evidence of civilization going back hundreds of thousands of years"? I doubt it. My guess is they did a little digging, found something of great interest, and turned the whole thing into a military zone until such time as they could plan to rob it blind.'

Mark was a little more on the curious side.

'What else does it say there?'

"The identity of the builder of the Layered Pyramid at Zawyet el-Aryan is not known with certainty, and there is no mention of his name in the monument itself. However, a nearby niched mastaba, designated Z-500, contained eight alabaster vessels with the name of Horus Khaba, a 3rd Dynasty King, impressed on the seal in red ink. Therefore, as it was customary for members of the nobility to be buried near their king, this has been taken as evidence that the pyramid was built for Khaba."

That really got Frank going.

'Oh, come on, can you believe these guys? Just because they found the vessels in the mastaba doesn't mean the mastaba belonged to that period, they could have been put there at any time after the reign of Khaba. That's like claiming the Cathedral of Notre Dame was built at the same time as the Eiffel Tower just because they're both in Paris.'

'It also says they found a pottery fragment with the name of the Horus Narmer.'

'There you go! Who's to say that the mastaba wasn't built by Narmer in the 1st Dynasty and then usurped by Khaba four hundred years later? And that makes sense to me, that the mastabas start when the dynasties start, but it doesn't mean the pyramid dates to the same period.'

'So when does it date to?'

'That's the sixty-four-thousand-dollar question! There's been no trace of a burial found there and even the surrounding galleries were found empty, which the Egyptologists would have us believe is because whoever built it died prematurely. Now wouldn't you think they'd still bury him there, or maybe the next pharaoh would finish it and use it? No, that would be too logical an assumption.

Despite that *minor* consideration, If you do choose to believe the Egyptologists, it dates to around the second half of the 3rd Dynasty, primarily because the substructure of the pyramid is very similar to the substructure of the pyramid of Sekhemkhet at Saqqara, which implies they must have been built around the same time, and because the Layered Pyramid at Zawyet el-Aryan is geographically located between Sekhemkhet's pyramid and the pyramid of Snefru at Meidum.'

'But from our visit to Meidum and Dahshur yesterday, we figured out the substructures predated the pyramids, and the superstructures were only repaired by Snefru.'

'Yeah, I know, and we figured it out in the space of…what…a few hours; they've had decades to examine the pyramids.'

'You think they're lying, covering up the truth?'

'Does a bear shit in the woods? They're either covering up the truth or they're as blind as bats and as dumb as dog shit!'

I looked for more clues, and what better place to start than with the subterranean chambers.

'The entrance to the substructure is a few metres north of the pyramid's north east corner and runs west for 36 metres until it terminates at the north-central axis of the pyramid with a vertical shaft.

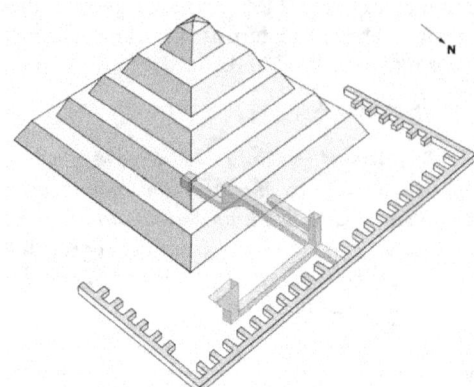

At the base of the shaft, to the right, a short corridor leads to a perpendicular U-shaped comb-like gallery, 120 metres long, 1.4 metres wide and 1.8 metres in height, running east-west, before doing a 90° turn to the south for a further 38 metres. Along the inner wall are 32 storage annexes, 1.6 metres wide and 5 metres long, intended for the burial equipment. 20 projects southwards from the east-west corridor and 6 from each of the two north-south corridors...'

'Nothing much there.'

I read on.

'...Another corridor, heading left from the shaft, leads 80 metres via a short sloping ramp and another final corridor directly to an empty burial chamber, 3.63 metres in length, 2.65 metres wide, and 3 metres in height, 26 metres below the surface, and located exactly under the vertical axis of the pyramid. However, this corridor is small, and it would have been almost impossible to move any decent sized sarcophagus through it to the burial chamber. In fact, there was no sarcophagus found in the burial chamber, nor evidence of any burial.'

Frank was unmoved.

'That's all very interesting, but it doesn't say what the substructure was actually made of.'

'My guess is granite, at least for the chamber...'

But I guessed that would have to wait until we saw it for ourselves.

'...Maybe there are some clues in the superstructure?...'

I returned to my notes.

'...A step pyramid in the early stages of construction, the superstructure of the Layer Pyramid is typical of 3rd Dynasty masonry, consisting of 14 accretion layers leaning inward against a central core, each layer having a dressed outer face, with coarser masonry backing, and all bonded with a thick, clay mortar. Had it been finished, it would have risen by 5 steps to a height of around 45 metres, but no trace of the casing stones has been found, indicating that the pyramid was never finished."

'Of course it was finished, it just wasn't what the Egyptologists think it should have been, and the reason they haven't found any casing stones is probably because there weren't any.'

'Though, according to this, they found *"considerable mud-brick around the pyramid"*, which would support the idea that the pyramid was cased in mud-brick, rather than limestone, and that it was a later addition.'

'You would think so, but most Egyptologists believe the bricks were used for construction ramps, left behind when the pyramid was unfinished.'

'That's crazy! It's clear the pyramid was finished in stages; subterranean chamber first, then possibly a ziggurat, then the steps. It's only the mud-brick additions after the structures have been damaged that have caused all the confusion.'

'You don't have to convince me, but try telling that to the so-called experts...'

As he spoke, the car pulled off the road and stopped outside a village shop.

'...Anyway, I wouldn't bother about it too much, we aren't headed there.'

That caught me completely by surprise.

'We're not? I thought we were going to Zawiyet el-Aryan?'

'We are, but not to the Step Pyramid, we're headed about a mile-and-a-half north of there, to the Unfinished Pyramid.'

'Can we detour?'

'Easier said than done I'm afraid; as the pyramids are in a military zone, it depends what our guide says, and, speak of the devil...'

When a middle-aged man approached the car, Frank quickly jumped out to greet him. After a brief discussion, they both climbed aboard, our guide in the back with Mark and me. After being reacquainted with Mark, Frank introduced our guide to me.

'Alex, this is Hassan. Hassan, Alex.'

'Assalaam Alaikum.'

'Wa Alaikum Assalaam, Mr. Alex.'

The car took off and I threw the question of the day back around.

'So, the Layered Pyramid?'

Frank brushed off my forthrightness and turned to our guide.

'Hassan, Alex was wondering, what are the chances of visiting the Layered Pyramid as well?'

The shake of his head and the look on his face said it all.

'Sorry, no, the Layer Pyramid it is not possible; not today.'

It was as if I had asked Hassan to go skinny-dipping in a pool filled with man-eating great white sharks. Frank simply shrugged his shoulders.

'Sorry, Alex, no go.'

'Such is life! Oh well, the Unfinished Pyramid it is.'

So, as Frank, Mark and Hassan exchanged formalities and discussed local politics, I took the opportunity to find out about our destination.

The Unfinished Pyramid

"Simply referred to as the 'Unfinished Pyramid of Zawiyet el-Aryan', based on its stylistic features, the pyramid was probably built sometime during the 4th Dynasty. It is not known for certain which king is responsible for its construction, although it has been speculated that it was built by Bakara, a little known king who ruled for a very brief time between the reigns of Khafre and Menkaure."

How original! I wondered how, if they didn't know which pharaoh it had been built for, how they knew it was built in the 4th Dynasty? Stylistic features? What if the Egyptologists were comparing the Unfinished Pyramid to other pyramids they had incorrectly attributed to the 4th Dynasty?

"Even less is known about the Unfinished Pyramid at Zawiyet el-Aryan than about the Layered Pyramid. Fragmentary hieratic inscriptions have been found that appear to indicate a name such as Nebka, or Wehemka, but they are difficult to read and may refer to a Baka who was also known as Nebkare or Beufre, the Bicheris on Manetho's king list."

Even if they did refer to Bakara, and that was by no means confirmed, that didn't mean the pyramid belonged to him; the inscriptions could just as easily be later additions, cartouches of the king who attempted to repair the pyramid.

"The pyramid was intended to measure about 200 by 200 metres, however, work probably ended after only one year, but, if finished, the pyramid would have been nearly as big as Khafre's pyramid at Giza."

If Frank was right, and the pyramid *was* completed, then how was the size of the pyramid relevant to its function, if at all? And was there any direct correlation and comparison between the size of one pyramid and any and all of the others? Or, was it not so much its size, as its location?

Did it have something to do with its proximity to the Nile, or was it more of a special relationship to the Layered Pyramid, and to all the other pyramids? Maybe it had something to do with both?

Cogitating my navel wasn't going to do much, and, since we weren't able to visit the Layered Pyramid, my guess was I'd find some answers, or, if not answers, clues, within my notes.

The first thing I found was a diagram showing the alignment of all the pyramids in the northern region of the Lower Nile. From Abu Raoush through Giza, Zawiyet el-Aryan, Abu Ghurab, Abusir, Saqqara, and on to the ancient city of Memphis, they were all there in a seemingly perfect straight line; too much of a coincidence to be ignored. But what was the significance?

The angle created between that alignment and the lines of latitude was 51.85 degrees, approximately the angle of the inclination of several pyramids, including the Great Pyramid, which was 51.50 degrees. That couldn't just be a coincidence, could it?

The next image seemed to be drawing a direct relationship between several of those pyramids on the ground and specific stars in the southern sky. Assigning the ancient city of Heliopolis to the star Sirius, Abusir was represented as Betelgeuse, and Abu Raoush was Rigel, both in the constellation of Orion.

It meant we were looking south, and something about that didn't seem right, as most things in ancient Egypt seemed to be related to the west, east, or north. But, if it *was* right, then what was the significance and what did Abu Ghurab and Zawiyet el-Aryan represent. In either case, it was a clue; the location of the pyramids probably had something to do with the stars.

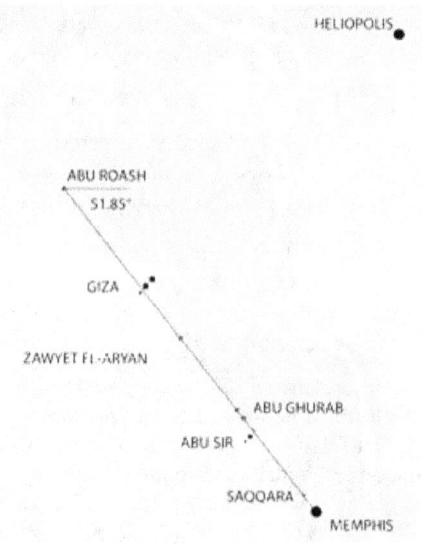

Moments later, the car left the cultivated area and headed out into the desert, stopping at what I presumed was the site of the Unfinished Pyramid. As we trekked through the sand towards the eastern side of the structure, we passed through the remains of an enclosure wall, made of fieldstone and clay that was at least four hundred metres long. Apart from that, according to my diagram, there was nothing else other than the pyramid, with its northern entrance and the inner chamber; it was the most basic site I'd been to so far.

'What exactly is it you're looking for, Frank?'
'Don't rightly know, but I'll know it when I see it.'

All I could see was the remainders of a square base, maybe ten to fifteen metres high, on or around which the core of the pyramid would have been constructed, hardly anything that was going to change the history of the planet, let alone ancient Egypt.

Frank may not have found what he was looking for, but I was seeing the evidence I needed to support my Thera theory. It was easy to see how a tsunami would have swept over the area. Perhaps the reason they hadn't found any mortuary temples or other structures was because they were obliterated or below thirty feet of sand and silt.

So was the pyramid unfinished, or had the top been completely swept away? Given the Giza pyramids were still in place, and visible only a few kilometres away to the north, if the Unfinished Pyramid was finished, it was highly likely it would have been similarly completed with limestone blocks, as, if it had, then like at Giza, there would still be parts of the superstructure in place. However, if it had been completed with mud-brick, then the blocks may well have been washed away. But that didn't ring true either, as there were no traces of mud-brick, like there were at Hawarra, Meidum and Dahshur. So, was it unfinished, or deliberately made without a top and finished?

We moved quickly around to the northern side, towards the entrance; it was like we were on a limited timeline, and, truth be told, going from Hassan's continued scanning of the horizon, we probably were.

The entrance itself was up the rise, and, unlike the usual small opening leading to a narrow descending passage, this was a wide open-cut trench, about six to eight metres wide, that descended about fifty metres or more inwards, and twenty metres deep, into the bedrock and the heart of the pyramid. The descending passage was steep, with no handrails or steps, and looked very treacherous indeed.

While I was primarily looking at the sedimentary layer, or layers, on top of the bedrock, which were at least twenty feet deep, Frank had thrown caution to the wind and headed straight off down the slope.
'No, no. It is not possible.'

Our guide looked at Frank as if he was about to step into a crocodile pit, and maybe, in some way, he was.
'I just want to have a look around; a few minutes at the most.'

Our guide clearly he wasn't happy and did another concerned scan of the horizon before gesturing for Frank to return.
'No, too dangerous, this it is not allowed.'

Frank was miffed, but respected the guide's decision and reluctantly stepped back up and out of the trench. Our descent into the 'burial' chamber thwarted, the only option left was to do a lap around the top of the trench, which we did, examining the fine cut walls.
'Look at the precision.'

Mark was right; the walls were almost gun-barrel straight. It wasn't the sort of technological precision you'd expect from people who used mud-bricks to build a pyramid.

And if the evidence of the tombs in the Valley of the Kings was anything to go by, it didn't make sense that you would quarry out massive amounts of limestone to create a burial tomb when they could have just tunnelled into the bedrock, unless it had something to do with the composition of the chamber itself. And what did they fill the trench in with, the very limestone blocks they had cut out? If so, where were they now?

'Oh, shit!'

Frank had stopped at the intersection of the trench and was looking down into where the inner chambers would have been.

'What is it?'

'They've filled it in.'

Sure enough, the bottom of the trench, where the chamber would have been, was covered with sand.

'What were you hoping to find?'

'According to excavation notes and photos from the early 20th Century by Jean-Phillip Lauer, the bottom of that long, sloping corridor was paved with huge blocks of granite and limestone, and there was a massive granite sarcophagus with an intact cover, but no body inside.'

That instantly got my attention.

'Granite! A massive granite sarcophagus just like at Hawarra, Mazghuna and Dahshur?'

'Not quite; this one is apparently in the form of an oval; I've got a copy of a photo of it on my ipad back in the car. There's also supposed to be evidence of underground chambers, but further excavations have "not been possible" because the pyramid is now part of a military reserve.'

I looked around at the desert that surrounded us.

'It seems a common pattern doesn't it, discover something extraordinary in the middle of nowhere and then declare the site a military site, Dahshur, Giza, here; that way the archaeologists and truth seekers of the world can't get access even if they wanted.'

Mark was right with me.

'And, in the meantime, the corrupt elite of the Supreme Council and the Illuminati, once led by your favourite megalomaniac and mine, Zahi Hawass, use the isolation and "off-limits" status to do their own five-fingered "investigations", unnoticed by prying eyes.'

'The perfect ruse!'

Looking back down into the sand-covered base of the trench, we were clearly all in agreement, and similarly all pissed off that having come this far we couldn't do our own investigation. However, by our guide's restlessness, our presence here was a tenuous one at best.

'It time, we must go.'

We'd probably been there less than fifteen minutes, but even that was too long for our guide, so, unable to get to the bottom of things and explore for ourselves the secrets beneath the sands, we cut our losses and started back to the car, Mark ever the optimist.

'Maybe we'll have better luck at Abu Raoush.'

As we walked hastily back across the desert to the car, hot on the heels of our guide, I pressed Frank for more details about the Unfinished Pyramid, and why he thought it was so important.

'Is it something to do with the 'T" shape trench?'

'Not directly, but it's probably part of it. I haven't figured it all out yet, but all my engineering training and experience screams out that the pyramids weren't tombs, they weren't built when the Egyptologists say they were, they weren't built how they say they were, and they weren't built in the order they say they were.'

'So, what's your theory?'

'Actually, it was your theory about the Thera tsunami that really got me thinking. It makes total sense and pretty much explains why the pyramids were left in their present condition, and, if we extrapolate that back through similar catastrophes, it might explain the various design and structural periods, although it doesn't complete the picture for me.

But, after listening to what you had to say earlier today when we were at Meidum and Dahshur, I'm now pretty convinced the core is the clue, the red granite chamber, its shape, its location relative to ground level.'

'And the answer is...?'

'I don't know...yet! I was hoping we'd be able to get down in the pyramid here and see the chamber with my own eyes, but it wasn't to be.'

As soon as we reached the car and were underway, Frank fired up his ipad and quickly pulled up an image of the interior of the pyramid.

'As you can see it's an old photo that dates back to the early 20th Century.'

'Jesus, will you look at the size of it; unless the guy on the right is a midget. And those shapes.'

'Actually I think the shape is because they've prized one of the blocks aside to the right, which must have been a job in itself because they're massive.'

'Is that a staircase they've revealed at the bottom?'

'Hard to tell for sure, but that's what it looks like to me.'

'Did they mention anything about it in their notes?'

'If they did, the notes have been lost.'

'Or locked away.'

'Is that what they called the oval-shaped sarcophagus in the centre?'

'It would appear so.'

'Hmm, it doesn't really look like a sarcophagus, more like a well. And how hard would it have been to carve a perfect oval out of the inside of the granite? Can you imagine what that would weigh?'

'What it weighs is not as relevant as how they got it there, and, more importantly, what was its function, because it most certainly was NOT a burial chamber.'

At that point Mark joined in the discussion.

'Clearly the granite must have come from Aswan, but how they cut it and transported it is a mystery.'

'Not if they had advanced technology; sonic saws and the ability to levitate objects.'

Frank was a little more specific than me.

'We know that modern scientist have been able to levitate objects and spin objects by using specific frequencies that match the atomic resonance of the object, and I know from my time at NASA that the military and the Illuminati have underground sonic drills that tunnel through rock, cut through it like butter, at the rate of up to seven miles a day.'

'And where did we get the technology to do that?'

'Ultimately from the same source as those who built the pyramids, an extra-terrestrial civilization that predated ancient Egypt by hundreds of thousands of years.'

Moments later, the car pulled up back outside the village shop and, after alleviating our pockets of a little baksheesh, we thanked our guide, bid him farewell, and continued on our journey. Although we hadn't been able to get down into the Unfinished Pyramid, I felt like we were on a bit of a roll.

'There's got to be so much more to all this, it's like we haven't even scratched the surface.'

By the beaming grin on Frank's face, I could see he was fired up as well.

'Oh, we've done more than just scratched the surface, we've unearthed the treasure; all we have to do it find the right key to the right treasure chest.'

It sounded great, but the reality was it often felt like we were trying to find the keys to the boxes that contain the *'Book of Thoth'* even though we actually hadn't pinpointed the exact location of the boxes. And that got me thinking about the places I'd been to on my trip.

'Hey, Frank, have you ever thought about how so many of the temples have been rebuilt on top of previous temples, not alongside or nearby, but directly on top of the original structure, and, given how so many of the pyramids appear to have been built in stages, maybe thousands of years apart, do you think the sites were just picked at random, or was there a purpose to their location?'

'If they were built at random locations, then it's the most amazing string of coincidences the world has ever seen.'

'What do you mean?'

It *is* written in the stars

'Well, apart from one or two exceptions, I don't think it's the location of the temples that's so important. I'm pretty sure it's more about where the pyramids are, perfectly aligned to stars in The Milky Way.'

'That's what Pieter said, that all the pyramids along the Nile correspond to certain constellations and stars in the Milky Way; Giza is Orion's belt, Saqqara is Andromeda, and like you said, Draco and Vega are at Dahshur.'

Mark piped up.

'Then this Pieter guy must have read up on Wayne Herschel's work.'

'Who's Wayne Herschel?'

'He's a South African who's correlated all the fifty pyramids on the western side of the Nile in Lower Egypt with the constellations on one side of The Milky Way.'

'You mean like Robert Bauval worked out back in 1993, that the pyramids at Giza represented Orion's belt, that they represented Osiris?'

'Bauval was just the first, but, at the time, he couldn't explain the significance of all the pyramids in Egypt, nor the Sphinx, so most of the academics refused to accept his theory.'

'But it's so obvious!'

That made Frank laugh.

'Of course it's obvious, and it's reinforced by one of the oldest known prophecies. As the thrice-lived Hermes claimed: "Egypt is an image of the heavens". Its pretty clear, even to a blind sea snail that each pyramid relates to a particular star, but if anyone outside the acknowledged field of Egyptology proposes anything like that, especially if it conflicts with the established "norm", then it's quickly denigrated and totally disparaged.'

'So, where we're heading, Abu Raoush, is Betelgeuse.'

'No, according to Herschel, Abu Raoush is Sirius, which makes the Unfinished Pyramid at Zawiyet el-Aryan the star Aldebaran in the constellation of Taurus, and the pyramids at Abusir correlate with the Pleiades.'

Frank pulled up an image and handed me his ipad.

'Check this out; I downloaded it a while back from Herschel's website, thehiddenrecords.com.

Back in 2003 he discovered that the angle at which the Sphinx intersects the line of the three Giza pyramids was virtually identical to the angle at which the brightest star in the constellation of Leo aligns with the row of stars that form Orion's belt.

Herschel thought that was more than just a coincidence, that it was a clue, so, he overlaid a transparency of the stars onto a map of the pyramids, and, after rotating it around, proved that all the pyramids in Lower Egypt represent the mirror image of the brightest stars within the known constellations in one complete three-hundred-sixty degree ring along side the Milky Way and around the Earth.'

That made much more sense than the other diagram I had in my notes. But then something Frank said tugged at my brain.

'Mirror image? What do you mean by mirror-image?'

'I guess it lines up perfectly reflected in the sky.'

'No, you specifically said, "mirror-image". Wouldn't that mean that either the map was inverted, turned upside down, or that the constellations would run clockwise rather than anticlockwise?'

Frank scratched his head.

'I've never thought of that. Why?'

Crystal's words reverberated through my head.

'I've run into this before, at Dendera. The current order of precession as we assume it to be, Taurus, Aries, Pisces etcetera, is represented reversed at Dendera. But it wouldn't be represented back-to-front if you were looking at it from the southern hemisphere.'

While Frank went into deep contemplation, Mark fired off the obvious.

'What are you getting at, Alex?'

'Well, if you look at the earth from above the north pole, it rotates anti-clockwise, but if you look at it from below the south pole, it rotates clockwise. The same zodiac order, but represented in completely the opposite way.'

Frank didn't need long to figure it out.

'What you're saying is that when the reliefs were made, when the pyramids were built, Egypt was in the southern hemisphere.'

'Exactly.'

'That's huge.'

I explained the mechanics involved in the pole shift as Bill, Pieter and I had uncovered them back on the felucca, the crustal separation, the magnetic repulsion between crust and core at the poles, the pivoting effect of the crust. Frank soaked it up like a bread stick in balsamic vinegar and olive oil.

'That's interesting, because Herschel proposes that there was at least a fifty-degree polar shift, another ten degrees of arc further from the old "Thuban star" theory proposed by some others.'

'The Thuban star theory? What's that?'

'The theory is that one of the shafts in the king's chamber was deliberately aligned with Thuban in the constellation of Draco around 4500 years ago. The problem with that theory is it aligns itself with the conventional position that the Great Pyramid was built around 2,500 BC, and we know that's not the case. But Herschel really opened the door when he proposed it was ten-degree shift beyond that. It means that the entire Milky Way now becomes positioned more on the equator, between Northern and Southern Hemispheres, and needs a whole new computer program.

But then you mention Egypt being in the southern hemisphere, and that means if the shift was fifty degrees directly *south*, then it would have placed the Great Pyramid at a latitude twenty degrees south of the equator. But in that scenario, west remains west and east remains east.

Alternatively, the shift may actually have been a hundred-thirty degrees,

15

basically a complete pole shift, and that completely opens a Pandora's box, because in *that* scenario, west becomes east and north becomes south; I don't think anyone's done any astronomical calculations around *that* proposition. But what it does do is totally explains Herodotus when he quoted the ancient Egyptian priests who said that the sun had twice risen where it now sets; it wasn't something strange about the sun, it was because the whole earth had turned upside down.'

I'd almost forgotten about the roadblock; that was until we were pulled over. Thankfully it was the same guy who'd been on duty yesterday; one look through the window at the three of us, Frank in particular, and he quickly waived us on.

'So, Frank, what stars do you think the shafts in the Great Pyramid were aligned with?'

'I don't think they have anything to do with *any* particular star alignments. I never believed it, Christopher Dunne didn't buy it, and neither does Herschel, although he does propose they were aligned to the galactic centre and equator, which does seem to make some sense. But the shafts didn't target specific stars, that's too basic, too obvious, and none of the star alignments put forward by any of the so-called experts actually match up with everything else.'

Mark made an attempt to sum things up.

'OK, so we know the locations of each of the pyramids had a design, to reflect the position of the stars on the galactic equator, but that still doesn't answer the questions of *why* they were built in that configuration.'

'I don't know if it's true or not, but, according to Pieter, the ancient Sumerian Clay Tablets describe how the Annunaki built pyramids all over Earth as astronomical markers to demonstrate which age of the Zodiac they were in, because their laws decreed a change of ruler with each new Zodiac Age.'

Frank wasn't convinced.

'Maybe, but maybe not; it still doesn't answer the questions of why the pyramids were built the way they were built, nor how they were built. The question remains, why build massive chambers of red granite that clearly had some functional purpose? Maybe we'll find some answers here.'

Abu Raoush

It felt like we'd barely hit the suburbs when the car pulled off the highway into what looked like a cross between a disused quarry and massive section of raised desert. Like some sort of clandestine mobster deal, a beaten up black sedan was waiting for us and we quickly disembarked to greet our 'guide'. I didn't catch his name, which was probably a good thing, and I don't think he was interested in mine, which was even better. It all felt very 'cloak-and-dagger' as we climbed back into our respective cars and he led the way up the escarpment.

When we pulled up, and everyone got out of the cars, I was buzzing with anticipation, looking around, searching for the pyramid.

'Where is it?'

Frank pointed to the slightly raised section of rubble that sat atop the plateau.
'That's it there.'

It was in a considerably poor state to say the least, better than the Edfu Pyramid, the one on Elephantine Island, and the Pyramid of Amenemhat II at Dahshur, but nowhere near as impressive as Meidum, the Bent or Red Pyramids, not even as complete as Hawarra's pyramid or Zawiyet el-Aryan; I couldn't see how it was going to prove to be so important.

'This is what all the fuss is about?'

'We'll just have to see, after all, according to Herschel, Abu Raoush corresponds to the star Sirius, the brightest star in the night sky.'

As we headed left, around the northern side of the "pyramid", Frank took over as tour guide pointing hither and thither as I fired up my iphone to compare his comments to my diagram.

'Like many of the other complexes we've seen, those at Meidum and Dahshur in particular, this one is oriented north-south and surrounded by an outer perimeter wall approximately two-and-one-half metres thick; that must be what's left of it over there.

This large open area between the northern perimeter wall and the pyramid, that we're walking through at the moment, should be the location of a mortuary temple, especially since the causeway leads away to the north over there....'

He pointed off to the left.

'...But they haven't found anything here as of yet, other than the possible foundations of an inner perimeter wall, about twenty feet from the northeast corner of the pyramid base, that heads east, and what could have been a covered corridor that led from the northeast entrance of the inner enclosure to the mouth of the causeway.'

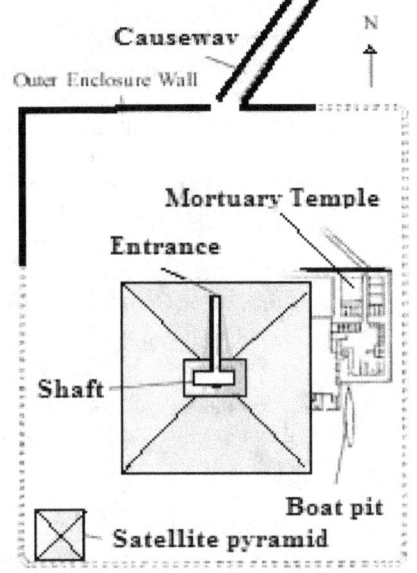

'How deep have they dug?'

'Maybe not deep enough, especially if your Thera tsunami really was six-hundred feet high.'

I wandered a little over towards the causeway.

'Is there a valley temple?'

'If there is, they haven't found one. But presumably, like most of the other pyramids, there would have been one at the other end of the causeway, and beyond that another connection would have led to a quay on the Nile, but it would have to have been at least a mile-and-a-half to have reached the pyramid complex through the Wadi from the Nile, arriving at a mortuary temple here before the pyramid.'

'So, clearly there *should* have been a temple here, right; the location of the causeway almost guarantees it, confirms it? But isn't the mortuary temple usually to the east? That's where they have it in this diagram.'

'And there *is* one there, we'll check it out in a minute. The problem is that eastern mortuary temples don't appear until the 4th Dynasty, and if Abu Raoush belongs to Djedefre, then that's the middle of the 3rd Dynasty, and that means, if the Egyptologists are correct, there should be a mortuary temple to the north.'

'So, are you saying that because the mortuary temple is to the east of the pyramid that the pyramid doesn't belong to Djedefre, that it belongs to someone who reigned during or after the 4th Dynasty?'

'No, but that's the sort of ridiculous "logic" you'd expect from some of the Egyptologists; that's if they could even put *that* together. What I'm saying is, the temple may have been built in the 4th Dynasty or later, but the pyramid must date to before *any* of the dynasties; possibly even before ALL the other pyramids.'

'What evidence do you have?'

'At the moment, none, that's why we're here, son, that's why we're here!'

I looked around; the area between the outer wall and the pyramid surrounded by random piles of rocks, rubble to most people, but not to me. As we wandered over to check them out, I recognized the texture and colour of some of the rocks straight away; granite! Jackpot.

From the proliferation of flush sides, the rocks were clearly fragments of some sort of structure, but it was hard to piece them all together and make some sort of sense of it all. There were no hieroglyphs or curved column fragments, like at Hawarra and Dendera, or on Elephantine Island, so that supported the theory they weren't part of a temple. Perhaps they formed part of the casing of the pyramid? I turned to Frank.

'Where does this granite come from?'

'My guess is Aswan.'

'Sorry, I meant where does it come from *here*; what part of the pyramid?'

'They certainly ain't part of any missing mortuary temple, that's for sure. My guess is, they came from in there.'

And with that, he pointed in towards the core of the pyramid.

'Then maybe it's time we took a look for ourselves?'

We made our way towards the pyramid, where several larger rectangular blocks of red granite had been lain along what would have been the northern face. Mark wasn't buying it.

'There's no way that's their original position.'

Neither was I.

'Which beggars the question, 'where *did* they originally sit?'

They were rough-hewn and, in some parts, very worn, aged. At the foot of one was a strangely shaped piece with a square base and a rounded top.

'Hey, guys, what do you make of that piece?

Mark had first bite of the cherry.

'It looks a bit like a fallen chess piece; a pawn, lying on its side. I know the ancient Egyptians had a game called senet, maybe was this a piece from a massive senet set for giants?'

I doubted it, but threw in an alternative.

'Maybe, if the gods were still on the planet, it was?

Frank's thoughts were more practical.

'If it was part of a dock, you could easily imagine it being used to tie up boats.'

That impressed both Mark and me, but, if that were the case, what was it doing here when the quay would probably have been over a mile and a half away?

Further along, on the next level up, another massive long piece of red granite was being used as part of the entrance 'staircase' that led to the inside of the pyramid.

It had an angled-shaped end, clearly related to its function, and that made me think it was possibly part of a portcullis or gabled ceiling. But, again, if that was the case, then what was it doing here?

The first surprise happened when we reached the 'entrance' to the pyramid. I'd expected to find a traditional shaft entrance, like the ones at Meidum and Dahshur, but, instead, we were greeted by a massive channel cut into the limestone and bedrock just like with the Unfinished Pyramid at Zawiyet el-Aryan.

'Interesting.'

Despite having not been here before, Frank resumed the roll as tour guide.

'You know it was here that one of the early explorers supposedly found a copper axe-head in part of the foundation, apparently buried when construction on the pyramid began.'

That didn't make any sense at all.

'A copper axe? And yet they had the technology to quarry and perfectly shape massive blocks of granite and transport them hundreds of miles, something we still can't do to this day. How do they know the copper axe wasn't left there when they tried to repair the pyramid?'

Mark put it into an even broader context.

'Let's face it, the axe could have been left there anytime.'

He was right, in fact the whole history of the pyramid was dubious, and the open channel before me seemed to reinforce it. Around six metres wide, the channel must have descended almost fifty metres long into the rock, to a depth of at least around twenty metres; it was almost a complete replica of the Unfinished Pyramid at Zawiyet el-Aryan. Was this the way they constructed the lower chambers in all the pyramids, by digging them out vertically from the surface first? It didn't seem right. It seemed in complete contrast to all the other pyramid entrances. This was a quandary, a quandary in a quarry.

Once again the descending channel was steep and slippery, maybe at an angle of forty-five even fifty degrees down into the bedrock, and lined with large blocks of Tura limestone, many of which were damaged or missing. With no rails to hang on to, or steady footing, the descent was going to be slow and steady, but this time, Frank had a green light.

'This is interesting; it seems the pyramid wasn't just built on top of this rocky plateau, rather, like some of the other pyramids, its foundation and internal substructure was housed deep within the bedrock.'

That got me thinking.

'What if there *was* no pyramid? What if it there wasn't even a ziggurat, just a hole dug into the limestone bedrock, with a red granite chamber made to fit, like at Hawarra, Meidum, Dahshur, and Mazghuna, then filled back in with limestone blocks and finished off as a mastaba?'

Having nearly reached the bottom of the channel, Mark paused briefly to respond.

'Actually, the early archaeological belief was that the pyramid here was probably never finished at all.'

'But I don't think that's likely, do you? Here, look at this.'

Frank had paused at the foot of the descent and was pointing to a cavity, high on the west wall, which marked the perpendicular ending of the descending passage and the start of the short horizontal passage that followed.

'Looking at the way the bedrock has been cut away, and the depth of the hole, I figure this would have been made to fit what would have been a massive granite lintel, probably the last ceiling block of the descending passage. That could mean the rest of this part of the passage was lined with granite, and it could also indicate the possible location of a portcullis.'

I read out a phrase I thought relevant.

'Though there's no conclusive proof the descending passage was built of granite, one of the granite fragments found in the descending passage bears a builders' graffiti mentioning the year of the first census of Djedefre.'

Frank scoffed.

'All that means is they found a piece of granite with Djedefre's name on it, any other conjecture, when it was put there, where the granite was originally, is purely speculative.'

The horizontal passage that followed was about five metres long, with a hole in the floor near the diagonally opposite eastern wall.

'Tomb robbers?'

'Possibly, if there actually was a tomb, but more likely chamber repairers just like at Dahshur. What it does show is there was more than likely a granite portcullis here…'

Frank pointed along the route of the excavated tunnel.

'…They would have started here, been unable to get passed the granite into the ante chamber, so headed down and west until they made their way further down and between the main chamber and the ante chamber, which means they must have had some idea of the internal structure. Apart from that, it's almost impossible to tell anything, even if it was a pyramid.'

'But, if it was a pyramid, even a step pyramid, what happened to all the stones?'

Mark rejoined the conversation.

'Apparently it was a popular target for early stone thieves.'

'Is that the truth, or is it just an archaeological fabrication to try and explain the missing stones, and it's been passed on like Chinese whispers or an urban myth?'

'That's a good point.'

Frank had a little more information.

'Well, I'm not sure how reliable it is, but there's supposedly documented proof from the end of the 19th Century that stone was being hauled away from here at the rate of around three-hundred camel-loads a day.'

I jumped on it like a hungry cat on a mouse.

'That may give an indication that stones were removed, but how many days did they remove them, and how big were the stones? There are lots of other factors to consider too, like, how much weight could a single camel carry before you broke its back, how many men would it take to lift that weight, and did they break the stones down into smaller sizes first?'

Frank volleyed the question back.

'That one I think I can answer. In the northeast corner of the inner enclosure, the archaeologists discovered workshops and housing they believe were used by the pyramid's builders. Part of their "proof" was the discovery of layers of limestone chips left from what was believed to be a stone-yard where the pyramid blocks were worked. But rather than working the blocks for the building of the pyramid, I think it's more than likely the layers of limestone chips are from the existing pyramid stones that were broken down into smaller transportable sizes for removal?'

'Either way you look at it, that's a lot of stones, and they may well have used the blocks to build new structures, but it may not have been the reason they wanted it all removed.'

'You think they just wanted to clear the site to find treasure?'

'Of course, back then, that's what their main objective was. It's more probably they carted the stones away and dumped then, and *then* they were appropriated to build new structures.'

Mark contributed to the mystery.

'And why here, why not at Giza, or Dahshur? If it was *just* to build other buildings, then surely all ancient sites would have been plundered to similar extents?'

'Unless Abu Raoush had a mud-brick superstructure as well?'

'So why quarry out red granite from the core of the pyramid, and then not take it away?'

It was my turn to raise my hand.

'I think I can answer that one, Mark. Because the limestone is easier to carve and shape, and could be cut down and used to build other structures, but granite, granite was too strong, simple copper tools couldn't cut it. The larger pieces would have been just too heavy for a camel to carry, and the smaller pieces seem to have resulted from being smashed into irregular unusable shapes, certainly not as practical as the limestone blocks'

'It would certainly explain why the pieces have just been left lying around.'

By then we'd all safely arrived at the bottom of the channel, more than twenty metres below the entrance, at what presumably was the "burial" chamber. Forming a 'T' shape, just like at Zawiyet el-Aryan, the corridor split at right angles to the left and the right, over twenty metres across, ten metres wide, and lower than the floor of the horizontal passage.

According to my notes, this was the site of an antechamber and burial chamber, but there was nothing left; it was empty, and by that I mean not even the chambers were there, just a partially 'reconstructed' foundation.

Frank and Mark headed west; I turned to the left.

"There is a depression in the middle of the eastern wall of the pyramid core that is believed to be a niche off the ante chamber, 1.6 x 2.1 metres, that might have held a false door or statue, in front of which would have been an altar and all been part of an offering hall."

No way! Who the hell would build an altar *inside* a pyramid; unless of course it was a later addition? There was almost nothing remaining, but, as usual, nothing had stopped the experts from speculating.

"The reconstructions provided by the excavators imply that the burial chamber was lying at a deeper level than the anteroom."

I looked at the diagram, especially at the eastern side; why go to all the trouble of moving tons of limestone, clearly as part of a design, and then put nothing there? What had the excavators missed, or deliberately left out?

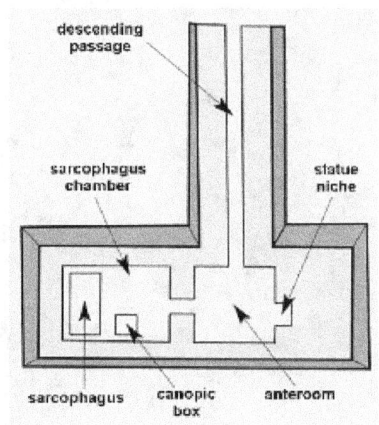

At the other end, Frank was looking around, shaking his head and grumbling away.

'This was supposedly an "open-pit" method of construction and a "throwback" to earlier times, rather just being an earlier pyramid, all because someone found a block here with Djedefre's cartouche on it. Forget the fact they didn't find any other blocks with any sort of hieroglyphs on them, let alone a cartouche. And, because of that one

21

stone, they ignore all the other evidence and ascribe the pyramid to Djedefre; imbeciles!'

There were the remains of about fifteen horizontally laid layers of smaller limestone blocks surrounding what would have been the core.

"The bedrock floor of the shaft was surmounted by five courses of fine limestone, probably bringing the level of the antechamber up to that of the horizontal passage. This disposition is similar to that of the Zawiyet el-Aryan pyramid."

The small size of the blocks to the sides instantly got me thinking the layers were clearly a later addition, possibly when the pyramid was being repaired by "Djedefre", or, more probably, as part of the 'modern' restoration and reconstruction.

Scattered around the floor were various size fragments of red granite: many of them seeming to have specific shaping. Frank was closely examining one.

'What do you make of the red granite, Frank.'

'Well, Petrie, as part of his investigations here, discovered a fragment of what he though was part of a pink granite sarcophagus in this area, but I don't think this is sarcophagus; too thick.'

'Part of the chamber walls? Or part of a massive granite vault, like at Hawarra, Senwroset III, the Black Pyramid, and those at Mazghuna?'

'That's the way it's looking to me, but not so much a massive vault, rather as large lining blocks, panels, like the ones we saw outside before we came in.'

We stepped down into the 'burial chamber', which sat about three metres lower than the horizontal passage. It was quite amazing to stand in the depth of the chamber and look up the walls. Frank was less amazed, more analytical.

'You know, they found mortar on the walls here, which means one of two things; either the chambers were buried and the shaft not just filled back up with limestone blocks, probably the ones they had quarried out, but they had gone to the trouble of using mortar to bind and seal them together, or, the shaft was sealed when they pyramid was being repaired during the time of Djedefre. The question is, why would you need to bind and seal massive blocks of limestone?'

'I'm sure the Egyptologists would say it was to stop tomb robbers from digging them up?'

'I agree, they would, but it would be easier for them to break into the descending shaft and use it to access the chamber. No, it wasn't to stop anyone from digging *down*, it had to have been to prevent something from escaping up.'

'Pressure?'

'Probably. Apparently previous excavators found a fragment of a large granite beam four feet wide, three feet deep and around seven-and-a-half feet long here. Normally I'd consider it was probably part of a doorway, more than likely the lintel, but two of its sides had been machined to form an angle of one-hundred-thirty-five degrees, which means it had a specific purpose and wasn't just a section of wall or door lintel.'

As he said it I pulled up a reconstruction of the structure of the burial chamber in my notes on Abu Raoush.

'You think it was part of a gabled vault ceiling?'

'Certainly looks that way.'

'But here the ceiling is made of granite, not limestone like it was at Hawarra and in the Black Pyramid at Dahshur.'

'Which means one was built before the other, but which is which? Limestone may have been the first design, but proved unreliable, and so latter models were built with red granite. Or, the limestone option was a cheaper, later choice, which, given the ease with which they cut and transported granite, is highly unlikely. The problem the logical engineering perspective of the limestone preceding the granite is, it means the "Middle Kingdom" pyramids of Amenemhat II predate the "Old Kingdom" structure here.'

'Unless, of course, they were all built tens, maybe hundreds, of thousands of years ago, and only repaired and claimed by Amenemhat II and Djedefre.'

'Precisely!'

We turned our attention from the ceiling to the floor, noticing several 'holes' that extended into the bedrock beneath what would have been the chamber.

'Situated beneath the chamber is a pit that sinks 3.1 metres into the bedrock.'

It didn't add up.

'Now it's possible these may have resulted from someone looking for secret passages in the cavities left after the 'sarcophagus' and the 'canopic chest' had been lifted out of their sockets in the floor, but anyone technologically advanced enough to 'lift' massive vaults of red granite out of a twenty metre shaft, would hardly make such primitive and brutal attempts at treasure hunting.'

Frank was on the same track.

'It's more likely the chamber was smashed apart, or even blown apart with dynamite by the earliest treasure hunters, dumping the rubble outside where we saw it all scattered around. But they failed to find anything of value in the chamber itself, so, frustrated, they used similar crude attempts to search beneath the chamber.'

'It's amazing what people will destroy in the name of greed.'

'Or religion.'

Exploring the rest of the chamber, Mark suddenly called out.

'Hey guys, check this out.'

In amidst the rubble on the floor was clear evidence there was much more hidden below, the entrances filled in with sand, dirt, and assorted chunks of limestone and granite.

'It looks like someone doesn't want us to know there are other chambers and corridors under here.'

'The plot thickens!'

Frank was right on to it.

'One can only wonder if there aren't similar staircases and chambers deep beneath here as there are at Giza and apparently at Zawiyet el-Aryan.'

Mark had another perspective.

'I bet there's more than a few mentions of Abu Raoush in those papers of yours.'

'If there are, it would give more evidence to support why this is a military zone, that's for sure.'

We all stood there, snapping photos, recording the evidence for ourselves. It seemed that despite attempts to conceal the truth, to the contrary, Abu Raoush was giving up its secrets. Well, all but one; what happened to the top? It seemed Mark was thinking the same thing.

'What do you think happened here, Frank? It looks like the top just blew off.'

'I suppose that's possible, and there's a recent theory to that effect, but being here and seeing it for myself, I don't think that's what happened.'

That surprised me.

'Why not? Surely it wasn't just carted away.'

'Don't be so quick to jump to conclusions, Alex, otherwise we might have to tar-and-feather you along with all the other "experts".'

'So what do you think *did* happen?'

Frank picked up a few fist sized fragments of red granite and gave them the "once-over".

'The first thing to determine would be, if there *was* an explosion, what caused it? They could check a few samples for signs of an explosion, but that might just be misleading as it's highly likely they blew apart the chamber, but I don't think that's what happened to the top'

It seemed obvious to me.

'What about if a pole shift caused the chamber to short circuit, go critical, surely it could have blown the top off?'

'Sure, possible, but how, with what?'

'Hydrogen gas? It seems the most likely and plausible explanation.'

'You mean like the Fukoshima reactor explosion?'

'Pretty much.'

'Then the blast would have had to have been massive to have blown off that many layers of stone, and yet it's not affected the side walls at all, so, no, I don't think the top was blown off.'

I looked around at the walls; he was right, the upper walls were even and unspoiled.

'So if it wasn't a blast, what was it?'

'Maybe sympathetic vibration.'

'Huh?'

Mark was as bemused as I was.

'What are you thinking, Frank?'

Frank looked around, and back up the channel, scratching his chin as he clearly formulated a concept in his mind.

'What if the channel was excavated a second time, post catastrophe?'

'Yeah? Go on.'

'Well, I've been thinking about what Alex said yesterday about the properties of granite, and about the different pyramid substructure designs. If we accept Christopher Dunne was right, that the Great Pyramid was, at least in part, some sort of power station, then let's assume, just for the minute, that Abu Raoush, which represents Sirius, the brightest star in the night sky, was the *first* power station ever built, perhaps even a prototype.

Let's assume they quarried down into the bedrock, carved the chambers out of the limestone, then lined them with granite, but not just with a single monolithic vault, but also with a ceiling of saddle panels.'

'OK, but what was the power source?'

'The earth.'

'In what way?'

'Nickola Tesla said that the earth rang like a bell, that it had a fundamental resonance. We know that all atoms have a resonance frequency, and all molecules and compounds similarly possess a specific spin resonance, so the chamber may well have been constructed in such a way that it's dimensions, or the very granite itself, resonated in sympathy with the "bell" frequency of the earth. The granite would then vibrate in sympathy, but at a subatomic level, absorbing the energy from the earth within its electron shells, forcing the electrons to higher shells.

That might make the compound unstable and it would almost instantaneously releases the energy as light or microwave energy when the electron falls back to its lower shell, thus keeping the granite stable. Thus, like in a computer, the silicon dioxide would generate a current that was possibly siphoned off through the entrance chamber, or even some other transfer device, like a crystal, to another receiver.'

'You're talking about free energy!'

'Exactly!'

'And that's just what you would expect from an advanced civilization.'

'Then the pole shift comes along, not the one in 1600 BC, but one way before then, possibly the one that wiped out Atlantis, and the reaction in the chamber gets supercharged and out of control. It causes a massive excitation of the vibrations, shattering the granite panels of the inner chamber and possibly the entrance shaft, causing both the chamber and shaft to collapse, and everything to cave in on top of it.

It sits there maybe tens of thousands of years until, in the 3rd Dynasty, Imhotep reappears and orders the repair of the major important structures, including the Great Pyramid and Abu Raoush. The first thing they have to do here is to excavate down to the damaged chambers.

Maybe it takes fifty, sixty years to clear away the debris, using the quarried blocks to build a mastaba around the opening. That done, they have to start rebuilding the chambers, this time using smaller limestone blocks to line the chamber and entrance shaft. This happens during the reign of Djedefre and his cartouche is carved onto one of the stones used to line the chamber.

But, maybe when Imhotep leaves to go to Greece, South America and the Indus Valley, those left behind don't know how to finish the job.'

I was stunned, it was brilliant, and made perfect sense of all the evidence.

'Frank, you're a fucking genius!'

He chuckled away.

'Not yet I'm not. But I *am* an engineer, and I'll figure out the solution....'

He scratched around like a rooster in a chicken coop, looking for stray seeds.

'...You see, there's also the possibility that when rebuilding the chamber, Imhotep realized the plan for the rebuilt design was flawed, and so he designed and built other power stations, still below ground level in the bedrock, but with modified designs, for example the "pyramids" at Mazghuna, Hawarra, and Dahshur, with saddle-vaulted chambers above the main chamber and modified portcullises to relieve the pressure of any future power surges.

From an engineering perspective, the next design step was the construction of corbelled chambers, first below the ground, and then later above the ground in the body of a ziggurat; Meidum, the Bent Pyramid.

The next step, as Alex has elucidated, was the addition of a pyramidal superstructure, then, the concaved-faced Red Pyramid, the pyramid of Khafre at Giza, and, ultimately, the Great Pyramid. That means all the mud-brick structures are probably merely dynastic-period repair-jobs done between the 3rd and 6th Dynasties, which in turn were devastated by the Thera tsunami.'

'But if the Great Pyramid was built in 50,000 BC, and if it was the *culmination* of all the pyramid building, the big ones that is, then that means all the other "big" stone pyramids, the ones that involve massive stone blocks and red granite vaults, etcetera, must have all pre-dated the Great Pyramid, that is, preceded 50,000 BC'

Frank raised an eyebrow.

'Hmmm. But I don't think the Great Pyramid was the culmination just because of its size. I think the size of the pyramid as it relates to importance is a red herring, the size of each pyramid was a simple reflection of the size of the corresponding star in the sky, that is, of its brightness.'

'Maybe the heart of each pyramid, the structure of the chamber, had something to do with the brightness of the star as well?'

'Now *that's* an interesting concept!'

We all stood there motionless looking at each other in mute shock. After what seemed an eternity, Mark broke the silence.

'If that's true, Frank, then not only will it totally rewrite Egyptian history, but throw it back at least, what, fifteen, sixteen pole shifts, fifteen, sixteen passings of Nibiru.'

'Maybe more. If the massive changes that occur with a full pole shift only happen say once every four passings of Nibiru, then we may have to go back hundreds of thousands of years.'

I was way ahead of him.

'And that's totally consistent with the history of the Zep Tepi, of the arrival of the Annunaki on earth, and the information detailed in the *'Book of Thoth'*.'

'Careful, Alex, we wouldn't want the world to know the truth, it would undermine every religion and almost every scientific assertion in the world.'

Clearly Frank had seen everything he needed to see, and took off back up the entrance channel, Mark following suit. I, on the other hand, still had unanswered questions and quickly scrambled after them.

'But, Frank, what makes you feel Abu Raoush was the first one, the first power station?'

'By comparing the internal structures of the pyramids, it's clear they fall into distinct groups, and each of those shows a progression of engineering techniques and design elements. That, and the fact it represents Sirius.'

'I'm with you all the way, Frank, but, playing Devil's advocate, the internal structure here is missing, all that's left is a hole in the ground and some rock fragments, so how can you be so sure?'

'I don't know, it just makes sense; I guess there's some obvious piece I'm missing.'

'Like the top of the pyramid?'

'Maybe, or perhaps what's back down there under the ground?'

'If you find it, you'll blow the lid on not only Abu Raoush, but all of the history of Egypt.'

I couldn't resist the pun, and it didn't go unnoticed by Mark or Frank, though Frank was less inclined to appreciate it. I wondered if that was a general American trend concerning humour, subtlety was totally lacking, if it wasn't set up, 1,2,3, and delivered with sledgehammer delivery, then it wasn't humour. Maybe it was because I didn't have the mandatory canned-laughter attached to it? In any case, the moment passed, no sooner had we extracted ourselves from the pit than we were continuing our lap clockwise and eastward around the base of the pyramid, if it ever was one.

"Originally, it was thought the pyramid had an extremely acute slope. Some even believe it might have been planned as a step pyramid..."

Ah, that was making more sense.

"...but the latest investigations have shown the casing blocks were not laid horizontally, but leaned slightly towards the middle of the pyramid creating, so instead of a steep 60º angle, a more standard 48º to 52º slope."

But, was the "leaning in" due to a subterranean collapse? Why else lay stones at an angle? Unless it was a technique used to prevent the stones from spreading? Even if it was, it still doesn't exclude the possibility Abu Raoush was still a step pyramid added at some later point.

We past more red-granite block fragments, corralled into rows on the plains of the plateau beside the pyramid, arriving at the site of the ruined mortuary temple to the east. I think Frank had summed it up as I had, that there wasn't really anything of interest to be found here. Never the less we wandered around, 'tire-kicking'.

Many of the wall foundations had been reconstructed out of limestone fragments and/or mud-brick, forming a number of compartments and chambers surrounding an open courtyard that still had some of its original pavement. In the middle of the north-eastern section was, what would once have been, a row of columns. Frank stood over them like the partner of a distant relative at the graveside of an aged great-aunt who'd died in her sleep, knowing they had to say something profound, but not really caring about the subject.

'Apparently, if the fragmentary evidence can be believed, these were once columns inscribed with Djedefre's cartouche. That, and the discovery of fragments of statues of three of Djedefre's sons and two of his daughters near here, may indicate who built the temple, but not confirm who built the pyramid.'

Having kicked enough tires, we headed south, passing more random red-granite fragments scattered through the temple site until we hit an excavated trench.

'A boat-pit?'

Mark shook his head.

'You'd think so from the shape, but no, they found the fragments of around a hundred-and-twenty statues buried here, most of which were representations of Djedefre sitting on his throne, and seemingly intentionally destroyed. '

'Djedefre, or Imhotep?'

Ever the grounded one, Frank brought things into focus.

'The question may not be so much who they were, but why they were buried in what amounts to a mass grave?'

'My first thoughts are the Amun Priests are behind it.'

'And why's that?'

'Well, they're responsible for most of the other destruction in ancient Egypt.'

Mark wasn't so sure.

'Couldn't it just as easily have been the Hyksos invaders of the 15th and 16th Dynasties?'

'I guess it's possible, but I doubt if they would have gone to the trouble of burying the statutes after defacing them.'

'What about the later Muslims?'

'Again, possible, but again, why bury them?...'

I looked around, noticing the remnants of another small temple or chapel between the pit and the pyramid.

'...It's more than likely the statues were associated, and probably housed in, whatever that building was over there.'

I read aloud a paragraph in my notes.

'A hollowing of the east face had been considered as a possible cult niche linked with the paved courtyard in front of it.. But now that the debris at the base of the pyramid has been removed, the hollowing appears to lie too high to have been a niche. It seems to be the imprint of huge granite beams of the casing, once lodged among the backing stones, and whose inclined resting facets can be seen on the bedrock core of the pyramid.'

That didn't tell Mark anything.

'Isn't it possible, the temple and its contents were flattened by the Thera tsunami, and, in the cleanup during the 18th Dynasty, they were simply buried because they were broken?'

'It's possible, but it sounds to me like the statues weren't just broken, they'd been systematically decapitated.'

'Who would do that to Djedefre?'

Frank had some thoughts.

'There was a theory that it could have been done by his half-brother and successor, Khafre, as revenge for Djedefre gaining the throne by murdering Khafre's older brother, Kauab.'

'Is any of that based on fact?'

'No, all speculation.'

And, with that, Frank meandered off, leaving Mark and I to toss around the topic of who were the culprits responsible for decapitating and burying the statues.

'Well, given the Egyptologists' track record on speculative assumptions, I don't give the Khafre theory much credence, especially if Djedefre was Imhotep, or even Imhotep's son. The finger still points back at the Amun Priests, they had the means and the motive.'

'What motive?'

'Well, if Imhotep was Annunaki and returned as Amenhotep I, then as Akhenaten, and the Amun Priests tried to eliminate all references to Akhenaten, then they may just as well have desired to eliminate all traces of the entire "hotep" lineage.'

'Just as plausible!'

Frank had moved ahead, towards the open plateau to the south, and was examining a block of red granite about five feet long. Along one of the edges were regularly spaced notches.

'What do you make of it, Frank?'

He ran his fingers along the edge like he was stroking the back of a prize-winning pet stegosaurus.

'Well, I don't think they're part of any interlocking system designed to hold the stone in place.'

'Do you think this might be evidence of the hidden sliding door mechanisms in the Great Pyramid?'

'That's pretty left field, what makes you say that?'

'They look like the sort of notches you'd see for a toothed wheel, that as the wheel turned it would slide the length of granite, perhaps closing or opening some sort of door or portcullis.'

'Maybe, although the notches may be too far apart for that; you'd usually expect them to be pretty much adjacent to each other.'

He wandered off towards another piece of red granite, this one propped up by a few stones.

'Oh, this is remarkable!'

It was indeed. The granite had been cut into a perfect rectangle about a metre wide, four feet long, and around nine inches thick. That in itself was pretty impressive, but nothing compared to the surface of the face. It had been shaped into a shallow but precise concave surface with grooved raised edges along the length.

'This "simple" block of stone could only have been accomplished by a level of skill, technology and accomplishment far in excess of that we possess today.'

Our guide must have been quite bemused that, of all the things to see here at Abu Raoush, the pyramid, the channel, the inner chambers, here were three obviously educated and intelligent "professors" totally obsessed and awestruck by a single simple slab of rock. I don't think he understood the significant of the piece, its geology, its machining, or its very presence here. We did.

Slowly we stood to our feet, each in a sort of self-induced reverence. As I stared out over the horizon I suddenly noticed it; it had been there all along, right before our eyes, but we had been so preoccupied with the pyramid we hadn't been able to see the forest for the trees.

'Frank, I think I found your missing piece,'

He turned around and looked in the direction I was facing.
'What?'

The view was spectacular, a panoramic view of at least one-hundred-and-eighty degrees; from the top of the pyramid it must have been the full three-sixty. In the distance, to the southwest, were the easily identifiable pyramids of the Giza Plateau.

'Pretty amazing view, hey; this must be the highest point around for hundreds of miles…'

Frank peered out into the distance.

'…You know, Frank, if this was any other city in the world, this would be prime real estate; with panoramic views that include the pyramids, this would be the Beverley Hills of Cairo!'

'Which beggars the questions, with all the corruption in Egypt, in a city of twenty million people, why is it a military zone, why hasn't it been swallowed up by development, and what is below the ground that they are covering up?'

Nope, he'd missed my subtle lead in.

'Yes, there is that, but I was thinking more along the lines of your proposition that Abu Raoush was the *first* "pyramid", because, if the Great Pyramid *was* built by Khufu, as a statement of how great he was, then surely he'd have build it on the highest point around, for all to see, right?'

Frank's eyes lit up as the penny not just dropped, it plummeted like a peregrine falcon in full attack mode.

'That's right, he would have. But he didn't, or rather he couldn't, because there was already something there, or rather here! Which means even if you bought the crap the Egyptologists put out about Khufu building the Great Pyramid, it's incongruent to suggest Djedefre built Abu Raoush *after* that. It makes total sense that Abu Raoush was the first site, just because of its location; how blind could I have been, it's so obvious!'

Mark had more to contribute.

'And that's totally congruent with Herschel's proposal that Abu Raoush represents Sirius, because Sirius is the brightest star in the sky.'

'I totally agree, but there must be even more to it.'

Mark looked out over the vast plains before us.

'Do you think it is a symbol of the Primeval Hill "on which the sun rose at the beginning of time"?'

'Perhaps, or maybe that was just an after thought.'

Frank scratched his chin and looked back and forth between the panorama, the pyramid and the ground.

'For some reason, I think it's got something to do with the limestone as well; it must form some sort of isolating foundation that maximizes the sympathetic vibrations. Perhaps, after Abu Raoush, Giza was the next suitable site, but only after considerable experimentation and trial at other locations further back up the Nile.

Perhaps the other ziggurats and pyramids, working their way up the Nile, and then back again, were substations or local power stations for the cities built there.'

I think at that point we each went into our own internal brain-space, running the ramifications of our discoveries through our respective CPUs. That was until our guide suggested our time was up and we best get going. It was one thing to be in a military zone without permission, totally different to be *caught* in a military zone without permission, and, even though I didn't have Kareem's papers with me, I didn't want them to detain me and put two and two together.

As we headed west, back to the car, we passed the ruins of a small subsidiary pyramid to the southwest of the main structure. Frank wasn't interested at all, and Mark barely gave it a cursive side-glance. Was it built at the same time, or later? Was it a queen's tomb as had been suggested by some Egyptologists? Frankly, I was with the others, it didn't really matter. What mattered was the history and function of the main structure. Find the truth out about Abu Raoush and maybe, just maybe, you had the key to the whole history of ancient Egypt?

Naturally the conversation in the car revolved completely around speculating on the significance of the location of Abu Raoush, about its importance, its correlation to Sirius, and about the possible significance of limestone being selected specifically as a foundation for the power stations; did limestone act as some sort of sonic or subsonic isolator, or possibly as a sonic filter? We debated the possibility it was because of limestone's organic molecular structure, $CaCO_3$, but, as none of us knew much about organic chemistry, we quickly ran into a dead end.

That everyone in the archaeological and New Age world was so preoccupied with Giza didn't mean Giza wasn't important, just that they probably hadn't thought outside the box or examine the *actual* evidence right under their noses; after all, we all knew the Labyrinth was important, Herodotus confirmed it, and the sheer presence of the Osireion at Abydos spoke for itself. Was it possible that every pyramid had hidden subterranean secrets waiting to be discovered?

Stealing home base

We'd no sooner crossed the Nile than the car pulled over and Mark pointed across the road and down the street.

'That's it over there, the Australian Embassy, what do you want to do?'

I weighed the options; if Frank and Mark were right, I could well just walk straight in and my problems would be over. But, and it was a big BUT, they could also equally be right and the Secret Police were waiting in ambush. Better safe than sorry. I turned sheepishly to Mark.

'Maybe you could go first, to check that the coast is clear?'

'No worries.'

Mark picked up the A4 envelope he'd prepared earlier, casually got out of the car, and sauntered down the street. There were several cars parked on either side, with occupants, as well as a number of "innocent" bystanders. When he was sure that everyone who was everyone had copped an eyeball of him, Mark crossed the road and headed directly for the Embassy gates. At first I thought he was going to make it, but, within the blink of an eye, gun-toting Secret Police appeared from everywhere and swarmed on him like a swarm of blowflies on a freshly-laid dog turd.

'Shit! If I'd known it was going to be so threatening, there would have been no way I would have let Mark do it.'

'Mark knows how to look after himself.'

While one of the officers took the envelope off him, opened it, and rifled through the contents, another was searching him. Mark was clearly protesting both his outrage and confusion.

'Right, I think that settles it; get the documents from the hotel and get to Alexandria and out of Egypt on a boat as soon as you can.'

Frank went to exit the car.

'But Saeed wont be here until this evening.'

'I wouldn't be waiting that long if I were you.'

'Maybe I can just lay low at the hotel until he gets here.'

'I don't think anywhere in Cairo is safe, especially your hotel. Before you arrived, did you write on your entrance card where you were staying?'

'Yes, the Cairo Palace.'

'Then it won't take long for them to check the records and stake out there as well.'

'Maybe I can rendezvous with Saeed in Saqqara this afternoon?'

'If you think that's the best option. But, seriously, either way, get your butt to Alexandria, FAST, and get out of Egypt!...'

Frank jumped from the car.

'...Now, get out of here!'

As the driver took off and turned down the first side street, the last I saw of Frank was as he made his way across the road to lend support to Mark's diversion.

'Where to, Mister Alex?'

No matter what, I had to get the documents first.

'The Cairo Palace.'

It wasn't that far from the Embassy to the hotel, but in that short time I had a thousand thoughts, all of which were at the very least laced with fear and trepidation at what lay ahead. As a consequence, rather than have the car pull up outside the hotel, I had the driver stop a few blocks away. Though he was probably heading back to pick up Frank and Mark, I gave the driver a hundred pounds anyway, for which he seemed most grateful, and set off for the Cairo Palace.

Trying to be as inconspicuous as possible, which was like a fluorescent pink elephant trying not to stand out in a herd of zebra, I made a few passes on the opposite side of the street. Having checked out every single person, cat, dog, and rogue camel within fifty metres of the entrance, I came to the conclusion it was safe to enter and made my way across the road and up in the lift to the Cairo Palace.

I didn't have to wait long to find out what was going on. As I walked towards reception, Abdo's face said it all. He held up a hand for me to stop, then dived under the counter, re-emerged with my backpack, and rushed towards me, meeting me in the corridor and whispering in an extremely agitated tone.

'Mr. Alex!…'

He thrust the backpack into my hands.

'…Quickly, we must go.'

I had a pretty good idea what it was about and that I was in no position to argue, but I couldn't leave without the papers.

'My laptop and the papers are still in the safe.'

'No, they are all in it the backpack; I have packed everything. Come, we must go.'

Abdo literally dragged me down the corridor, then up the stairs to the roof and we jumped across to the building at the rear, then down another flight of stairs; Abdo on the phone barking orders in Arabic while all the time looking back to see if we have been followed. Eventually we emerged in the street at the rear, where Magdy was waiting beside a car.

'Oh Mister Alex, you have made it the cobra very angry!'

'No shit, Sherlock.'

The truth was I hadn't just stirred the hornets' nest; I'd used it as a football and kicked it from pillar to post. But this was no time or place to discuss the finer points of political etiquette and, as if to emphasize the point, Abdo bundled me unceremoniously into the back seat.

'Lie down!'

Without question, I did as he said; I had little choice. Abdo jumped in the driver's seat, said something in Arabic to Magdy that sounded a matter of life and death, which it probably was, mine, and we set off into the amorphous quagmire that was Cairo traffic.

'Where are you taking me?'

'Somewhere safe.'

'Why? I mean, thanks, but why are you helping me?'

'This morning, not long after you have gone, the Secret Police, they come to the hotel. They have it the copy of your passport and ask it many question about you, if you are stay at Cairo Palace. They check the record and know you are stay here. What can I do, what can I tell them? They go and search it your room, come back with it your empty backpack and ask many more question about government paper. I think, these must be it the paper you have left in the hotel safe.'

'You didn't give them to them, did you?'

'No. But they tell me you have killed the Government official in Luxor and stolen secret paper, that you are very dangerous man. This it is true?'

'It's a long story, but no, I didn't kill anyone. They did, the Secret Police killed him.'

'Yes, I am believe you.'

'You do?'

'Many thing they have changed in Egypt since the revolution of the people, but some thing they have not changed for the good. When you kill it the king lion of the pride, the younger male they all fight to take over his rule. You understand this?'

'Totally.'

'They ask where you have gone and how long is it you will be. I tell them I do not know, but I think it you have gone to Giza to see it the pyramid and will be back in it afternoon. They leave here a man to wait in the lounge.'

'That's why you rushed out to meet me?'

'If you had made it to reception, he would have seen you.'

'Shit, that was close, thanks. So, why didn't you give me up?'

'I worry about the paper in the safe so I have to have it the look. You know it what these paper, they say?'

'Not exactly, but I guess they're pretty full on.'

'These paper, they are very dangerous. Where was it you did get them?

I filled in Abdo on the whole story, Saeed, Kareem, the papers, the train trips, the brushes with death, and overall the importance to get the papers out of Egypt and tell the truth to the world. He listened intently then, when I'd finished calmly responded.

'When I was it the boy, I work at Giza on it the excavation. My brother and me, we carry it the sand and stone from the dig site in the bag, one on each side, you understand?'

'Yes.'

'It hot and very hard work; my brother and me, we only fill it half the bag. Zahi Hawass he stop us, and yell and hit us for be lazy.

'How old were you?'

'Ten, eleven; just little boy. Hawass he not good man, very greedy.'

'Do you remember anything about anything special being discovered?'

'Not really, but we hear many thing, of Hawass search for the treasure of the pharaoh, of many secret room under Giza that Hawass he cannot get in. There is much corruption, many of the younger lion who challenge the King. Many of them lose their job or die in the accident.'

'Do you know Dr. Bakr?'

'He was the good man, and a lucky man.'

'Lucky, why, he got fired?'

'He was lucky he was not killed; he knew much of the corruption and the people involved.'

'It seems there are lots of people who know the truth.'

'Many people.'

'Why don't they speak out?'

'They know the consequence. It is easier and safer to follow the cobra than to confront it.'

I took a moment to fully comprehend the level of fear and corruption that ruled Egypt; it was endemic. Not only that, it had probably been this way for the greatest part of over five thousand years! There may well have been a political puppet show going on for the world to see, but the really was the military were still pulling the strings and things were not going to change in a hurry.

'You can sit up now, Mister Alex, we are out of the city.'

I sat upright and stretched my back out.

'Where are we heading?'

'To my home in Abusir, here you will be safe.'

'Abusir? Isn't that near Saqqara?'

'Yes, Saqqara it is only a few kilometre further south.'

'Saeed is taking some tourists to Saqqara, maybe you could take me there and I could meet up with him? Then I wouldn't be putting you or your family in any more danger.'

'Yes, this I can do. Do you know where they are go to in Saqqara?'

'No, why?'

'Saqqara it is a very large place, about five mile long and one mile wide. Do they visit South Saqqara, to the pyramid of Pepi I and Pepi II, or to north and the Step Pyramid of Djoser?'

'I don't know.'

'It is most likely to North Saqqara; South Saqqara it is not so easy to reach and it is closed to tourist, unless they have it the permission, they may not be allowed to go there.'

'Then let's head for North Saqqara.'

'Very good.'

I pulled out my iphone.

'And I'll read up on South Saqqara just in case.'

Saqqara

"About 30 km south of Cairo, Saqqara, a name possibly derived from the ancient Egyptian funerary god Sokar, is a vast, ancient burial ground, covering an area of 900 hectares. Around 7 km by 1.5 km, it served as the necropolis for the Ancient Egyptian capital of Memphis and was designated as a World Heritage Site by UNESCO in 1979."

Alarm bells went off straight away - UNESCO! Clearly there were things here of interest to the Illuminati.

"Saqqara features a number of mastabas and pyramids, built by as many as 17 pharaohs, and encompasses the entire span of the dynastic periods of Ancient Egypt."

Well, that's what the Egyptologists claimed, but was there more to it? Certainly there was evidence supporting that there was something happening during the entire dynastic periods, but did that extend far before the beginning of the dynastic periods?

I was now convinced there was strong evidence supporting the alignment of all the pyramids to specific stars in the sky, and, if that were the case, it was strong evidence suggesting the pyramids were all built around the same time, not spread out over numerous dynasties. So, were the locations of the pyramids at Saqqara random, or did they line up with the positions of specific stars? I went online and pulled up an image of Saqqara from Herschel's website.

The star map was centred around the galaxy of Andromeda and clearly showed a correlation between the major stars and the pyramids at Saqqara.

The formation included the stepped pyramid of Djoser and the pyramid of Sekhemkhet, both attributed to the 3rd Dynasty, the pyramids of Userkaf, Djedkare

Pepi I ☒

☒   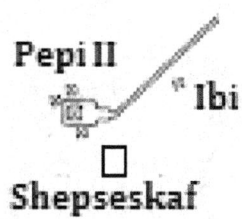
Merenre   **Djedkare**

Pepi II
    "Ibi
☐
Shepseskaf

N

Khendjer ☒
Unfinished ☒
Pyramid

and Unas supposedly from the 5th Dynasty, and the pyramids of Teti, Pepi I and Merenre purportedly from the 6th Dynasty; that spanned a period of over four-hundred-and-fifty years.

There is no way this ancient civilization, that barely existed from one ruler to the next, whose average life-spans were perhaps seventy to eighty years at the most, devised a 'plan' to build a series of pyramids, in direct correlation with the stars, that would take that the best part of five-hundred years to fully implement. Come on, guys, common sense rules it out; they had to have been built at the same time, and at the same time as the Giza pyramids, Abu Raoush and Zawiyet el-Aryan.

I probably wasn't going to get to see the pyramids of South Saqqara for myself, but perhaps I could extract enough information from my notes to support my thinking; if they had monolithic red-granite chambers, then it confirmed my thinking.

The southern section of Saqqara not only included the pyramids of Pepi I, Merenre and Djedkare-Isesi, but also, further south, an 'unfinished' pyramid, the pyramid complex of Pepi II, the pyramids of Ibi and Khendjer, and the mastaba of Shepseskaf. And if the pyramids of Pepi I, Merenre and Djedkare-Isesi correlated with the 'mouth' of the Andromedan snake, then that meant the structures further south most likely correlated to stars in Pegasus or possibly Altair. I decided to tackle the southernmost pyramids first.

The Unfinished Pyramid

"Southwest of Khendjer's pyramid at South Saqqara is the substructure and minimal core remains of a mud-brick superstructure of an unfinished pyramid that had an impressive side length of 78.75 metres."

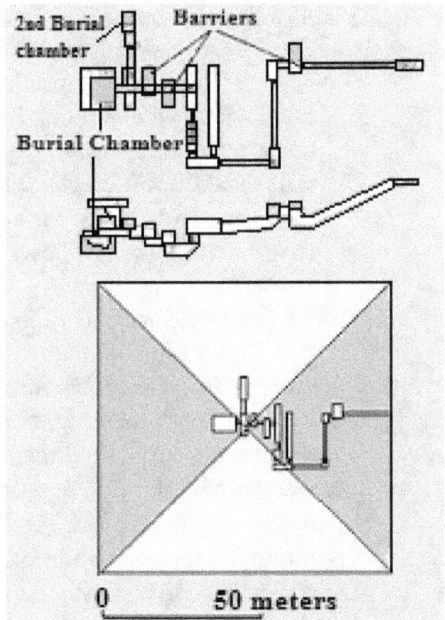

Was it unfinished, or had the superstructure just been swept away by the Thera tsunami?

I briefly scanned a comment that spoke of a wavy, undulating perimeter wall built of mud-brick that ran around the pyramid, but quickly dismissed the wall as either an Old Kingdom structure or a later addition from one of the post-Thera dynasties; I was focused on the substructure, which was pretty much all that remained.

"The Pyramid has an elaborate and complete substructure, one of the finest, and is not unlike that beneath the pyramid at north Mazghuna."

That sounded promising.

"The entrance to the pyramid lies on its central axis at the foot of the east side and leads to a long stairway and ramp that descends to the first of three large side portcullis barriers."

That sounded even more promising.

"After the first barrier is a small chamber that opens to the south into a second corridor that leads to another small chamber. This in turn has a corridor heading west through a narrow passage that leads to a third, longer chamber. Here, a wide, dead-end corridor leads to the north. Just beyond that, another stairway and short corridor also leads to the north and to another long chamber-like corridor. In the centre of this chamber's west wall a final, narrow corridor first passes the two remaining portcullises barriers before arriving at the antechamber in front of two burials chambers. The king's chamber, the larger, was west of the antechamber, the queen's chamber to the north. "

It was sounding exactly like the substructures at Mazghuna.

"Regular rows of black-painted stripes decorate the white limestone walls of almost every room in the substructure."

It sounded like the intention was to cover the walls with text but that they never got around to it. Surely not all these pyramids were left 'unfinished'? There had to be a reason.

"The burial chamber was formed from a monolithic quartzite block weighing around 150 tons, with niches carved out for the sarcophagus and canopic chest."

That was a layout with which I was becoming particularly familiar. This too was a structure built way before the Middle Kingdom period suggested by most Egyptologists.

"The chamber was meant to be closed by a system of sand filled shafts where generally three huge limestone slaps sit atop the burial chamber. Two slabs were usually in place, while the third slab rested upon blocks that in turn set atop sand filled shafts, so that the coffin and canopic chest could be introduced to the chamber. In this case, however, the "lid" was never lowered."

The oversight of not lowering the 'lid' seemed the case with many if not all of the pyramids; surely the ancient priests were not that forgetful?

"An unusual feature of the substructure is the existence of a second burial chamber to the north of the antechamber, accessed by a small stairway. Also made from a monolithic quartzite block, the second burial chamber varied slightly in that the canopic chest was provided with a separate compartment in a niche off one corner of the chamber. Here the closure system was similar to those found in the pyramids of Ameny-Qemau and north Mazghuna, consisting of a much simpler lid sliding horizontally over the chamber."

Was this a similar development, as seen in the Bent and Red Pyramids, of additional chambers that had something to do with the actual functionality of the 'pyramid'?

> "Regular rows of black painted stripes decorate the masonry of white Tura limestone walls that line almost every chamber and corridor within the substructure."

I'd read about them in the northern pyramid at Mazghuna, but the last time I'd seen anything similar was in the tomb of Thutmoses III in the Valley of the Kings. If the lines were meant for text, then clearly the interiors were unfinished, but when were they added, and why were they left blank? Another mystery possibly answered by the Thera tsunami?

Reading on, there was further reference to the discovery of two black-granite pyramidions outside near the entrance, one polished smooth, while the other was roughly finished and had a truncated top, but...

> "No inscriptions were found on either pyramidion, nor anywhere else within the substructure, to indicate the identity of the builder."

Was that evidence to support that the inscriptions on 'Amenemhat III's' pyramidion, found at the Black Pyramid, were a much later addition? It was possible.

Clearly the 'pyramid' was of major significance, and yet, despite its intended size, the masonry of fine Tura limestone casing the corridors, the massive red-granite monoliths used to create both 'burial chambers', and the elaborate closure system of portcullises, the 'experts' have virtually no idea who the owner may have been. Perhaps I should go and scrawl my name on it somewhere and the Egyptologists can ascribe it to the little known, but mysterious, King Alex.

What was becoming clear to me was that there was much more to be discovered about these so-called lesser-known and rarely visited sites. Why were they closed, why were they off limits, and why were they military zones? These sites posed a myriad of questions and held the keys to a true understanding of not only the history of Ancient Egypt, but also of the world. Why keep that knowledge from the people? Simple, control!

Fully excavating these sites would not only create thousands of jobs for the Egyptian people, but create an even greater reason for tourists to come to Egypt for extended periods, or several times. Economically, it makes sense to fully excavate these sites, archaeologically, it makes sense to fully excavate these sites, but, if you wanted to keep the truth and the discoveries for the elite few, then it makes sense to keep it all buried under the sand.

Anyway, I had enough evidence to support my theory, so, as Abdo stopped to pick up a few supplies, water and fruit, it was time to move on to the next structure, which, according to the Egyptologists, was contemporary with the 'unfinished' pyramid I had just 'explored'.

The Pyramid of Khendjer

> "Located between the pyramid of Pepi II in far South Saqqara and the pyramid of Senwrosret III in the north of Dahshur are the slim remains of the only 13th Dynasty pyramid to be completed, the mortuary complex of Khendjer."

According to my revised dynastic chronology, Khendjer, was perhaps the last pharaoh before the breakaway 14th Dynasty. By now it was obvious to me, if not to the mainstream Egyptologists, that all these pyramids were structures that predated the dynastic period. I couldn't help but think that by claiming the pyramid as his own it was perhaps a last ditch effort to legitimize his place on the throne?

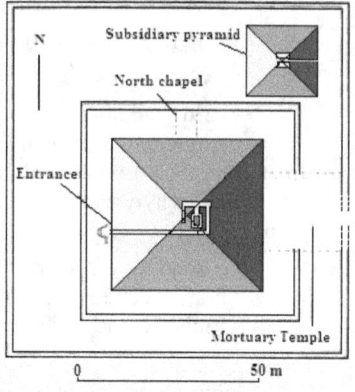

Reading on, I discovered, as with many of the other pyramids at Dahshur, the complex was enclosed by both inner and outer walls; the outer wall of mud-brick, the inner wall of limestone, with niches and panels. This inner wall apparently replaced an even earlier wavy wall. That was all totally consistent with my theory the inner wavy wall was probably Old Kingdom, replaced by the niched wall in the Middle Kingdom, and the outer mud-brick wall, post-Thera.

Between the inner and outer enclosure walls, at the northeast corner of the complex, sat a subsidiary pyramid, supposedly the only known subsidiary pyramid dating to the 13th Dynasty, that is if in fact it does date to then, which is highly questionable. If it aligned with a star then it was definitely contemporary with the 'Khendjer' pyramid, and I had a feeling the evidence was going to strongly suggest it was built way before the 13th Dynasty.

"The subsidiary pyramid has a simple substructure consisting of a stairway and ramp that leads to a corridor and through two barriers before arriving at a central antechamber. There, two burial chambers are found, one to the north and one to the south, for two of Khendjer's consorts, each containing quartzite coffers."

Hardly 13th Dynasty!

"The lids were propped on blocks and the coffins never apparently used."

As Abdo jumped back in the car and tossed me a welcome bottle of water, I pondered over how many times the Egyptologists had to have it put right under their noses before they could see the truth: no closed lids, no mummy, not used? Guys, it's time to come up with another theory, one that doesn't centre on tomb robbers capable of shifting thirty-ton blocks, instead, one that incorporates there *were* no bodies, it wasn't a tomb, and the massive red-granite chambers and portcullises had some functional purpose.

There were also several shaft tombs discovered within the enclosure walls, which several Egyptologists purport most likely belong to Khendjer's family members, however, the reality is, they could have belonged to anyone, as, like at the Black Pyramid, they could have been usurped at the same time Hor usurped the ones at Dahshur, which was only about twenty years earlier. But their location outside the inner limestone wall certainly appeared to date them post-pyramid.

Once again the mortuary temple was located on the east side, in this case encompassing both the inner and outer enclosure walls. This would have allowed for the outer section of the temple to be located outside the inner wall, leaving the inner sanctuary on the inside of the inner wall, or the halves may have been built at different times, however, according to the notes, the only remains of the temple are parts of the pavement and bits of reliefs and columns, so it's hard to tell.

There was also a north chapel, which was raised on a platform reached by two stairways and contained a yellow quartzite false door in its north wall, built out from against the pyramid face to the inner enclosure wall, of which fragments of reliefs from this chapel have been recovered, revealing standard scenes of offering. But I knew where I was headed, the substructure and 'burial' chamber.

"While the pyramid was once about 37.35 metres (123 ft) tall, today it is reduced to no more than about one metre, a sad but common result of using a mud-brick core."

Unless of course the mud-brick was a much later attempt to repair and renovate the structure.

"Over the mud-brick core were backing stones and a casing of limestone, which, when quarried by stone robbers, left the core to disintegrate."

Or it was washed away *then* pilfered.

"A mostly whole, but fragmentary pyramidion was found on the east side, which has now been restored, bearing the inscription of the cartouche of King Userkare on one side, believed by many to have been the king's throne name."

Or it could have been somebody else all together! Isn't it more likely that Userkare was in fact Userkara, son of Teti I, father of Pepi I, and 2nd pharaoh of the 6th Dynasty? That this wasn't the pyramidion of a 13th Dynasty pyramid at all, but had been appropriated in the 6th Dynasty? Wasn't that more logical? It could even have belonged to the 5th Dynasty 'pyramid' of Userkaf and been washed south by the Thera tsunami.

"It is possible that the pyramid was earlier suppose to have a somewhat different substructure plan, for there is an aborted stairway in the southeast corner that was later blocked."

Blocked by whom? Maybe the 'aborted' stairway was the entrance to a much older subterranean structure? Maybe Zahi Hawass and his vultures had already robbed it, but the information left behind, possibly on the walls and ceilings, was too confronting and controversial to expose to the scrutinizing eyes of the world? An aborted entrance; I doubted it!

The 'actual' entrance to the pyramid was apparently at the base of the southern end of the west face.

"Here, we find a not untypical arrangement of a stairway leading down into a portcullis room. The barrier was never engaged, but this might not mean that there was no burial."

Oh, please, another forgetful priest? Maybe it wasn't closed because it wasn't meant to be. Then I got the idea that maybe the first portcullis door in all these structures acted not just like a pressure valve but perhaps like a fire-door, a safety measure just in case something went wrong deeper inside?

"Another stairway leads down to a second barrier room, once closed by a double-leaf wooden door. From here, the corridor continued for a short distance before taking a 90-degree left turn to the north. Apparently the burial chamber could be reached from here, or from corridors that continued along the northern and western sides of the burial chamber that changed levels no less than four times."

Initially that didn't make sense, until I included the possibility of 'maintenance' tunnels, like the one in the Bent Pyramid, excavated in an attempt to repair the substructure, or later actual tomb robber tunnels. In either case, without being able to investigate first hand, I could only speculate. But, I was arriving at my destination and I was confident of what I would find.

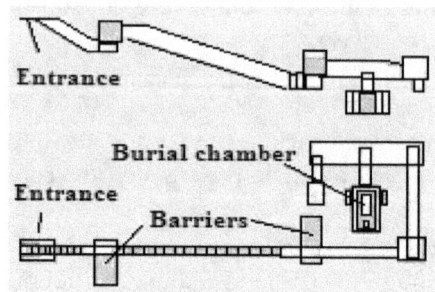

"The burial chamber was built prior to the construction of the superstructure in a ditch just beyond the second barrier."

That sounded exactly like the structures at Mazghuna and Hawarra, and very similar to the lower chamber of the Bent Pyramid and possibly those at Abu Raoush and Zawiyet-el Aryan.

"The burial chamber was a monolithic block of quartzite in which separate niches were created to hold the king's coffin and canopic chest. These niches were covered by a roof formed of two huge quartzite slabs. The method of sealing the burial chamber was the same as that found in Amenemhet III's pyramid at Hawara and in the south Mazghuna pyramid."

Snap! Frank would have a field day.

"After building the final barrier and the burial chamber, they roofed the corridors and built a gabled roof of limestone beams above the burial chamber."

There was that pressure relief structure again; these pyramids were far to advanced to have been built by the Ancient Egyptians of the 3rd to 6th Dynasties.

"They also constructed a brick vault above the limestone construct to help relieve some of the stress created by the superstructure."

And there it was, that absolutely ridiculous logic of the Egyptologists sprouting forth again; do these guys actually think things through and get structural engineers to validate their speculations, or do they just mindlessly regurgitate what another boneheaded parrot has postulated? A vault of mud-brick would not disperse the weight of the rest of the pyramid any more than the gabled limestone blocks themselves. No, I was convinced; the gabled limestone blocks were a remarkably simple pressure release system.

"After the burial took place, they filled the corridors with masonry and paved over the openings into the corridors."

Now part of that may have been true; maybe they did fill the corridors and pave over the openings, but it may have been after they attempted to fix the interior. Or maybe they did think of entombing someone here, though I highly doubt it. Above all, I was totally flummoxed that, apart from the work of Christopher Dunne on the Great

Pyramid, it seemed as if no one had studied ALL the 'burial' chambers of ALL the pyramids purely from a purely structural engineering perspective? And had anyone bothered to examine all the properties of red granite? I doubted it.

I was going to skip the next structure to the north because it was a 'just a mastaba', but on second thoughts, when I considered the size of it, I decided to check it out.

The Mastaba of Shepseskaf

"Once ascribed to Unas, last pharaoh of the 5th Dynasty, since 1925, primarily due to the work of the French Archaeologist Gustave Jeuier, the mastaba has been ascribed to Shepseskaf, last pharaoh of the 4th Dynasty, based on scant and circumstantial evidence at best; a fragmentary stela found at the site that contained part of the last letter of the king's name."

That didn't mean Shepseskaf built the mastaba, just that he placed a stela there at some time during his brief four-year reign.

"Independent of the site, Jeuier also discovered that the name of the king's tomb was 'Shepseskaf is purified', which concluded with an explanatory sign in the form of a mastaba, suggesting that Shepseskaf's tomb was of that form. Finally another stela, dated to the Middle Kingdom, showed that during that period, Shepseskaf's cult was still active on the site of Mastaba Fara'un."

None of that was conclusive; that Shepseskaf had built, or even appropriated *this* site. And yet modern Egyptologists had just accepted, based on Jeuier's scant evidence, that, despite ruling for only four years, Shepseskaf was not only was responsible for completing the pyramid of his father, Menkaure, the smallest of the three large pyramids on the Giza Plateau, although that was now considerably in question, but that Shepseskaf also built the mastaba at Saqqara. I wondered what fresh eyes and a fresh mind might make of the *actual* evidence.

The first thing that struck me about the structure was that there was a Mortuary Temple and Valley Temple connected to it by a Causeway, although, from my notes, "the remains of the Valley Temple have never been unearthed". I wasn't aware Mortuary Temples were usually associated with mastabas, so was this evidence that it was what was beneath the mastaba that was worshipped? If the chambers were made of red granite it would strongly support the notion that the 'pyramids' were built in stages, and that the mastabas were one of those stages.

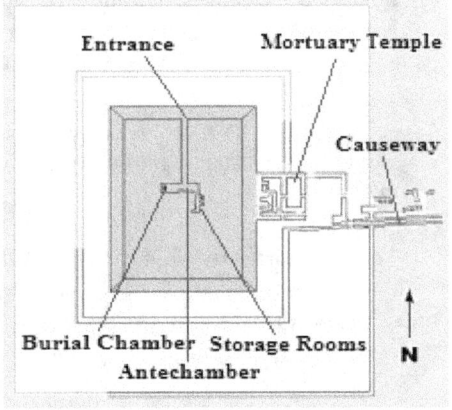

"The Causeway was built entirely of white-painted mud-brick, and seems to have taken the form of a corridor with a vaulted ceiling."

The design reminded me of the limestone corridors that led to the Osireion at Abydos, but the mud-brick placed the Causeway more in the post-Thera era, as did the two mud-brick enclosure walls. And, even though I was pre-occupied with the mastaba's subterranean structure, several other irregularities about the surrounds stuck out.

First, that the causeway, that normally connected valley temples with their mortuary temples, did not directly connect here, rather it led to the southeast corner of the Mortuary Temple before running along the south wall into the open courtyard that surrounded the mastaba.

Second;

"The Mortuary Temple that stood, as was the norm, in front of the east wall of the mastaba, varied significantly in that instead of facing east it was oriented north-south."

It may not have seemed such a big deal, but it made me think there was some incongruity.

Thirdly;

"Based on the material employed for its construction, the Mortuary Temple seems to have been constructed in two or possibly three phases; the earlier parts in stone, a paved courtyard of limestone, with later mud-brick additions."

The periphery was giving up some clues but it was the mastaba itself that could provide real evidence.

"Oriented north-to-south, Shepseskaf's mastaba was huge, measuring 99.6 metres (327 ft) long by 74.4 metres (244 ft) across. The core of the mastaba was built in two steps of enormous blocks of greyish-yellow limestone that originated in the stone quarries west of Dahshur. The mastaba was encased with fine white Tura limestone except for the very bottom course of red granite."

How interesting; I knew red granite meant pre-dynastic. It indicated the limestone steps were definitely a later addition, probably during the Old or Middle Kingdoms.

"On some of the casing blocks are inscriptions of Prince Khaemwaset's later restoration of this monument."

And, as Khaemwaset was a son of Ramses II, pharaoh of the 19th Dynasty, that would be consistent with the damage being caused by the Thera tsunami. But what was underneath?

"The substructure is entered by a sloping passage on its northern side, very similar to a pyramid entrance, about two metres above ground level. Lined in pink granite, the corridor descends about 20m into a second corridor originally blocked by three portcullis slabs."

There it was, a corridor, not of limestone, or carved out of the bedrock, but specifically of red granite.

"Beyond the barriers, the corridor flattens out leading to the subterranean antechamber, built entirely from pink granite, including its false-vault ceiling. From the antechamber a narrow passage runs from the southeast, leading to six niches or store-rooms, while another short passage descends westward from the antechamber allowing access to the burial chamber, similarly made of pink granite and again with a pink-granite false-vault ceiling, but containing little else but a few fragments of a dark basalt sarcophagus."

Bingo; red granite! But, according to the photo that accompanied the file, it looked as if the chamber was made of large granite blocks rather than from a single monolithic slab, which must have had some relationship to the chronology of its design.

All that said and done, one thing was certain to me, the subterranean component of the mastaba wasn't built by Shepseskaf, or *any* dynastic pharaoh for that matter, it couldn't have been, because if they had the technology to quarry and transport red granite, then surely they would have used it extensively in the Mortuary Temple, if only for its aesthetic appearance.

I had a feeling this mastaba had a lot more importance than Egyptologists considered it to have. If it aligned with a star, perhaps even a big star, then that confirmed it.

I brought up one of Herschel's star maps, and there it was. Not only was the mastaba of Shepseskaf significance, but so were the next two pyramids, those of Ibi and the complex of Pepi II. I didn't really have any choice, I had to check them out.

'Abdo, how long to Saqqara?'

'About five, maybe ten minutes.'

I dived back into my iphone.

The Pyramid of Ibi

Northeast of Shepseskaf's tomb, near the causeway of the pyramid of Pepi II, is the badly ruined pyramid attributed to Qakare Ibi. According to the 'experts', Ibi, whose reign only lasted about two years, was the only pharaoh of the 8th Dynasty who attempted to build a pyramid: "the last pyramid and royal funerary monument to have been built at Saqqara".

But, is it possible they got even *that* wrong, that the Ibi who had appropriated the pyramid was the Ibi who ruled for five years at end of the 6th Dynasty? That would seem to be more logical and in keeping with the other structures nearby. And, again, did Ibi claim it as a last ditched attempt to legitimise his claim to the throne? Perhaps there were clues or some hard evidence within the pyramid? But first, I perused the information about the pyramid's chapel.

"Beside the north-east side of the pyramid are the remains of a small mud-brick chapel containing an offering hall with a rectangular alabaster basin in the floor and the foundations of a stele or a false door."

Unlike the majority of pyramids, Ibi's pyramid is not oriented to any cardinal point, rather it's on a roughly northwest–southeast axis. Why, I had no idea.

"The pyramid's dimensions, a base length of 31.5 metres (103 ft), with a slope of 53°7', and an estimated height of 21 metres (69 ft), are very similar in plan, dimensions and decorations to the pyramids of the queens of Pepi II, the last great pharaoh of the Old

Kingdom. Consequently it was proposed that the pyramid was originally that of Ankhnespepi IV, a wife of Pepi II, and was only later appropriated by Ibi."

Perhaps it was appropriated by both?

"Even though the foundations for the outer casing of the pyramid were laid, the casing itself was never mounted. As a result, the monument appears today as a 3-metre-high pile of mud and limestone chips."

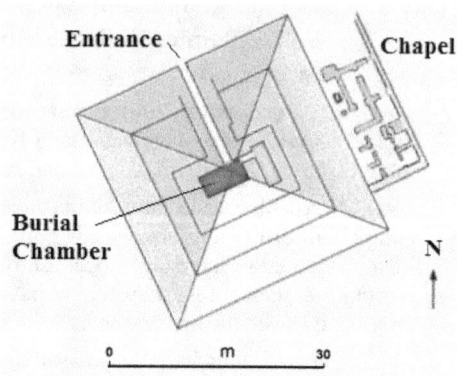

Or was it severely damaged by tsunamis, firstly the Thera tsunami, and possibly later by the tsunamis of 369 BC and 365 AD?

"Among the debris of limestone chips and clay, a number of limestone blocks from the core, were discovered on which were crude inscriptions in red ochre paint of 'Prince of Libya' for which Egyptologists seem to have no explanation."

"Crude inscriptions", "Prince of Libya"; they seemed quite clear to me. If Ibi was the last pharaoh of the 6th Dynasty, and his priests or servants saw that he was kowtowing to the invading Libyans, then they may well have written graffiti over the most sacred of Ibi's monuments. Calling the king a prince would have been insult enough, but suggesting he was subservient to the Libyan king would have been a greater insult to his Egyptian heritage. But, just because the graffiti was there, it didn't mean Ibi had built the pyramid; that would require digging deeper.

"The pyramid's core was constructed of small limestone blocks of local origin, most of which are now gone. They formed a girdle around the subterranean chambers which are entered from the north-west wall via an 8 metre (26 ft) long limestone-clad descending passage: inscribed with Pyramid Texts, the most recent version to be found in a royal pyramid, and seemingly directly inscribed for Ibi rather than appropriated by him. "

I wondered at the need for the limestone cladding in the passage, was it a later addition so as to add the Pyramid Texts?

"The descending passage leads to a large granite portcullis."

Ah, there it was, some of the evidence I was looking for, a large granite portcullis.

"Beyond the portcullis lay the king's burial chamber, also inscribed with Pyramid Texts. Its ceiling, once flat and decorated with stars, was probably made of a single 5 metre (16 ft) long block of Tura limestone, but is now missing and has been replaced with modern concrete."

"Missing"? How does a five-metre-long slab of limestone, that probably weighs a few ton, just up and disappear? The term "replaced" is a clue, it tells me that, like with the ceiling at Dendera, the ceiling here has been 'appropriated'. But by whom, and where is it now, and, more importantly, what is on it that is so significant? The plot thickened with every chamber.

"On the east side of the burial chamber is a serdab for the statue of the Ka of the king, and, on the west side, a false door and a huge granite block on which once stood the king's sarcophagus."

There was the granite again, but where was the sarcophagus? What if there wasn't one? What if the granite slab was in fact a lid, and the burial chamber was in fact just an antechamber and the real chamber lay beneath the granite slab just like at Hawarra and Mazghuna? Had the Egyptologists overlooked this pyramid because of its small size and poor condition? It seemed so.

I figured we maybe had a few minutes more before we arrived in Saqqara, so turned my attention westward to the complex of Pepi II, not so much to *who* the pyramids were ascribed to, or even the peripheral structures such as the Valley Temples, Causeways, and Mortuary temples, but to the actual relevant evidence of the superstructure and substructure of the pyramids. That said, I did pick up a few useful titbits from my notes.

The Pyramid Complex of Pepi II

The Valley Temple was very different to the usual plan in that it was fronted by a large rectangular terrace with harbour ramps on either side. That gave an indication the level of the Nile during the 6th Dynasty was much higher than it is now.

"In the centre of the wall of the terrace was a single red-granite doorway, inscribed with Pepi's names and titles."

I would have loved to have seen it with my own eyes, but my gut was telling me that the doorway came from some previous temple, contemporary with the Osireion at Abydos, and that the inscriptions were probably crude and added when the granite was reused to create the river entrance to Pepi II's complex.

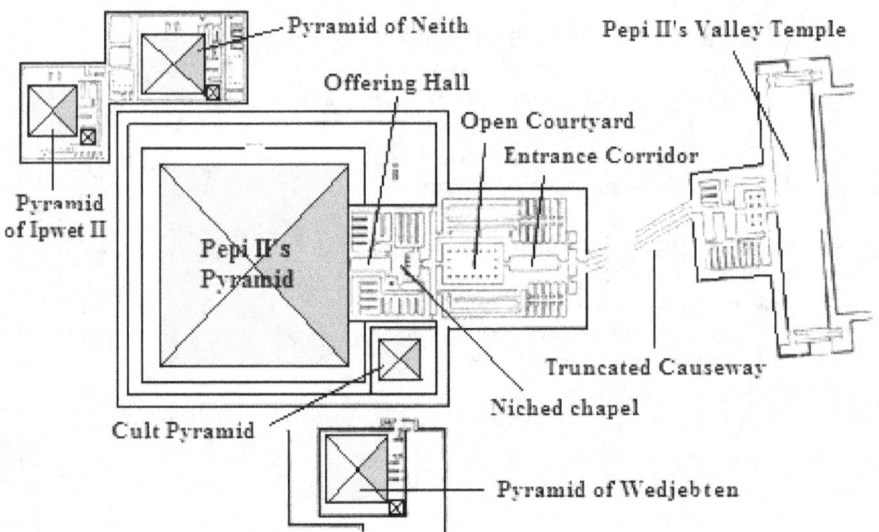

45

Reading on, I discovered that scenes within the remains of the 400-metre causeway apparently included; a depiction of the king as a sphinx and as a griffin massacring prisoners and enemies of Egypt, as well as scenes showing a funerary procession of servants bringing offerings from the mortuary estates and various divinities approaching the ruler on his throne. Normally I might have been interested, particularly at the beginning of my trip, but now it was barely of interest. I did however find something of interest in the Mortuary Temple.

"The Mortuary Temple is quite large and of a more traditional design, with an open-porticoed court paved in limestone that originally contained 18 rectangular reddish quartzite pillars, one of which remains in situ and depicts the figure of Pepi II embracing Re-Horakhty."

"Rectangular quartzite columns", I wondered how big they were, as the only other rectangular granite columns I'd seen were in the Osireion, and they were massive.

"In the inner sanctum of the temple is the cult chapel, with its five niches framed in red granite and lined with pink granite. Behind the chapel is the antechamber that once had a single reddish quartzite pillar. Here the ceiling had an astronomical theme, decorated with stars."

Even more red granite; could it be there was the remains of another ancient temple forty to fifty feet below the surface here at South Saqqara? Oh if I only had the time to investigate! If only *someone* had the time to *really* investigate. Or maybe they had, and the whole thing was hush hush, after all, someone had stolen the ceiling of Ibi's burial chamber.

Then, while looking just at the image of the pyramids of the Pepi II complex, and at the usual satellite 'cult' pyramid, that here lay at the south-east corner within the enclosure wall, I had a flash of brilliance. If all the pyramids along the Lower Nile corresponded to specific stars in the Milky Way, then that included all the satellite pyramids as well, all the 'queen's' pyramids, *and* all the satellite pyramids of the queen's pyramids.

And surely it included the smaller pyramids further up the Nile at places such as Edfu, the pyramids at Deir el Bahri, and the one on Elephantine Island. Then there is the location of the temples, surely they had some significance as well, particularly if the 'current' temples were built on the sites of previous much older temples that, given the presence of reused red granite, are more than likely contemporary with the pyramids. Each 'answer' posed even more questions.

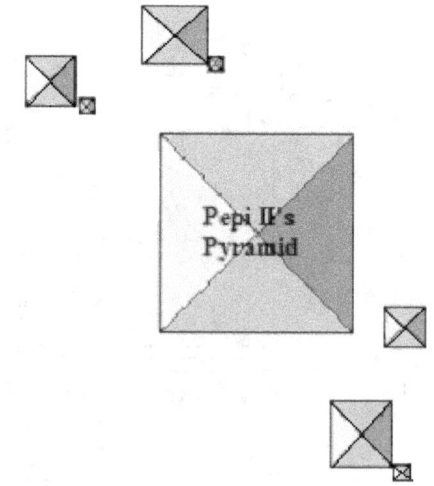

Before I realized, Abdo pulled the car to a halt.

'Please to wait here, I will go and get it the ticket.'

'Hang on.'

I pulled out a hundred and handed it to him.

'Let me know if you need any more.'

'This it will be fine.'

Abdo disappeared towards the ticket office while I returned to my iphone.

I didn't know specifically which star Pepi II related to, or any of the three 'queen's' pyramids, but I did know that Abu Raoush represented Sirius, and, if that was the case, then did that mean the satellite pyramid at Abu Raoush represented Sirius B? If it did, then that really set the cat amongst the pigeons because modern astronomers weren't even aware of Sirius B until radio telescopes confirmed it was a smaller neutron star companion in the 1960's; something the 'primitive' Dogon tribe of Africa had known all of their existence. It was all making sense; were all these satellite pyramids representations of Binary Star Systems? That sparked even more thoughts.

If the locations of the pyramids outlined a detailed star map of the Milky Way, then it must have a purpose, as maps aren't just for show. Maps are usually designed to get you from one place to another, a 'lay of the land' with the purpose of outlining a series of directions to get to an ultimate destination. And by using the Nile, the flow of the water, as the journey, it would seem to indicate that the destination was Sirius, which just happened to sit at the mouth of the river before the Nile delta, on the highest point around. Also, given the ancient Egyptians calculated by Sothic zodiacal cycles of 1,460 years tied to the heliacal rising of Sirius, the brightest star in the sky, it gave even more importance to the site of Abu Raoush.

The other purpose of a map is to find the location of somewhere important, a sort of treasure map where X marks the spot. I just wasn't sure where the X was, and what was the real treasure. Perhaps there was something buried at the complex of Pepi II?

I started looking around, wondering what was taking Abdo so long, when I notice the ruins of what looked like a valley temple on the opposite side of the road to the ticket office. I took a quick look at the map of Saqqara and figured it was most likely the Valley Temple of Unas, last pharaoh of the 5th Dynasty.

Now somewhat 'stranded' in the desert, it would once have been situated on the bank of the Nile, or on a canal, with a quay to give access to the causeway that led up to the Mortuary Temple and Pyramid of Unas. I returned to my iphone to see if I had anything on Unas's Valley Temple. There wasn't much, but I did find this gem.

"In the 1970s archaeologists excavating the lower parts of the valley temple, found a greywacke sarcophagus, similar in style to those of Menkaure and Shepseskaf, on a terrace of the Valley Temple. The sarcophagus contained a mummy of an elderly man identified by an inscription on his golden belt as 'King's son, Ptahshepses'."

I wasn't sure who Ptahshepses was, but I found it rather bizarre that a sarcophagus was discovered on the terrace of a valley temple. Surely it wasn't meant to be there, so, was it being transported when something untoward happened and it was left abandoned, then buried, or, was it washed there during some catastrophic tsunami? The latter seemed more logical, even if it was more calamitous. Time to keep digging.

In my quest for more evidence, I decided it was time to examine what I could about the pyramids themselves, starting with the three 'queens' pyramids, but, before I could, Abdo returned to the car with the ticket.

'OK, Mister Alex, where do you wish to meet your friend?'

'Saeed!'

I'd been so preoccupied digging under the sands and dodging bullets I'd forgotten to call him. I put Abdo on hold and hit the number.

'Saeed, it's Alex.'

'Indy, how are you my friend?'

'Good, good! Well, not so good, I had to get out of Cairo; the Secret Police had staked out the Embassy.'

'Did I not tell you?'

'Yeah, yeah I know. But don't worry, I still have Kareem's papers.'

'Where is it you are, my friend?'

'Saqqara.'

'Saqqara! What is it you are doing there?'

'Waiting for you, Ahoya. Where are you?'

'I am at Hawarra; we are having it the lunch with Mohammed.'

'Hey, give him my best wishes, and my thanks to his family. Tell him I'm going to send him a little thank you as soon as I get safely out of Egypt. When will you be at Saqqara?'

'Maybe two hour.'

'OK, well, give me a call when you arrive.'

'Very well, but, Indy, please, keep it your head down, the vulture they are everywhere.'

'I will. I'll see you later, Inshallah!'

'Ma'asalaamah.'

'Ma'asalaamah, Ahoya. Assalaam Alaikum.'

'Wa alaikum assalaam.'

Just hearing his voice was reassuring; things were going to be OK,…Inshallah.

'Alright, Abdo, I've got about two hours, where do you suggest we go?'

'Perhaps first we go to the museum of Imhotep.'

'Sounds good to me.'

As Abdo drove us to the museum, I got back to my notes.

The Queens' Pyramids of Pepi II

What was surprising was that each of the three 'queens' pyramids also had a 'cult' pyramid, as well as a mortuary temple. Was each a binary system in its own right?

"Located at the northwest corner of Pepi II's complex, the Pyramid of Neith, Pepi II's half-sister and cousin, is the finest and oldest of the queens' pyramids. The entrance to the Mortuary Temple was flanked by two small limestone obelisks bearing the queen's name and title."

Did the pyramid really belong to Neith, or had it just been ascribed to her in the 6th Dynasty? Isn't it just as possible it once belonged to, or was once ascribed to, Neith-hotep, wife of Narmer, first pharaoh of Egypt, eight-hundred years earlier? After all, they had found a lot of 1st Dynasty stuff in and around Saqqara.

That the obelisks were made of limestone and not red granite supported my theory about the alabaster/limestone belonging specifically to the Old Kingdom. There were other mentions of a false door and a stepped altar, but not what they were made of.

Similarly the 'cult' pyramid, about five-metres square, had a miniature passage leading to a small, rectangular chamber, but no mention of the nature of the stone.

"The Pyramid of Neith, with a base of 23.5 metres, had a three-step core built of local limestone, with a fine white limestone for the casing. The entrance was through the pavement of the pyramid's open courtyard, located in a chapel in the middle of the pyramid's north side. On the south wall of the chapel was a granite false door that sealed the entrance corridor."

Why would you use a false door of granite when the rest of the pyramid was made of limestone? You wouldn't, unless the granite was recycled, like it had been at so many of the other temples back up the Nile.

"The entrance corridor descended to a pink-granite barrier placed at the point where it levelled out, a second barrier in place just prior to arriving at the burial chamber."

Just what I expected, more red granite.

"Oriented east-west, the burial chamber is located on the pyramid's vertical axis. It has a flat ceiling with astronomical decorations of stars on a dark background, and Pyramid Texts decorate three of its walls, the fourth, west of the sarcophagus, having a symbolic palace facade. Neith's empty red-granite sarcophagus remains in the chamber, along with her canopic chest of the same material."

That got me wondering if the red-granite sarcophagus and canopic chest had been 'cut' from the one of the monolithic chambers found in one of the other subterranean structures.

Pulling up in the car park of the Imhotep museum, which had a vague resemblance to the edifice of the Seti Temple at Abydos, I hoped there was plenty of time to consider it all later whilst lying beside a pool in Greece. But, for now, it was time to see what the museum had to offer; I knew that the Illuminati would have pilfered anything of value or significance, so my hopes in that respect, of finding something profoundly astonishing, were minimal at best, but you never go, you never know.

As we made our way inside and through 'security', I quickly reviewed the other two queen's pyramids; soon glad I'd locked my backpack in the trunk of the car.

The next pyramid was ascribed to Ipwet II, thought to be a daughter of Merenre and one of Pepi II's less attested queens. Although now badly damaged, it was smaller, with poorer finishings, and didn't apparently differ that much from that of Neith. Once again, there were two obelisks, and a red-granite false door. In addition;

"A granite sarcophagus, supposedly ascribed to Ankhesen-Pepi IV, another consort of Pepi II, was discovered in the westernmost storeroom of the mortuary temple."

I found that curious; four wives but only three pyramids. It confirmed my thoughts that there were only three pyramids to usurp and that poor Ankhesen-Pepi IV, being fourth in the pecking order, missed out.

"Inscriptions found on both sides of the basalt sarcophagus lid contained part of the royal annals of the 6th Dynasty, lending support to the rule of a King Userkare near the beginning of the 6th Dynasty, perhaps for a period of around four years."

That supported my belief that Userkare was Userkara, second pharaoh of the 6th Dynasty.

The third queen's pyramid, southeast of Pepi's pyramid belonged to Wedjebten, believed to have been a daughter of Pepi I, and wife of Pepi II. According to my notes, both the pyramid and the Mortuary Temple were completely ruined, the only openly visible evidence of its existence being an alabaster offering table bearing an inscription of the queen's name.

Apart from the absence of a serdab adjoining the antechamber, the substructure of the pyramid didn't differ much from that of the pyramids of the other queens, the walls of the burial chamber and possibly the corridors again covered in fragments of the Pyramid Text. What did catch my eye was that part of an inscription was also found in the Mortuary Temple claiming that the pyramidion was sheathed in gold, and, if that were true, it would certainly raise interest in further investigation of the site, something I was keen to do.

I didn't dwell on the 'cult' pyramid; all my notes told me was;

"It was about 15.75 metres square, with a T-shaped passage and a small chamber, all of which was left rough."

But I just knew that, at the very least, there must have been red-granite portcullises beneath the surface. And that got me scratching my head. If all the pyramids were power generators, why would you need so many, so close together? OK, they weren't tombs, and it looked as if they weren't power stations, well, not as we would normally consider them. So what were they apart from markers in a massive map? I started looking for alternative answers.

No two pyramids were exactly the same; the only discernable difference between all the pyramids was their base length and the angle of the slope of their faces. Now it's possible two pyramids could have the same volume, but would they have the same resonance qualities? Everything so far on the trip had come back to vibration, to frequency: was that what the mystery of the pyramids was all about, that they each had a different 'pitch'? Perhaps the museum held some clues?

Opened in 2006, the interior of the Imhotep Museum was vastly different to the museum in Cairo; rather than exhibits 'piled up' and crammed in, here they were aesthetically 'presented' as one would expect in a modern museum. Beyond the 'security' gate was an area dedicated to the Egyptologist Jean-Philippe Lauer, who worked for much of his life at Saqqara, restoring many of the monuments. Whether he restored them as they actually were, or rather if he reconstructed them as he *believed* they once were, is questionable. There was also the base of a statue, supposedly belonging to King Djoser, 2nd pharaoh of the 3rd Dynasty, with just part of his feet and the name, Imhotep, Chancellor of Lower Egypt, written in hieroglyphs, remaining; hardly awe inspiring. I guess they had put it there because they had to have something relating to the name of the museum.

Although I had a brief look at the model of the Djoser complex, I elected to skip watching the video on Saqqara, I just couldn't bear the thought of yet another minute of Zahi Hawass self-promoting himself, and of him using and abusing the history of Ancient Egypt to do so. Instead, I moved on into the main hall where I was greeted by a boundary stele of Djoser, this time with his Horus name of Netjerikhet.

Beyond that, in the centre of the main hall and taking pride of place, was a headless seated statue of Djoser; perhaps they should've called it the Djoser Museum as they seemed to have more artefacts of his, than of Imhotep. At the far end of the hall, opposite the entrance, was a long wall covered in magnificent blue-green faience tiles collected from the burial chamber of Djoser's pyramid and the South Tomb of the Step Pyramid complex. They had been 'reconstructed' as a whole wall, including doorways and reliefs of the king running in the Heb-Sed, and, whilst it may have appeared aesthetically pleasing, it wasn't a true reconstruction, rather a possible representation based on Lauer's beliefs.

The rest of the room contained various architectural elements including stone pillars and columns, a stone arch, and stone cobras from the enclosure wall of the Step Pyramid, nothing of significance that caught my eye as I slowly circled around. Perhaps the 'tomb' room off to the side had something of interest?

Here, the designers of the museum had reconstructed a small tomb, complete with a wooden coffin of Merenre, and a mummy, as well as displays of many of the objects found in burials; ceramic jars, shabtis, several alabaster canopic jars, limestone mace-heads, jewellery, several small statue heads, and various wooden models. There was also a large limestone sphinx of King Unas and limestone reliefs from his causeway that depicted starving Bedouins.

Further along was a piece that did grab my attention; it was another limestone block, this one depicting part of the Pyramid Texts from the Pyramid of Pepi I. It took me back inside the pyramids, but not to the Pyramid of Pepi I, I could see that for myself soon enough, it took me back to my notes on the pyramids further south, in particular that of Pepi II.

The Pyramid of Pepi II

My notes indicated that Pepi II was Ancient Egypt's longest ruling pharaoh, supposedly reigning for ninety-four years. If that was so, then he must have been a child when placed on the throne. His pyramid, named "Pepi's life is enduring", had a base of 78.75 metres, which was fairly conventional, but, from there, that's when things started to get interesting.

"The core was constructed in five steps from small pieces of limestone set in clay mortar, with casing stones of fine white Tura limestone."

That fitted my thoughts about the pyramid possibly being built in stages. The question was, was it built around a ziggurat?

"For some reason we don't understand, at some point during construction, after the casing was laid and the north chapel built, the structure was enlarged with a girdle of mud-bricks about 6.5m wide around the level of the third step of core blocks. This necessitated the dismantling and rebuilding of the already completed north chapel and enclosure wall, the wall rebuilt back a little further from the pyramid."

One suggestion in my notes was that the addition might have been to strengthen the pyramid after it was damaged by an earthquake, but there was no way mud-brick was strong enough to do that. The answer seemed obvious, and the key seemed to be the north chapel and enclosure wall.

Blind Harry could figure out the chapel and wall weren't so much dismantled, as destroyed, along with the three-step structure, not by an earthquake, but by a tsunami. The next obvious conclusion was that if the rebuilding was then done by Pepi II, expanding the pyramid and rebuilding the chapel and wall, then the subsequent decimation of the site was due to the Thera tsunami. All that made perfect sense, but it raised the issue of when the previous tsunami struck, which, going by the evidence of the layers at the Osireion, surely had to be pre-dynastic, and that meant the three-step structure also had to be pre-dynastic.

There was also the possibility, primarily because of the use of mud-brick rather than alabaster and limestone, that part or all of the rebuilding could have been post-Thera, as, although there was no clear evidence, it was reinforced as a strong possibility because of the name of Khaemwaset, son of Ramses II, on the casing stones of Shepseskaf's mastaba just to the southeast.

Heading underground, the subteranean layout was pretty basic.

"From the entrance chapel on the northern wall, a sloping passage leads to the vestibule, beyond which, the horizontal corridor, inscribed with Pyramid Texts, is blocked by three huge portcullis slabs of granite."

There they were again, three portcullises! Why three; when, if tomb robbers we going to be able to get through one, then they were going to get past three? Then I had another idea, was it brilliant, time would tell. Perhaps the portcullises weren't designed to keep 'tomb-robbers' out, they were designed to keep 'something' *in*?

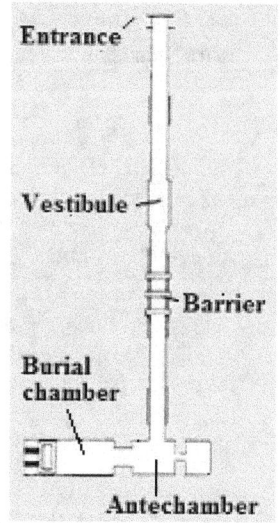

If they did act as some sort of safety valves then their 'operation' must have something to do with their resonance frequency. It was way beyond my area of knowledge and expertise, but it was just as crazy an idea as the portcullises being there to keep out tomb-robbers. How did I know that? Because, from my research, not one single mummy was found inside a sarcophagus inside the burial chamber of a pyramid where the portcullises were intact and sealed.

"After the barrier, the Pyramid-Text inscribed corridor continues into the antechamber, where, 90-degree to the right, is the entrance to the burial chamber, both of which have a vaulted ceiling painted with stars. All the walls are covered in Pyramid Texts except the west wall behind Pepi's black-granite sarcophagus, which is decorated with motifs of a stylised palace facade."

Initially it all sounded very much like the Pyramid Texts and decorations were added to the chambers during the Old Kingdom, probably during Pepi II's reign in the 6th Dynasty, but it didn't mean the chamber dated to then.

"The sarcophagus was decorated at the head and foot in green-painted false door motifs and topped with the name plate of the king, though the King's mummy has never been recovered. At the foot there was a niche in the floor for the canopic chest though only the lid of the chest was found in the tomb."

That didn't add up. If you have the technology to carve a massive sarcophagus, why would you then just paint such important details on the exterior?

No, I was convinced; the consistent presence of numerous red-granite portcullises and sarcophagi was consistent with all the subterranean chambers here pre-dating a pole shift. In addition, the red-granite doorways reused in the temples indicated there may well have been some pre-poleshift temples here as well, probably anything up to forty feet below the surface. Clearly, the visible ruins were the remains of structures rebuilt and claimed by Pepi II during the 6th Dynasty, but the devastation of the site was totally consistent with the effects of the Thera tsunami.

I'd left the 'Tomb room' and was wandering in and around the room off the opposite side of the main hall. It contained stone bowls and jars from the Early Dynastic Period as well as statues of people such as Ptahshepses, Akhethotep and Ptahotep. The statues were of mild interest, mainly because of the 'hotep' component of their names, but I found myself more interested in one particular Old Kingdom relief that clearly showed the image of a person with an elongated skull. It took me back to thinking about the Annunaki, and about their descendants; this was a relief from the Old Kingdom, but it could just as easily have been an image of Tutankhamen, the shape of the head was almost identical.

The final room left to explore, the 'Saqqara Missions', contained artefacts found by the Louvre's excavations at Saqqara and objects found in some of the more recent excavations. The most obvious was a brightly-painted, gilded, but unnamed coffin from the 30th Dynasty, found in recent excavations around the Teti pyramid, that looked like it was painted yesterday.

On the chest, painted in yellow, blue, red and black, was a magnificent pectoral with a winged scarab. To either side were five gods holding scepters. There was also an image of the winged goddess, Ma'at, with two feathers. Further down, on the legs of the mummy, were several scenes of Anubis performing the mummification ritual. It was an exquisite piece of craftsmanship and showed that the ritualistic beliefs of the Ancient Egyptians were still very strong in the 30th Dynasty, at least in and around Saqqara.

Among the other objects in the room was a display of about twenty, Late Period, bronze statuettes, a gathering of gods and goddesses including; Osiris, Isis, Horus, Ptah, Anubis, even Imhotep. They were apparently found while excavating near the recently discovered tomb of Qar, a physician and dentist from the Old Kingdom. Just imagine having a tooth extracted four thousand years ago, or even worse, a root canal. Ouch!

As I scanned along the collection, I found myself inextricably drawn to the statuette of Isis. She sat on her throne nursing her son, Horus, a set of bull's horns with a sun disk between them, on her head. Something was niggling me about it, like it was telling me something. I knew the Ancient Egyptians often represented things very symbolically, but what did a set of bull's horns have to do with the sun? Was it some reference to the star-sign of Taurus, to Horus or Isis being born during April/May, or was it something to do with the precessional era of Taurus? I felt like it was so obvious I should know it, but I didn't. I made a mental note, and moved on.

Below the statuette case, another contained 'surgical tools' from Qar's tomb. They reminded me of the carved relief on the back wall of the enclosure wall at Kom Ombo; how far I'd come since then.

It seemed an eternity ago I was drifting innocently down the Nile without a care, trading thoughts with Bill and Pieter, admiring Candy's tits, lusting after even one glimpse of Crystal's tight ass. Now I was stranded with just one lifeline to get me out of Egypt, Saeed. I checked my iphone; he was still at least ninety minutes away.

'You like?'

As we exited the building I turned to respond to Abdo. The museum had offered up little or no real surprises, I guessed all the best discoveries were whisked off to some private cache of the Illuminati.

'It was OK, nothing extraordinary.'

'Maybe you will like it the pyramid more?'

'It's a lot harder to steal a pyramid than it is to run off with its contents, that's for sure.'

As we jumped back in the car and headed back towards the main part of the complex, I tried to catch up with the other pyramids at South Saqqara that I still hadn't 'explored'. First stop was the Pyramid of Merenre at the southern edge of the northern necropolis of Saqqara, part of the mouth of the 'great snake' of Andromeda.

The Pyramid of Merenre

Merenre was the son of Pepi I and half-brother to Pepi II, and, although his pyramid was once called "Merenre's beauty shines", according to my notes and the accompanying image, it is apparently now mostly in ruin and barely noticeable next to other nearby monuments.

"Much of what we know of the pyramid comes from biographies of high officials such as Uni, who provided valuable information on the origin of the materials used to build the pyramid; there was pink granite from Aswan, alabaster from Hatnub, and dark-grey wacke from Ibhat, which was used to build the pyramidion and sarcophagus."

That *was* valuable, but it really only told us *what* the structures were built of, not *when* they were constructed. And were the materials used to build the original structure, or build the extensions and repairs? The truth is little is known about most of the complex, in fact nothing is known of the valley temple, though there must have been one because there was reference to a causeway about two-hundred-and-fifty metres long that went around the pyramid of Djedkara-Isesi. There was a scant reference to a mud-brick perimeter wall but virtually nothing about the pyramid's mortuary temple. Even the plan of the pyramid was in question.

However, there was a simple ground plan of the interior of the pyramid, which was consistent with the interior of many of the other pyramids of this type at this location.

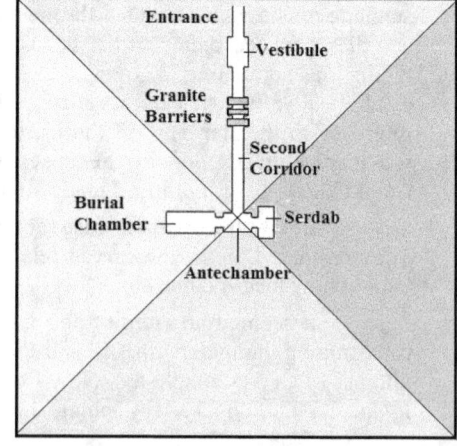

"The pyramid is entered from the north side which leads, via a descending corridor, to a vestibule. It then continues along a second, level corridor, until it reaches a barrier made up of three huge granite blocks. Beyond the barriers, the corridor leads to an antechamber; to the left is a small Serdab, or annex, to the right, the burial chamber."

The consistency of these subterranean chambers, and the use of massive blocks of red granite, further convinced me most of the Egyptologists were barking up the wrong tree and that the whole history of Ancient Egypt needed a complete rethink and overhaul. And these diagrams may have only been the bare bones; there may well be other hidden chambers and corridors, deeper, waiting to be unearthed.

In the burial chamber, the ceiling had an astronomical theme of white stars on a black background, and a sarcophagus, decorated with coloured reliefs including the royal palace façade motif, stood before the west wall.

"In 1880, Maspero entered the tomb and found the mummy of a child, its hair combed into a side curl. Because of the mummy's wrappings, scholars at first decided that this was a latter burial, perhaps of the 18th Dynasty, but, today, Egyptologists are rethinking this decision, deciding that it might be the mummy of Merenre after all."

I think Maspero was probably half right and the modern Egyptologists half wrong; the mummy either belonged to the 18th or 19th Dynasty and was placed there after the tsunami, or, and my money was on the latter, that the mummy belonged to the Old or Middle Kingdom, possibly even being Merenre, and was relocated during the 18th or 19th Dynasty from its original flooded tomb as part of the rebuilding and reconstruction after the Thera tsunami. And that's probably how the pyramid was attributed to him, and all the other pyramids to *their* 'owners', including the next pyramid on my hit list, the Pyramid of Djedkara Isesi.

We pulled up in the parking area outside the Step Pyramid of Djoser and Abdo turned to me.

'Step Pyramid, we start here?'

'Not quite…'

I'd been working my way northward, down the Nile, and wanted to maintain my 'flow'.

'…Let's start with the Pyramid of Sekhemkhet, to the south.'

'OK...'

He tossed me a bottle of water.

'…then we must be head across the desert.'

As the local guardian joined us, I decided it was best to take the backpack with me. So, Kareem's target once again on my back, Abdo led the way as we trekked south, out of the car park and across the sand, with me using the time to review the next pyramid in line, that of Djedkara.

The Pyramid of Djedkara Isesi

Djedkara Isesi was Menkauhor's successor in the 5th Dynasty, and was either Menkauhor's son, his brother, or his cousin. The way the ancient Egyptians interbred, who knows, he could have been all three. Although he might have usurped the pyramid, I now strongly doubted he was responsible for its construction; its repair, and the construction of the Mortuary Temple very possibly, but not the subterranean chambers.

"No systematic investigation of the pyramid was begun until the 20th Century, when Abdel Salam Hussain and Alexandre Varille examined it, but unfortunately their work was interrupted and their work research lost. The same thing happened when Fakhry investigated it during the 1950s."

How does someone's research just get 'lost'? Stolen, yes, locked away in someone's safe, sure, but "lost", I don't think so. And not once, but twice, concerning the same pyramid, I think the odds well and truly put that beyond mere coincidence.

"It was further investigated by Mahmud Abdel Razek in the 1980s but at this point damage has made it difficult to excavate."

What sort of damage could possibly have been done in the thirty-odd years between 1950 and the 1980s, certainly not natural damage due any tsunamis that I know about? Remember, this was around the same time the Russians were here with Project Isis and the building of the Aswan High Dam. I smelled a rat; a big one by the name of Muburak.

"Varille began excavations of the Valley Temple but did not get very far, however, a later report by Leslie Grinsell and Fakhrey, indicates they found the remains of walls with reliefs, along with a few pink-granite blocks scattered about under the first houses of the nearby of village of Saqqara."

Pink-granite blocks: that was strong enough evidence for me.

'Abdo, do you know if the villagers have unofficially found anything under the ground in the village of Saqqara.'

He looked at me, at the guardian, then back at me like I'd just told a state secret.

'You know about this? It is in these paper you have?'

'Geez, I don't know, probably. So they have found things?'

'Yes, but no one here they talk of this because the Antiquities Police they will take over and the people they will get nothing for the find of these thing.'

'And so they go on the black market, never to be recorded or studied.'

'Exactly.'

Djedkara's complex looked very similar to many of the others, the Mortuary Temple to the east and a 'satellite' pyramid to the southeast.

"The temple's entrance hall was apparently paved in alabaster, and, judging from its massive walls, probably had a vaulted ceiling. The alabaster continued into the courtyard, which had sixteen pink-granite palm-columns inscribed with the names and titles of Djedkara."

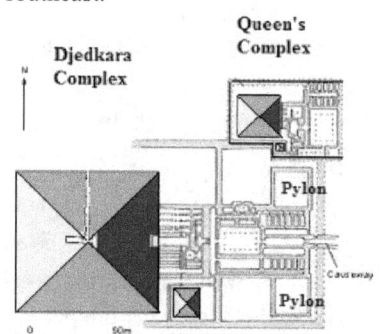

The paving and the inscriptions were definitely Old Kingdom, but the granite columns may well have been recycled from a previous era. If the wear and tear and aging of the granite was similar to that of the columns on Elephantine Island and at Dendera, then, in my book, that was conformation they were pre-poleshift.

"A passage led through the five-niche chapel and the antechamber to the offering hall where there were more pink-granite columns bearing Djedkara's name and titles."

That told me there must have been quite a temple here before the earth changes.

"Another interesting aspect of the offering hall is that its western part was incorporated within the masonry of the pyramid and would have incorporated a false door so that the dead pharaoh could enter the room for his symbolic meals."

That was food to my soul; the way I read it was that, like at other sites such as the Pyramid of Khendjer, the temple containing the false door, probably of granite, predated the pyramid or extensions to the pyramid. Is this what Hussain, Varille and Fakhry had discovered, and why their reports disappeared, they had discovered the truth about the age of the ruins? Keep digging, Indy.

Moving on, the 'cult' pyramid near the southeast corner of the main pyramid appeared to be just like all the others; a base of around fifteen metres, made of three cores, entered from the north wall, with a descending corridor leading to a single subterranean chamber. But no notes on whether any or all of the elements were made of red granite.

Thankfully there was a little more information on Djedkara's pyramid.

"With a base of 78.5m and a slope of around 52 degrees, the Pyramid of Djedkara was originally about 49-52 metres (163-173 feet) high. It had a core of six steps, however the upper three layers no longer exist and today the pyramid is only about 24 metres tall.

Each step, approximately seven metres high, is built up from fairly small, irregular pieces of limestone bound with clay mortar. Most of the casing is long gone, but some parts of the pyramid, such as the north side, are well preserved."

The use of "irregular pieces of limestone bound with clay" hardly sounded like the construction techniques one would employ to *build* a pyramid, more like those used to *repair* and *rebuild* a structure.

"The entrance is from the north, located in the pavement of the courtyard of a chapel that once stood over the opening, although the chapel is now all but gone, a small ceiling block with astronomical decorations that probably was a part of the chapel, near the entrance."

So was the entrance contemporary with the chapel, or had the chapel been built over, and to incorporate, the entrance? It seemed highly likely it was the latter, and, if that were the case, then that meant the subterranean elements pre-dated the Old Kingdom.

"The entrance corridor angles slightly east as it descends, first leading to a level vestibule, then to a barrier consisting of three huge plugging blocks of pink granite. Beyond the barrier, which still partially blocks the corridor, the corridor leads to another granite barrier just before the antechamber."

It was all sounding so very familiar; I could see how the Egyptologists had simply assumed they were all constructed around the same time, and they probably were. Their problem was in allocating the first pyramid to an Old Kingdom ruler. After they'd made *that* error, it was easy to keep perpetuating the mistake and name pyramids based on the names of those rulers who had tried to repair the pyramids, reconstructed them, augmented them, or built Mortuary temples beside them.

"To the east of the antechamber is a storage chamber with a flat ceiling, while the antechamber itself, and burial chamber to the west, both have gabled ceilings constructed of three superimposed layers of huge limestone blocks."

Seriously, a gabled ceiling "constructed of three superimposed layers of huge limestone blocks", how could the Egyptologists keep overlooking the obvious evidence that was right before their eyes?

"The burial chamber once held a dark-grey basalt sarcophagus in which the mummy's head was oriented to the north. In front of the sarcophagus, on the southeast corner, was a small, square hole for the alabaster canopic jars. However, only fragments of the sarcophagus and canopic jars were found, along with the mummified body of a man, thought to be around 50 years old, believed to be that of Djedkara."

If they only found fragments of the sarcophagus, how do they know the head was to the north? And the mummy may well have been that of Djedkara, placed there during the Old Kingdom, but it could also have been someone else relocated from somewhere else after the Thera tsunami. The truth is, that without any positive identification, it could have been anyone. And that was the big danger of modern Egyptology; it was mostly putting round pegs into square holes based on triangular assumptions of the early treasure hunters.

By now I was confident that the pyramid of the unknown queen and its satellite pyramid to the northeast of Djedkara's pyramid was not built to house an unknown queen of Djedkara, or any pharaoh for that matter, it was representative of another binary star system that formed part of a mini constellation. Then I started thinking about Ptolemy's eight-eight constellations; were all the pyramids and satellite pyramids of Lower Egypt encompassed in Ptolemy's constellations? Now *that* would be interesting to explore!

The unknown 'queen's' pyramid consisted of only the pyramid, a tiny satellite pyramid of its own (which meant it was in itself a binary system), a mortuary temple, and its own enclosure wall; there was no causeway or valley temple.

"The entrance to the mortuary temple is unusual in that it was south of the pyramid and from the west, where a corridor led to a five-columned hall, the six-papyrus-stemmed columns made of fine white limestone aligned in a single row. The hall led to an open-columned courtyard, oriented north-south, with sixteen six-papyrus-stemmed columns skirting the inside walls."

Apart from the unusual arrangement of its rooms there was nothing to suggest it was anything other than an Old Kingdom or Middle Kingdom structure.

"With a base of 41 metres, a slope of 62 degrees and a height of 21 metres, the pyramid was not much larger than some of the cult pyramids of other complexes. It consisted of three steps and the construction methods were similar to that of Djedkara's pyramid."

All the evidence was pointing towards a unified concept, a star map, with a unified building plan that contained perhaps two or three variations in the underground chambers.

We'd walked between some boat pits on the right, attributed to Unas, and the mastabas of Nefer-her-Ptah and Ptah-iry-ka to the left, and on, just south of the causeway of the Pyramid of Unas, when we hit a stretch of desert covered in what looked like a dig site.

'What are these?'

'These, they are the tomb of the New Kingdom. Between 1977 and 1988, there was around thirty-five important New Kingdom tomb discovered here in some row west of it the Monastery of Saint Jeremiah.'

I scratched my head. I knew that during the New Kingdom, Memphis had taken second place as the country's capital, but it was still the administrative and military centre for the whole of Egypt, so where were all the official buildings?

From the 18th Dynasty onwards, many high officials, who lived around the palaces and religious institutions, supposedly built tombs at Saqqara or were buried in the Saqqara necropolis. Supposedly here were their tombs, but no sign of their houses? I was on to something.

I wasn't sure if there was any reason, or anything of relevance, to bother bribing our guide to try and enter the closed site so, first, I dived into my notes.

"Unlike their Theban counterparts, the tombs at Saqqara generally consist of free-standing chapels, or miniature temples, above a complex of funerary chambers hewn out of the rock and accessible via deep shafts. The tombs can be divided into three main types of construction – a simple single-roomed chapel; a cult-room flanked by chapels and an open courtyard; and a more complex 'temple tomb' reserved for the highest of the elite such as Horemheb. The chapel walls were generally decorated with limestone reliefs, colourfully painted on plaster"

Of the thirty-five tombs, initially I was only interested in one; that of the final pharaoh of the 18th Dynasty, Horemheb, apparently built when he was still just a general.

"The tomb of Horemheb at Saqqara, built in three stages, is a vast complex resembling a mortuary temple."

Maybe because it *was* a temple, or even a dwelling?

"It is approached by way of a once massive pylon and a paved columned courtyard, but many of the original reliefs from here were destroyed. A statue room and second courtyard lead to three chapels at the rear of the structure. As Horemheb was buried in his royal tomb in the Valley of the Kings, the tomb in Saqqara was used for his anonymous first wife and his second wife Queen Mutnodjnet."

The question remains, was it really a tomb, it didn't look like one? Couldn't it just have been a dwelling? Were the Egyptologist totally misled by believing that because the structures needed to be excavated, that because they were found *below* the ground, that they therefore *must* have been tombs? Had they totally overlooked the possibility that these structures may well have once been above-ground structures buried by something like the effects of a tsunami?

Supposedly there have been no dwellings found of any of these officials, and surely you would build your home or office, close to the 'featured' buildings, those being the pyramids. So, were the underground chambers and shafts pre-existing, and did Horemheb and the others simple build temples, even houses, on top of them? It was feasible, possible, and just as plausible, if not more so, than the explanation offered up by the 'experts'.

And how could they suggest the 'tomb' was used for his anonymous first wife, whom he probably married whilst still just a general, *and* his second wife Queen Mutnodjnet, whom he married as part of legitimising his reign by marrying the *sang réal*? They would hardly have shared the same house let alone the same burial place; one was a commoner, the other, of royal blood.

In referencing Mutnodjnet, who was more than likely a maternal half-sister of Nefertiti, it drew my attention to several other New Kingdom 'tombs', discovered in the past twenty years, that related specifically to the Amarna years and to Akhenaten. They had not yet been full explored or documented, perhaps because they revealed too much controversial information, but their very presence posed some interesting questions.

The first 'tomb' was discovered in 1997 and is believed to belong to Maia, Tutankhamen's wet-nurse; clearly a wet-nurse held a high position within the court. I wondered if Maia may have been the nurse portrayed carrying a baby in a mourning-scene in the royal tomb at Amarna? So why wasn't she 'buried' in or around Amarna? Was this just her Saqqara 'residence', where she would have nursed the royal children when the royal family was in Memphis?

The second, discovered in 2001, belonged to Meryre, High Priest of Memphis during the reign of Amenhotep III and Akhenaten. He held the titles 'Overseer of the God Aten,' and 'Overseer of the Fields of Aten'. Around the same time, a third 'tomb' was discovered, just east of Horemheb's, that belonging to Meryneith, High Priest in the Temple of the Aten and the Temple of Neith, 'Steward of the Temple of Aten' and 'Scribe of the Temple of Aten in Akhet-aten'. The final 'tomb' of interest was discovered as recently as 2007 to the east of the tomb of Meryneith and belongs to Akhenaten's 'Royal Butler' Ptahemwia.

Seriously, it made sense that all these officials have houses or offices side by side when they were alive, but wasn't it a bit much to expect they would all be entombed the same way? However, the presence of these three latter 'tombs' strongly suggested two things; one, that Akhenaten spent a considerable amount of time in Memphis/Saqqara, and, if that is the case, then, two, that there *must* have been an Aten Temple at either Memphis or Saqqara, or both, and that it may still be there, buried beneath the sands.

Speaking of things buried beneath the sand:

"Early Dynastic structures have recently been located beneath the New Kingdom tombs of Maya and Meryneith."

That supported my theory of the Thera tsunami, that it covered the area, and that sometime in the New Kingdom structures were built on top of the buried buildings, which were in turn buried by the 369 BC and/or 365 AD tsunamis. But were the Early Dynastic structures tombs, or were they free-standing structures? And did the New Kingdom builders actually know what they were building on? And, were *they* tombs? Tombs have bodies, mummies, right? So, where were the mummies?

And did I need to 'baksheesh' my way into the closed site? No, unless there was any specific mention of red granite, and there wasn't, then it wasn't really calling me to explore further, so we continued on, towards the Pyramid of Sekhemkhet.

But first, back to review the last of the pyramids to the south, that of Pepi I.

The Pyramids of Pepi I

Pepi I was the second ruler of ancient Egypt's 6th Dynasty and my earlier map of the pyramids along the Nile hadn't shown anything unusual about his pyramid, even Herschel's maps hadn't shown anything out of the ordinary. However, the minute I opened the specific file on Pepi I and saw a close up of the complex, I was literally stopped in my tracks.

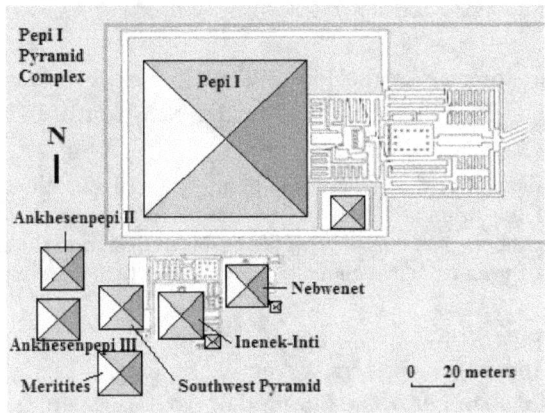

It suddenly became glaringly obvious to me having also examined the layout of the 'queens' pyramids at the Pepi II complex, that if you were going to add smaller pyramids for the pharaoh's queens around the pyramid of the demised king, then surely you would add them evenly spaced around the perimeter. But nowhere in Egypt was that the case. So, clearly their positioning was not random; there had to be some meaning to it as it made no sense to clump them all together, unless they were a copy of something like a star map. So what did we have at the Pepi I complex?

The biggest star, the 'Pepi I Pyramid', was part of a binary system. It was 'accompanied', as part of the 'constellation', by six other 'smaller' stars, two of which, Nebwenet and Inenek-Inti, were also binary. It was important to see the layout was a two-dimensional representation of a three-dimensional perspective, and that the stars were represented as they appeared from earth, not with their actual magnitudes; that meant the smaller stars could be massive, just further away. Basically we were seeing "as above, so below", the representation of the sky on the earth.

If the unique arrangements of the complex of the Pyramids of Pepi I, including the identification of binary star systems, correlated to an actual arrangement of stars in the night sky to a distant time in the past, then surely that had to be absolute proof the "queens' pyramids" theory of the Egyptologists was way off track. Sure they may have been usurped later, but it wasn't why they were built. All that said, theories are fine but now it was just a matter of looking for the corroborative evidence below the surface.

Given there was a mortuary temple, it would be fair to assume there was also a valley temple and causeway, although I couldn't find any information in my notes on either. The mortuary temple itself was predictable, having a columned courtyard, five-niche chapel, and an offering hall with a false door in the back wall adjacent to the pyramid, all later additions, most likely during the reign of Pepi I.

Of the six 'queens' pyramids;

"There is little left of Nebwenet's pyramid, enough to estimate its basic layout, that it was built of limestone, and its entrance was in the pavement of the courtyard of the north chapel. The entrance led via a descending corridor through a small vestibule, then a simple pink-granite barrier to the burial chamber, which had a flat ceiling, and no inscriptions on the walls. Fragments of a pink-granite sarcophagus were recovered."

I had my evidence, my granite portcullis, as well as fragments of a granite 'sarcophagus'. And that got me thinking, why was that such a common finding: "fragments of a granite sarcophagus". What happened to them, were they smashed from the outside, which is hard to comprehend given many of the pyramids were sealed? Or, did the 'sarcophagi' shatter from within, because of what was inside, and if that were the case, what was in them that caused the 'explosion'?

Moving on:

"The mortuary temple of the Pyramid of Inenek-Inti, was unusually wrapped around the pyramid on the east, north and south sides."

To me that clearly indicated it was a later addition, squeezed into the inter-pyramid space, and not part of the original placement of the queen's pyramids. All I found about its subterranean chambers was that they were similar in design to the other queens' pyramids, no mention of granite, but then again, no mention that there wasn't. Of the other queens' pyramids:

"Parts of a pink-granite sarcophagus were found in the burial chamber of the South-western Pyramid. Similarly, in the badly damaged burial chamber of the Pyramid of Ankhesenpepi III, a sarcophagus was found which was cut from a huge sandstone block and embedded in the floor, the lid of the sarcophagus formed from a huge roughly-dressed block of pink granite. Further, the burial chamber of the Pyramid of Ankhesenpepi II contains an enormous, carefully-crafted basalt sarcophagus with the queen's name and titles inscribed upon its lid and on the partially exposed east and north sides."

Everywhere I looked below the ground seemed to reveal granite or basalt, evidence that supported my 'red-granite theory'. Sure, I hadn't seen the inscriptions, but I was pretty sure they would be quite crudely carved and could easily have been added when the chamber was usurped during the Old Kingdom. But, did the evidence carry through to the main Pepi I pyramid?

"With a casing of fine white limestone, Pepi I's pyramid was constructed with a base of seventy-eight metres and slope of around fifty-three degrees, giving it an estimated height of around fifty-two metres, though today it is no more than a twelve-metre-high ruin. It had a core of six steps constructed from small blocks of limestone bound with a clay mortar."

It sounded very much like a reconstruction job to me.

"Blocks from queen Sesheshet were discovered within the core of the pyramid."

That was interesting, and it went towards my reconstruction theory, because

Sesheshet was Pepi's grandmother, and it seemed to be strong evidence the first period of repair work may have begun well before Pepi I finished the work and built a temple beside it to celebrate.

> "From the fragments of the restoration text of Khaemwaset, Ramses II's eldest son, we know the pyramid was in good shape during the 19th Dynasty, with few improvements."

At first that seemed confusing, as it sounded like the Thera tsunami hadn't had much effect, but then I realized it *was* a translation, perhaps a rather poor one, and that Khaemwaset could just as easily have written that he had been responsible for the repairs, that it was he who made a few improvements, and then summed it up by saying it was *now* in good shape. But the real 'concrete' evidence, or rather 'red-granite' evidence, was below the surface, and, even though I couldn't do it personally, that's where I was heading.

> "The pyramid's entrance is from the north, in the courtyard pavement next to its face. There was probably a chapel here, but nothing of it remains today."

Perhaps it was omitted with the extensions to the core.

> "The subterranean levels begin with a descending limestone corridor that leads to a vestibule. After the vestibule, the next corridor is level but reinforced at three places with pink granite."

Pink granite, just as expected, although the term "reinforcement" sounded a lot to me like a later rebuilding.

> "Located about the middle of the second corridor are three portcullis blocks also of pink granite."

The evidence just kept adding up.

> "Beyond the barriers, the corridor leads to an antechamber on the pyramid's vertical axis. To the east is a serdab with three niches, to the west, the burial chamber. The gabled ceilings of the antechamber and burial chamber, decorated with astronomical scenes of white stars on a black background, consist of three layers of blocks, each layer having sixteen blocks. All together, these ceilings weighed around five-thousand tons."

That's a lot of additional weight to put above the sarcophagus just to support small limestone blocks. If it was for that purpose, and I doubt it, then why have a gabled ceiling over the antechamber when it's unnecessary?

> "Fragments of a sarcophagus that once stood on the west wall of the burial chamber suggest that it was probably a substitute, the original having broken in transportation or perhaps developed flaws."

And where is this supposed 'original' sarcophagus? If the fragments found don't fit your theory, don't make ridiculous speculations, rethink your theory!

> "Fourteen shards of yellow alabaster canopic vessels were discovered along with a fragment of a mummy that could have been that of Pepi I, but is uncertain."

The alabaster canopic vessels definitely suggest the era of Pepi I, but they, along with the fragment of the mummy, could have been placed there during the repairs to the pyramid, or even later. And why place a fragment of a mummy? Doesn't that suggest some traumatic event happened that dismembered the mummy? It could even have been some sort of replication of the Osiris myth? Without knowing for sure to whom the mummy belonged, it was anyone's guess.

We'd walked about two hundred metres or so beyond the site of the New Kingdom tombs when the guardian stopped and pointed to a very unimpressive plateau of sand ahead.

'Pyramid, Sekhemkhet.'

Abdo looked at me for my reaction, which was probably akin to asking to be taken to the famous historical location of a castle only to find it had been razed to the ground and was now overgrown with blackberry bushes. There wasn't going to be much 'exploring' going on, probably just sand-scuffing and lots of checking my notes. But, we'd walked this far.

'Once around the park!'

The 'Buried' Pyramid of Sekhemkhet

"This was a 3rd Dynasty pyramid, because the ornamented outer enclosure wall, cased in fine, white Tura limestone, with rows of deep niches alternating in a regular intervals with false doors, was very similar to the nearby enclosure wall Djoser had built for his complex. The wall probably stood about ten metres tall, with a walkway, sentry posts and probably only one real door in the entire complex, which has never been found."

No, folks, "This was a 3rd Dynasty *wall*, because the façade of the perimeter *wall* was very similar to the 3rd Dynasty *wall* of the Djoser Complex"; the construction of the pyramid was a totally different matter, and as for the subterranean chambers, I was sure *that* would prove to be a whole other story. Geez!

By now I was totally ignoring to whom the Egyptologists had attributed each of the pyramids, in fact I believed the chances the 'pyramid' before me was built by Sekhemkhet were less that those of the Eiffel Tower being built by Bob the Builder. In fact;

"The only evidence of Sekhemkhet's existence outside of his unfinished 'buried' pyramid is a military scene of Sekhemkhet, with his raised mace about to smite his desert enemies, at Wadi Maghara in the Sinai."

There was no actual proof Sekhemkhet was even buried here. But that didn't stop the Egyptologists from making it sound as if he did.

"If we consider his attempted pyramid as evidence, Sekhemkhet came to an abrupt end. In fact, most Egyptologist seem to agree that he probably only ruled for about six years and perhaps died in some remote expedition or battle, his body never again seen."

That was so typical of the Egyptologists; using a false premise of "his attempted pyramid" as evidence to support another unfounded theory that he died in battle, and vica versa, was a total insult to scientific methodology and should assign the majority of Egyptologists to the same gaggle as fortune tellers, religious zealots, and snake-oil sellers. Wouldn't it be novel to just look at the actual evidence?

"The perimeter wall was built in two phases. In the first phase, the original perimeter wall was a much less radical rectangle, 262m x 185m, and encompassed the South Tomb. Later it was extended south, and particularly north, to a length of 500m, making it close to the size of the nearby Djoser complex."

That implied the South Tomb predated the outer enclosure wall, which seemed totally logical, though it didn't mean the South Tomb and the inner enclosure wall were built at the same time. But why was the outer enclosure wall added, what did it enclose? Given there was little exploration done here, it could have been a temple, or even another tomb or group of tombs just like at the Black Pyramid.

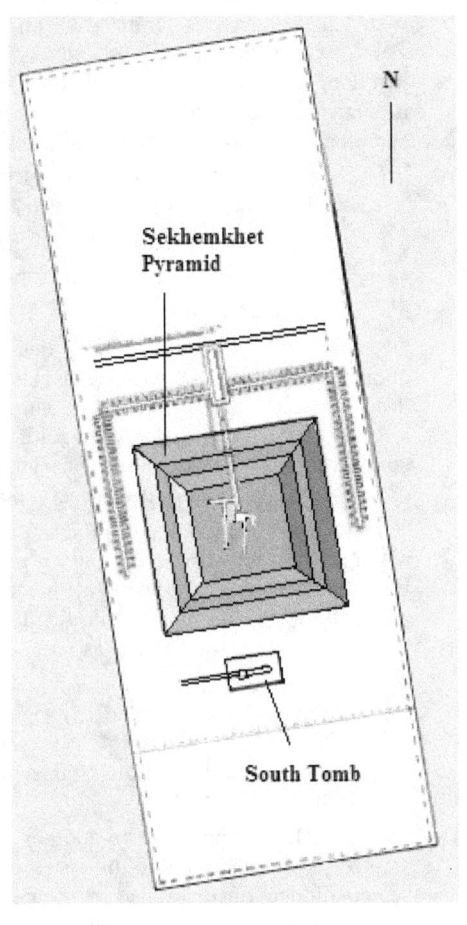

"No one yet has excavated the mortuary temple or the rest of the grounds, so many questions still remain about this pyramid."

That was an understatement. The map gave no indication of the location of the mortuary temple, whether it was north of the pyramid, or to the east. If it was to the east, as might be expected, then it would have required considerable 'groundwork' to prepare the site, as the ground was quite steep, that is unless the current lay of the land was caused by the tsunami and the temple was simply washed away and collapsed into the waters. Either way, the current site gave no clues as to the location of the mortuary temple, if there even was one, so Abdo and I set off on a clockwise circuit of the ruins, via the South Tomb.

Just over a hundred metres further along were the buried remains of the superstructure of the South Tomb; a mastaba, maybe thirty-five metres long and twelve to fifteen metres wide, built of limestone blocks. The entrance was from the west, but not accessible.

"From the entrance, a long corridor descends eastward, however, like in the main pyramid, it is interrupted by a vertical shaft. Further down the corridor, the excavators found the fragments of a small coffin that had held the remains of about a two-year-old-child. Beyond that is a small burial chamber."

There was no indication of when the tomb, if it was a tomb, was built, or if the remains belonged to the tomb, or if they were a later addition. It was all guess work, and without any concrete evidence, I wasn't going to buy into it.

A further few hundred metres west was Gisr el-Mudir, the 'Great Enclosure' and supposed massive funerary complex of king Khasekhemwy, last pharaoh of the 2nd Dynasty.

> "The first royal burials, comprising underground galleries, date to the 2nd Dynasty."

Nothing much showed up on my maps, and there was very little to see of it from beside Sekhemkhet's pyramid. Had it been properly investigated? The notes said it had underground galleries, but there was nothing on the map, nothing like at Abydos with Khasekhemwy's Umm al-Qa'ab 'tomb' and the massive enclosure at Shunet el-Zebib. If something had been found, why was there nothing written about it? Had they just done a superficial exploration some time at the dawn of modern Egyptology and the modern Egyptologists decided there was nothing there? Or, was there a cover up? Would a deeper excavation reveal a veritable trove of treasures?

> "Even though the last king of the 2nd Dynasty, Khasekhemwy, was buried at Abydos, he also built a large rectangular funerary enclosure at Saqqara. It probably inspired Imhotep to build the monumental enclosure wall around Djoser's Step Pyramid complex."

Or, it was Imhotep who designed and built them all; after all there was only about seventy years between Khasekhemwy and Sekhemkhet. As I looked out over the desert towards the enclosure, I wondered if there was any corresponding star that aligned with it. And that's when it hit me; just as the pyramids defined stars in the sky, so the stars in the sky could define unknown locations in the Egyptian desert. The map of the Milky Way could just as easily be a treasure map of as yet undiscovered riches.

I'd been interested in space and the stars when I was a child, but suddenly I had a passion for astronomy like I'd never imagined, and I was sure Randy would have been the first one to join me at the local planetarium, a map of the known pyramids along the west bank of the Nile firmly in hand. I made a note to connect with him and let him know my 'discovery' as soon as I got safely out of Egypt and reconnected with Dwight.

Meanwhile, back to my right, I could see why Sekhemkhet's pyramid was called the 'Buried' Pyramid as it was almost completely swamped in sand; there were probably no more than a few courses of masonry and it was maybe only seven metres high at its highest point.

There seemed to be another pattern emerging here in Egypt, that, unless you wanted to turn a site into a tourist attraction, or perhaps because you wanted to keep its secrets hidden, once you had 'explored' the site, or robbed it blind, you reburied it so no one could re-examine the evidence. That certainly made it difficult for a new set of eyes and an open mind to make its own conclusions about the site, rather one was put in the uncomfortable position of often just accepting the opinions of others as verbatim.

One of those 'opinions' generally regarded as fact was that, based on its design, the Pyramid of Sekhemkhet itself, if it ever was one, was, like the Step Pyramid of Djoser next door, supposedly built by Imhotep. That may well have been the case, Imhotep *may* have built them both, but it may have been just that the subterranean chambers were attributable to Imhotep, and possibly during an earlier incarnation.

"Why Sekhemkhet chose this site for his pyramid is a bit of a mystery as the pyramid was built upon uneven rock and the builders were forced to level the terrain, building large terraces, some of which were more than ten metres high. Perhaps it was because of the nearby 2nd Dynasty royal tombs?"

It seemed obvious to me; the location was predetermined by the alignments in the star map. Assuming Sirius, as the brightest star in The Milky Way, was built first, on the highest peak in Cairo beside the Nile, then the locations of all the other pyramids were subsequently aligned with it. Besides, who would build next to the tombs of people you probably weren't even related to?

"Like that of Djoser, Sekhemkhet's pyramid was also intended as a step-pyramid."

Or, maybe it wasn't! Maybe it was deliberately 'unfinished', like the pyramids at Zawiyet el-Aryan, Mazghuna, and Abu Raoush. I mean, really, did the Egyptologists honestly believe there were so many pyramids left 'unfinished' in Ancient Egypt? Obviously they did! I guess it was a convenient explanation that supported their beliefs the pyramids were constructed when they believed they were.

"The pyramid probably had a base of about 119 metres and, if it was built in seven steps, it would have risen 70 metres (230 ft) above its base, higher than Djoser's Pyramid."

The truth was, they didn't know how many steps were intended, it could have been six; it may only have been three and been a mastaba.

"It was constructed using the accretion layer method, where the stones are laid inwards at an angle of 15 degrees with sloping courses of relatively small stone blocks laid at right angles to the incline, but, since the pyramid was left unfinished, there was never any casing applied."

Maybe it wasn't the original structure that was unfinished, that used the accretion method, rather it was the repairs and reconstruction that was left incomplete? As we rounded the corner to the northern side of the pyramid, the guardian was waiting for us at the entrance to the 'pyramid'; I wasn't sure I'd get in, but I was sure the real answers were underground.

I stood before the entrance, which was in the ground in front of the north wall, outside of the actual pyramid, much as it would have been before the north chapel would have been built. Alas, the entrance was once again unfortunately closed.

"Originally discovered blocked by an intact wall, the entrance leads into a descending corridor, past three sets of blocks, which appear intact, and eventually communicates with the burial chamber. However, the corridor is bisected by a wide vertical shaft that enters the ceiling of this passage and extends up through the rock and into the masonry of the pyramid itself."

There was some suggestion the vertical shaft was used to lower blocks into the passage when the tomb needed to be sealed, and it was possible, but I wasn't so easily convinced, it would have been much easier to position the blocks during construction, as they were in other subterranean corridors. No, the shafts had some other function, what it was, for the present I had no idea.

"There were 62 papyri from the 26ᵗʰ Dynasty, written during the reign of Ahmose II, found within the shaft, as well as the bones of various animals, including cattle, rams and gazelles, no doubt offerings to the deceased. Below these were some 700 stone vessels and remarkably a gold treasure cache from the 3ʳᵈ Dynasty containing 21 bracelets, small mussel shells and faience corals covered with gold leaf. It was no doubt a part of Sekhemkhet's funerary goods, but how it ended up at the bottom of the shaft rather than stolen with the rest of the tomb's content remains a mystery."

What contributed to the mystery was that the 'offerings couldn't have just been dropped into the shaft, as the top of the shaft was up inside the body of the superstructure. So was the shaft originally outside the superstructure, and was the width of the pyramid extended after the 26ᵗʰ Dynasty, or were there more chambers to be discovered?

"Further along in the corridor a number of clay vessel stoppers were discovered bearing Sekhemkhet's name, another reason why the pyramid is attributed to him."

Oh, sure, that nails it; nothing on the walls, just a few pots with Sekhemkhet's name on the lids and that means he built the whole shebang – hardly!

"A subterranean set of 132 galleries or magazines built in a U-shape around the North, East and West side of the pyramid was never finished."

If they didn't know what the underground galleries were for, how did they know if they were finished or not?

The underground galleries looked exactly like the comb-like arrangement of rooms under the Layered Pyramid at Zawiyet el-Aryan, just here there were one-hundred-and-thirty-two galleries, a hundred more than at Zawiyet el-Aryan. What were they really for?

If the structure really was for Sekhemkhet, which I didn't believe, and he only ruled for six years, why the need for so many 'storage' rooms? I mean these things were carved out of the bedrock like nuclear bomb shelters. Was that a possibility?

"The main descending corridor passes a transverse corridor just before the burial chamber that leads off to the right and to the left, each then making a 90 degree turn back to the south, past the burial chamber. These galleries are unfinished, and may have been intended to lead to a larger mortuary apartment. The burial chamber itself is about 100 feet below the base of the pyramid, oriented north-south, and precisely aligned with the pyramid's vertical axis."

North-south? That would normally make perfect sense, *except* for the fact the pyramid above, and the compound around it, were offset from north-south by about ten degrees. Here was clear evidence the subterranean chambers were built at a separate time to the structures above. It also made sense of the vertical shaft originally being in the open. Was the superstructure built after a pole-shift?

"The walls within the burial chamber are unfinished. Inside is a rare, highly-polished alabaster sarcophagus cut from a single stone, the only others being the coffins of Queen Hetephere I, of the 4th Dynasty, and Seti I, of the 19th Dynasty."

That instantly made me think that Seti I had probably usurped the sarcophagus from an Old Kingdom king or queen, just as he had done with his temple at Abydos. It might have been an explanation for why a 'finished' sarcophagus was found in such an unfinished chamber, it was a much later addition, one possibly made through the vertical shaft and before the pyramid was constructed over it.

"The sarcophagus had no lid, rather a sliding partition, and was found sealed, which seems to indicate, though not with certainty, that it never held his remains."

Yet another empty sarcophagus, and this one in a pyramid that was supposedly found sealed; surely it was about time someone proposed another theory, one that postulated an alternative function for the granite and alabaster boxes other than their subsequent usurping as sarcophagi. And if the boxes were usurped to hold the mummified bodies of the pharaohs, why, what was the significance?

Abdo had been pretty quiet, allowing me to explore in silence, however the pensive look on my face must have sparked a curiosity within him.

'Mister Alex, what is it that you are look for?'

'The truth, Abdo, the truth!'

'This is why you have it the paper?'

I'd almost forgotten the backpack and its precious cargo.

'I guess so, but that was more fate I think.'

'Then if Allah he choose you, it must be so.'

'You think Allah chose *me* to get these papers out of Egypt?'

'Of course, how many time now it is you have escaped the Secret Police; they shoot at you and you get away. It must be the will of Allah.'

I didn't want to destroy Abdo's illusion about who Allah really was, but at that point I could have had an armed escort in an armoured vehicle, and still had doubts. But something in Abdo's faith in a higher power reassured me everything was going to be OK.

'Insh'allah, yes, if the truth be told, then let it be told.'

'And Allah he bring your friend to you here at Saqqara, and then you will be out of Egypt and safe.'

'Then let's move on and see as much of Saqqara as we can in the meantime.'

'Where is it you would like to go next?'

I pointed northward towards the Pyramid of Unas, which was little more than a barely-noticeable pile of rubble about two hundred metres away.

'I know, Scarecrow, let's keep following the yellow-brick road.'

My reference to "The Wizard of Oz' went totally over Abdo's head, although he politely nodded as if he understood and led the way off across the sand. Approaching the southern face of the pyramid, I paused briefly to look down a few shaft tombs, probably Persian tombs from the 27th Dynasty, but they were of little interest to me, so I moved on to the pyramid.

The last ruler of the 5th Dynasty, Unas had a long reign of around thirty years, so, according to the experts, he should have built a much larger pyramid, however, the one before me was far from that.

"With a base of 57.75 metres and a slope of 56 degrees, the pyramid would have risen to a height of 43 metres."

Those same 'experts' have suggested the reason for its small size was because it was at "a time of decreasing wealth", that Unas was being economically frugal. If a star map shows the reason the pyramid is smaller is because of its magnitude and size relative to the other pyramids, then I think that would pretty much leave the self-proclaimed 'experts' up shit creek without a paddle.

When I examined the diagram in my files, the layout of the pyramid complex looked almost identical to that of his predecessor Djedkara-Isesi, as well as the main cores of the complexes of Pepi I and Pepi II, even down to the size and relative position of the 'binary-star' satellite pyramid; it couldn't have been a coincidence. The same architect, sure, but when? Time for a little more exploration.

Virtually nothing remained of the satellite pyramid, so I decided to leave the mortuary Temple and Causeway until last and set off to the left, clockwise around the main pyramid.

The first section I examined was a section of the fine, white limestone casing stones that remained at the base of the southern face. It was here that Prince Khaemwaset, son of Ramesses II, had added an inscription to commemorate his restoration of the pyramid, part of which still remained. To me, that was strong evidence of major damage done to the superstructure some time before the 19th Dynasty. Khaemwaset would hardly have taken such credit for minor maintenance or repairs, it would had to have been something substantial, the sort of damage done by a tsunami only three-hundred years earlier.

"The structure's core of rough limestone blocks diminishes in size towards the top of its six layers and had a casing of blocks of fine white limestone (now only remaining on the lowest levels). The core of the pyramid consists of six layers, constructed from rough blocks of local limestone, decreasing in size as the builders reached the top layer."

I wasn't doubting the evidence at all, just the interpretation of it. How can the Egyptologists know what was the original structure, and what was a result of the repair work done by Khaemwaset?

Moving around to the northern face, the north chapel was all but gone.

"Originally it was a single room, and on its south wall next to the pyramid itself, there was an altar shaped in the hieroglyphic sign for a hetep (offering table). Behind the altar was a stela."

Sure it may have been usurped later for other reasons, but my belief was the chapel may simply have served to 'house' the entrance to the subterranean chambers.

As with the other similar pyramids, the entrance was through the pavement in the courtyard of the north chapel.

"The entrance slopes down, via a descending corridor and horizontal passage, originally blocked by three granite slabs, to an antechamber and burial chamber, both of which originally had gabled ceilings painted with yellow stars on a blue background."

As expected, the three granite portcullises confirmed the earlier dating of the subterranean chambers.

"The antechamber lies beneath the centre of the pyramid, with a room containing 3 niches to the east and the burial chamber to the west. In both chambers, Pyramid Texts were written in bas-relief, painted in a blue green on all but the west wall of the burial chamber, Unas being the first king to adorn the subterranean chambers in his pyramid with Pyramid Texts. White alabaster lined the walls of the burial chamber, the western wall incised with designs in black, white, yellow, blue and red, the five colours of the royal palace façade, intended to imitate the wooden structure covered by reed wall hangings of a royal palace or a niched archaic mastaba."

It was a shame the subterranean chambers were closed, but apparently moisture from the breath of visitors had damaged the decorations. I'd have to rely on my notes.

"Columns of beautifully-carved blue-painted hieroglyphs on the remaining walls of the burial chamber, antechamber and parts of the passages, depict 283 'spells', part of a body of texts known today as the 'Pyramid Texts'."

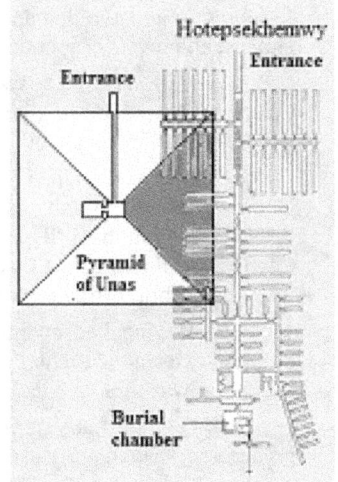

The 'Pyramid Texts', forerunners to the 'Book of the Dead', comprise almost eight-hundred known 'spells' or 'utterances' that describe the different stages of rebirth and were presumably to be read by the deceased and intended to safeguard and assist the deceased in their journey from death through the Underworld, to the Afterlife.

Interestingly, there was no single pyramid that contained the whole collection of spells, possibly because of the lack of space, and there was no standard edition, which may mean they were tailor-made for each occupant.

So was this proof the burial chamber was a tomb? I still wasn't convinced; the texts and decorations could easily have been a later addition. For me, the jury was still out.

> "Little was found within the pyramid; Unas's sarcophagus of greywacke was sunk into the floor on the western side of the burial chamber, with his canopic chest in the floor to the southeast. Only a few mummified fragments of bone were found, but it is not clear whether they belonged to Unas, as well as parts of two small knives used during the Opening of the Mouth ceremony."

A few mummified bones hardly confirmed the presence of a mummy in the sarcophagus; sure the bones might belong to Unas, but, without DNA testing, they could also belong to anyone from any dynasty. Just imagine if they DNA tested *all* these mummies, including Scota in Ireland and those of Robert the Bruce. Add to that list Cleopatra Selene II and whoever is entombed in Srinagar, Kashmir, and you might have a very interesting study.

There was another, longer, subterranean entrance further along to the east, the entrance to the tomb of Hotepsekhemwy, first pharaoh of 2nd Dynasty.

> "Very close to the Pyramid of Unas, with extensive galleries partly underlying the pyramid, is the immense tomb of Hotepsekhemwy. It was identified by numerous seal impressions bearing the King's Horus names and those of his successor Nebre, but his tomb was otherwise empty."

When I looked back at the image, at exactly how that 'part' of the massive tomb actually was positioned beneath the eastern part of the Pyramid of Unas, I had a revelation. For starters, it didn't look like a tomb to me, more like a compound; much like the other 2nd Dynasty complexes.

In any case, the 'official' belief was that the 'tomb' of Hotepsekhemwy predated the Pyramid of Unas by about five-hundred years. The question is, why did Unas build on top of Hotepsekhemwy's tomb when he could have built it fifty metres further west and avoided any overlap? Surely Unas would have known of the location of Hotepsekhemwy's compound?

Well, the first answer is that the pyramid's position was determined by the star map, but that meant the pyramid must have come first, or rather, not the superstructure, but the subterranean chambers.

Now if the Unas burial chamber *was* built first, it would then make sense why Hotepsekhemwy's tomb 'wrapped around' it. It would then make sense that some time later, possibly in the 6th Dynasty, the extended pyramid superstructure was added. It was totally logical to me, but I would bet my last dollar the so-called 'experts' would scoff at it as the ramblings of a rank amateur.

Having had no problem building over Hotepsekhemwy's complex, whoever built the extensions to the pyramid most likely built the Mortuary Temple and Causeway as well. It was time to check them out.

The mortuary temple was largely destroyed, but followed the plan of his predecessor, Djedkara-Isesi. The inner part of the temple consisted of an offering hall abutting the pyramid, with the usual false-door made of pink granite, parts of which were still in place. I headed out through what would have been an antechamber and chapel, with five statue niches, into the outer temple. It had several large Late Period shaft tombs to the side of an open court that would have once had eighteen red-granite palm-columns around the perimeter depicting the names of Unas.

> "These columns are no longer here, but some have survived by being reused in the Delta at modern Tanis, and in the Louvre and British Museums."

Surely it was about time these pilfered trophies were returned and the temple rebuilt? What good are a few columns in the corner of a museum compared to visiting the actual reconstructed location? Besides, with today's technology they could easily replicate the columns for their museum displays.

The shaft tomb was huge, too big for my liking to consider it a tomb. It seemed to be just outside, or very close to, the north-eastern edge of Hotepsekhemwy's tomb, and that seemed too much of a coincidence. Was it really a shaft tomb, or a shaft cut to remove large objects from beneath the surface, because that's what it looked like to me? And if it was a looters' shaft, was it really dug in the Late Period, or were we just being told that to cover up some 20th Century treasure hunting?

Moving out through the entrance hall, I noticed remnants of the floor paved with alabaster, then through the remains of a red-granite gateway at the entrance to the temple, built and commemorated not by Unas, but by Teti, Unas's successor. Two weather-worn square columns formed the doorjambs, crudely carved with hieroglyphs, including Teti's cartouche. Was this an indication that the outer temple was built by Teti from the remains of an even older temple, and the inner temple by Unas? Unlikely, but worth considering as it was a definite 'trend' during the New Kingdom.

As I moved on down the walkway, the main question running through my head was, did they usurp the red granite from some previous temple? To the left were several recently reconstructed structures. I stopped briefly.

'Abdo, do you know what these are?'

'Private mastaba of Nebet and Khenut, two queen of Unas.'

I turned to Abdo.

'Mastabas? Any half-blind amateur can see these weren't tombs, they were residences.'

'How is this?'

'For starters, they don't even look like mastabas; and they're not underground structures. They look like houses, including having a porticoed courtyard, and they line the causeway and are positioned outside the temple. Looks like houses of the rich and famous to me.'

Abdo pondered my words as he gave the structures a second perusal.

'This it is interest me, yes!'

'Is it that the Egyptologists are so preoccupied with finding "tombs", that any structure they discover beneath the surface, that has to be excavated, must be a tomb, despite the evidence to the contrary and the fact they have never found any corresponding residences? If they woke up to the fact the Thera tsunami, and possibly other tsunamis, had buried the civilizations, then maybe we could get some intelligent discourse happening, and get to the real history of ancient Egypt.'

I shook my head and moved on.

The causeway linking Unas's mortuary temple to his valley temple must have been very impressive in its time, and there had been considerable work put into restoring sections of it. It once consisted of a covered passageway, over seven-hundred metres long, making two turns, probably to avoid other buildings and to connect to the lower section of causeway, which, going by the map, may have originally run from Djoser's complex to the Valley Temple, which may have actually originally belonged to Djoser. The interior was lit through a slit in the roof that would have run along the full length of the causeway.

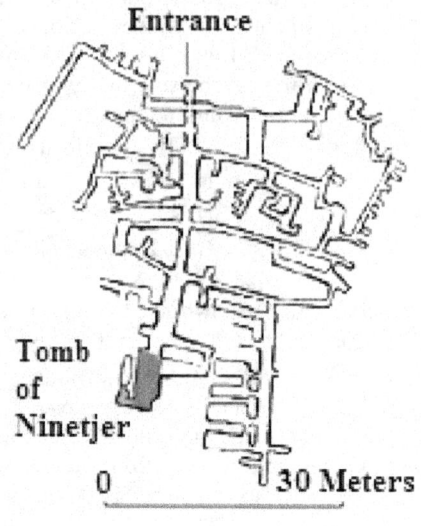

Entrance

Tomb of Ninetjer

0   30 Meters

"The interior surfaces of the causeway were decorated with high-quality multi-coloured reliefs depicting a range of scenes including; royal rituals, vignettes from heb-sed ceremonies, and the transportation of granite palm-columns from Aswan."

Ah, but did that mean the columns were actually quarried and made in Aswan, or were they usurped from other older ruined temples there; like the ones I had seen on Elephantine Island for instance?

"Other reliefs included hunting scenes of giraffe, lions and leopards, agriculture, metalworking, and battle scenes with Asian enemies. There was also a haunting representation, on the lower part of the causeway, of emaciated Beduins that appears to show the hardships during the Old Kingdom and may be connected with the 'Famine Stela' on Sehel Island at Aswan, which supposedly documents a 7-year famine during the reign of King Djoser."

Was this the seven-year-famine that Joseph/Moses had supposedly interpreted from pharaoh's 'dream' and that he wrote into his 'memoirs' as part of his own 'extraordinary' life-story? I wouldn't put it past him.

We strode past a few more 'tombs'/dwellings, those of Idut, Mehu, and Neb-kau-hor, and past the entrance to the tomb of Ninetjer, 3rd pharaoh of the 2nd Dynasty. Ninetjet's 'tomb' worked its way under the causeway and looked as if the irregular network of tunnels might even have negotiated around the 'boat pits', if that's what they really were. If the tomb *did* navigate around them, then surely that meant the 'boat pits' predated the reign of Ninetjer.

Although Ninetjer reigned for forty years and a mere ten years after Hotepsekhemwy, and his tomb similarly reached out to the south, towards the area of the New Kingdom tombs, Ninetjer's tomb lacked the regular planning, symmetry and precision of his predecessor. That didn't add up. So did it really belong to Ninetjer, or was it from the 2nd or even 1st Dynasty.

"When it was first discovered it was found to contain hundreds of Late Period mummies from later burials."

Surely that was proof that just because you found a mummy or part of a mummy in a tomb, it didn't mean the mummy originally belonged to that tomb? I kept digging.

There were even more subterranean chambers running beneath the western terrace almost the full length of the compound: these ones systematically regular in the precision and alignment of their layout. One in particular was over four-hundred-and-fifty metres long and must have had over five-hundred chambers; it appeared to be contemporary in design to that of Hotepsekhemwy which aligned with it on the other side of what was apparently a dry moat. There was no way it was a tomb! But if it wasn't a tomb, what was it?

It was just another question that arose as I paused, in line with the house of Ka-Irer, to briefly examine the 'boat pits' on the south side of the causeway. There were two of them, forty-five feet long, carved out of the bedrock and encased in limestone blocks. The experts made the obvious conclusion that "at one time they would have probably held long, slender wooden boats". No shit, Sherlock. But I wondered if maybe they had some other function, perhaps as some sort of dry-dock to make repairs.

We still had at least an hour before Saeed arrived, so we moved on northwards to the big show, the main event at Saqqara, the complex of 'Djoser'.

The Funerary Complex of Netjerikhet

Known to the ancient Egyptians as kbhw-ntrw, 'libation of the deities', since the New Kingdom the Step Pyramid has been attributed to the 3rd Dynasty pharaoh, Djoser, but, the reality is, the only name that has ever been found on the monument is that of 'Netjerikhet'. Were Djoser and Netjerikhet the same person? Everyone seems to think so. But what if they weren't?

By now, after visiting so many temples and seeing that the deeper you went within the further back in time you went, I'd strongly considered the possibility that the subterranean chambers, the various stages of the pyramid, and the different elements of the surrounding compound, could all have been built by different people at significantly different periods. Was the complex of Netjerikhet going to be any different? With that in mind, my objective was the Step Pyramid itself, but best check out the surrounds just in case.

Oriented north-south, the entire complex covered around fifteen hectares in a rectangle about two-hundred-and-fifty metres wide by six-hundred metres long, and was once enclosed within a stone wall about eleven metres high and over sixteen-hundred metres long.

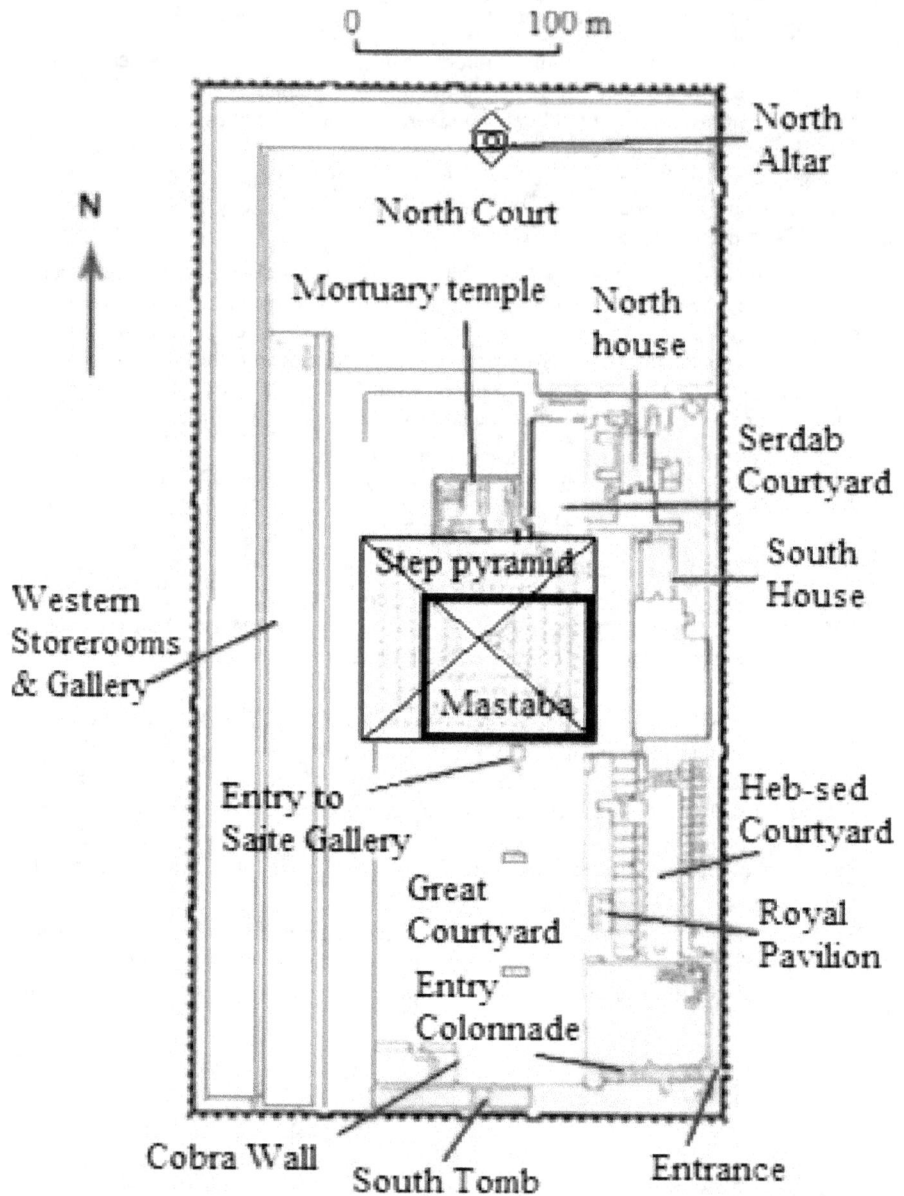

North Altar

North Court

Mortuary temple

North house

Serdab Courtyard

South House

Step pyramid

Mastaba

Western Storerooms & Gallery

Entry to Saite Gallery

Heb-sed Courtyard

Great Courtyard

Royal Pavilion

Entry Colonnade

N

0   100 m

Cobra Wall   South Tomb   Entrance

"There were fifteen entrance towers, made of fine white Tura limestone, spaced around the niched wall. Of the fifteen doors, fourteen were imitations, complete with door- leaves and a lock, carved into the wall after it was built.

Some archaeologists believe it may have represented the earthly residence of the King and so the term 'palace façade' became used for this type of decoration."

Did they consider it may actually have been his residence, that it *was* a palace;

not built around a tomb, rather a palace built around some significant site perhaps connected to the generation of some energy source? Just looking at the map it was clear the terraces predated the 'Step Pyramid' and were possibly contemporary with the Mastaba. And tiered terraces would indicate viewing platforms for some rituals or celebrations held in the Great Court.

The southern wall had been partly reconstructed, as well as near the single entrance to the enclosure, on the southeast rampart, and that's where we were headed.

The entrance led to a corridor lined by a colonnade of twenty pairs of columns, each resembling bundles of reeds or palm ribs. To either side, between the columns, was a total of forty-two small chambers, perhaps representing the nomes of Upper and Lower Egypt.

"Several statue fragments were found in the entrance colonnade but the most important was a statue base inscribed with the Horus name and titles of Netjerikhet as well as the name of a High Priest of Heliopolis and royal architect, Imhotep."

If you believed the Egyptologists, pharaohs were originally buried in rectangular mud-brick mastabas and 'Djoser's' pyramid was a revolutionary design in which Imhotep created a pyramid by stacking six mastabas of stone on top of each other. It was supposedly the first structure ever built of cut stone; the oldest of the Seven Wonders of the World, and the beginning of an evolutionary period that would eventually see the polished, smooth-faced true pyramids of the 4th Dynasty master-builders seen at Giza and elsewhere. Well, I didn't buy it for one second; all I needed to find was the proof.

Inside the enclosure wall were the ruins of terraces, stairways, platforms, shrines and chapels with finely carved facades, ribbed and fluted columns, and life-size statues, plus a number of buildings, some of which the 'experts' believe were;

"...dummy buildings filled with sand, gravel and other rubble, included solely to confuse would-be invaders".

Were they serious? That's like saying, "most DNA is junk DNA", or "we only use ten percent of our brain". Hey guys, just because you don't know the answer, don't come up with asinine ideas and pass them off as fact. Isn't it possible the rooms were flooded by and filled with the sand, gravel and other rubble of a six-hundred-foot tsunami? Dummy buildings, what a laugh!

I spotted the frieze of cobras, a symbol of royalty and apparently worshipped as a goddess in this region, on part of the southern wall near where the South Tomb was supposed to be. Heading off in that direction, I made my way up an external set of stairs to what I thought was the top of the southern wall. Imagine my surprise when I found another massive shaft descending into what I presumed was the South Tomb. There was a second larger one further along. Were they part of the original design? I doubted it!

I wanted to go down and check it out, but there was no safe entrance visible, and I was pretty sure the guardian shadowing us wasn't going to oblige.

"The South Tomb appears to be a miniature replica of the subterranean chambers of the Step Pyramid as three essential features of the substructure of the pyramid have been replicated: the descending corridor; the central shaft with the granite vault; and the king's palace with its blue-tiled chambers.

Or, should that read, "the Step Pyramid is an enlarged copy of the subterranean chambers of the South Tomb"?

At first the granite vault confused me; if it *was* a model made by Netjerikhet, then the granite vault threw a spanner in the works of my red-granite theory. But then I wondered, that as the Step Pyramid had no 'satellite' pyramid, if the chamber and descending entrance corridor of the South Tomb belonged to the binary-star companion of the main pyramid? If that *was* the case, then the granite chamber would already have been in situ when Netjerikhet appropriated it and my red-granite theory was still intact.

"Remarkably, the wooden beam used to lower the granite plug was still in place with traces left by the ropes still visible."

Isn't it just as plausible that the wooden beam and rope were used to *raise* the granite plug in an attempt to rob the 'tomb'?

"The granite vault is similar to the one under the pyramid, but it is much smaller, too small for a human burial, and its interior was covered in green traces of copper."

Copper? The first thing that came to mind was that copper was a great conductor and used in electrical circuitry. Was this evidence that the South Tomb was an energy 'sub-station'?

"The walls of the manoeuvre chamber are made of large limestone slabs with the underside of the stone ceiling beams rounded to imitate palm logs. Incorporated into the ceiling were blocks of fine limestone with relief-carved stars - remains of a previous vault."

How do they know the star ceiling blocks were from a previous vault? I tended to agree, but it was also possible they were reused from the same vault.

"The 'inner palace' is far more complete than that beneath the main pyramid. Chamber I has six panels identical to those under the pyramid, with blue faience tiles laid on a limestone backing imitating reed-mat facades with a vaulted top supported by djed columns. One contained the real door from the vestibule. In another chamber, three more panels contain false-door stelae, while the fourth contains the real door that exits to a short corridor. Two more chambers are covered, like their counterparts under the pyramid, with blue faience inlay. The reliefs and text depict the king in perpetual communion with the *netjeru*, the gods and denizens of the Nether world."

I scratched my head: it didn't make sense that the South Tomb was so intricately decorated.

"The interior also contains a relief of Djoser running the Heb-Sed race; a ritual marking the 30th year of his reign in which he was required to run back and forth between thrones to represent the union of Lower and Upper Egypt, however the burial chamber is too small to have ever contained a sarcophagus."

That the interior was decorated with the same sort of tiles as those I'd seen in the Imhotep Museum, and that it was so small, too small for a body, got me again wondering if it was in fact a tomb; maybe it was a private spa and sauna? Some

Egyptologists had even suggested it was a tomb just for the canopic chest.

Anyway, more questions unanswered, I snapped a few photos then headed on, back down via the western terraces to the Great Courtyard, which measured about two-hundred metres by a hundred metres. In the centre of the court were two strange structures with low walls and shaped like the letter 'B'. the whole court reminded me a bit of 'Ben Hur', of the Circus Maximusin Rome and the scene of the great chariot race; the ancient Egyptians had chariots, maybe they used to race them here? Surely, at the very least, this area was for public celebrations, perhaps it was associated with the Heb-sed ceremonies.

"The Saqqara complex was designed for the performance the rituals of the jubilee festival, or Hebsed. The complex consisted of many other buildings, as well as ornamental posts some 37 feet high sculpted into drooping leaves, blooms of papyrus, and sedge flower. These carved stone, imitations of the images of Hebsed, were finished with a bright green ceramic to make them more colourful and lifelike."

That told me this wasn't a necropolis, this was a place of celebration. The Heb-sed was celebrated by a *living* pharaoh, and living pharaohs hardly celebrated their lengthy reign in a mortuary complex that was supposedly built to honour their death. That it was celebrated at a place of great reverence and power, yes, but not a funerary complex. And that brought me to the source of everything, the focal point:

The Step Pyramid of 'Djoser'

It dominated the site, rising above the plateau in a series of six 'stepped' mastabas to a height of around sixty metres. But there were other factors that made this 'pyramid' different; with a rectangular base area of a hundred-and-forty metres by one-hundred-and-eighteen metres it wasn't the 'traditional' square pyramid base.

"The Step Pyramid was first constructed as a square mastaba, which was enlarged and expanded through six stages over twenty years, eventually becoming a 4-step mastaba and then a 6-step structure, which was no longer square but had become a rectangle oriented east-west. When completed, it was covered in smooth fine limestone, although the casing was removed long ago."

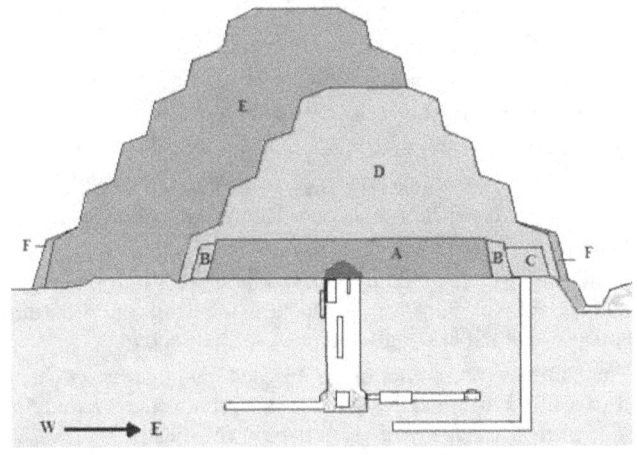

What if the casing was never there in the first place? What if the 'construction' period of twenty years was not for the whole structure, including the subterranean chambers, but only for one stage, or for the repairs to the pyramid?

I couldn't believe what I was reading, there were some 'scholars' who suggested that the whole structure was planned as a rectangular pyramid from the outset, simply because earlier mastaba tombs were always rectangular. Other 'Einsteins' had an equally ridiculous proposal:

"Perhaps the pyramid wasn't initially imagined as a step pyramid, but rather as a large, square mastaba. However, the fact that the first stage is square, whereas most all mastaba style tombs are usually rectangular, suggests that the builders may have, from the beginning, planned a stepped pyramid."

Oh, right, and then they screwed up and built a rectangle; it didn't make any sense. What did make sense was that the original 'mastaba', if that's what it was, was far removed from not only the final superstructure, but probably from the subterranean chambers as well. I couldn't dissect the actual pyramid, but I could check out the diagram.

Clearly there was a lot going on here, or rather, had gone on here. The first thing that struck me was to start below the surface; all the other pyramids had indicated the subterranean chambers existed way before the superstructure, so best start at the bottom and work my way up.

'Can we go down, inside the pyramid?'

The guardian, who had been silently shadowing my every move, pointed eastward.

'Permit from office.'

Abdo filled in the blanks.

'You must first get it the special permission from the office of the Antiquities Inspectorate. I do not think this is wise, they will ask many questions.'

I wasn't going to upset that hornets' nest, not while I was so close to getting out of Egypt, I'd have to rely on my notes. I sat down on the 'B' shaped structure in the courtyard, and tuned in.

"Below ground, Djoser created a complex system of corridors on a scale previously unknown, quarrying out more than 5.7 kilometres of shafts, tunnels, chambers, galleries and magazines. A central corridor and two parallel ones extend over 365 metres connecting 400 rooms. These and other subterranean features surround one of the most complicated tangles of tunnels and shafts the Egyptians ever created."

Well, I didn't think 'Djoser' was responsible for building what was underground; that he usurped it and used it for a variety of reasons, most probably, but built it, no!

Man, they weren't kidding, this was a maze. In my mind I tried to simplify it, ignoring the peripheral corridors, first just focusing on the 'burial chamber', the entrance corridor that led to it, and the massive shaft above it.

The shaft seemed to dominate proceedings, just by its sheer size and position, but, was it part of the original design or a later shaft dug for some other reason, before the first stage of the mastaba/pyramid was built overhead?

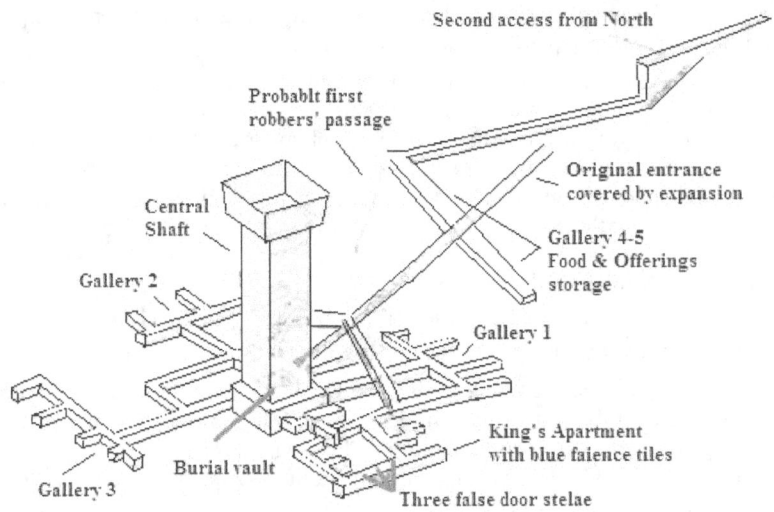

Second access from North

Probablt first
robbers' passage

Central
Shaft

Gallery 2

Original entrance
covered by expansion

Gallery 4-5
Food & Offerings
storage

Gallery 1

King's Apartment
with blue faience tiles

Burial vault

Gallery 3

Three false door stelae

"Visitors enter via a tunnel in the south face, cut by robbers during the Late Period, though a series of passageways and wooden ladders to the central burial shaft, as the original entrance, from the north and sealed with a three-tonne granite plug, has been blocked up because it is unstable."

OK, there was my first clue. First it was granite, which convinced me this was pre-dynastic and pre-poleshift. Second, why seal the entrance with a massive granite barrier if the whole burial chamber was easily accessed by lowering yourself a mere twenty-eight metres down the vertical shaft? Surely the shaft must have been a later 'addition'.

"The burial chamber is lined with Aswan pink granite but little was found inside, only a few small fragments of bone wrapped in linen in Old Kingdom style, including a left foot and part of an arm, which have been radiocarbon dated and prove to be from a burial much later than Djoser's reign."

It sounded like it was just a granite chamber with no actual sarcophagus. But it was granite, and that supported my theory it was pre-poleshift. And the human remains just showed how dangerous it was to assume they belonged to the place they were found because clearly they didn't belong to the early part of the Old Kingdom. You would wonder that while they were doing a radiocarbon dating of the remains no one thought to do a DNA test as well! But it didn't give me a solid explanation for why the vertical shaft was there?

"Numerous fragments of limestone or 'alabaster' were also discovered nearby and some limestone blocks carved with stars were found to have been re-used, with their decoration hidden and it is thought that Djoser's burial chamber may have contained the first example of a star ceiling."

Bingo! There it was! There must have been a gabled limestone ceiling in place above the chamber, just as there had been at many of the other pyramids. The difference was, that instead of combining the entrance corridor in a trench, like they had at Abu

Raoush and Zawiyet el-Aryan, here they built a slightly different design, digging a vertical shaft with a separate entrance/maintenance shaft.

Maybe the ceiling then fractured due to the vibrational overload caused by some massive catastrophic event, the same one that short-circuited Abu Raoush, the Bent and Red Pyramids, and the ancient Egyptians tried to repair it. But, unable to open the granite block in the original entrance, they created a second entrance from the north, circumnavigated the granite block and set about attempting to repair the damage. However, finding the ceiling blocks were not repairable, the chamber was abandoned, as many others had been, such as those at Abu Raoush and Zawiyet el Aryan. But who claimed the chamber as their tomb?

"In a passage north-west of the burial chamber a wooden box was found inscribed with Netjerikhet's name."

It's possible then, that during the Old Kingdom, the chamber was usurped by Netjerikhet, who decorated the ceiling with stars, like in the chamber of Pepi I, built a simple mastaba over the top to claim it as his own, and built his palace around the site. It's also possible the box was placed there at some later stage, perhaps as an heirloom.

Then I thought, wait a minute, maybe the chamber was usurped way before then? That there were so many 1st and 2nd Dynasty 'tombs' discovered at Saqqara was clear evidence the rulers of those dynasties must surely have known of the significance of the star map sites; the close proximity and evidence of the 'tomb' of Hotepsekhemwy, in it being built around the chamber of the 'Unas' pyramid, seems to confirm that they did. And if that is in fact the case, then it also raises all sorts of questions.

Was the chamber originally usurped by a 1st Dynasty ruler? Most of the 1st Dynasty rulers had tombs at Saqqara: Djet, Djer, Merneith, Aha, Qa'a; so could the lower galleries that run off the main chamber and under the western terraces have been excavated by someone such as Narmer? Was this, in fact, originally used by Narmer, perhaps as his burial site; his name is notably missing from the list of tombs discovered here?

Was Narmer the first to decorate the ceiling of his tomb with stars? It would make sense. And what happened to the limestone ceiling; did it collapse, or was it deliberately removed and reused elsewhere by a later usurper, Netjerikhet, perhaps in the South Tomb? Who knows? Ultimately, the significance is not where it is now, but that it was there in the first place.

"Many galleries and magazines surround the central burial vault. In one of the galleries on the eastern side, three false doors were carved from limestone and the walls were decorated with exquisite tiny blue faience tiles inter-spaced with rows and motifs of limestone to represent wall-hangings of natural reed matting."

From my previous discoveries I was fairly confident the civilization that created the red-granite temples and chambers was too advanced to bother making corridors of limestone decorated with 'primitive' blue tiles; so I didn't believe the burial chamber was from the same period as the galleries that surrounded it, they were much later.

"Reliefs of the King wearing the red crown and the white crown, and running or walking, probably depict the heb-sed."

Perhaps the real significance was the representation of the king wearing the red *and* the white crowns, that he had united Egypt; was this Narmer?

"Another series of galleries extends westwards from 11 shafts on the eastern side of the pyramid. Thought to be for the burial of the King's wives and children, one of them was found to contain an empty alabaster sarcophagus as well as a wooden coffin belonging to a small boy.

Netjerikhet's name was also found on a seal-impression in one of the shafts. In other shafts around forty thousand vessels were found, with a wide variety of shapes and made of a variety of materials; alabaster, dolomite, aragonite, and other precious materials, many bearing inscriptions of Djoser's ancestors."

That didn't gel. Why build eleven more vertical shafts when you could use the existing main shaft and just extend the lower galleries? The eastern shafts had to have been created later, after the initial mastaba had been built over the main shaft, and before the second extension to that superstructure. That was consistent with the eastern shafts having been created during the 3rd Dynasty reign of Netjerikhet, and it explain why the galleries contained so many vessels bearing the names of Netjerikhet's ancestors.

"As a final measure, the king's treasure was lowered through vertical shafts around the tomb into a long corridor 100 feet below ground. The protection of the king and his endowment of burial gifts was the primary function of the burial site."

No, it may have *become* the primary function when Netjerikhet built his enclosure around the Mastaba, even using the subterranean chambers to store his valuables, but it certainly wasn't its original purpose.

So, was the South Tomb really Narmer's 'model' of what he wanted to achieve, or, did it belong to Netjerikhet? Maybe it belonged to somebody else all together? I didn't have anything in my notes to check it out, but if the South Tomb didn't have a corresponding series of eleven eastern shafts then as far as I was concerned it strongly supported the notion the South Tomb belonged to Narmer.

Was the whole thing all too far-fetched a concept? It made more sense to me than the current theories ever did, but did it make sense of what was happening above the ground; what did the superstructure tell us? Perhaps I could figure it out as I walked around it.

"About 200 metres north of the original mastaba, the South Tomb, Imhotep began the Step Pyramid with another mastaba structure twice the traditional size, approximately 110 metres on the north and south walls by 130 metres on the east and west."

Well, there was a contradiction straight away; the experts couldn't decide if the original mastaba was rectangular, or square. Were they just guessing, as usual? To me, it made absolutely no difference if it was rectangular, square, or pear-shaped, the real questions to answer were "who", and thus "when". But was there any way that could be determined from the structure itself?

"The pyramid was raised on top of this structure in five successively smaller steps, or accretion layers, When the builders began to transform the mastaba, they began by building a crude core of roughly shaped stones with a fine limestone casing and a layer of packing in between.

Abandoning horizontal beds, they began to build in accretions, where limestone blocks were laid in courses and inclined towards the centre of the pyramid, employing larger and better-carved blocks that no longer needed to be packed with large amounts of mortar.

In the initial stage, they encased the king's mastaba in fine limestone, and then only a few years later entirely covered it with the Step Pyramid."

There were a few clues; that the initial mastaba was encased in limestone seemed to indicate a definite stage. Also the shift to larger blocks seemed to hint at something, but there wasn't really anything conclusive. Or was there?

I was looking at the picture of the cross-section when I realized it was the very structure that told the story.

The vertical shaft, 'burial' chamber and descending entrance corridor from the north were built first, cut down into the bedrock most likely before the last pole-shift. Next, sometime shortly after the pole shift, the second northern entrance was built as a way to bypass the granite barrier, access the descending passage, and repair the interior. It seems the repairs may have failed.

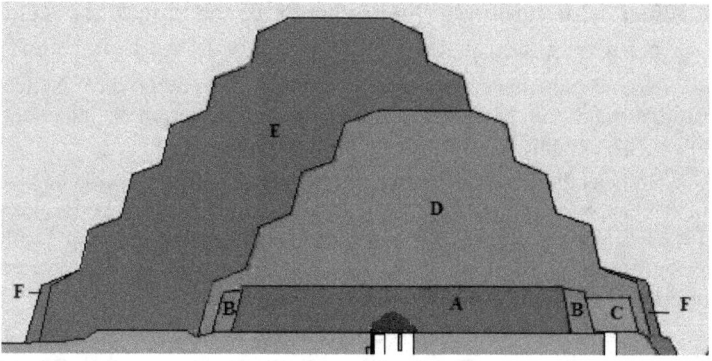

The beginning of dynastic history sparked the next stages, with construction of the South Tomb by Narmer, built as a model of what he planned beneath the ground. Narmer then excavated the various lower galleries off the 'burial' chamber at the base of the shaft, decorating the limestone ceiling of the chamber and erecting the originating mastaba above the vertical shaft. He probably also built the South House as it aligns with the dimensions of the mastaba, and possibly built the North House as well.

Just under three-hundred years later, at the beginning of the 3rd Dynasty, Netjerikhet encased the mastaba in limestone and claimed it as his own, excavated the eleven eastern shafts and galleries, filled them valuables, built the massive limestone enclosure wall, Hed-sed Courtyard and other structures, and turned the site into a palace.

The next addition, still a minor one, was basically to cover up the shafts built by Netjerikhet, in effect burying him and his ancestors. That was most likely also done in the 3rd Dynasty, possibly by one of his successors, Khaba or Huni.

It was the next two alterations that significantly changed the skyline. The first added a further three levels to the mastaba, turning it into a four-step 'pyramid', and probably happened during the 4th Dynasty. It was most likely part of Snefru's handiwork, although it could have been done by Bakara as no pyramid has been found that has been attributed to him.

The second big expansion, and the penultimate one, turned it into the six-stepped structure that we see today. But, was the structure completed as a proper pyramid, fully encased in smooth limestone? If Snefru was responsible for the previous stage, then it could be attributable to Bakara. In either case, it is highly probably that the structure was fully encased in smooth limestone, as with those of his immediate predecessors. Also, simply by observing where it aligns with the 'pyramid', the Mortuary Temple to the north would most likely have been added at this stage. So, where is it?

It was after this stage that the Thera tsunami would have struck, damaging the pyramid, stripping it of its limestone casing, razing the Mortuary Temple to the ground, and burying most of the area in up to fifteen, maybe twenty feet of silt and sand.

However, this stage of expansion may also have been done post-Thera, and, if it was, then it was most likely done by Thutmoses IV, who restored many structures. Alternatively it may possibly even have been done by Horemheb, as he seemed to have a significant presence here at Saqqara.

The final stage, casing the lower level in limestone, was clearly attributable to Khaemwaset.

"A limestone block was found here bearing a text of Prince Khaemwaset, son of Rameses II, who was known to have restored many of the Old Kingdom monuments in his role as High Priest of Memphis."

Or was it? Was Khaemwaset attempting to repair the already existing remains of the lower level of casing stones of the Bakara Pyramid? Perhaps he was finishing the work started by Horemheb? It was extremely common for Ramses II to claim temples, statues, or anything significant as his own, why should his son be any different?

It seemed there was a distinct possibility the history of the pyramid may not be as cut-and-dried as the Egyptologists would have us believe; as far as they were concerned, the Step Pyramid was built by Imhotep. The question remained, where was Imhotep while all this was going on?

I'd made my way back southwards towards the entrance, where, immediately to the north of the entrance colonnade, was a series of reconstructed buildings "thought to have been connected with the King's heb-sed, or jubilee festival". Maybe the Egyptologists actually got something right.

"A rectangular building known as Temple 'T' is suggested to have been a model of the King's palace and contains an entrance colonnade, antechamber and three inner courts leading to a square chamber decorated with a frieze of 'djed' symbols."

Maybe because it *was* a palace; if it looks like a duck, walks like a duck, and quacks like a duck. Hardly a funerary compound at all!

Beyond that was a deep trench, something like a moat, about thirty metres deep, that ran along the inside of the outer wall. Clearly it was an important structural aspect; was it for defence? That would seem to correlate with there only being one entrance to the compound. So, was it part of the original Narmer compound, after all he was responsible for uniting Upper and Lower Egypt? The massive outer limestone wall may have been Netjerikhet's but could it just as easily have been built by Narmer?

At the corner was a zigzag staircase descending maybe forty metres below the ground. Of course it was off limits, and I could only speculate where it led, and why it was there; more chambers? If so, why no mention of them on the map or in my notes? Curious! Were there things down there the Egyptians didn't want us to know about? Perhaps. Was the truth down below? It seemed so.

I headed north into the southern end of the Hed-sed Courtyard. Two chapels at the south had a staircase leading to a statue niche, while the other buildings to the west had more simple façades and may have been robing rooms or other buildings connected with the Heb-sed festival.

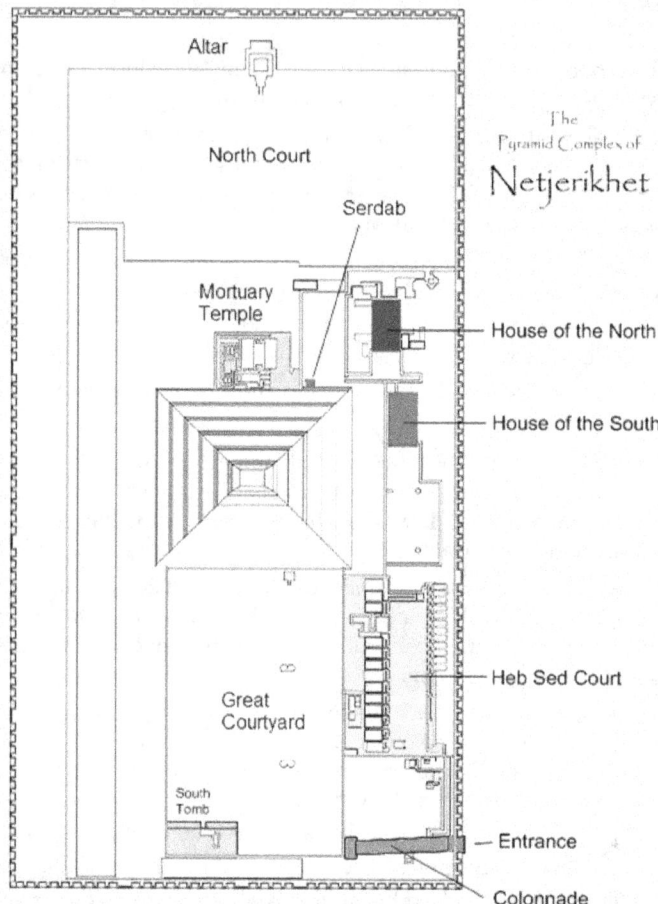

At the southern end of the court was a large elevated dais which possibly held the thrones of Upper and Lower Egypt, where Narmer may have been crowned as the first pharaoh of a united Egypt, where each subsequent pharaoh celebrated the union. Was the original Heb-sed Festival meant to celebrate the union of Upper and Lower Egypt, but, over time, as hundreds of years rolled past, was hijacked to celebrate the glory and longevity of the reigning pharaoh? That's the way it was starting to look to me.

"The eastern wall of the courtyard was originally lined with twelve chapels in the shape of Lower Egyptian shrines, each with a curved vaulted roof and having a statue niche which would have contained statues of the King."

There had been some reconstruction work done on both sides of the courtyard; whether it was authentic or not was another question.

"To the west, the wall contained thirteen chapels, modelled on the shrines of Upper Egypt, with three-fluted half-columns, simulated doorleaves at the entrances, topped by an arched vaulted roof. All these buildings are dummy buildings; purely symbolic structures to serve the king's ka in the Afterlife."

What a crock of crap. Of course you'd make up some load of bollocks like that if you believed the whole complex was a funerary complex, because you believed the whole western bank represented the Afterlife, but what if all your presumptions and beliefs were wrong?

I had a different view, a common-sense perspective. This location was decided as the 'Camp David', the 38th Parallel, selected as the place were each of the warring sides met to sign the unification treaty. Each of the two sides would have required chapels or chambers to represent their respective 'nomes' or political states, twelve to the east and thirteen to the west, which may well have predated or even been part of an existing forty-two-nome system.

The 'bipartisan' elected ruler, Narmer, would have been presented on the throne, crowned with both the white and red crowns and perhaps the united crown of Upper and Lower Egypt. It would have been witnessed by all the official interested parties on both sides, then ceremoniously Narmer would have emerged into the Great Courtyard where the populace, were amassed on the western terraces, as the first pharaoh of a united Egypt. THAT made a hell of a lot more sense of the evidence I was discovering and seeing than the waffle I was reading in my notes.

Heading on, north of the Heb-sed Courtyard with its own courtyard, was the 'House of the South'. A continuous 'khekher' frieze existed over the entrance and the walls, which, to me was reminiscent of the decoration in the tombs in the Valley of the Kings and indicative of the New Kingdom.

"Inside are many pieces of New Kingdom graffiti, written in ink by ancient visitors, naming Djoser as the owner of the complex."

"Written in ink", not in reliefs? Was this where the Egyptologists got the name 'Djoser'? For all we know 'Djoser' was a New Kingdom priest or scribe under the rule of Khaemwaset. He could even have been an interior decorator responsible for the frieze, or a brickies-labourer, who scrawled his name on the tea-room during breaks: "Kilroy was here", "Foo was here", "Djoser was here". How embarrassing would that be for the 'experts'!

By the time I hit the northern side of the pyramid, I was pretty sure I had seen everything I needed to see here at Saqqara, however there was still over half-an-hour until Saeed arrived, and the guardian was pointing to the north-eastern corner of the pyramid.

'Serdab. Djoser.'

He led us over to the remains of a small structure leaning against the north face of the pyramid, two large holes drilled into the wall; yes *drilled* into the wall; smooth, and perfectly round. Where did the ancient Egyptians get circular masonry drills?

Through the hole was a life-sized statue, supposedly of 'Djoser' seated on his throne, staring back at me. Apparently it was a replica, the original being in the Cairo Museum.

Clearly this structure and the statue within it were not contemporary with the latter two stages of the pyramid's expansion. Were they part of an original north chapel that was 'swallowed up' in the expansion, but somehow survived? And who was the statue really of; Netjerikhet, Huni, maybe even Narmer?

Further west, in front of the northern face, were basically the partially reconstructed foundations of the Mortuary Temple. According to the Egyptologists it was Djoser's Mortuary Temple, but by my reckoning, that couldn't be possible. My thinking was it originally belonged to Snefru, or maybe even Bakara.

It was a little bit difficult to make out the ground-plan but, according to my notes, it differed considerably from the mortuary temples of other pyramids. The one structure I could make out was the original entrance shaft into the Vertical Shaft, which could still be seen in the floor, even though the entrance was closed.

"In excavations of the temple, clay sealings were found bearing the name of a King Sanakhte, previously thought to have been a predecessor of Djoser, and these may provide evidence that he actually ruled after Djoser's time."

What a ridiculous proposition! According to the Kings Lists, Sanakhte *was* Netjerikhet's predecessor, so making the suggestion Sanakhte *followed* Netjerikhet, just because you were erroneously conditioned into believing the complex was built by Netjerikhet, was a prime example of the closed-minded approach and 'logic' most Egyptologists applied to Egyptology.

That clay seals belonging to Sanakhte were found here was clear evidence the complex pre-dated Netjerikhet. To me, it was hard evidence, and, if that is the case, then it points the finger very strongly towards this place at one time being the unifying palace of Narmer, first pharaoh of Egypt.

Having made yet another history-shaking discovery, I continued on my star-map journey northward, eastward, towards the next pyramid in the galactic line. Meanwhile, Abdo pointed back south, towards the entrance.

'Mister Alex, it is this way.'

'No, I'll keep going. You go back and get the car, and I'll meet you at the next pyramid.'

'Very good.'

Abdo headed south and I pointed east.

'Userkaf.'

The guardian nodded and led the way, passing the 'House of the North'. Inside, it contained a shaft, about twenty metres deep, with an underground gallery. Common sense dictated the shaft was probably contemporary with the eastern shafts of Netjerikhet, which may mean the house above it also belonged to Netjerikhet, rather than Narmer.

"Currently believed to represent the archaic shrines of Nekhbet and Wadjet, evidence suggests that the builders originally partially buried these two dummy structures, along with the South Tomb and Sed Chapels, almost immediately after they built them, which would have given them a funerary significance."

There they were again; "Dummy structures", "structures categorized by dummies" more like it. The burying of all the structures was simply explained by the tons of silt and sand dumped on and in everything by the Thera tsunami, most of which I just happened to be trekking over. But, then again, if you had your head up your own ass, and hadn't looked outside the box, you wouldn't even consider that as a possibility, now would you?

The guardian had led me eastward, out of the northern section of the 'Djoser' complex and to the complex of Userkaf, founder of the 5th Dynasty.

The Pyramid Complex of Userkaf

The southernmost element, about ten metres south of the main enclosure, was the Pyramid of Queen Neferhetepes, wife of Userkaf and mother of Sahure. The pyramid was little more than a small mound of rubble.

"With a base of 26.25 metres and a slope of 52°, the Pyramid of Queen Neferhetepes would originally have stood around 16.8 metres high. The core of the pyramid consisted of three horizontal layers of roughly-hewn local limestone blocks and gypsum mortar and was undoubtedly covered with a fine Tura limestone outer casing, now removed."

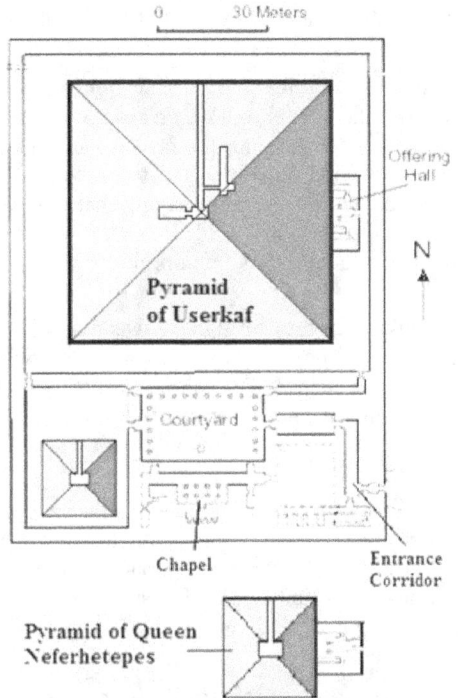

As my notes weren't revealing much, certainly not anything new, I quickly made my way anticlockwise around the rubble to the eastern side where it appeared the queen's pyramid once had its own mortuary temple. All I could see was sand and more rubble.

"From the ruins, archaeologists propose that the temple comprised an open colonnade, possibly made of granite, a sacrificial chapel adjoining the pyramid side, three statue niches and a few magazine chambers. No traces of a cult pyramid were found onsite."

Whilst it was easy to speculate, and support my theory, I wasn't going to accept there was a granite colonnade unless actual evidence existed. Basically there was nothing left to speculate about, as it appeared the pyramid had been extensively used as a source of building blocks in later times.

Rounding the northern side, to the pyramid's entrance, I did see a surprising benefit; its internal chambers were now exposed, so maybe there was something of note beneath the surface.

"The entrance to the substructure consists of a descending passage leading to a T-shaped chamber located under the tip of the pyramid and oriented on an east-west axis. It has a gabled roof made of large limestone blocks."

OK, that confirmed it for me; the gabled ceilings were definitely NOT to relieve the weight of the pyramid above the chamber. This was only a small pyramid and I couldn't see the purpose of using such a unique structural device in such a small pyramid if it was to do with weight distribution. These gabled ceiling surely had a functionality of relieving pressure in the other direction.

Turning to the north, I took in the remains of Userkaf's main complex. To the left, occupying the southwest corner of the complex, were the lowest two levels of the core of the now familiar cult pyramid, or as I now considered it, the 'binary star' pyramid.

"Originally it stood 15 metres high, with a base of 21 metres, and its slope of 53° identical to that of the main pyramid. The core was made of roughly-hewn limestone blocks disposed in two layers and finally clad with fine Tura limestone. Entered from the north, a descending corridor leads just below ground-level to a T-shaped chamber, with a gabled roof, constructed in a shallow open pit dug into the ground before the construction of the pyramid above it commenced."

That was consistent with many of the pyramids, but the question remained as to how long after the chamber was built was the superstructure erected over it? I was suddenly reminded of Chernobyl; the reactors were dug into the ground, and when the accident happened, years later, meltdown happened and they had to erect a concrete 'tomb' over the top to contain the radioactive material. I wasn't saying that is what had happened here, or at the other sites, it just popped into my head. But what was it Frank was saying about the nuclear reactor under the Temple of Solomon, under the Dome of the Rock? Could there be something to it?

It made me think of Mark and Frank; were they all right? I was tempted to call them; it had been over two hours now. But what if they had confiscated Mark's phone? I would call and they might let him answer it, and then they would use GPS to track me down. What the hell had I got myself into? In the end I decided that once Mark and Frank were clear they would call or send a text, or maybe they would wait a few days to make sure I was out of Egypt safely.

These were not good thoughts to be having whilst standing out in the desert at an archaeological site guarded by the very people you were trying to escape from; exploring a mortuary temple of all things while you have a suicide pack crammed with incriminating evidence on your back. So much for a fun couple of weeks in Egypt!

Unusually, the Mortuary Temple was built south of the pyramid rather than to the east.

"The mortuary temple was most likely built to the south because there was insufficient room to the east due to a great trench."

I couldn't see it now, it was probably filled in with sand and silt, but I wondered if this trench was somehow connect to the deep trench I had seen earlier in the main compound. In any case, if it was true, then it was strong evidence that the locations of the pyramids was determined way before any associated temples were even planned, meaning the mortuary temples couldn't have been contemporary with the pyramids they abutted, and any reference to the builder of the temple was just that, to the temple, but not to the pyramid.

It was almost impossible to make out any detail of the temple, because, in addition to the damage of the Thera tsunami, during the 26th Dynasty a large shaft tomb was built in its midst, and all that remained were sections of the basalt paving in what was the courtyard, and the large granite blocks framing the outer door.

"The entrance to the temple, from the causeway leading from Userkaf's valley temple, which remains unexplored and unexcavated, was at the southeast corner. Inside the entrance, the corridor takes right then left turn before arriving at the pillared courtyard, paved in basalt and surrounded on all sides except the south by monolithic pink-granite pillars inscribed with Userkaf's name and titles.

The walls were adorned with fine reliefs depicting scenes of life in a papyrus thicket, a boat with its crew, and the names of Upper and Lower Egyptian estates connected to the cult of the king. Near the south wall, once stood a five-metre-high colossal statue of Userkaf, the head of which is now in the Cairo Museum and shows him wearing the Nemes and Uraeus."

Was this the evidence they relied on to attribute the pyramid to Userkaf? If it was, it was pretty scant; the statute, assuming it really was of Userkaf and not appropriated by him, could have been placed there any time. Similarly, the pink-granite pillars in the courtyard could also have been appropriated by Userkaf from an earlier temple. But the sheer size of the statue and fact it was of red granite, as were the pillars, seemed telling. And whilst the evidence may have indicated the temple was most likely built, or appropriated, by Userkaf, it did not confirm Userkaf was responsible for building the pyramid. In fact, the position of the temple seemed to totally prove the pyramid was already existent before the temple was even planned.

"Two doors, at the south-east and south-west corners of the courtyard, led to a small hypostyle hall, the inner sanctum, with four pairs of red-granite pillars and a chapel with three to five niches where cult statues of Userkaf were placed."

Even more red granite; I would have loved to have seen it with my own eyes, because, if it was as worn as the red-granite columns on Elephantine Island and at Dendera, then it clearly predated the surrounding stone by thousands of years.

Looking at the diagram, what I also found interesting about this particular mortuary temple was, that whilst the inner sanctum was located on the south side of the courtyard, separating it from the pyramid, the offering hall that should follow it was not located in the inner sanctum, but rather it existed as a small, separate limestone temple in front of the pyramid's east wall. Was that again because they ran out of room as the satellite, or 'binary' pyramid, like the main pyramid, was already there, and had been for centuries? Or was it because of the existence of the pyramid of Queen Neferhetepes? Or maybe because of the large enclosure wall that surrounded the main pyramid, the 'binary-star' pyramid, and the space in which the mortuary temple was built?

It made a lot of sense that something was in the way; it was as if the mortuary temple had been chopped up and shuffled around to fit in the space between the pre-existing pyramids, and that could mean only one thing, they weren't planned and built by the same person or in the same period.

I skirted around the eastern side of Userkaf's pyramid, checking out what I could of what remained of the offering chapel, which was barely visible.

"A small offering chapel, floored with black basalt, adjoined the eastern side of the main pyramid. It consisted of a central two-pillared room with a large quartzite false door and two narrow chambers on the sides. Its walls were made of Tura limestone, adorned with fine reliefs of offering scenes, with granite dadoes decorated with scenes of sacrifice gracing the upper sections of the other walls."

I had a fair idea that the red granite predated the limestone by centuries, possibly thousands of years, but where did the basalt fit in? Was it an early attempt to replicate the red granite, but proved unsatisfactory or difficult to work and was replaced with limestone? There had to be some reason for both its appearance, and then its decline. Perhaps the pyramid had some answers.

The Pyramid of Userkaf

"The pyramid originally had a base of 73 metres, and, with a slope of 53°, rose 49 metres high. The core was built of small roughly-hewn blocks of local limestone set in horizontal layers in a step-like structure. This meant a considerable saving of labour compared to the large and more accurately-hewn stone cores created using the accretion layer method of 4th Dynasty pyramids. The outer casing of the pyramid was made of fine white Tura limestone."

Was this simpler method of construction actually an indication this pyramid was an earlier model, meaning it predated the accretion method structures? Given the pyramids were not originally built by any dynastic rulers, it was a distinct possibility, but would that be reflected in the subterranean chambers?

The entrance to the pyramid was again from the north, and would have been through the pavement of the pyramid's northern courtyard, if it hadn't been for the fact an earthquake in 1991 had buried it beneath rubble.

"The pyramid itself does not have internal chambers, rather they are located underground, constructed in a deep open ditch dug before the pyramid construction started and only later covered by the pyramid."

That was very similar to Abu Raoush and Zawiyet el-Aryan.

"The entrance was hewn into the bedrock and floored and roofed with large slabs of white limestone, most of which have been removed in modern times. It descends 18.5 metres southward to a horizontal tunnel 8 metres below the pyramid base. The first few metres of this tunnel were roofed and floored with red granite. The tunnel was blocked by two large portcullis of red granite, the first one still having traces of the gypsum plaster used to seal the portcullis."

There was my granite, as expected, though not just the portcullises, also used for the ceiling and floor: curious! What was more enlightening were the "traces of gypsum used to seal the portcullis". If the granite portcullis was a physical block to prevent entry by unwanted persons unknown, there would be no point "sealing" the block as tomb-robbers could just chip the gypsum away. If, however, at a later time you needed to air-seal the portcullis, perhaps as an attempted repair, then that would make sense.

"Just after the plugging block, to the east, was the entrance to a storage annex shaped like the letter 'T'. The presence of such a storage chamber, located under the base of a pyramid, is unique of all the 5th and 6th Dynasty pyramids."

Could that be because it *wasn't* a 5th or 6th Dynasty pyramid? It was consistent with the South Tomb and descending passage of the 'Djoser' pyramid, and the extensions to those sites appeared to date back to the 1st Dynasty.

"At the southern end of the horizontal corridor is the antechamber, exactly on the pyramid's vertical axis and oriented east-west. Here, the gabled ceiling is made from two huge blocks of fine white Tura limestone, the walls lined with the same material.

From the antechamber, the interior plan takes a 90-degree right turn westwards into the burial chamber, which is constructed nearly identically to the antechamber, but about twice as long. Near the west wall of the burial chamber were found fragments of an empty undecorated basalt sarcophagus that would have sat in a depression in the floor."

I'd thought I pretty much had it figured out; red granite was pre pole shift, alabaster and limestone linked things to the Old and Middle Kingdom, and mud-brick from the New Kingdom on, but where did the basalt fit in, was it early dynastic, a transitory link between the red granite and the limestone? Yet another question! Thankfully there were more pyramids to explore and more chances to stumble across the answers. I pointed northeast.

'Teti pyramid?'

The guardian nodded, he was right with me, and we set off down the road towards the Pyramid of Teti.

I wished Bill was around, he might have been able to shed a bit of light on things. I wondered where he was and how he was getting on, and how Pernille was. They were an odd couple, the 'Okker-bloke' billionaire and the 'Danish delight', but I was so happy for them both. She was so much better off with Bill than that asshole Jacques; thank God I never had to put up with his arrogant French presence ever again. I wondered where he was, back in Paris filing for divorce and plotting to make Pernille's life as difficult as possible no doubt.

I wondered about the others, where they were now? Pieter and Yuko were probably blissfully backpacking their way down the Nile somewhere between Abydos and Hawarra, Dwight most likely had his head buried in his books somewhere in Cairo, while Randy was more than likely back at Princeton boasting of his exploits in Egypt to impressionable freshman college girls like Candy, who was more than likely back in LA on her back somewhere taking 'direction', or giving some talent agent the best blow job he's ever had. Oh, for the good life! And Crystal, where was she now, and would I ever see her again?

As if on cue, when we reached the cross road, Abdo pulled up in the car. The guardian and I jumped in and we made the short trip around the corner to the Pyramid of Teti.

Teti

Teti was the first ruler of Egypt's 6th Dynasty, even though the Egyptologists believe he was possibly the son of Unas, the last ruler of the 5th Dynasty. It was yet another reason to have severe doubts over Manetho's 'arrangement' of the King's List into dynasties; rather than make it clearer it only seemed to complicate matters. Or was it a coded reference to the path of the *sang réal*?

Unas reign for about thirty years, and had at least two wives; Nebet, and Khenut. But he also had at least four sisters, one of which was Kekheretnebti. Is it possible Nebet, Khenut, and Kekheretnebti were all one and the same person, or that Nebet was the name Kekheretnebti assumed once she married her brother? He may well have had other wives who were not siblings or blood-related. So Teti may well have been the son of Unas, but not to a woman of the lineage of the *sang réal*, not to one of his sisters, or possibly Teti's mother was a cousin of Unas, a different lineage? Is that why Manetho considered it a different dynasty? What *is* sure, is that Teti married Iput I, the eldest daughter of Unas, and thus justified his rule by marrying the *sang réal*.

The other thing to consider was, despite ruling for thirty years and having at least two consorts, there were no 'queen's' pyramids associated with the pyramid of Unas. The Egyptologists propose that's because times were tough and they couldn't afford it. That didn't gel with me; I was sticking with the star map theory, and Teti's pyramid corresponded directly with it.

The Pyramid of Teti

Although the pyramid's ancient name was "Teti's places are enduring", it had not lived up to expectations and not endured very well at all. As usual there were the remains of an enclosure wall and within it would have been an open courtyard, if it had not been for all the sand.

"In the northwest part of the courtyard was a forty-metre deep shaft, probably used as a well by the original builders of this complex."

Forty metres, that was pretty deep. Possibly it was a well, or just as possibly it was a later shaft tomb? Or, it delved down to the level of the pre-pole-shift civilisation? As it was full of sand, there was no way I was going to find out.

Beyond that was the pyramid; the core built in five layers with a base around eighty metres and an original height thought to have been just over fifty metres, it was now little more than a rounded hill of rubble.

"Teti's pyramid consisted of a core of five levels of masonry encased in small locally-quarried limestone blocks, some of which are still in situ on the eastern side."

It seemed the east side was the most protected. Was that because of the direction the tsunami hit? Nah, the tsunami would have come from the north and obliterated everything; it was probably just coincidence. Or, had the temple on the eastern side offered some protection? It seemed possible, so I took off around the southern side of the pyramid to check it out.

'Mister Alex, where is it you are going?'

'Just doing a lap of the pyramid. You might as well wait here; I'll only be a few minutes.'

'Yes? Very good.'

According to my diagram, which, apart from the absence of accompanying 'queens' pyramids, had a floor-plan that looked almost a duplicate of those of Pepi I's, Unas, and Djedkara-Isesi., the satellite pyramid stood on the opposite, southeast corner of the main pyramid and sure enough, there is was; enclosed within the remains of its own perimeter wall

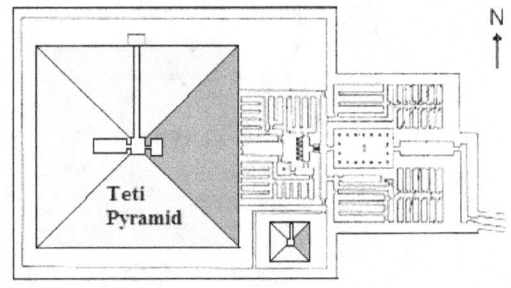

and especially well-preserved considering the passage of time. I wondered if that was because the mortuary temple had shielded it from the initial impact of the tsunami?

Like most of the other 'binary-star' pyramids, it had a base of around fifteen metres and stood about the same distance high.

"The entrance to the satellite pyramid is on the northern side and gives access to the single chamber through a descending passage."

I quickly moved on to the east, to the ruins of the mortuary temple; if the main pyramid had "not endured well", the Mortuary Temple had fared far worse.

To the southeast, part of the causeway was visible at the point where it met the mortuary temple, however;

"Teti's valley temple and the three-hundred-metre-long causeway that leads to it have not been archaeologically investigated."

And that was about the extent of discerning anything, as most of the masonry was gone, supposedly robbed in antiquity, but more likely washed away by the tsunami. In either scenario, there was little to see as no clearing or reconstruction work had been done, so, I had to revert to my notes.

"The causeway connects to the mortuary temple via a small north-south courtyard that runs along the southern part of the east façade."

There was some suggestion the entrance was modified because of an 'earlier' 5th Dynasty pyramid, tagged Lepsius XXIX, just to the east. There was nothing to see there now, but if a star map confirmed a star in that position, then odds-on there was another red-granite chamber awaiting discovery somewhere under the sand.

"From there, entry into the mortuary temple was through a heavy, single-panelled wooden door over a quartzite doorstep."

This time the red granite formed the doorstep, as it had at many of the temples further up the Nile; Kom Ombo, Edfu, Dendera. Was it really the door lintel of another, much older temple buried underneath?

"The entrance corridor had a high, vaulted ceiling decorated with stars, an alabaster floor, and decorated walls showing the king and gods, the sed festival and the smiting of Egypt's enemies.

It led to an open courtyard with a portico of 18 pink-granite pillars, some of which were square and harked back to the 4th Dynasty, all inscribed in deep relief with the king's name and titles."

That told me that the courtyard had been built from both round and square columns, from two separate previous temples, both usurped by Teti, but without seeing the columns with my own eyes, and the extent of their wear-and-tear, it was impossible to say which were older.

"A short staircase in the western wall led into the inner temple through granite doorways inscribed with the names and titles of the King."

As expected!

"The niched chapel that followed led to the offering hall, where the monolithic quartzite base of a false door still remains in situ on the western side of the offering hall."

How could the modern Egyptologists not have noticed this; first the use of granite in key locations, secondly, its different weathering, and third, how could they not have asked the simple question, why granite?

After briefly examining the remaining casing stones at the base of the eastern face of the pyramid I made my way back to where Abdo and the guardian were waiting at the northern entrance to the pyramid. Its subterranean corridors and chambers were similar to those beneath the pyramids of Djedkare-Isesi and Unas, including having the entrance down through the pavement of a north chapel, which was now gone and replaced with a modern concrete entrance.

Fortunately the concrete quickly made way for the descending passage, lined with pink granite, but, alas for my rather robust and lofty frame, only about four-feet high, and the same wide: definitely not constructed for regular human traversing, unless you considered Snow White's dwarves or a tribe of pygmies from the Congo to be the norm.

However, despite the cramped conditions, and the fact it had only been a day since I was inside the Bent and Red Pyramids, adrenalin started surging through my body. Yes, this was something!

The passage levelled out to a horizontal corridor, again only four-feet tall, but even less, wide, which once contained three granite portcullis blocks in the middle. How any tomb-robber could have worked in here by the light of a few candles or a lighted torch is beyond imagining. And there wasn't just one granite block to get through, there were three!

As I scrambled my way along, I found it extremely difficult to accept this was the grandiose entrance to the tomb of a pharaoh.

I paused at the remains and opening of one of the granite portcullises to admire it; smashed open no doubt to access the treasures that supposedly awaited within the 'burial' chamber. It was amazing, not just the technical design aspects, but to be able to work such massive stones with such precision.

Moving on, the corridor emerged at the antechamber, directly under the central axis, where thankfully I could finally stand erect. It had a vaulted ceiling made of huge limestone blocks, three layers of them apparently, stars decorating the surface.

Parts of the walls were decorated with stylised reliefs painted to resemble a 'palace façade', and the ceiling was painted with stars, but the highlight was the end walls, which were covered in Pyramid Texts.

> "The Pyramid Texts are indicative of the Old Kingdom, being found in five kings' pyramids of the 5th and 6th Dynasties, those of Unas, Teti, Pepi I, Merenre and Pepi II, as well as a few of the queens' pyramids, plus the 8th Dynasty pyramid of King Ibi."

According to the Egyptologists, the Pyramid Texts describe the King's journey from the land of the living to the Netherworld and were intended to guide the pharaoh, whose cartouche was easy to pick out amongst the hieroglyphs, successfully towards his eternal life with the gods. But, the translations by Champollion are poor at best, so what do the Pyramid Texts *really* represent? Is there more to it, is it more of an attempt to represent a spiritual journey of consciousness, from the 3rd Dimensional realm to a higher realm? And were the texts connected to the chamber in any way? I took a closer look at them.

Yes, the hieroglyphs were cut reasonably cleanly, in columns into the stone, but they didn't seem to be of the standard you would expect from the same people who would have cut and positioned the massive stone into which they were cut.

> "Teti possibly died before the decoration of his burial chambers was complete as the texts were never completed and are more damaged than those in the Pyramid of Unas."

Once again it seemed the priests were not as intent on making sure the pharaoh had all he needed to journey through the Afterworld. Perhaps the adjoining chambers held some answers.

To the left, a low square-cut opening in the massive block that was the eastern wall led to a small annex with three niches or magazines, which, according to the Egyptologists, would have originally contained statues of the pharaoh. And, perhaps they did, once the chambers had been usurped by Teti that is. However, before then, there may not even have been any niches in the wall.

To the right, another dwarf-sized square-cut entrance in the western antechamber wall led to the burial chamber. They hardly befitted a tomb; they were more like access doors. Why have such small 'doors' into the chambers? After all, there were so many false doors in the temples abutting the pyramid; surely they would have created similar doorways within the chambers? But they didn't, which surely shows the temple and chambers were not designed or built by the same person, and that the chambers pre-date the mortuary temple.

Like the antechamber, the burial chamber contained a vaulted ceiling of huge limestone blocks. However, when I looked closely I realized that some of the massive stones had dropped considerably.

Looking at the star patterning that had been added to the limestone blocks on the ceiling, it was clear the movement of the stone had occurred after the decoration had been added. That meant it was possibly due to the Thera tsunami, but in reality, it could have been any earthquake after the reign of Teti, if in fact he was the first one who usurped the chamber.

What was more noticeable were the sidewalls; not smooth limestone carved with column after column of pyramid texts, but rather slap-dash bricks that didn't look consistent with the original chamber. Running the full length of the chamber, it was clear these had been added at some later stage to either cover up what was on the walls, or, more likely, to sure up the walls and support the collapsing ceiling.

Against the western wall stood a grey basalt sarcophagus, supposedly belonging to Teti, its lid partially opened and broken, one would presume, by previous tomb robbers.

Of particular note was the orientation of the lid and the way it abutted the base. It appeared the lid could only have been lid into place from the western side, the side abutting the wall, which would have been impossible in the location it now resided; the lid had to have been in place when the sarcophagus was placed against the western wall.

Speaking of impossible, there is absolutely no way the sarcophagus could have been transported down the narrow entrance corridor and through the small wall openings; the sarcophagus had to have been put into the chamber when the pyramid was still being constructed, before the limestone ceiling was put into place.

"The lower part of the sarcophagus, although unfinished, is well-preserved and was originally decorated with a single band of gilded Pyramid Texts."

Again the question arose, were the inscriptions contemporary with the granite box, or had they been added at a much later date, when Teti usurped the box to use as his sarcophagus, if it was Teti? After all, all that was found here was an arm and shoulder of a mummy, who the Egyptologists presume to have been Teti; discovered among the rubble on the burial chamber floor. It sounded to me more like the partial remains of someone who had been drawn and quartered. Or was this symbolic of the dismembering of Osiris? And to whom did the remains really belong?

Many things about this pyramid just didn't make sense, not to the 'official' story anyway. But I had what I needed and headed back out, through the antechamber and into the confined space of the horizontal passage. As I scrambled along, I heard a low-pitched hum, or maybe I thought I did, but it was enough to cause me to take a moment to pause near the remains of one of the portcullises. I wasn't sure where it was coming from, I even considered it was just inside my head, so I closed my eyes, placed my hand on the granite portcullis beside me, and tried to tune in.

The stone was somehow 'alive', and suddenly I found myself toning, "aw". Almost instantaneously I felt vibrations through the walls and floor of the corridor and the sound of stone rumbling against stone, movement somewhere behind the walls. It scared the shit out of me; the last thing I wanted was to have one of the portcullises suddenly seal me in. Like a rat up a down-pipe, I scurried out of there as fast as I could.

'Teti Pyramid, good, yes?'

The guardian was waiting for me just outside the entrance, Abdo a little further along.

'Are all the stones in there secure?'

The guardian looked at me bewildered, not understanding what I was asking. Abdo quickly translated for me and the guardian nodded.

'All safe, yes, stone no move.'

OK, now I was either having major hallucinations or some pretty heavy shit had just gone down. I took a deep swig of water, just in case I was dehydrating, then reviewed what had just happened; no, I was certain, something started moving behind the wall of the horizontal corridor.

'Where to now, Mister Alex?'

I checked my iphone; Saeed was due in about ten minutes.

'Let's keep going north, check out the smaller pyramids and other structures here; I'm not so sure this was all originally built because of Teti.

On the other side of the path, just north of Teti's pyramid was a cluster of private 'mastaba tombs' belonging to the officials of Teti's reign, including the 'tombs' of Mereruka and Kagemni, viziers of Teti.

'This, largest mastaba tomb in Saqqara, belong to Mereruka, marry to Teti eldest daughter, Watet-khet-her.'

That meant Mereruka must have been a powerful person in the court if he was married to the *sang réal*. However, that raised the question as to why he did not assume the throne upon Teti's demise?

It also raised the question of who Userkara, Teti's successor, really was. There is some belief amongst scholars that Userkara may have been a son of Teti to a lesser, non *sang réal*, queen by the name of Khuit. But is it possible, as the majority of scholars suggest, that Userkara wasn't Teti's son at all, but rather a son of Unas, meaning he was possibly a younger brother of Teti, which would make sense, or, is it more likely, that Userkara was married to one of Teti's sisters, or, even more likely, to a younger daughter of Unas? I was sure the *sang réal* held the key.

In any case, as it was the largest 'mastaba', and Mereruka was held such an esteemed position, I decided that as Saeed hadn't rung, I had time to have a look and indicated for our guardian to lead the way.

Straight away I had doubts the 'tombs' were tombs, as they had clearly been built above ground and looked more like dwellings or offices of administration; even looking at the map seemed to support that. The interiors did nothing but confirm my beliefs.

Mereruka's mastaba contained thirty-two rooms! If he built such a large place to be buried in, then surely he would have built an even bigger place to live in, right? You would think so. So where is it? The Egyptologists will no doubt say it was quarried in later times and no trace remains. But they can't even say *where* it was. Bollocks!

Doesn't it make much more sense that, given Saqqara was the administrative centre of Egypt during the 6th Dynasty, Mereruka, being vizier, would built his residence as close as possible to his place of work? Sure it does. Doesn't it make sense that when the Thera tsunami swept over Egypt it buried Mereruka's residence in twenty to thirty feet of silt and sand? Sure it does.

The walls were decorated with painted reliefs, not of Pyramid Texts as one might expect of such an esteemed person, but with images of everyday Egyptian life: sailing, hunting, fishing, metalworking with dwarfs, even images of force-feeding animals, including a hyena. Hardly the sort of scenes one would expect in a tomb, but very likely the sorts of scenes one might have painted on the walls of their home or place of work. Don't people put photos of their home-life, family, and holidays on their desks at work? Surely this was just the same.

In another room was a statue of Mereruka, standing dynamically within a niche, surrounded with a doorframe indicating he was entering or emerging from somewhere dark and mysterious, possibly the Underworld; there was even a set of stone steps for him to walk down. Or, were they there for others to walk up and pay reverence?

"The statue marks the centre of Mereruka's cult and the place for offerings."

Perhaps people may have placed offerings at his feet, but as to it being a "centre for Mereruka's cult", I wasn't so convinced; I'd seen many modern buildings with statues of the person who had built the building, or to whom the building was dedicated, erected in the lobby, foyer, or outside the main entrance.

Was Mereruka simply marking his territory and instilling in any peasant or lower plebiscite coming to plead their case, that they should respect Mereruka as they would a god? That made more sense to me than a cult to a vizier when there was not even a cult following to the pharaoh.

I was getting pissed off now: "tombs", what a romantic glorification! I continued on, wandering through the adjoining mastabas; all very similar, with similarly beautiful well-preserved reliefs and murals of day-to-day life in ancient Egypt. It beggared disbelief to propose that the tombs of all these people had been found, all beautifully decorated, and yet not one actual residence had been found. Was it possible, sure, but was it likely, no.

In the last of the tombs, that of Ankh-ma-Hor, I spotted what looked to me like food preparation areas; what need would a mummy have for preparing food? So, was it an actual functioning kitchen? There was also what appeared to be a shallow bath, a bathroom? Or was it a place were one was anointed with oils? Either way, it appeared one had to be upstanding to be washed or anointed, hardly something that would be done to a mummy, and in any case would have been done prior to entombment.

I took particular note of several square shafts in the floor that descended into the floor and beneath it. They were similar to others I had seen, those of the North Tombs and South Tombs at Amarna in particular. Clearly there was something else beneath the surface. The question was, what? Were the shafts for storage? Rich people have wine cellars, right?

By the time I'd left the final mastaba I was convinced beyond any doubt these were residences, and how anyone else could have come to the conclusion they were tombs was totally beyond, or rather beneath, my comprehension.

Further north were two small pyramid complexes, attributed to Khuit and Iput I, two of Teti's queens. Little remained of the pyramid attributed to Khuit, not even its dimensions were discernable, in fact, until the fairly recent excavation of part of the mortuary temple, it was though to be a mastaba; and maybe at some point it was.

"The mortuary temple sits in front of the east wall of the pyramid although little of this has been excavated, however the previously excavated offering hall has the usual false door and altar."

I wondered if the door was made of granite, most probably, but I couldn't find any evidence of it as I scuffed around in the sand. But, I was sure that if the pyramid had subterranean chambers, and they contained granite, then this pyramid, despite its dilapidated condition, was part of the star map as well.

"The pyramid's original entrance was on the north side of the pyramid in the floor of the courtyard. It accessed a descending corridor leading to the solidly constructed underground compartments of the pyramid that comprised a burial chamber beneath the vertical axis of the pyramid, containing a pink-granite sarcophagus, and a storage room east of the burial chamber."

Immediately north of Khuit's pyramid were the remains of the second of the 'Teti queen' pyramids, the pyramid complex attributed to Iput I. If Iput I was the daughter of Unas and thus the *sang réal*, and the principal wife of Teti, most likely legitimising his claim to the throne, why was her pyramid further away from Teti's that

that of Khuit?

According to my notes, the whole of the complex was surrounded by an enclosure wall of limestone, but had no valley temple, causeway or cult pyramid. Further:

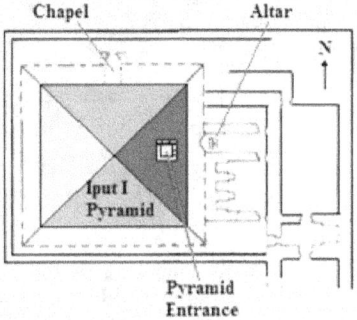

"On the eastern side of Iput's pyramid is a small mortuary temple with an unusual floor plan. Entered from Teti's pyramid to the south, the entrance hall had four limestone pillars and walls engraved with military scenes. An antechamber follows, comprising a pillared courtyard with two pillars. The inner part of the temple consisted of an offering hall with reliefs of offering bearers, sacrificial scenes, and a ritual performance held at the palace."

It made sense that the "palace" was the complex of Netjerikhet?

"In the western wall of the offering hall was a limestone false door and, before it, a pink-granite altar inscribed with, 'Queen mother Pepi's splendour is enduring'."

Why wasn't the false door made of granite? Maybe there weren't enough pieces left from the original pre-dynastic structures to go around. Perhaps Iput got the altar but the false door was used somewhere else, meaning Iput's false door had to be carved from limestone?

Although there had apparently been some 'recent' excavations by our master-villain Zahi Hawass, most of the temple was now covered in sand so I wasn't able to confirm anything. However, I was positive that the red-granite altar would have been like those in the temples at Philae and Edfu, considerably more weathered and aged than the limestone or sandstone around it, which would clearly indicate the granite was possibly tens-of-thousands of years older.

Get the picture? No? OK, imagine this: imagine looking at a ninety-year-old woman wearing a modern g-string bikini, not a pleasant sight I agree. Now imagine that standing next to her is a nineteen-year-old girl in the same brand of bikini and that you are trying to convince everyone the two women must be the same age because they are wearing the same period bikini. I think you get my point.

"North of the offering hall was a storeroom, to the south, rather than a complete chapel, there were three deep niches for statues of the queen."

Was there only room for three niches rather than five, or did the difference in number relate to a different period of worship and thus point to a different period of construction of the temple? As usual, the real answers would most likely be found underground.

"When Pepi I ascended the throne, he expanded his mother's tomb from a stepped-mastaba to a small pyramid with a base of 21 metres, slope of 63°, and a height of 21 metres."

Only the original mastaba section remained.

"Although there was a small chapel on the northern side, there was no entrance there, rather a vertical shaft led to the burial chamber from the second layer of the core."

Apart from the absence of a descending passage, it was sounding very similar to the South Tomb and original vertical shaft of Netjerikhet.

"A rough limestone sarcophagus was found in the burial chamber, containing fragments of a cedar coffin and the bones of a middle-aged woman."

Which could all have been added when the chamber was usurped.

"Also discovered in the burial chamber were five limestone canopic jars."

As opposed to the usual four, which could mean the fifth belonged to a separate burial, possibly the middle-aged woman.

"An alabaster headrest was also found, along with fragments of a necklace, a gold bracelet, a small alabaster tablet with the names of the seven sacred oils, and several copper tools, all discovered amongst the debris of models of alabaster vessels."

I was disappointed there was no mention of what the burial chamber was made of, but the rough-hewn limestone sarcophagus seemed to indicate it was an Old Kingdom addition, probably lowered down the vertical shaft before the final stage of the mastaba was added.

At last my iphone rang.
'Saeed!'
'Alex.'

It was Mark.
'Mate, are you OK?'
'I'm fine.'
'What happened?'
'At first they thought I was you, I'm sure they were deceived by the envelope, but I quickly set them straight by showing them my passport. They weren't easily convinced and started rifling through the pages, but by the time Frank arrived and started name dropping and throwing around his NASA connections, they were more than a little embarrassed and apologetic and backed off.'
'So they left you alone?'
'No, they took us aside and showed us a picture of you, taken from your passport, and asked if we knew you.'

I started feeling uncomfortable, and with the guardian looking on, I walked away from the pyramid and whispered into the phone.
'What did you say?'
'We told them the truth…'
'What!'
'…That we met you for the first time at Hawarra, that you joined us in exploring Meidum and Dahshur, and then we simply gave you a lift back to your hotel in Cairo.'
'Did you tell them I went with you to Abu Raoush and Zawiyet?'
'Why would we do that, they're military zones and not open to the public?'
'And the papers?'

'What papers?'

'Kareem's papers.'

'Mate, I've got no idea what you're talking about.'

The penny dropped, Mark was playing dumb.

'Brilliant, thanks, so everything's under control?'

'Oh, I wouldn't say that; they asked if we knew where you were?'

'And…?'

'We told them we thought you were heading to either Hurghada or Sharm el Sheik for a little R&R, and then catching a plane to London from there, so I suggest you get the first stage coach out of Dodge before they figure out the truth.'

'I will, I'm just waiting on a phone call from Saeed, I'm meeting him here at Saqqara.'

'Saqqara? You're at Saqqara?'

'Yeah, the police were waiting for me back at the hotel; thankfully Abdo, one of the hotel's owners, came to the rescue and was taking me to his house in Abusir. I contacted Saeed and we arranged to meet up here at Saqqara.'

'Well, if you think that's your best option; the good thing is you're out of Cairo. Just remember, if you need help, just call.'

'Thanks, Mark, much appreciated.'

'All the best, and hopefully we'll hear from you once you're safely out of Egypt.'

'Cheers.'

I hung up and checked the time, 3:18 pm; still no word from Saeed. I looked at Abdo.

'Yes, Mister Alex, where to now?'

'Let me have a quick look.'

According to my notes there were supposedly seven mud-brick tombs and a pyramidion, all dating to the New Kingdom, recently discovered somewhere around Teti's pyramid.

"Each of the tombs belongs to a high-ranking priest or official and consists of an entrance, an open courtyard containing a burial shaft and a vaulted chapel at the rear. Artefacts discovered include statues and stelae, amulets and scarabs and most significantly a limestone pyramidion from the tomb of Thener, a scribe in the Temple of Ptah."

Who puts their tomb shaft in the middle of a courtyard *before* the chapel? No, this sounded more like New Kingdom tomb shafts, if they were tombs, dug into the courtyard of older, possibly Old Kingdom residences, offices, or chapels. I looked at the map, but it didn't show any of them, presumably because they were new discoveries.

Further north was a row of 1st and 2nd Dynasty 'tombs' that ran along the eastern edge of the North Saqqara escarpment, along what would surely then have been the riverbank. According to the Egyptologists, the necropolis was begun during the reign of Hor-Aha, second king of the 1st Dynasty. Generally the 1st Dynasty mastabas followed the eastern ridge with the 2nd Dynasty tombs arranged behind them.

"Despite the fact the only pharaoh names positively linked with tombs at Saqqara are those of Hotepsekhemwy and Ninetjer, the names of other early kings are attested here, with several tombs positively identified, those being; 3503 owned by Queen Merneith,

3504 by Sekhemka, 3505 by Ka'a, and 3507 by Queen Hernieth, possible wife of King Djer."

The reality is, most of the information we have from the Early Dynastic Period has been gleaned from the numerous seals, impressions, inscribed ivory and wooden labels, stelae, and stone vessels found in this area, artefacts that give the names of many individuals who were supposedly buried here. But wouldn't an administrative area just as likely have contained such objects?

"The rectangular mastabas were either filled with gravel or divided into chambers, many of them used as storerooms to contain the rich trappings of burials and decorated with reliefs or paintings."

Government offices and private residences of the elite would also contain such "rich trappings", and given their proximity to the river, were surely more than likely not tombs, which could easily be flooded, but rather offices or private riverside residences? Just because they were discovered below the ground, didn't mean they were tombs. If their roofs were more than thirty feet below the surface, below the pre-Thera tsunami ground level, then maybe they were tombs, but as their floor was most likely at that level, then when they were built they were most likely free-standing structures above the ground and not tombs. And that didn't discount the possibility that, like in other parts of the world, people dug tombs and buried their dead under the very houses in which they lived.

"Unlike the earlier tombs at Abydos, that were basically pits lined with mud-bricks, heading into the 2nd Dynasty, as they did with the royal tombs at Abydos, the Saqqara mastabas became increasingly more elaborate, with subterranean chambers cut from the bedrock, some of them incorporating a rudimentary funerary temple. In the later tombs, the 'palace façade' decoration became simpler, but with two false doors added to the outer walls, and the underground chambers were arranged to represent a typical contemporary house, while the unfired brick superstructure was filled with a solid core of rubble or mud."

Maybe the underground chambers represented a typical contemporary house because they *were* contemporary houses, just underground, and, as to being filled with rubble or mud, that was totally consistent with the tsunami. Anyway, all of this was despite the fact the royal burial ground during this time was supposedly at Abydos. So, were they actually burials, or admin buildings?

To the northwest were more 'tombs', these dating to the 3rd Dynasty, along with several animal cemeteries, including tomb galleries cut into the rock containing vast numbers of mummified baboons, ibis and falcons. I was all set to go and check out the 1st Dynasty 'tombs' until I read the next paragraph.

"The area of the large Early-Dynastic mud-brick mastabas at North Saqqara has been uncovered and re-buried over many years. Today, little can be seen as they have all been back-filled, their superstructures barely visible, and are now covered by wind-blown sand."

I looked northwards, out over the sand.

'Shit, they've done it again.'

'Who has done what, Mister Alex?'

'Zahi Hawass and his vultures; they've robbed the tombs and buried all the evidence.'

'This, it is not unusual.'

'What do you mean?'

Abdo raised his eyebrows towards the guardian, as if he couldn't speak in his presence.

'Come, we will go to see mastaba of Ti, this it is still open to see. I will tell you as we go.'

I handed over a healthy thank-you of baksheesh to our grateful guardian and Abdo and I made our way back to the car. Once inside and underway I was quick to pick up the conversation where we had left it.

'You know more about what's buried here?'

'Not so much here at Saqqara, there are many looter now, but in Giza.'

'Under the plateau?'

'No, under the village of Nazlet El Smaan.'

'The village; what's under there?'

'Several year ago, 2009, some people they were dig under their house and they find it their way into the buried temple.'

Saeed mentioned this in Luxor, the temple under the Giza village, but now it had even more relevance.

'That would be consistent with the Thera tsunami.'

'What it is this Thera tsunami?'

Without freaking out Abdo with the whole Nibiru scenario, I quickly explained the eruption of Thera, and the size of the wave that would have hit Egypt.

'This it is very interesting, there are many buried temple in the Nile Delta and also under the sea at Alexandria. This tsunami, yes, it make it the sense.'

'And the house in the Giza village?'

'The people they were dig under the house, yes, and they find it the ruin of the temple. Zahi Hawass he find out of this and he take over the house and they continue to dig it in secret. They find many thing; statue, gold, all these they take them away. They dig very deep but there is it the accident and the house it fall in, and six men, they are buried and die. Zahi Hawass he do nothing for the family, and he tell them that if they talk of this that many bad thing they will happen to them. Many family they are angry, but also they are scared of Zahi Hawass, he is very close to Mubarak.'

I decided to fill Abdo in when I spotted something off to the left.

'What's that?'

Abdo pulled the car over,

'This it is the Philosopher Circle. It is from the Ptolemaic Period.'

It didn't look like much was left, but I decided to check it out in my notes, just in case.

"Just before the resthouse, towards the Serapeum, there is a curious semicircle of Greek statues known as the 'Philosopher's Circle'; a monument to important Greek thinkers and poets including Hesiod, Pindar, and others. The statues were set up at the end of the Avenue of Sphinxes by Ptolemy I as a wayside shrine. The best-preserved figures include Plato, Pythagoras and Homer."

'You wish to see it?'

'It's not calling me at the moment, but there must be some significance to it just because of what it is and where it is. Maybe we can stop on the way back?'

'Most certainly, Mister Alex.'

We continued on to Ti's Mastaba.

'You know, Abdo, the house you were talking about in the Giza village, I think it must be the house Saeed was telling me about...'

I pointed to the backpack now beside me on the seat.

'...Apparently there's some papers about it here in Kareem's documents. And the owners didn't get any compensation, right?'

'What it is, this compensation?'

'They weren't given any money, the Supreme Council didn't buy their house.'

Abdo laughed.

'The Supreme Council they do not even know of this; there is no money. Even when they do know of this, like in Luxor where they excavate it the avenue of the Sphinx, still they do not pay the people for their home.'

'So how did they evict them?'

'The owner of the house they are forced out by the soldier.'

'The military?'

'Everywhere in Egypt, whenever something important it is discovered, the military they take over.'

As Abdo pulled the car to a stop and we climbed out, I thought more about it. Dahshur, Zawiyet el Aryan, Abu Raoush, Giza itself, the whole thing went all the way back to Project Isis. Actually it probably went back even further than that, but that's when the Illuminati took over through the Russians and the Military. And when Anwar Sadat didn't tow the line they simply took him out and put Muburak in charge, whom they previously had been grooming for years.

Then the question hit me: if the Illuminati had been in control for over fifty years, how did they let a small uprising of students grow and grow and throw a spanner in the works; it was just like the French Revolution. The Illuminati always have their claws all over everything; the Secret Police could simply have murdered or arrested the ringleaders as they had always done?

And then the penny dropped, yes, it *was* just like the French Revolution; they had seeded the whole thing, they *made* it happen, Muburak was just a pawn they were prepared to sacrifice for some greater strategic move. The question now was, what was so strategic they needed to turn the whole country on its head?

As we walked down the narrow track towards the Mastaba of Ti, I thought back to the 'Revolution', to what *really* happened. First, a female member of the media was attacked and raped by several men in the public square, with thousands of people around. After that, all the media were so scared, so much in fear of their lives, they were confined to their hotels for their own safety. That meant they could not film or report on anything that wasn't visible from their balconies.

Second, Hawass had staged several lootings, such as the 'break in' at the Cairo Museum and other sites, which justified the military into throwing all sorts of forces, not to protecting the foreign press, but to encircling and shutting off the archaeological sites, Giza, Saqqara, etcetera, to protect them from looting. They had done exactly what they did with the Luxor massacre; if it worked once, why not do it again. How anyone was going to steal a pyramid weighing sqizzillions of tons was beyond me!

Then I got it! Hawass was finishing the job he started in 2010, the one in which he used the 'front' and distraction of the Red Bull games to dig a deep shaft into the ground before the Sphinx, the very one where he was caught in the middle of the night looting from beneath the Giza Plateau. This was the 'Big Job', and to pull it off the Illuminati needed a massive distraction; and what better distraction than a 'Revolution'.

But then Hawass was arrested, so how could he have been involved? That was easy, what better way to take the heat *off* yourself, than to supposedly have it put it *on* yourself. I didn't think we had seen the last of Zahi Hawass: the great 'protector' of ancient Egypt, the great vulture that has spread his wings over everything to hide his actions while he ripped at the flesh of ancient Egypt with his razor-sharp talons and gorged himself on its tastiest morsels. Somehow I was sure that when the political 'unrest' died, the cock of the vultures would return as sanctimonious as ever about protecting Egypt's great treasures, sprouting about how many things were looted during the turmoil, all supposedly from sites protected by the military.

As we stopped before the entrance to Ti's mastaba, I turned to Abdo.

'You know Abdo, I don't think this People's Revolution is so much a revolution of the people, more a matter of turning the people in circles like pigs slowly roasting on a spit. I don't think that Morsi or the Muslim Brotherhood are the ones really in control here.'

'But yes, they were elected by the people.'

'There's no way the puppet-masters would allow it unless it was part of their plan. Don't be surprised if things don't change much, if at all, here in Egypt. And don't be surprised if Zahi Hawass returns to his position.'

'If this is true, then this it is not good.'

'No, not good at all.'

'Then you must get these paper out of Egypt.'

I suddenly realized, on my back, I was carrying the future freedom of a whole country of honest hardworking people, most of whom lived in suppressed poverty imposed by a clandestine junta.

'Whatever it takes, my friend.'

Ti

To be fair, I didn't know much about Ti, or Ty depending on which spelling you preferred, just that he was a reasonably important official in the middle of the Old Kingdom. I was about to flick through my iphone files to find out more about him when Abdo unexpectedly stepped into the role of tour guide.

'Ti he was hold it the high office during the middle of Dynasty five. He was "Overseer of the Pyramid of Niuserre", and 'Overseer of the Sun-Temple of Sahure, Neferirkare and Niuserre".'

'You seem to know a lot about him.'

For a brief moment I even contemplated Abdo was Ti reincarnated.

'I am born and grow up in Abusir; I know much about this area.'

'Then maybe you know why, if Ti was Overseer of all the pyramids at Abusir to the north, he was supposedly buried here at Saqqara?'

It was a bit of a rhetorical question, but Abdo still did his best to answer it.

'Because Saqqara, this it is the burying place.'

Unfortunately his answer was the conditioned one I had half expected.

'But, Abdo, what if Saqqara wasn't a necropolis at all, what if it was a thriving bustling administrative centre where the rich and famous all built condos on the riverbank?'

'You think this?'

'I do, it's exactly what happens today, and maybe the proof is waiting inside, so let's go.'

Modern walls flanked the gently sloping ramp that ran down from the north to what was the entry and original ground level of Ti's mastaba; it was as if I was seeing first hand the depth of the silt and sand deposited by the Thera tsunami, at least twenty feet, more likely twenty-five. As we descended I pointed it out to Abdo and briefly explained the size and effects of the tsunami in more detail. Within seconds he had it.

'Yes, yes, I see this.'

Despite what was strikingly blatantly obvious before us, that Abdo could see and comprehend within a few sentences, other 'experts' had different opinions:

"The mastaba was originally built on top of the sand but it has sunk entirely into the sand it was placed on top of."

Guys, seriously! Once you realized it was originally a freestanding structure that sat above the ground, it was hard to conclude it was a tomb; even the entrance looked more like an official place of doing business.

Ti for two

Measuring about thirty metres wide and forty metres long, the tomb had been restored and reconstructed by the Antiquities Department.

"The body of the building is constructed from pieces of stone and clay, partitioned by mud-bricks, and in some cases, enhanced by a cladding of limestone slabs."

Sounds like a patch job to me; different stages, different periods.

"In the middle part of 5th Dynasty, most of the mastaba was formed by the central solid core; hallways and rooms occupying a restricted portion of the mass."

It didn't sound right, time to investigate.

The entrance consisted of a portico with two pillars sitting in a recess of the outside wall. The floor was paved, but I couldn't tell if it was original or part of the reconstruction. The square pillars on the other hand, were clearly reconstructed. About four metres high and, on the front face from about a metre from the ground to about two metres high, contained the remains of now colourless decorations of Ti with a naked chest, wearing a kilt with a triangular front, a short square beard, and a long striped wig descending behind his shoulders. In many ways it reminded me of a modern judges wig.

Around his neck was a large necklace, and, in one hand, he carried a long staff, in the other the sekhem-sceptre, his emblems of office. Interestingly the two images faced the entry from either side, not standing guard defiantly, but as if in welcome. Now why would you welcome someone to your tomb?

As we walked through, Abdo resumed his role as guide.

'Ti he live under many king, at least twenty year, from Neferirkare-Kakai, then Shepseskare Isi, Neferefra, and last, Niuserre. This we know it from the hieroglyph on the wall of the tomb. Ti he control it the many farm and animal that belong to the royal family, and he is also do the haircut to the royal family.'

'Seriously? That would mean he actually touched the heads of the pharaoh and his queen, which would indicate Ti himself must have been considered part of the royal family.'

'Yes, his wife, Neferhetepes, was relate to the royal family, as the children of Ti they are said to be of royal descent.'

For a moment I was confused.

'Neferhetepes was the wife of Userkaf, possibly even his sister, and thus the *sang réal*...'

Then I started thinking through it.

'...Neferhetepes was also the mother of Sahure, who must have assumed the throne at a young age following the death of his father. Then, at some later stage, Ti must have married Neferhetepes, which means he must definitely have been of royal blood, possibly her cousin, and they had a daughter, Neferetnebty, Sahure's half sister, the *sang réal*, who became Sahure's consort. Brilliant! No wonder he held such high positions. How come the experts couldn't figure that out?'

Abdo wasn't really listening to, or understanding, my mumblings.

'Mister Alex, here, Serdab of Ti.'

In the eastern corner was a slit in the wall, in the thickest part of the northern wall of the mastaba, that revealed a Serdab. I must admit it was a very strange place to have one in a 'tomb', just as you enter; it was like a cloakroom where you could get a sneak peek at Ti. Some Egyptologists suggest the ka spirit of the deceased would look out through these slits in the wall. Well, he wouldn't have much of a view; this would have to be a sideways glance that only showed who was coming in the front door.

Now Serdabs were clearly either for the statue, the ka of the deceased, to look out, or for others to look in. If it was for the statue to look out, then a slit wouldn't do the trick, you'd need a window, or you'd need to position the statue with its face flush against the wall to see out.

So, as far as I was concerned, Serdabs were *not* for the "ka to look out", they must have been solely for outsiders to look in, and, if it was that, then why; especially if it was a tomb that was supposedly off-limits to everyone? There was a second peephole from the adjoining courtyard, and that's where we quickly headed.

The open court that followed measured around fifteen metres long by maybe a little over ten metres wide. Twelve square pillars, spaced about a metre-and-a-half apart and each decorated on all faces with a standing figure of Ti, stood around the edge creating a portico about two metres wide around the perimeter; this was no tomb, at least not this part of it.

The entry to the 'burial' chamber was through the courtyard floor in the southeast corner.

'I'll get to that later, let's check out the rest of the above ground structure first.'

Just looking at the diagram of the mastaba told me heaps. The diagonal path and

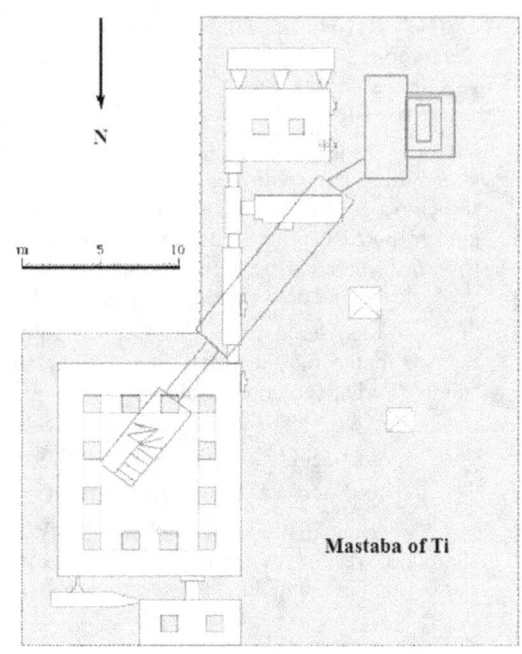

Mastaba of Ti

position of the substructures was clearly not consistent with the design of the superstructure, and I found it incredulous to believe the bulk of the mastaba was just a mass of rock surrounding the 'shaft tombs' of Ti's wife and son. It just didn't gel; the courtyard and inner chambers were clearly a later addition to some other structure that was itself built over the subterranean layout.

Unfortunately little remained of the courtyard decorations; the upper part of all of the walls was lost, as well as part of the middle and lower registers on others, though what scenes did remain included reliefs of Ti being carried in his official chair, agricultural scenes, and scenes of daily life.

These were hardly the sort of scenes you would expect to find in a tomb, an official building of someone who governed agriculture and animals perhaps, but not exclusively in a tomb.

But, if it was a burial place, where were the Pyramid Texts so common to this period? Nothing about this building so far rang true, not the diagram, nor the hard evidence; I was starting to think the Egyptologists had this building totally summed-up all wrong as well.

At the south-west corner of the courtyard, adjacent to the entry to the chapel, was a false door stela supposedly attributed to Ti's son, Demedj. I wondered if, like the doors discovered in the Great Pyramid by the 1976 'truth-seekers', it really opened into a hidden chamber within the bulk of the mastaba. Maybe if I toned like I did in the horizontal passage of Teti's pyramid the stones would start to rumble and the door would open to reveal a secret chamber filled with golden treasure. I placed my hands on the side panels and closed my eyes, trying to tune in.

'Aaawwww.'

'Mister Alex, what is it that you are doing?'

Clearly this was not the time nor place.

'Just seeing if the welcome mat was out.'

Abdo scratched his head and kept walking.

Beyond the false door was a dark, narrow, but decorated corridor, about six metres long, just over a metre wide, but about four and a half metres high. About half way along, on its western wall, was another false door. Abdo stood just beyond it.

'This is false door which Ti dedicate to his wife, Neferhetepes.'

On the door, Neferhetepes was represented as a symbol of fertility in a slinky slim-fitting dress with two shoulder straps, which should have covered her breasts, but somehow didn't. She was adorned with a large usekh-necklace on her chest, a tight choker necklace, bracelets around her wrists and ankles, and on her head, a long tripartite wig, clearly a sign she was royalty.

'It line up with tomb of Neferhetepes in centre of mastaba.'

I looked at my diagram; it was a pity it didn't show the subterranean aspects of the two shaft tombs, especially how they aligned with the subterranean floor plan of Ti's 'tomb'. Perhaps my notes held a clue.

"The entrance to the well tombs, or shaft tombs, of Demedj and Neferhetepes, is from the roof of the mastaba, however entry and access to the burial chambers is not permitted."

What if the shaft tombs came first? Which raised the question of what their chambers were made of; red granite perhaps? And if so, did this location align with a star or stars in the night sky?

"Ti's wife and eldest son were also placed in the tomb although their remains were stolen along with the goods that were inside."

OK, if they were stolen, who stole them, and where are they now? Or are the Egyptologists making another blind assumption, based on no actual evidence, that because something is empty it means there was something there before and that it had to have been stolen? Of course you would make a stupid comment like that if you were clutching at straws to support your false premise that the building was a tomb, because if it wasn't a tomb, if it was an administrative building where people came to make offerings and plead their cases, then you would never find a mummy buried here, which seemed to be exactly the case with almost all these mastaba buildings at Saqqara.

So, did all the underground tombs originally belong to Ti and his family, or, like so many other subterranean chambers, had they been usurped, these by Ti during the 5th Dynasty? What if there was a smaller first part of the mastaba constructed around and over the two subterranean shaft chambers, and the corridors and courtyard added much later? I put my thinking cap on and, like a modern day Sherlock Holmes, switched on my powers of deduction.

Examining the diagram, it seemed clear to me that the subterranean chambers clearly existed before the superstructure was built above it, but which of the two types of chambers was built first, the shaft tombs, or Ti's tomb? I kept coming back to the diagonal passage, with its opening in the previous courtyard; I felt it held the key, but couldn't find the missing piece to the puzzle. Perhaps it was waiting discovery underground?

The next corridor was much shorter, less than three metres, divided in half on the right by a long narrow chamber decorated with colourful reliefs of food preparation, including cooking and brewing, pottery production, as well as scribes recording the activities. Again, these were hardly the sorts of scenes you would logically put into a tomb. Was it possible this was what it actually appeared to be, a food preparation area? My god, wouldn't that be radical!

My sarcasm running on all eight cylinders I moved on into the larger chamber at the end of the corridor. About seven metres east-west by five metres north-south, and nearly five metres high, the roof of the 'chapel' or 'offering hall' was supported by a beam running down the centre of the length of the room, itself supported by two square pillars painted to appear like red granite. The tops of the walls were decorated with a narrow frieze comprising a simple geometric pattern.

Above the door were images of musicians and dancers; surely these were signs of celebration, not of mourning. However the main portion of the northern wall was dominated by a beautiful relief of Ti standing on a papyrus boat and presiding over a hippopotamus hunt, the boat floating on a swamp full of different types of fish, hippopotami and a crocodile; yet again more celebrations of the good life and not a single mention of the underworld.

On the eastern wall were numerous scenes of Ti overseeing a variety of agricultural activities as well as scenes of boat-building. If I wasn't convinced before, now I was totally convinced, these reliefs were not meant for a tomb, not here to remind the 'deceased' of the wonderful life he led, they were the signs of a wealthy, influential man, strategically placed so that any person who visited the structure was constantly reminded of Ti's importance, and thus appropriately acted with respect and reverence.

Turning my attention to the western wall, I discovered it had not one, but another *two* false doors, supposedly for Ti, that stretched the full height of the wall; one door still had an alabaster offering table in front of it. Now why would a tomb need *two* offering tables and *two* false doors?

Surely the 'deceased' only needed one doorway in and out of his 'tomb', which, by the way, was not directly in line with the doors on the same level, but rather metres below the surface. Clearly the builder of this room, this structure, was anticipating a considerably regular stream of traffic of living people making offerings.

The final wall, to the south, was covered in numerous scenes of Ti amid various industrious activities such bird-catching, carpentry, sculpture and metal-working; just the sorts of activities the deceased would be focused on in the afterlife, right? Spaced along the wall were three 'spy-holes' that revealed, behind the south wall, a second serdab: a completely enclosed oblong section about ten metres wide and maybe a metre-and-a-half deep.

Unlike the 'offering hall', the serdab was completely devoid of any decorations or inscriptions, and only contained a replica of the original life-sized statue of Ti once visible through the openings.

"Ti would have communicated with the world of the living and witnessed his ritual offerings through these apertures."

No, I wasn't buying that, I'd already figured out the slots were for looking in, not out; besides, the whole superstructure was plastered with images of daily life, agriculture, fishing, butchery, hunting, but there was not one single Pyramid Text. Given they were prevalent at this time, and this was supposedly a tomb, I found their absence more than just surprising.

And why the need for a second 'serdab', were the ancient Egyptians suggesting that Ti's spirit didn't trust that the living would honour him? Like the first one, this serdab was supposedly enclosed and yet someone had been in there long enough to restore it and add a lighting system to illuminate the statue. A 'sealed' room with no doors made no sense, surely you would at least need access for maintenance and to touch up the paint job on the statues? So, was there a secret entrance in the floor, or walls, and was that an indication of the real function of these weird little rooms?

'OK, Abdo, I've seen enough, let's see who and what's buried in the cellar.'

We made our way back out through the corridors into the open courtyard and stood before the descending staircase. The first thing I made note of was that this would have descended from what was, at the very least, the pre-Thera ground level. Ignoring the obvious modern 'restoration', the ramshackle arrangement of the staircase told me many things, firstly, that it was not contemporary with the mastaba that surrounded it; the standard of the workmanship was shoddy and makeshift, second, that the twisted staircase had been built to fit an existing shaft, because if the staircase had been part of the original structure it would have made far greater sense for it to have been a smooth descending passage, as existed in most of the other subterranean chambers.

Thirdly, the only reason to put in a staircase would be if you wanted permanent access in and out of the subterranean chambers. If you were stocking the tomb, it would be much easier to simply lower objects down a shaft as there would be more space available, thus making the whole process easier. Similarly, if you were a tomb-robber wanting to remove objects, a staircase would hinder operations. No, the steps were clearly a later addition, and a poor one at that.

I took a few steps down when the phone rang.

'Indy?'

'Saeed; it's good to hear your voice. Where are you? Are you here?'

'I am at Saqqara, yes, I have arrived five minute ago.'

'Whereabouts; it's a pretty expansive piece of real estate.'

'We go into the Serapeum.'

'The Serapeum...'

I vaguely remembered seeing it somewhere on my map.

'...I'm at the mastaba of Ti.'

Abdo chipped in, pointing off to the southwest, coincidently in the direction of the tunnel.

'The Serapeum it is very close, maybe one-hundred-fifty metre.'

'Brilliant. Saeed, I'm just about to check out the basement of Ti's so-called tomb, I can be there in about five to ten minutes.'

'This it is very good, I will be wait for you at the entrance.'

'Thanks, Ahoya.'

This time Abdo brought up the rear as I negotiate my way carefully down the steps; the last thing I needed this close to escape was to stumble and break an ankle; an arm I could deal with, but a broken or even badly sprained ankle would definitely not be a welcome event.

I thought somehow that the small opening I had seen from the top of the stairs was going to magically open to admit my large frame. I was wrong; if anything it appeared to get smaller with each approaching step.

'How the hell am I going to get through there?'

On my ass, feet first, that's how. And even then it was a tight fit, as I had to reluctantly remove my backpack to squeeze through.

The narrow opening led through a short, very low and narrow descending passage to a much wider one, about two-and-a-half metres wide, a little over two metres high, and a little less than fifteen metres long. Continuing downwards in the same direction, the walls were rough and undecorated.

As I looked back, it suddenly hit me that the corridor was still half-filled with mud from the tsunami, that the low, narrow 'entrance corridor' was actually a doorway, and the corridor I was standing in would have originally been perhaps another two to three metres higher, or rather deeper.

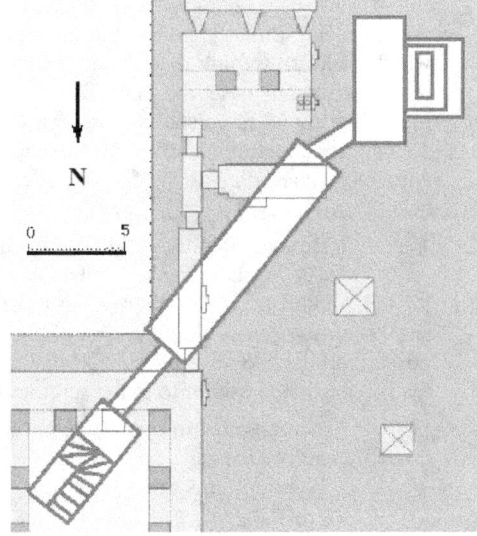

I couldn't help but speculate how interesting it would be if they dug down a few feet, took a few samples, examined them, and lo and behold found evidence of a variety of marine creatures native to the Mediterranean Sea? How would the experts explain THAT?

Beyond the 'wide' corridor, another 'low bridge' doorway veered right through another short transition corridor around two metres long, less than a metre wide, and barely a metre high, into the totally undecorated and unimpressive 'burial' chamber; an oblong 'room' measuring around five metres north-south by just under three metres wide. The only thing of interest was the 'sarcophagus', which sat in an excavation in the west wall.

Rather than a separate sarcophagus of granite, basalt or limestone, the top third of the west wall had been excavated to provide a large niche around four metres wide by just over three metres deep. The bottom two thirds, under the niche, had been shaped to form the large stone sarcophagus that supposedly belonged to Ti, leaving the niche itself as room for the placement of the stone lid. But neither the lid, nor the sarcophagus showed any signs of decoration, and the sarcophagus, like so many others, was found empty.

So how do the experts get off on suggesting, no, *claiming as fact,* that this was the tomb of Ti, was it just because he built an office building on top of it? That's just plain-and-simple BAD SCIENTIFIC METHOD. I was certainly no expert, but clearly the evidence I was seeing with my own eyes just didn't correlate with the fairytale they were spouting as fact.

'How could anyone in their right mind honestly believe that Ti excavated this space, that he didn't add one scratch of decoration to the walls, ceiling, or the sarcophagus, not one Pyramid Text, but then went ahead and built and extensively-decorated large Mastaba on top of it?'

Thankfully Abdo had followed me 'down-under'.

'You do not think this it is the tomb of Ti?'

'Abdo, I think the only things that definitely belong to Ti are the decorations on the walls upstairs and maybe the courtyard and entrance; the rest could have been built by anyone before him, especially the shaft tombs and the underground chambers.'

'What is it you think it really was?'

'I'm not sure, and I doubt if there's anything earth-shattering about it in these papers I got from Kareem, but I've got a few ideas; I'll tell you about them on the way out. After you, my friend.'

Abdo ducked down and led the way out as I ran through the thoughts in my head out loud.

'OK, here's my thinking. I think the diagonal chamber we're now in is the key; usually it would have been aligned north-south, or in some cases from the east, but this is neither, which means they had to navigate around something.'

'I do not understand.'

'If Ti's chamber was the first thing built, they would have started with the entrance, dug directly south, and then excavated the chamber, simple. But they didn't, which makes me think that Ti's chamber may well have been a shaft tomb just like the other two. In any case, the Ti chamber was covered when someone built a small mastaba incorporating all three shafts, but for some deliberate reason they covered Ti's chamber. To compensate for this they dug the corridor from the inside out and created a new entrance, a shaft outside the first, smaller mastaba.'

We scrambled out of the entrance and up the stairs.

'But why is it they did not just dig it the corridor to the east, it is much closer?'

'Yes, and, going by other 'tombs', a totally acceptable direction. The only logical conclusion is that there must have been something in the way, another building, another subterranean chamber, possibly another shaft tomb, directly east of Ti's chamber, possibly under the offering hall, or just to the east of the mastaba. I think whoever built the final mastaba used it to gain secret access to the second serdab off the offering hall.'

The conversation continued as we exited the mastaba and made our way back down the path to the car.

'You think this other room it is still there?'

'I do.'

'And when is it you believe this was built?'

'Going by the lay of the land and the locations of everything else, my totally uneducated deduction is that it's consistent with the row of excavations attributed to the officials of the 3rd Dynasty.'

'This it is very different idea. And Ti he take over this tomb in Dynasty five?'

'Pretty much, but the building wasn't a tomb, at least not the superstructure. Ti expanded the mastaba, adding the offering hall and serdab to the south, and the courtyard and entrance to the east and turned it into an administration office, a taxation office where the populace came to appease Ti and make offerings for favours, to pay homage and their taxes.'

'This it is a crazy idea, but, yes, I can see this.'

We reached the car and I went to get in.

'No, Mister Alex, the Serapeum it is just here.'

Abdo pointed south; we had parked at the common restroom to both places, and the entrance to the Serapeum was less than fifty metres away, which meant the minivan parked beside us must be Saeed's.

'Brilliant!'

I used the short walk to check my notes.

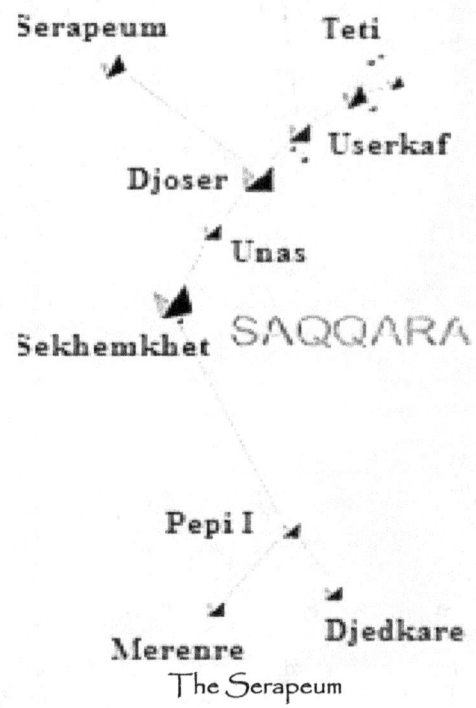

to Abusir

Serapeum   Teti

Userkaf

Djoser

Unas

Sekhemkhet   SAQQARA

Pepi I

Merenre   Djedkare

The Serapeum

"The Serapeum was discovered by the Greek writer Strabo in the 1st Century BC, who described a road of lonely windswept sphinxes, some half submerged in the sand, stretching out across Saqqara to a temple of the god Serapis. The row of 600 sphinxes, added by Nectanebo I during the 30th Dynasty and stretching all the way from Memphis, led to the remains of two pylons which, in turn, originally led to a temple, of which virtually nothing now remains. However, one of the chambers in the temple led to a vast subterranean vault."

"All the way from Memphis", it sounded like a pro-mo for Elvis; the Serapeum must have had more than just moderate importance and significance.

According to Herchel's star map, the Serapeum was the location of another star, and of another pyramid at least the size of the pyramids of Userkaf and Teti. So where was the pyramid? There were scant remains of a temple, yes, but how could they miss the remains of a pyramid that large, unless they just hadn't looked hard enough, or, unless there wasn't one. If there *wasn't* a pyramid here, then it all lent support to my theory that it was what was below the surface that was important, not what had been erected above it.

"Nearly 2,000 years passed before, in 1850, Auguste Mariette, having spotted the head of a sphinx in the sand, and remembering Strabo's writing, rediscovered the Serapeum. Mariette used explosives to clear the entrance, and excavated most of the catacomb. Inside, he found one undisturbed burial, which is now at the Agricultural Museum in Cairo, along with 24 other massive sarcophagi, including three sarcophagi Mariette reported to have identified in a chamber too dangerous to excavate and which have not been located since, all of which had been robbed. Unfortunately, Mariette's notes were lost."

Lost? That seemed a far too common occurrence with the early Egyptologists. Were they all that careless, making reams and reams of detailed meticulous notes, then simply misplacing them, or leaving them carelessly lying around to be swept away by the cooling zephyrs of the Nile? I doubt it. More likely, they've been deliberately withheld and have never been seen by public eyes.

As I turned the corner and started down the gentle slope that led to the subterranean entrance of the Serapeum, I spotted Saeed chatting to the guardian. A surge of relief went through my body.

'Ahoya!'

'Indy...'

Saeed swaggered towards is his typically nonchalant way, then wrapped me in a most-welcome bear hug.

'...It is good to see that you have not become it the meal for the vulture.'

'I would have been a veritable feast for them if it wasn't for Abdo; he virtually pulled me from their claws.'

I introduced my two Egyptian brothers to each other, who shook hands and embraced. Saeed was extremely grateful, for many reasons, and for a minute or more the two men exchanged many words, but all I really understood was "Shukran, Abdo, Shukran jazeelan". Formalities over, Saeed continued, turning to me with his infectious grin.

'Indy, you have it more life than the temple cat.'

'Perhaps, but I have no interest in losing any more; when can we get going?'

'There is no hurry, maybe you should first visit the Serapeum, it was just reopen after twenty year of being closed.'

'Closed? How come?'

Abdo had the answers.

'In 1992, there was it the earthquake which cause it much damage to ceiling of Serapeum; it become not very safe. Zahi Hawass, he take many year to make it the roof safe, with steel arch and inject of the stone with glue to make strong the rock and stop it the roof from collapse.'

'So he could rob it safely, right?'

Saeed laughed.

'But of course.'

'And I bet there's a veritable dossier all about it in my backpack.'

He had that smirk on his face.

'All thing in good time. I think, perhaps Indy, you will find what it is inside the Serapeum much more to your liking. After this we can talk more and make it our plan.'

'Whatever you say, Ahoya, so long as I don't have to get dressed in women's clothes again or hide in the trunk of a car.'

Now he was grinning like a Cheshire cat; oh, how I'd missed that smile.

'Indy, you disappoint me; where is it your sense of the adventure?'

'Somewhere back in Luxor with the rest of my clothes and my innocence.'

Saeed chuckled away, then said something to the guardian in Arabic that included the word "Dottore". It invoked an immediately grinning response, the guardian nodding with respect and gesturing for me to enter. I took off my backpack and tossed it to Saeed.

'Do me a favour, Ahoya, and take this monkey off my back for a while.'

Saeed suddenly appeared serious and indebted.

'But of course.'

A weight off more than just my back, I graciously accepted the guardian's invitation, leaving the three 'locals', the three 'amigos', to chew the fat. I had visions of the three of them playing 'pass the parcel' like three Irishman in a Belfast pub. I casually walked on, for some bizarre reason not wanting to appear too much like a tourist, passing a closed door to the left and on towards the main entrance at the end of the descending ramp, reading up on my notes as I went.

> "For over a thousand years, from the 18th Dynasty and the reign of Amenhotep III to the Ptolemaic Period, the Serapeum was the burial place of the Apis bulls; living manifestations of the god Ptah. It also contains the tomb of Khaemwaset, son of Ramses II, who supposedly enlarged the Serapeum and was buried in it during the 55th year of his father's reign."

But was the Serapeum built in the 18th Dynasty, or was it usurped then, like it was 'usurped' by Khaemwaset and many other pharaohs up to and including the Ptolemaic Period? Given it was buried beneath the sediment of the Thera tsunami, which predated the 18th Dynasty, I was confident it was much older, and that I would find answers inside.

> "Until the reign of Psamtik I during the Late Period, each Apis bull would be laid to rest in a wooden coffin and buried in a large niche leading off from one long corridor, called the Lesser Vaults by today's Egyptologists; which was extended and a new niche carved from the rock as each bull died.
>
> From the 52nd year of Psamtik I to perhaps the Ptolemaic

reign of Cleopatra VII, a second tunnel, known as the Greater Vaults, approximately 350 m in length, 5 m tall and 3 m wide was excavated. Now the spacious niches would contain large granite or basalt sarcophagi, each weighing around 80 to 85 tons."

Granite! It seemed a lot of trouble to go to bury a few dead cows, and the weight of the sarcophagi and their being made of granite raised major questions about their original date of manufacture and usage, especially when, according to the 'experts', they seemed to imply the sarcophagi dated to the 26th Dynasty.

In contrast, I was hedging my bets that the presence of the granite was an indication of an advanced civilization that not only existed before dynastic Egypt it pre-dated the last pole-shift. Was the presence of the sarcophagi here a confirmation of my thinking, or did it bury it once and for all?

And was it purely coincidental, possibly even speculation, that the use of the Serapeum culminated with Cleopatra, mother of Caesarion, because of the invasion of the Romans? Or was it as a result of the earthquake in 27 BC? That was unlikely, because, according to Strabo, writing in the 1st Century BC, it would have already have been buried.

I thought it was more likely the use of the Serapeum ceased half way through the Ptolemaic Period, because of the earthquake of 224 BC; that would be consistent with the evidence I had seen on the West Bank at Luxor. Whatever the reason, how is it possibly that over the next two thousand years the Serapeum was basically buried and forgotten beneath the sands of Egypt? I stepped inside hoping to find out.

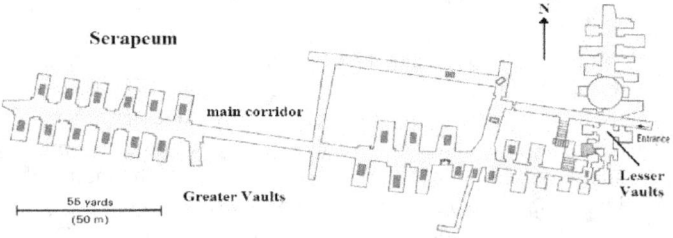

No sooner had I walked through the door than I was amazed, not at the modern cavern-like atmosphere they had created with the modern reinforcements and improvements, including a modern wooden floor, 'mood' lighting in the floor, and brick reinforcements of the arches and walls, which was all great, but by a massive block of red granite just to the left of the door, propped up on what looked like shaped limestone blocks.

The block must have been ten feet long, six feet wide, an incredible two feet thick, and weighed maybe ten ton. It wasn't polished to the extent of most of the sarcophagi I had seen, but it had clearly been 'cut' with considerable precision. This was pay-dirt, proof of my red granite and tsunami theories. Saeed was right; it was to my liking.

'Alex! I'd know that hat anywhere.'

I swivelled around.

'Bill! Pernille! What are you two doing here?'

'Checking out the latest in subterranean rock dwellings.'

They were up at the other end of the corridor beside another massive granite sarcophagus lid. I quickly moved back passed the entrance to greet them.

'You're here with Saeed?'

'Yep.'

'I thought you were heading off to Hurghada.'

'Slight change of plans. It's a bit of a long story but after your rather rapid and dramatic departure in Abydos we went back to Luxor, where, after an hour or so of grilling by the local constabulary, we joined Diane and her group that evening for a circle. They were off on a cruise-ship the next morning heading for Aswan, so naturally most of the session focused on Isis. Pernille broke down in tears; she felt lost, like she had some unfinished business back at the Temple of Isis. So, first thing the next morning, we jumped on a plane to Aswan and headed straight out to Philae Island. Just as we're about to reach the dock, Pernille sees this huge boulder sticking out of the ground on an adjacent small island and feels this strong urge to go there instead.'

'P'aaleq?'

'Yeah, that's it, how did you know?'

'I felt a pull to go there as well; it's where the original temple once stood, probably still does somewhere beneath the water...'

I put my hand in my pocket; I couldn't believe I still had the pieces of red granite I'd found there, and that I'd been carrying them around ever since. I held them out.

'...I found these in the shallows. I'm pretty sure it's where I first got my idea about the red-granite civilization...'

It was also where I'd first seen Crystal.

'...In fact, the more I think about it, it's where all this whole bizarre dream started.'

'Mate, it ain't no dream.'

Bill nudged Pernille who took up the story, acting it out as she spoke.

'I was standing in the shallows as well, just near the boulder. I had my eyes closed and my hands out, as if I was feeling the water. When I opened my eyes and looked down, something caught my eye, I saw a glimmer of light, a sparkle of something in the sand. I put my hands down into the water and washed away some of the sand...'

As she continued, she reached into her bag, fishing around for something.

'...and suddenly this appeared right in front of me.'

She held it out, perfectly nestled in her hands: an exquisitely crafted sphere about five inches in diameter, mostly clear, like glass, but through it were waves, flames, of pink and gold.

'What *is* that?'

'A crystal ball.'

'I can see that, Bill, but what's it made of; I've never seen anything like it?'

'As far as I can figure, it's clear quartz with veins or streaks of rose quartz and gold running through it. I didn't think it was possible, or, if it was, that it would be structurally fragile and fall apart, but here it is. And neither clear quartz nor rose quartz are natural to the region at all, quite remarkable.'

'It's beautiful!'

'Crystal said it might possibly be connected to the prophecy of the Lamp of Isis.'

'Crystal went with you?'

'No, I showed it to her when we returned to Luxor later that day.'

I motioned as if to hold it.

'May I?'

'Sure.'

It was extraordinary.

'The Lamp of Isis?'

I contemplated closing my eyes, tuning it, but somehow it seemed to draw me deeper into it.

'Crystal said that it has been recorded that during the time of an eclipse, and just before a possible disastrous break could occur in the Aswan Dams, an important discovery would be made among the stones beneath the Kiosk of Trajan at Philae.'

'Well, maybe not on Philae, but where you were standing pretty much describes where the Kiosk of Trajan *would* have once stood, before it was moved.'

'Apparently sacred objects of gold and silver will be brought into the light, one of which, a Golden Lamp, will have inscriptions revealing directions for finding the Hall of Records at Giza.'

'That is if Zahi Hawass hasn't blasted his way in and robbed it.'

'The objects will be given to certain people, known only as "The Openers", when they come to the Temple of Isis to re-dedicate themselves to the Mother Goddess. They will re-light the Lamp of Isis for the first time in over a thousand years and use the sacred objects to initiate a new awakening on the planet.'

'"The Openers", hey? What are you going to do with it?'

'I don't know, but, when the time is right, I'm sure I'll know what to do.'

I handed the ball back to Pernille, who carefully returned it to her bag, then started circling the granite sarcophagus lid that sat right at the corner of two corridors, Bill and Pernille following me around the stranded monolith.

Beyond the corner, the corridor continued on for a short distance. Re-examining the map, there seemed to be similar extensions to all the corridors; I wondered if this was purely to assist in the navigation of the massive blocks around the corners. What was the lid doing here; it was like it had just been abandoned in transit?

'It sounds like things are all coming to a climax, and that you might be a part of it all.'

Bill chipped in.

'Not just Pernille, Crystal went on to say that around the same time, "The Lost Books of Gold" of Imhotep will similarly be found in the area of the Step Pyramid here at Saqqara.'

I started running through in my mind any places that I had seen where the books could have been hidden, but nothing instantaneously sprang to mind, they were all too obviously, except, maybe, perhaps under the Philosophers' Circle. The original site would surely have been encompassed by the now dilapidated temple, so was it built on top of the location of the books as a type of marker?

'Is that why you're here, Bill, to find the books?'

He chuckled.

'I've found my treasure... '

Pernille blushed, then Bill continued.

'...No, I don't think so, I'm not sure I'd know where to begin to look, but, you never know who I was in a past life, an Egyptian High Priest perhaps; I could have been responsible for burying anything, the Books of Thoth, the Dead Sea Scrolls, even the Holy Grail.'

'The Holy Grail, you mean the *sang réal*?'

'Well, that's where it gets interesting, because if the Holy Grail really is a misreading of the old French, then that means the references in *'The Bible'* are coded, which is exactly what the Australian biblical scholar and theologian, Barbara Thiering, wrote in her book 'Jesus, The Man'; she calls it the *pesher* method.'

'You've lost me.'

Bill wrapped his arm around my shoulder.

'Come on, I walk around with you and tell you about it on the way.'

We set off around the corner and along the westward corridor towards a massive sarcophagus base that almost completely filled the corridor.

The search for the Holy Grail

'Thiering proposes that Jesus was the leader of a radical faction of Essene priests and was not of virgin birth, and that being technically born out of wedlock, his fortunes changed depending on the views of inheritance of the high priest in power.'

'Well, she was right, Jesus was a bastard, his father was Caesar and his mother was Cleopatra, but the change in his fortunes was probably more linked to the allegiance of the Sadducees and Pharisees to either Rome or Egypt.'

'She also says that Jesus didn't die on the Cross, that he married Mary Magdalene, fathered a family, but later divorced her, and died sometime after 64 AD.'

'Pretty much what we worked out.'

'And that the texts in *'The Bible'*, and the teachings of Jesus, were written in a series of metaphoric parables so that only those initiated could understand them.'

'Which would make sense given the political turmoil of the times.'

It all seemed cut-and-dried, game-set-and-match, until Pernille had another question?

'But how does all that relate to the Holy Grail and Saqqara?'

Bill was quick to answer.

'Saqqara is supposedly the place where Joseph of Arimathea commissioned the Holy Grail to be produced.'

Not being an aficionado of Christian religion, I quickly dredged my memory but couldn't place him.

'Who was he again?'

'Depending which text you read, Joseph of Arimathea was either the uncle of Mary, Jesus' mother, and/or the great-uncle of Jesus.'

'A member of the exiled Egyptian Royal family, who fled Egypt with the invasion of the Romans.'

'Probably.'

'The story of Joseph of Arimathea is told in all four gospels. He was supposedly a wealthy Jew, a good and righteous man, who asked Pilate for permission to take Jesus' body and bury it properly after the Crucifixion. Permission was granted, the body was taken down, wrapped in linen, and laid in an unused tomb hewn in the rock, that Joseph may have intended for himself.'

'Except Jesus wasn't dead.'

'Exactly; which probably explains why they anointed his body with myrrh and aloes, and other healing balms.'

'And that probably meant Joseph of Arimathea was most likely an Egyptian High Priest.'

'Even a member of the Tat Brotherhood; he was supposedly both a member of the Council of the Sanhedrin and yet a secret supporter of Jesus, which would explain why he didn't join in the Council's actions against Jesus.'

'It would also explain why the Grail was commissioned in Egypt?'

'It would indeed.'

We arrived at the sarcophagus and I was somewhat amazed. At over six feet tall, at least four feet wide, and over ten feet long, it was the perfect match for the lid, and, like the lid, was unpolished; it reminded me of the massive shrines in the Temple of Khnum on Elephantine Island and in the Inner Sanctuary of the Temple of Edfu.

'Wow!'

Bill agreed.

'You can say that again; it's like it was specifically designed for a purpose.'

I thought about its dimensions; four foot by six by ten and quickly did the math.

'Yeah, four feet wide by one-point-six would make it six-point-four feet high, which was about right. Six-point-four by one-point-six, make that by four and then by zero-point-four, makes it ten-point-two-four feet long, which seems to match as well. You may be right, Bill.'

'If I am, then it appears as if the "sarcophagus" was designed according to the harmonic ratio of phi, Φ, the Golden Mean. The question is, why?'

'And how did they get here, where were they headed, and why were they just left abandoned here right in the middle of the corridor?'

'Something must have interrupted their relocation; an earthquake perhaps?'

'It must have been something serious enough that they not only downed tools and walked off the job, but they never came back to finish it.'

'Now you're talking pole shift, I know it.'

'It would fit the bill. I mean, it's clear why they're where they were now; we simply don't have the technology to move them one nanometre.'

'All the renovation work would have had to have gone on around them, including putting in the modern floor.'

'But that doesn't explain how they got here; they certainly weren't dragged on logs by thousands of slaves. And these were supposedly placed here when, around 650 BC during the 26th Dynasty? Yeah, sure, and the Eiffel Tower was built by a primitive tribe of one-legged pygmies from the deepest darkest reaches of the Congo using bamboo and vines.'

The corridor called me on to explore its mysteries. But where did it lead, there seemed no point to it; was it just a corridor to nowhere? Pernille was less concerned about the sarcophagus and more interested in picking up on our talk about the Holy Grail.

'Why would an Egyptian High Priest need another cup of gold when he probably had dozens of them lying around?'

I agreed.

'Even less reason to fashion a cup of wood, like the one put forward in *'Indian Jones and the Temple of Doom'*.'

As usual, Bill was a mile ahead of us.

'Actually 'grail' could be a misrepresentation of *graal*, meaning platter.'

'Well, that would hardly fit in with the Last Supper, now would it? Just imagine Jesus passing around a platter of hors d'oeuvres with cocktail frankfurts and Swedish meatballs on it and saying "This is my body you eat".'

'It would certainly put a new slant on Jesus' second coming.'

Once we'd finished laughing at our irreverent attack on the Last Supper, Bill focused back on Pernille's question.

'Seriously though, if it wasn't a platter, or a cup, but as you suggest, a royal bloodline, a "vessel to hold the sacred seed", then, if we think it terms of DNA, it implies there was some sort of Genetics Laboratory, Blood Bank, or even a Sperm Bank here at Saqqara. Joseph "commissioning the Holy Grail" could mean that Mary's uncle "created a female offspring", a daughter or cousin of Mary Magdalene, Cleopatra Selene II, or even through Arsinoe IV, Cleopatra's younger sister, using DNA and some sort of in-vitro fertilization and possibly surrogacy.'

I was totally open to the idea, but Pernille found it a bit far-fetched.

'In-vitro fertilization? Two-thousand years ago?'

Though initially enthusiastic, even Bill was finding the plausibility of in-vitro fertilization hard to grasp, until he had another idea.

'Or, the term "commissioned" was code for he was "in charge of" or "the guardian of" the sang réal, meaning he "looked after" Jesus' half sister, Cleopatra Selene II.'

'Brilliant! Perfect.'

'Then the legend says that after its use during the Last Supper, Joseph of Arimethea eventually took the Holy Grail to Glastonbury for safe-keeping.'

'Which is exactly what Joseph of Arimathea did with Mary, he took her to Ireland via South France and Glastonbury.'

The corridor made a left turn into another empty corridor that also seemed to fulfil no essential function. Maybe the two corridors were by-pass corridors, created to circumnavigate a tunnel collapse in the main corridor? Maybe they were part of an extension designed to create more niches for more sarcophagi? Perhaps this was the extension the Egyptologists had attributed to Khaemwaset?

Meanwhile, though Bill had decoded part of the story, the rest was still playing on his mind.

'It all makes sense so far, but how do we explain how, five-hundred years later, Percival, a knight of Arthur's round table, received the Grail, and, as part of his Quest, returned it to the city of "Sarras" or Saqqara, where it's still hidden beneath the ruins of the Coptic monastery of St. Jeremias.'

'Simple; he searched all over Britain and Europe until he found Mary's grave, dug up the remains, and reburied them beneath the floor of the Coptic monastery?'

'Now that *would* be interesting. I was thinking more along the lines that over the centuries the lineage of the bloodline had somehow been lost, that the search for the Holy Grail was a search to find the rightful heir, your *sang réal*.'

'You mean Percival was actually looking for a living descendant?'

'Yeah, if he found the bloodline, a girl, and escorted her back to Saqqara, then he either stored a sample of her blood or tissue, or maybe even buried her body there, which makes me think, there's a story that Joseph of Arimathea took two vials containing the blood and sweat of Jesus to England, maybe that was the "vessel" Percival was searching for?'

'I think you're back on the DNA red-herring again, Bill, I've got a more plausible alternative.'

'Fire away.'

'Maybe Percival, as a knight of the round table, was a member of the Tat Brotherhood, and returned her so that she could be married to a High Priest of the Tat Brotherhood, and re-ignite the lineage in Egypt?'

Bill jumped straight aboard.

'Maybe Percival married her himself, after being initiated here at Saqqara and beneath the Great Pyramid?'

Finally the south corridor connected with the main corridor and the Greater Vaults, and, as we arrived, Bill connected one thought after another.

'You know there's a prophecy that says that one day the Grail will be taken back again to Glastonbury by three of Percival's "offspring", when the Etheric Gemstone Temple in which it is to be housed will appear over Glastonbury Tor.'

'That would mean three blood descendents of Percival and of Cleopatra Selene II will return to Glastonbury at a time when some sort of higher vibrational crystal temple manifests over the Tor in Glastonbury, and one of them will take up residence.'

Pernille piped up.

'I've always wanted to visit Glastonbury, and Stonehenge, and Ireland.'

I looked at Bill, who looked at me at exactly the same time, and I'm sure we were thinking exactly the same thing; the three blood descendants were Pernille, Crystal and …? Rather than embarrass Pernille, I diverted the conversation.

'So why do you think you're here, Bill, the Holy Grail, or the Books of Thoth?'

'Don't get me wrong, I wouldn't complain if I stumbled upon either.'

'Remember, Bill, a bird in the hand is worth two in the bush.'

He wrapped his arm around Pernille's waist.

'Very clever, Alex, don't think I don't know how fortunate I am.'

He gave Pernille a loving and grateful kiss, but, before they got too involved, I kept things moving.

'Anyway, back to business, have you checked out the Philosophers' Circle outside?'

'Not yet, what is it?'

'A semi-circular stone wall that contain statues of famous Greek poets and philosophers from the Ptolemaic Period.'

'Oh yeah, I caught a glimpse of it on the way in; I wondered what that was.'

'Maybe the *'Book of Thoth'* is under one of the statues, Plato perhaps?'

'That's an interesting proposition! I like your logic. And, speaking of books, maybe your papers have something to do with all this, with exposing the truth? You do still have them, don't you?'

'Don't get me started. Yes, I gave them to Saeed outside to mind for me. But the papers aren't even the tip of the iceberg; there's so much to tell you and ask you. Where are you heading after this?'

'Saeed is taking us into Cairo; we're going to meet up with Diane's group again tonight and early tomorrow morning we're taking a camel ride at dawn into the Giza Plateau from the desert, then visit the King's Chamber of the Great Pyramid for a circle.'

'Sounds amazing, wish I could join you, but I think I'd better get out of Egypt as fast as I can.'

'Actually, Saeed and I have been talking about that; we've got a plan. We think the quickest and safest way out of Egypt is via boat from Alexandria to Greece.'

'Agreed, the airports are out, and the Embassy was a no-go zone; they've got it staked out.'

'Now, I've got a little boat moored in the Greek Islands that I keep for holidays around the Mediterranean. I've arranged for it to come here straight away. It should be here by tomorrow night, which means you *could* come with us to the pyramid if you really wanted to, and didn't think it was too risky.'

'It's tempting, let me think it over.'

'OK, well I'm off to check out the Philosophers' Circle.'

'And I might check out the Lesser Vaults on the lower level first.'

'Lower level?'

'Yeah.'

I showed Bill the diagram. He shook his head.

'Not open...'

He pointed down the corridor to the left.

'...It must be what's behind the closed door at the end of the corridor. Only the upper level's open for viewing, but I'm sure you'll find it worth it...'

Pernille went to say something, but Bill politely stopped her.

'...Now, now, let's not spoil things, let's just leave the man to enjoy the discoveries for himself...'

Pernille just smiled and together they headed out.

'...We'll see you outside later. Enjoy looking around, I'm sure you'll be stunned by what you see and find.'

With the Lesser Vaults closed, I decided to explore the Greater Vaults and headed to the right, into the dead end, where there were twelve massive granite sarcophagi, six alternating to each side, each housed in a huge niche or alcove carved out of the solid rock and now protected by modern steel arched frames.

"Oh, Wow!

Excluding the site of Crystal coming out of the shower, this was clearly the most amazing thing I had seen on the trip so far.

Made of red, grey, or black granite, most of the sarcophagi were around ten feet long, six feet wide, and over eight feet tall; so tall that I could have stood under the lid. Each one was carved from one singular piece of granite and they must have each weighed maybe a hundred-and-twenty ton or more.

Most of the sarcophagi were perfectly cut and polished; the faces were perfectly finished and flat, the corners perfectly square and precise, and most of the lids had wide bevelled edges along the side.

The end of one lidless sarcophagus contained the same 'palace' facade I had seen on the walls of the Complex of Netjerikhet. The question now became, what came first the chicken or the egg; were the walls copied from the sarcophagus, or the sarcophagus from the walls?

On the end of the lid of another granite box were two short rows of tiny hieroglyphs, hardly what you would expect for such a massive piece of rock. I didn't recognise the cartouche, but clearly they were a later addition to the stone.

The last alcove on the right permitted access via a set of steps to get close and walk around the sarcophagus. This one was made of black granite, not just dark grey, but really black, and it was massive, possibly the largest of them all. It felt alive, like it had its own history, its own personality, its own presence. The sides were perfectly 'machined' and polished, so much so you could almost see your reflection in them. They were perfectly straight; the angles where they intersected were meticulously exact. The technology to create this magnificent object was far in excess of anything we possessed today.

And yet it was 'inscribed' with what could best be described as chicken-scratching; it was as if someone had taken a nail and scratched into its side like a teenage graffitist.

Once again there was the 'palace' façade imagery, or false-door imagery, as well as a row of basic hieroglyphs, but anyone who put forward the opinion that the inscriptions were contemporary with the sarcophagus should go back to Archaeology 101.

The official explanation is that these sarcophagi were made for sacred bulls, but the truth is not a single mummified bull's testicle of a single Apis bull was ever found in any of them. Even if it was, why would you need to make them six feet high, unless you were planning to entomb them standing up. And if that were the case, you wouldn't need them four feet wide. Apis bulls? Bull's bollocks!

For some reason I wanted to jump up and climb inside one, but, no matter how hard I tried, it just wasn't possible, they were too damn high. I circled it once again.

So, what were they used for: they weren't used to bury bulls, they were much much older than that, they weren't buried separately, rather all together in a 'community', and they were far too big to have been made for humans? I was getting ideas so I decided to tune in see what Nemo had to say.

I put my hands on the side wall, rested my forehead against the stone as well, took a few deep breaths to clear my mind and focus, and slowly started to tone a very low pitched 'Aw' into the stone. Within a few breaths Nemo appeared inside the sarcophagus flipping and flopping around like he was in a fish tank. Slowly the tank filled with water and the lid was place on top, sealing him in. But it wasn't bad, Nemo wasn't dead, he was well and truly alive and well, and he was happy, looking forward to what was about to happen.

Next, the sarcophagus and its lid began to hum, the very molecules of the stone vibrating, resonating; the whole box became a massive resonating chamber. It was as if the whole monolithic box had come to life, breathing *for* Nemo, his body totally engulfed in every wave. Time seemed to stand still as Nemo went into a state of suspended animation. And then something extraordinary happened; Nemo started to regenerate, his whole body was being recalibrated, rebooted, reconfigured. Slowly it morphed into a tall humanoid form, into a member of the Annunaki, into Akhenaten, no, into Aak-en-aten, Aak-of-the-aten, Aak-of-the-consciousness-of-the-sun.

On the next breath I found my awareness spreading, from within the walls of the black sarcophagus, to the next 'sarcophagus', and then the next, and then across the corridor until in encompassed them all. They were all 'occupied', with 'beings', tall humanoid beings. These 'granite boxes' belonged to them, to 'the gods', to the Annunaki, or the hybrid offspring of the gods, and they used them like we would use a day spa.

All of the granite boxes were 'humming' in an amazing symphony of cosmic cyclic evolution, but one 'instrument' was standing out. At first I put it down to Nemo, but as I tuned in to it more and more I realized it was the sound of a woman's voice. I stopped toning and listened closely; it was still there. I opened my eyes; it was still there. I took my hands off the stone; it was definitely still there, resonating through the Serapeum.

I left the alcove and made my way back down the corridor, scanning from side to side to locate the origin of the voice. It was coming from the far end, past the intersecting corridor. And then I found it, on the left; there was a sarcophagus that had been smashed open at the end and someone was lying inside, toning, the soles of their feet visible from the corridor.

I climbed down to look inside; there was only one woman I could think of who would tone while lying inside a massive granite sarcophagus.
'Crystal?'

No response. I stooped down so my head was looking inside.
'Crystal, is that you?'

She stopped toning.

'Yes.'

'What are you doing?'

'Getting a fake tan in the tanning salon.'

She recommenced her toning, and I didn't need to be told twice to piss off; clearly she was busy connecting to the rock and I'd interrupted her flow.

'Sorry.'

Tail between my legs, I climbed back up out of the alcove and into the corridor: I couldn't believe it, I'd wanted to see her again so much and the first thing I did when I got my wish was to act like a totally inconsiderate epsilon semi-moron.

Moments later she stopped toning and emerged from the hole in the wall, looking like an Athenian goddess. Maybe it was her white dress and shawl, maybe it was just the lighting but she looked like she was glowing, radiating with energy. She stood calmly looking at me.

'It is good to see you, Alex. Would you mind giving me a hand up?'

I scrambled to step forward and offer my hand.

'Sure, sure; I'm sorry if I disturbed you.'

'It's fine, I was nearly finished anyway.'

As soon as she was up she thanked me and sauntered off along the corridor like a super-confident supermodel on a Paris catwalk; me stalking her like a lovesick puppy.

'Tell me, these weren't sarcophagi, were they?'

'When ever will you learn not to make statements and then question them?'

'So they *weren't* sarcophagi?'

'What do you think?'

'They *couldn't* have been.'

'Oh, they *could* have.'

'They could?'

'Yes, …but they weren't.'

I felt like Crystal was toying with me, the way a cat plays with a mouse. We passed the locked door, the sarcophagus lid next to the entrance and out the door where Bill and Pernille, along with Abdo, Saeed and the guardian, were waiting outside at the top of the ramp. Bill chuckled.

'Ah, I see you discovered the Serapeum's secret mystery, our very own Sleeping Beauty. Right then, all present and accounted for, let's go.'

'Where to?'

'Abusir; Abdo lives in the village and has invited us all to his house for dinner.'

'I thought Abusir was closed to the public; don't tell me it's another military site?'

Abdo cleared things up.

'The village it is not closed, and the pyramid they are actually not really closed, but you have to arrange it the personal visit with the guardian, and it is very expensive.'

Bill was right on to it.

'I don't think money is an issue, my shout, so how do we contact this guardian.'

'I will make it the phone call; he is best friend of my brother; we all are grow up in Abusir together.'

'You think you can get us in?'

As he hit speed dial, Abdo smiled and nodded.

'We can first visit Abusir pyramid, then I will arrange it for dinner by sun temple of Abu Ghurab, yes?'

'Sounds great.'

I couldn't understand the rush.

'But, Bill, you just got here, don't you want to see the rest of Saqqara first?'

'Is it more impressive than what we've just seen in the Serapeum?'

'Well,..no!'

'Then, seen one step pyramid, seen 'em all.'

'Yes, true, but it's what's under them that's important.'

'Sand? Rocks? The Lost Books of Thoth?'

'Red granite chambers actually.'

'Hmmm, now that *is* interesting.'

Abdo wound up his phone call.

'Yes, very good, it is all arranged, we can go to Sahure Pyramid now, then we will cook it the meal and have it dinner at Abu Ghurab. Come we go.'

Abdo set off for the car as Bill gave the guardian a very healthy baksheesh handshake. I followed suit, and we made our way off towards the cars, though I admit I was still a little bemused by things.

'Did you check out the Philosophers' Circle?'

'Indeed I did. I think you might be on to something there old chat!'

'So there's lot's to talk about.'

'Indeed there is! And we can talk about it over dinner, so let's go, I'm starving.'

Bill and Pernille climbed in the minivan, followed, much to my dismay, by Crystal. I guess it made sense, after all her bags were in the minivan, but somehow I'd hoped she might have shared the ride with me.

'I guess I'll see you all there.'

Saeed threw me the backpack.

'Unless your car it gets stopped by the Secret Police and your hat it gets filled with more bullet holes.'

'Very funny.'

Laughing away, Saeed got into the minivan and they set off. I climbed into the back of Abdo's car.

'Follow that cab!'

CHAPTER 29 - MIND YOUR ASP

Abusir, which means the "Place of Osiris", was only a few kilometres north of Saqqara, so the trip was only going to be five to ten minutes. Saeed and the others waited as we exited for Abdo to take the lead, which he did, driving one-handed as he chatted away on his phone obviously organizing the dinner. So, rather than fritter the time away going over how stupid I'd acted in the Serapeum, I used the time to go over my notes on Abusir.

"About 12 kilometres south of the pyramids of Giza, Abusir has 14 pyramids, belonging to the 5th Dynasty, and several small mastabas, that seem to have perhaps had as many as three steps and date back to the second half of the 1st Dynasty. All of the pyramid complexes are badly ruined, as much by stone thieves as from the ravages of time."

The ravages of time, what about the effects of a six-hundred-foot-high tsunami?

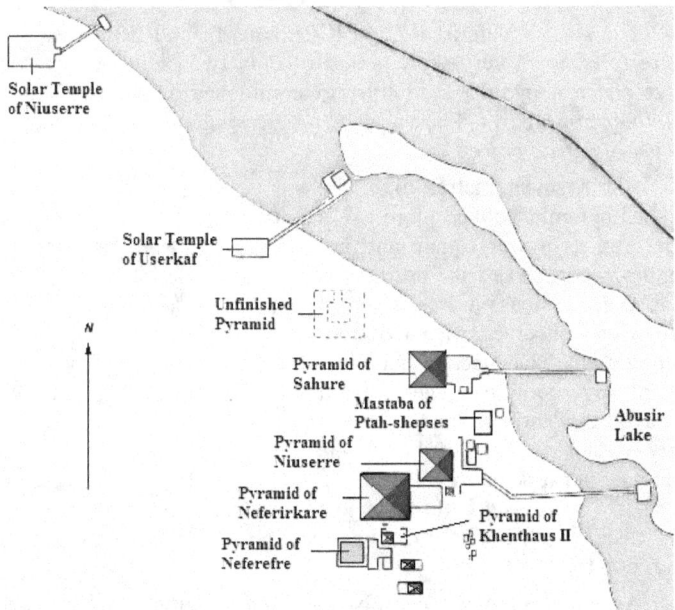

The layout of the structures was clearly deliberate and it drew me back to Herchel's star maps.

According to Herschel, Abusir represented the constellation of the Pleiades, the "leg of the bull".

"The Pleiades is a young constellation comprised of hot blue giant stars which has uniquely retained its leg-shape constellation almost unchanged for a staggering 20,000 years."

So, sure, it was possible, highly probable Abusir represented the Pleiades, and it certainly had enough pyramids, but if it did represent the Pleiades then it wasn't exactly as it appeared from planet earth. So why the preoccupation with the Pleiades, what was the significance, and was it more important than Giza, Orion, and the Sphinx? If so, why? Or were they all part of a massive galactic scheme?

I knew it wasn't some random concept; the ancient Egyptians weren't the only ones preoccupied with the Pleiades; almost every ancient civilization and every modern New Age story of extraterrestrial visitation seemed to include some tall, fair Pleiadean emissary from the Galactic Federation come to earth to assist humanity.

It would have been great to have been able to grab Frank and Mark and wander around tire-kicking and turning over stones at Abusir, picking their brains, however, that wasn't going to be possible. Maybe there were papers about Abusir in the backpack on the seat beside me? Abusir was clearly an important site; was that why it was so expensive, and not promoted to tourists, the vultures hadn't finished covering up the truth and picking the bones clean yet?

It was now approaching 4:30, and the day was fast getting away from us. It was unlikely that even if I wanted to, and assuming it was permitted, we would get to explore anything other than the Pyramid of Sahure. That being the case, just to be sure, I decided to check out my notes on the other pyramids, working my way up from the south.

The Unfinished Pyramid of Neferefre

The son of Neferirkare and Khentkaus II, and fifth ruler of the 5th Dynasty, Neferefre ruled for a very short period of only two or three years. Despite this short reign Neferefre apparently had time to commence a large pyramid, with a base of around sixty-five metres, known as *"The Pyramid which is divine of the Ba spirits, Divine is Neferefre's power"*.

About seven metres high, the 'unfinished pyramid' looked more like a mastaba, but, as it was square and not rectangular, nor was it northsouth oriented like mastabas, it was believed to have been conceived as a pyramid. Why couldn't it have been a mastaba? Was there any proof to suggest that it might have been? In addition, a number of early explorers had attributed the pyramid to Shepseskare-isi, Neferefre's predecessor. I wondered if this was just

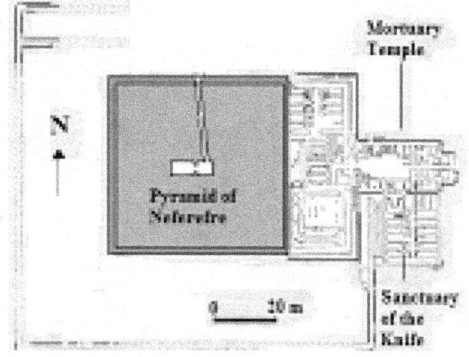

another case of attributing the construction of the 'pyramid' to the earliest name discovered in the Mortuary Temple?

As had become blatantly obvious from my time at Dahshur and Saqqara, it was the norm for a 'mortuary temple' of a pharaoh to be built in front of the east face of a pyramid. But it didn't mean it was a 'funerary' temple, just a temple of worship, nor did it mean that the temple and the pyramid or mastaba it was built in front of, were contemporary with one another. Time to do a little detective work.

"In the 1970s, the University of Prague did a systematic investigation using geophysical surveying, specifically with magnetometry, of the ground in front of the eastern wall of the structure. The tests revealed a huge, highly articulated building of mud-bricks, in the shape of the letter 'T', a shape characteristic of mortuary temples in the 5th and 6th Dynasty..."

Nothing out of the ordinary so far.

"Then, by piecing together various clues, they arrived at the conclusion that it was indeed Neferefre's pyramid. "

Just because you find a few rolls of toilet paper in the outdoor dunny doesn't mean the main house was built by Sorbent.

"On a five metre wide part of the pyramid's base, originally created by two layers of huge limestone blocks intended as foundation for the pyramid's smooth limestone casing, was a very small mortuary temple, with a north-south axis, constructed of small blocks of fine white limestone and entered by a stairway and ramp from the southeast."

There were several things about the quote that instantly struck me; firstly that the site of the structure must have been levelled first, just like with the blocks added at Abu Raoush, second that the base of the 'pyramid' had possibly been a rectangle, which would be consistent with it being planned as a mastaba. Third, that there was a smaller temple built first, possibly belonging to Neferefre's predecessor, Shepseskare-isi.

"It's uncertain who build the original small temple, but nearby were found two clay seals engraved with the Horus name, Sekhemkhau, probably king Shepseskare, who most likely only ruled for a few months, perhaps only for a few weeks."

Surely that one piece of evidence ruled out the possibility that the 'pyramid' was built by Neferefre; expanded perhaps, possibly even repaired, but was he responsible for the original subterranean structures, highly unlikely. Unfortunately there was no mention of any red-granite false door in the western wall of the offering hall either, although, before it, an apparent depression in the floor supposedly marked the spot where an altar once stood. Was *it* made of red granite? Who knows?

"The small temple was extended to the north by a group of ten, two-story storage magazines for the papyri of the priesthood, and, to the south, by an east-west oriented hypostyle hall with 20 wooden six-stemmed lotus columns, in four rows of five, which supported a flat wooden ceiling at a height of about four metres."

Wooden columns? Did that indicate that all the ancient red-granite columns had already been usurped, or, were wooden columns the norm for this period?

"About the hall were found fragments of statues of Neferefre. Made of diorite, basalt, limestone, reddish quartzite and wood. They included six relatively complete, though mostly broken statues, the most beautiful of these, as well as the smallest at about 35 centimetres, being an incomplete rose-coloured limestone statue, in fragments, depicting the young pharaoh sitting on a throne and holding a hedj, the emblem of royal power, to his chest.."

It seemed pretty obvious to me that Shepseskare's small temple was extended and modified by Neferefre into a larger rectangular temple, made almost entirely of mud-brick, that stretched along the whole eastern side of the 'Unfinished' 'Pyramid'.

"The entrance to the new temple was in the middle of the east façade, through a portico with two four-stemmed lotus limestone columns. In the centre of this addition, between the entrance and the offering hall of the older temple were five storage annexes."

Again there were no red-granite columns, however this time they were made of limestone.

"The last major building phase in the temple's development consisted of a new entrance, supported by a pair of six-stemmed papyrus-columns of fine white limestone, and a large open rectangular courtyard supported by 24 columns, at which point it acquired the characteristic "T" shape."

It seemed logical that this final stage was attributable to Niuserre, Neferefre's successor, and probably also his brother, who ruled Egypt for the next twenty-five years. As for the "Sanctuary of the Knife" to the southeast, it was basically an abattoirs, or slaughterhouse, and could have been built by any of the three pharaohs previously mentioned, though most likely by Neferefre. But the 'pyramid', *that* was another question.

"The outer face of the first step of the pyramid's core comprised a retaining wall seven metres high made of huge blocks of dark-grey limestone, some up to five metres long, bound together with clay. A second, inner wall, built of smaller blocks, made up the walls of the rectangular trench of the substructure of the tomb. Between these two walls there were no accretion layers, rather pieces of small, poor-quality limestone, sometimes stuck together with clay mortar and sand, sometimes packed dry, alongside little compartments of rough stone lumps filled with rubble such as fragments of mud-bricks and potsherds."

To me, the evidence was clear; the first part of the superstructure constructed was the inner wall that surrounded the trench of the 'tomb', which meant the trench must have preceded it, and that's where I was sure I'd find the real evidence.

"The first step of the core then resembled a truncated pyramid, which was then faced with blocks of fine white limestone. The outer surface, which had a sloping angle of about 78 degrees, was carefully smoothed down, and thus what had been planned as a pyramid became an atypically square mastaba."

I think they had it the wrong way around. The way I figured it, at some later stage, after they had surrounded the trench, it was obviously decided to build a mastaba to encase the 'tomb', preparing the ground, but then they changed their mind from building a mastaba to building a step pyramid, much as had been done at Saqqara with the Step Pyramid of Netjerikhet, using whatever rubble was lying around to fill in the first step.

However, for some reason they either aborted the project after the first level, or, the upper layers were swept away by the Thera tsunami and it was repaired much later. But, by now, it was what was below the ground that I was interested in.

"In the middle of the prepared base, a rectangular trench, east-west in orientation, was dug down into the bedrock to house the royal tomb. Next, a deep ditch was dug down to intersect the trench from the north, intended to be for the passage leading down to the underground chambers."

It sounded exactly like the subterranean floor plan at Abu Raoush and the Unfinished Pyramid at Zawiyet el Aryan, and very similar to the Pyramid of Userkaf. It was hardly a coincidence that so many of these 'unfinished' pyramids had the same subterranean structure.

"The entrance passage, lined in the lower regions with pink granite, curves slightly to the southeast as it descends towards the antechamber."

As expected, there was my red granite, but why did the descending passage have a curve in it; that baffled me? Whether the trench was dug first, or the ditch, the ditch would surely have been dug perpendicular to the trench. It looked like there was a change of mind along the way and it was decided to intersect the trench at the antechamber rather than the burial chamber, but why?

"Prior to arriving at the antechamber the passage was sealed with several huge barrier blocks made of pink granite, still partly in situ and unique to this pyramid. Normally, the portcullis blocks would slide vertically, however, here an ingenious system of pairs of stones with lugs and holes was used."

Right on cue, the granite portcullis blocks appeared, confirming for me the pre-dynastic, pre-pole-shift origin of the subterranean chambers.

"Past the barrier, the antechamber and burial chamber, both lined with fine white limestone, are aligned very precisely east-west. Above them sat a gabled roof, anchored at the foundation level of the pyramid, consisting of huge limestone blocks; the vacant space above the roof filled with lumps of stone and rubble arranged in diagonally running walls crossing over the pyramid's centre."

It was following the usual pattern, although clearly there had been some modification when the mastaba was reduced to one level or repaired.

"Only scant remains were found within, including fragments of a pink sarcophagus, four alabaster canopic jars, alabaster containers and offerings, and parts of a mummy, including the complete left hand belonging to a 20 to 23 year old man, probably Neferefre."

The remains could have belonged to anyone, but my bet was if they dated to the 5th Dynasty, and not some later usurped burial, then they were more likely to belong to Shepseskare. While I was deep in thought, Abdo suddenly pulled up outside a house in the village.

'I will be it one minute; we must get him Haakim.'

Knowing that in Egyptian time 'one minute' could be anything from thirty seconds to a quarter-of-an-hour, and rather than jump out to strike up an obvious conversation with Crystal in the other car, I kept reviewing my notes.

The Pyramid of Khentkaus II

The next pyramid to the north, a much smaller pyramid complex, belonged to Khentkaus II, the mother of both Neferefre and his successor and brother, Niuserre. Khentkaus II was also the wife of Neferirkare Kakai, possibly even his sister, which would mean she was a daughter of Sahure and Neferetnebty, or perhaps a half-sister, but I was purely speculating. What I was sure of was that she must have been the *sang réal* for Neferirkare Kakai to have married her, which means Khentkaus II's mother may have been Khentkaus I, who may well have been a full-sister to Sahure. Anyway, there'd be time to examine the lineage of the *sang réal* if I ever got out of Egypt alive.

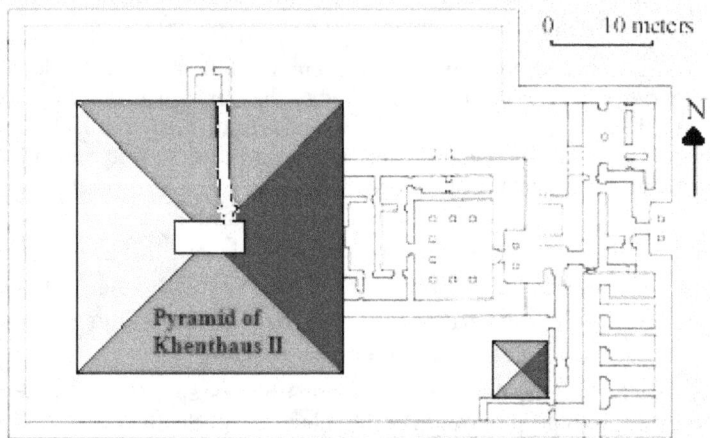

The first thing I noticed was the satellite pyramid, or 'binary-star' pyramid as I now saw it. The Egyptologists had referred to these satellite pyramids as 'queens' pyramids, but here was proof that couldn't be correct, why, because Khentkaus II was a queen already. So how did they explain that a queen had a queen's pyramid? They didn't. Maybe they couldn't. It just didn't make sense. So, until someone could disprove my binary-star theory, I was going to run with that.

"The original plan of the pyramid complex, including the original Mortuary temple, called for it to be enclosed within a high wall built of limestone blocks. Later the complex was reconstructed and the temple extended towards the east with the addition of a new entrance, adorned with twin limestone pillars, erected precisely on the east-west axis of the pyramid complex. The entrance hall allowed access to a group of five magazines in the southeast and a group of domestic rooms in the north-eastern corner, while also communicating with the original temple to the west. Most of the new construction was plastered mud-brick, whitewashed and sometimes adorned with painting."

Given the original temple was probably constructed by Neferirkare Kakai for his wife *because* she was living essence of the *sang réal*, it makes sense that the extensions were probably done by Neferefre and/or Niuserre, as sons of Khentkaus II, after Neferirkare's death. I'd already dismissed the claim by the Egyptologists that the queens pyramids were built *for* them, rather they were usurped and attributed to them, but now I took it a step further, I was now thinking that only those queens that were of the *sang réal* had pyramids attributed to them; a direct connection between their 'royal' blood and the stars. What better way than have a 'star' dedicated to you as acknowledgement that you in fact were a descendant of the gods.

"In front of the east wall of the pyramid was the earliest part of the mortuary temple, modest in size, made from limestone and entered from the south-east through a pillared portico decorated with twin monolithic limestone pillars coloured red and bearing, on the exterior side, vertical hieroglyphic inscriptions in sunk relief with the queen's titles, name and depiction."

Clearly painting the limestone pillars red was to imitate red granite, because, firstly, there were no more red-granite columns to usurp, and second, they didn't have the capability to quarry and transport new granite columns themselves.

"An open courtyard followed, decorated with similar pillars, leading to a room with niches for the statues of the queen, an offering hall with a false door made of pink-granite, an altar and storage annexes."

I wondered if the altar was also made of red granite, and, if it and the false-door were still in situ; unlikely.

"The rooms in the western part of the temple were decorated with a wide array of scenes and inscriptions in coloured low relief including sacrifice, agricultural work, and processions of offerings to the queen. On the fragment of one scene, the queen's name is preceded by a title naming her 'King's Wife', on another as 'Mother of the Two Kings of Upper and Lower Egypt', indications the temple was constructed at various stages. In another scene, Khentkaus II is sitting on a throne, holding a wadj-scepter in her hand, the queen's brow adorned with a uraeus."

There is also the possibility that when Niuserre assumed the throne, probably due to the untimely death of his elder brother, Neferefre, he was still a child, and that Khentkaus II acted as Niuserre's co-regent for a period of time, effectively acting as the ruler of Egypt, much as Hatshepsut did almost a thousand years later.

"With a base of 25 metres, and slope of 52°, the pyramid would have risen around 17 metres, however it is now mostly in ruins and measures only four metres high. A simple design, it comprised a core of three layers, bound with mortar made of clay, a casing of high quality white limestone, and once had a dark-grey granite pyramidion, of which fragments have been found."

But did the pyramidion belong to *this* pyramid? And what was below the surface?

135

"The entrance to the pyramid is near ground level in the middle of the north wall. The initial corridor, made from small blocks of fine white limestone, first descends, then becomes level, leading slightly to the east where it is terminated by a simple stone barrier just prior to the burial chamber. The burial chamber is also lined with white limestone, but with larger blocks serving as it flat ceiling."

Again, there was that bizarre deviation of the descending passage to the east; it was in the diagram, and it was in the notes. Alas, the notes failed to indicate why, nor did they reveal the nature of the stone barrier, though convention led me to believe it was more than likely made of granite. Not much was found within the pyramid either, just a few small remains including fragments of a pink-granite sarcophagus, bits of her mummy's wrappings, and some shards from stone vessels.

While I was scratching my head, Abdo returned to the car with Haakim, who joined Abdo in the front seat. Introductions over, we set off for the Pyramid of Sahure and I took the remaining time to complete my review of the pyramids; next was that of Neferirkare.

The Pyramid of Neferirkare-Kakai

According to the notes, the pyramid was built without a valley temple or causeway, but one look at the map convinced me there was indeed once a valley temple and causeway, but that they had been usurped by one of his successors, his son Niuserre, so I flicked a few pages to the file on Niuserre.

"Because of its proximity to the Nile, the valley temple of Niuserre's is almost gone. Its floor was originally around five metres below the present ground level and was probably built upon a foundation originally laid by Neferirkare, as was the causeway."

That confirmed it; the Valley Temple was originally Neferirkare's. Also, that the original floor level was five metres below the present ground level was, as far as I was concerned, totally consistent with the depth of deposits from the Thera and post-Thera tsunamis.

"It had two columned entrances, the west one having two colonnades with four pink-granite six-stemmed papyrus-shaped columns bearing Niuserre's names and titles. This entrance led to a harbour ramp, paved with basalt, and a granite dado."

I still wasn't sure about where the basalt fitted in, but these six-stemmed papyrus-shaped columns made of red granite regularly appeared in temples that were clearly much older than the 5th Dynasty. In addition, they would not have been carved with reliefs, and it would have been great to have been able to examine the standard of the carving; if it was like the chicken-scratchings on the Serapeum 'sarcophagi' then it was clearly inferior and a much later addition.

"In the middle of the valley temple there were once numerous statues including statues of Niuserre in three niches on the west wall, statues of captive enemies, an alabaster head of Queen Reputnebu, and a pink-granite statue of a lion, all of which only fragments have been discovered."

The alabaster definitely related to the Old Kingdom, but the red-granite lion took me back to the weathered one on the Island of Philae outside the Temple of Isis, I was sure it wasn't 'Roman' but rather much like the lion statues of Sumer; the Assyrian lion. It all raised the question: was the current valley temple built on the site of an even older structure, or was it originally built as part of, and connected via the causeway, to the original pyramid substructure attributed to Neferirkare?

The causeway itself didn't provide much information, it hasn't even been fully investigated, other than confirm my thinking that the lower section was originally part of Neferirkare's complex. I guess any real answers would, as usual, be found in the mortuary temple and below the pyramid.

The pyramid complex itself was apparently once surrounded by a great mud-brick wall, parts of which are barely distinguishable today, that encompassed the pyramid and a mortuary temple, built in stages.

"The eastern part of the temple was built mostly from mud-brick with a floor of packed clay and consisted of a four-columned portico of wooden columns, a columned entrance hall with six pairs of wooden columns, all in the shape of four lotus stems, and an open columned courtyard with 38 lotus shaped wooden columns."

Here again was proof the ancient Egyptians of the 5th Dynasty surely didn't have the technology to quarry and move red granite; if anyone was going to have red-granite columns it would have been Neferirkare, but he didn't, he had columns, not even of limestone, but made of wood.

"The oldest, inner section of the temple, located immediately to the east side of the pyramid, is built of limestone on a small stone platform, perhaps the site of an earlier structure. It consisted of an offering hall, three annexes, and five niche chapels"

That didn't shed much light on things; other than if the pyramid predated Neferirkare, then the inner section of the mortuary temple could have predated him as well. As for the pyramid, though the days of the step pyramids were supposedly long past, the plans for this pyramid apparently called for a step pyramid of six layers, however:

"As the original step casing reached the top of the first layer, the architects decided to enlarge the structure to eight core levels and make it into a true pyramid, the blocks in the upper several levels clearly not cut as finely as those on the lower levels."

Although, according to the 'experts', it was probably never finished, Neferirkare's pyramid, with a base of one-hundred-and-five metres, a slope of around fifty-three degrees and height of seventy-two metres, was the largest structure in the region. Ironically, it was because of its ruined condition, and its exposed core steps, that it became the 'model' upon which generations of early Egyptologists based their theories of inclined accretion layers.

"The entrance to the pyramid is about two metres up on the north wall. From it, a descending corridor built of limestone leads to a vestibule about two-and-a-half metres below the base of the pyramid and a granite barrier. The corridor, which is unique in that its roof is flat but has a second gabled roof above it, extends beyond the barrier, making two turns until it arrives at an offset east-west aligned antechamber and burial chamber, both of which are of the same width, though the antechamber is a little shorter than the burial chamber, and have gabled ceilings."

Although the granite portcullis was now expected, generally I couldn't believe that such an important pyramid had been so little investigated; perhaps the Pyramid of Niuserre held some answers. However, as if exactly on cue to interrupt my research, that's when we arrived at Abusir; all gathering in front of the cars; Niuserre would have to wait.

The Pyramid Complex of Sahure

'Welcome to Abusir. My name it is Haakim and today we visit it pyramid of Sahure, second pharaoh of five dynasty. Pyramid of Sahure is first pyramid for it to be build at Abusir. We start valley temple and walk up causeway to pyramid. This way, please to follow'.

Abdo bid us farewell, he was going on to oversee dinner, and I took the opportunity to position myself next to Crystal.

'It was a pleasant surprise to find you in the Serapeum. Was your visit there part of your trip to awaken the goddess within you?'

'It was.'

'Part of letting go of your fears?'

'No, I had done that earlier; at Kom Ombo and Luxor.'

'So what exactly were you doing in the Serapeum?'

'Fully remembering all of who I am.'

'And who is that?'

Before she could answer, Haakim started speaking.

'It is most normal for it valley temple to have it one ramp, it from the east, from the Nile, but the Valley Temple of Sahure it line-up north-to-south and have it two landing ramp, one from the east and the another from the south.'

Crystal leaned in and whispered.

'We will talk later.'

'East entrance it have eight pink-granite column; to the south it have four column...'

There were my red granite columns again.

'...Both entrance they lead it to central room with roof of stars and wall cover with many relief in many colour of Sahure as it Sphinx, yes? Him trade the enemy of Egypt .'

The truth was there wasn't much left to see, most of the stone had been pilfered, and what was left of the temple was overgrown with bulrushes, although I did find part of a red-granite column that had been painted white, probably by a later usurper. What there was, was a floor made of basalt, cut into irregularly sized and shaped stones.

'Hey, Bill, what do you make of this?'

He joined me, looking at a large piece of stone.

'Basalt! Interesting. Clearly it's been precision cut, not bashed with a piece of diorite.'

'I've been trying to figure out where it fits in.'

'In the floor?'

'No, in the history of things.'

Before we could get into it, Haakim interjected.

'Basalt, yes, more in mortuary temple, much better, come.'

We nodded and joined the procession, led by the girls, leaving the valley temple and entering the causeway that made its way two hundred metres up the slope to the pyramid. Unlike the causeway of Unas at Saqqara, very little remained of the Sahure causeway except for the large, rough limestone blocks of its base ramp.

'Causeway it was once corridor, with roof that have it small open space for light, and wall to either side cover in many colour relief.'

Whilst Haakim was rolling off his tourist talk, I was on a different station.

'You know, Bill, I don't think we're seeing the full picture here.'

'What do you mean?'

'Don't you think it's a bit strange that the surface of this causeway is so irregular, hardly what I'd call a smooth walking path.'

'Yeah, doesn't make sense.'

'It does when you realize this whole area was buried in fifteen feet or so of tsunami sediment around 1600 BC, because then we're not walking on the *floor* of the corridor,…'

'…we're walking on the roof!'

'Exactly; there must be another corridor, the original one, underneath the ground.'

'You think maybe it was a double-decker causeway?'

'Is George W a wanker?'

As we chuckled away, scuffing at what we believed was the roof, we approached the upper section of the causeway, Haakim continuing his discourse.

'1994, Zahi Hawass he decide him to open Abusir pyramid to tourist. He remake part of causeway, but, here he find it very big limestone block with relief on stone of performing and of it celebrate the finish of pyramid and the bring it of gold cover top for pyramid of Sahure.'

'Was the stone a part of the causeway, part of the wall, or part of something else?'

At first Haakim seemed bemused by the question, then clicked into what was surely a standard response.

'Yes, stone it was part of causeway.'

I wasn't so convinced, and headed back to my notes for more information, and to get the plan of the temple in my head before entering.

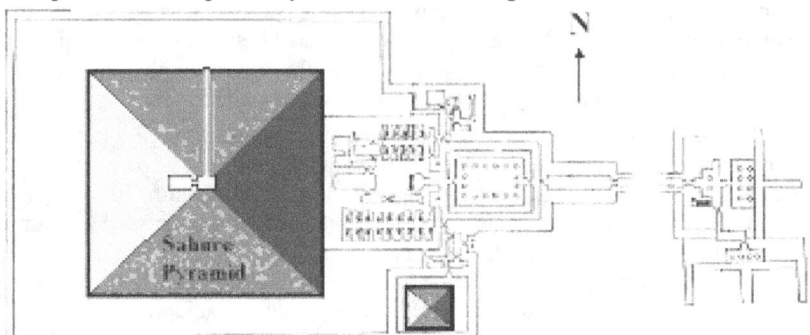

It looked very similar to most of the other sites I'd visited or read up about here and at Saqqara, the only difference being that this was supposedly the first of its kind. Sure the Pyramid of Userkaf had a small offering hall to the east, and a courtyard and chapel to the south, but this was the first 'formula' arrangement of the mortuary temple abutting the eastern face of the pyramid as it was to become known.

"The mortuary temple lies on the east side of the pyramid on a foundation of two layers of rough limestone blocks. It is divided into an inner section and outer section by a central corridor, that also served as a central lane connecting the pyramid courtyard and the small cult pyramid."

'Hey, Alex, check this out...'

Bill was kicking the sand away from the centre of the path.

'...What do you make of it?'

There was a long trench, a few inches wide and deep, running from the inside of the temple, down the entrance passage, and down the causeway.

'It looks like a drainage channel.'

'Bizarre place to put a drainage channel, right in the middle of an important walkway.'

'Unless the floor was covered in paving tiles.'

'You mean the ceiling.'

'I'm not sure what I mean; wouldn't you love to just do a little digging around and find out for yourself?'

We joined Haakim and the others who were waiting in the entrance passage.

'This pyramid complex of Sahure, which he call "Sahure soul it shine". Temple very important because it first temple with new design, and build of these stone, and first temple to have it such magnificent relief on it the wall. Temple very famous in ancient time for it art work. Relief in valley temple, causeway, and mortuary temple cover ten thousand square metre, all very rich in different type of scene, in artist concept, and quality of it the workmanship. It represent it highest level of this type of temple that have it been discovered from Old Kingdom.'

I was sure the reliefs were great, but they could have been added at any time; it was the walls of the entrance passage that caught my attention, or what was left of them, not because of what was on them, but what they were once lined with; thick slabs of red granite. Built of fine quality limestone, over the years they'd been heavily quarried, but at least a third to a half of the stone that would have made up the walls, and the granite lining, still remained.

Straight away, I started thinking; clearly this was no ordinary entrance. Did it mean this temple may well have been on the site of a much older temple. In fact, if the ceiling had been of red granite as well, which was likely, then maybe, given the prolific use of granite in the entrance passage, it *was* the older temple, and had merely been usurped by Sahure. I couldn't wait to explore what awaited within.

Haakim led the way into the courtyard passing through a pair of massive red-granite columns shaped like the trunk and crown of a palm tree. They were extraordinary; around eight metres tall, each one carved from a single monolithic piece of granite, they were the remaining pair of sixteen that once formed a perimeter around the rectangular open courtyard.

'Column they have it name and title of Sahure, also have it vulture goddess, Nekhbet, in south part of courtyard, and cobra goddess Wadjet in north half.

At one time the columns would have supported an architrave bearing the royal titles, on it resting limestone ceiling-slabs decorated with stars, all forming an ambulatory around the perimeter of the open courtyard. There were still several large slabs of limestone from the ceiling at various locations around the perimeter, leaning against the remains of the courtyard walls.

'On wall of courtyard were it scene of victory of Sahure over Asian and Libyan.'

I circled clockwise around the courtyard; not much of the wall survived, at best, fragments of the reliefs did. Beyond the walls was what appeared to be a surrounding corridor. Why build a corridor all the way around the courtyard when you could simply walk through the courtyard, unless the outer corridor was a later addition by a later pharaoh.

"A corridor encircles the courtyard, its walls containing scenes of Sahure fishing and hunting birds and other desert game. There is also a significant scene of the royal entourage and under the depiction of Neferirkare, we find text that was added, stating, *'Neferirkare, King of Upper and Lower Egypt'*."

Were the columns and inner wall original, dating back to who knows when, usurped by Sahure who had his name scratched all over them, then at some later stage the outer wall and corridor of limestone was added, most probably by Neferirkare? It made sense, it was plausible, but who built the original temple? I was pretty sure it wasn't Sahure.

Circling around to the northern side of the courtyard I couldn't help but notice what at first I thought was a fallen obelisk of red granite propped up off the ground on a few stones and blocks of wood. At maybe ten metres long, it was the size that deceived me.

On closer inspection I noted that it was rectangular-cut, not tapered like an obelisk, and broader than it was deep; this had been a massive lintel that perhaps sat atop the columns or part of the northern inner wall.

Confirming all my thoughts was the orientation of the hieroglyphs on the stone, indicating the massive lintel once horizontally spanned part of the open courtyard. On it, the cartouche of Sahure was clearly visible.

But all that did was confuse me; sure it was added during the reign of Sahure, but the standard and execution of the carving was far superior to the chicken-scratches I had seen in the Serapeum, and more in keeping with the hieroglyphs on 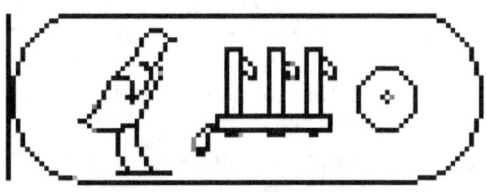 some of the New Kingdom monuments. I wondered if anyone had done an extensive examination on just how these sunken reliefs had been executed?

As I finished examining the lintel and continued scanning the periphery of the courtyard, looking for more chunks of red granite, I noticed Bill was kneeling in the centre of the courtyard, head down, examining the floor.

'What's up, Bill, lost a contact lens, or praying to Allah for forgiveness?'

'Praying for inspiration more like it...'

As I wandered over to join him, I could see he was tracing his finger around the outline of the floor blocks.

'There's no way these blocks were randomly cut or put in place.'

It was then I realized that the whole floor was made of a jigsaw of irregular basalt slabs.

'Basalt again! Why basalt?'

'I don't know, basalt weathers relatively fast compared to other rocks like granite or sandstone; it's such a strange choice for the floor of a valley temple or open courtyard. It was usually just used in ancient Egypt for more important objects like small statues and the decorative accents on buildings and other structures.'

'How come?'

'Primarily because of its hardness, it's a seven on the Mohs scale, and because of its rareness.'

'I thought basalt was pretty common?'

'It is, it's one of the most common types of rock in the world, but most of it makes up the floors of the oceans. Those deposits that are above sea level are in hot spot islands and volcanic arcs where the crust is thin, or in continental floods.'

'So it's rare in Egypt?'

'Yeah, for the most part Egypt is made up of granite, sandstone, limestone, and mudstone, loose sediment like sand and mud, with a few scattered deposits of basalt in a corridor that runs southwest to northeast from Gilf Kebir in southwest Egypt, through the White Desert, Black Desert, Baharya Oasis, Minya, Fayoum, Cairo and up into the north part of the Sinai Peninsula. But most of the basalt used in pyramid construction and the temples came from Widan el Faras, an Oligo–Miocene flow of tholeiitic basalt between twenty to thirty-five metres thick located at the northern edge of the Fayoum Oasis.'

'OK, Bill, I was with you up until the thioletic…?'

'Tholeiitic. It means the basalt is relatively rich in silica.'

'And the Oligo–Mio, thing thing …?'

'Oligo–Miocene boundary; it was around twenty-three million years ago, when the continents were approaching their current positions.'

'Twenty-three million…?'

It sparked a thought.

'… Bill, did you ever read a book called "Nemesis"?'

'No, can't say I have.'

'It's by a Berkeley professor called Richard Muller who put forward the theory there was a brown dwarf star with an orbit of around twenty-six million years that caused regular extinction events on earth.'

'There's certainly geological evidence to support it.'

'But how does that fit in with the Nibiru theory, there's a big difference between twenty-six million and thirty-six hundred?'

Bill started thinking, then pulled out a calculator.

'Not really.'

'You carry around a calculator?'

'I confess, I'm a geek; always carried one since my ventures into the gold market.'

'Fair call.'

'Anyway, its just over a factor of seventy-two hundred. Let's say the extinction events correlate with comet or asteroid impacts. The brown dwarf would drag in its wake tens-of-thousands of pieces of flotsam and jetsam from the Kuiper Belt and the Oort Cloud; asteroids, comets, maybe even planets.'

'Yeah?'

'When it passes around the sun, lets say that there's a three day period in which the earth passes through its wake. That's a one in one-hundred-and-twenty chance of the earth passing through its wake in the earth's yearly orbit of three-hundred-and-sixty-five days around the sun. Twenty-six million divided by one-hundred-and-twenty is…around two-hundred-and-seventeen-thousand.

From there, dividing it by thirty-six hundred,…you only need a one in sixty chance of an extinction-level asteroid striking the earth.'

'That's pretty high; one in sixty!'

'Hmmm, yes it is. Once every two-hundred-thousand years the earth passes through the danger zone, and every time it does, there's a one in sixty chance it gets hit by an extinction level asteroid.'

Bill and I were contemplating the significance when Haakim joined us, eager for us to move along and join the girls, who had meandered on and into the inner temple.

'Basalt, you like?'

We both looked back at the floor; somehow it seemed symbolic of everything we were thinking.

'We sure do.'

'We go, see pyramid, then I take you Pyramid of Niuserre; much basalt, very interest for you.'

'Sounds good to me. Come on, Bill, we can mull it over on the way.'

We didn't even make it out of the courtyard when Bill stopped and climbed between the ruins of the inner and outer wall.

'Will you take a look at that!'

'What?'

He was looking between two thick pieces of red granite.

'The weathering of the limestone and the granite.'

'Yeah, I see it. What are you getting at?'

'This was the *inside* of the wall. The outside is almost perfectly preserved.'

'That doesn't make sense. How does the inside of the wall weather that much but the outer side stays almost pristine?'

'Well, it means it's not weathering.'

'Then what caused it?'

'To affect both the limestone and the granite the way it has, very high temperatures and water or some other reactive agent.'

'What are you saying?'

'That at some time the courtyard was more than just a courtyard.'

'Do you think it had something to do with the basalt floor?'

'It must have.'

Before we could continue, Haakim gave us a hurry up.

'Yes please, more basalt in pyramid temple of Niuserre, but first we go pyramid of Sahure.'

The entrance to the inner section of the temple was up a few steps that ran between the lower sections of another two six-stemmed papyrus-shaped pillars of red granite and through the middle of the west wall of the central, dividing corridor. It led to the Chapel that once contained five niches. The walls were covered in decorated limestone and the floor made of alabaster, however the niches were made of granite. From basalt, to alabaster, limestone and granite; but which came first? I was sure it was the granite, but was the basalt contemporary with it?

A door to the south of the Chapel led via a westward corridor that supposedly only the priests could use, towards the pyramid. Suddenly Bill scaled the low remains of the southern wall of the corridor.

'Will you have a look at that!'

Naturally I followed him.

'What is it?'

Haakim held his ground with the girls.

'This it just many storage room on two level where priest keep valuable.'

Bill wasn't so easily convinced.

'Why build a two-story structure with dividing walls of massive blocks of fine Tura limestone, that's not local to this area, when it would be much easier to make them from smaller local blocks?'

I examined the blocks closely; the walls were enormous, made from one single block of limestone over six feet tall, two feet wide and maybe twelve feet long.

'Stability?'

'What event would you be expecting to necessitate such massive blocks; it was only two-story?'

'An earthquake?'

'Possibly.'

Then I realized he was on my wavelength, even before I was.

'A tsunami perhaps?'

'Perhaps! Can you think of any buildings recently that failed the 'structural test' of a tsunami?'

'You mean the Fukoshima reactors, you think this might have been a nuclear reactor?'

'Perhaps not nuclear as such, but maybe some sort of power station.'

Before we could explore it more, Haakim called us back.

'Please to come now, much to see, and sun it go down.'

He was right, the sun was definitely on its downward journey, and if we wanted to see the pyramid of Niuserre we would have to get a move on. We scrambled back over the wall and on into the westernmost chamber adjacent to the eastern face of the pyramid.

'This Offering Hall, it once have roof of stars.'

It also had a floor of alabaster. I wondered what else it once had; a false door of red granite?

"The ceiling of the Offering Hall was decorated with an astronomical scene of stars and the walls were decorated with scenes depicting divinities carrying offerings for the dead king. On the west wall there is an enormous, granite false door, that should have had inscriptions of magical spells, and the names and titles of Sahure, but it does not, which has led some Egyptologists to believe it was once covered in either copper or gold that was inscribed with this information."

Where was it? Clearly whoever had written the article had done so when the false door was in place, but now there was no trace of it. And was its 'naked' state the norm for all false doors prior to them being usurped and defaced in the dynastic eras?

'Haakim, where is the false door?'

He looked briefly at Saeed then shook his head and scoffed.

'It gone, taken.'

'Stolen?'

'*Taken.*'

Clearly he didn't want to state the obvious and get into trouble.

'Who by?'

'Zahi Hawass.'

'Where is it now?'

He shrugged his shoulders.

'I do not know.'

The big question was, did anyone?

Rather than get caught in any further discussion, Haakim led us northward out of the Offering Hall into several small annexes.

'Hey Alex, guess what I found?'

Bill was scratching in the floor again.

'Sand?'

'More drainage channels.'

We both examined the grooves in the floor; they were clearly part of some sort of pre-designed plumbing system, but I thought I'd ask anyway.

'Haakim, do you know what these are?'

'This part of drain. Many copper pipe in floor, one-hundred-eighty metre. All connect it to main channel. Over here basin, and here. There five basin, made of stone, lined with it copper.'

He showed us where each of the basins were once positioned in the 'annexes'. As usual, Bill was streets ahead.

'What if they didn't just take liquid away, what if they brought water up and into the temple as well?

'A modern plumbing system.'

'At least three-thousand years before the Romans.'

'Probably a lot more!'

We headed east out through the northern 'annex' rooms back to the central corridor and then north out of the temple via the side door, where the flooring changed from basalt to limestone, Bill still fascinated by it.

'Look at this stone, look at the way it's been cut, into maybe ten sides, and how it's connected to all the others. It's not as if the ancient Egyptians didn't know how to make perfect rectangles or squares. It's like the whole floor has been carefully and deliberately planned to be irregular.'

'Why would they do that, surely it would be easier to cut and lay uniform paving stones?'

We moved on.

'It would, but uniform structures are easily disrupted by specific vibration frequencies, whereas a random pattern has a far greater level of tolerance and resistance.'

'Look at this piece.'

It was even more convoluted.

'And check out this one, it's actually had shapes cut out of it presumably to hold things.'

'So, what you're saying is that the whole structure of the floor, the whole temple base, has been deliberately designed to withstand vibration?'

'Yep, but not earthquakes, the vibrations caused by the very function of the building itself.'

'*And* the pyramid.'

'Yes, *and* the pyramid.'

And that's where we were headed next.

"Due to the pyramid's ruined condition, the exact specifications and the pyramid's original appearance are impossible to determine, however, with a base length of 78 metres, a slope of around 50° and an original height of 48 metres, the Pyramid of Sahure was around the same size as that of his predecessor, Userkaf."

That was of course assuming the pyramid *was* built by Sahure and not just usurped by him, as it appeared the others had been by other pharaohs.

"The Pyramid of Sahure is much smaller than previous 4th Dynasty pyramids, using a reduced volume of material for its construction in comparison with 4th Dynasty examples, though this was compensated for by better quality and more diverse types of stone."

Looking at the collapsed pile of rubble before me, I found it hard to see how anyone could believe this was an 'advance' in technological building techniques from the massive 4th Dynasty pyramids at Giza.

"The pyramid is probably founded upon a platform of at least two layers of limestone blocks, however this is an assumption as the foundation has never been investigated. On it, the core was built of six horizontal layers of rough limestone blocks, with a casing of fine, white limestone. It is interesting to note a design flaw within the pyramid's architecture that resulted in the southeast corner being 1.58 metres too far to the east. Therefore, the pyramid is not completely square."

I couldn't believe it.

'How could the Egyptologists not have done a proper investigation of this site and yet still make such sweeping assumptions?'

Bill was pensive.

'Maybe they want to, but they just haven't been given permission?'

I was more accusative.

'Maybe Hawass did, in 1994, and he stripped it of all its valuables, *then* opened it to the public, and he blocked any further investigations because he doesn't want to let anyone in to discover what he did?'

Bill raised a sarcastic eyebrow.

'What, someone looting the sites for their own profit, surely that wouldn't happen nowadays!'

The truth was, that since the overthrow of Muburak and the 'election' of the Muslim Brotherhood, looting of all the ancient sites of Egypt had become something of a national pastime. In fact most of the theft was being done by the very people charged to protect them, right under the eye of, and often with the 'baksheesh blessing' of, the antiquities police.

It was understandable; with all the political turmoil in Egypt, tourists were staying away in their droves, and that meant thousands of people who made their living from the tourist trade, the hawkers and store owners at the sites, the camel-ride owners, the kalash and taxi drivers, perfume and oil sellers, the very guardians themselves, were all struggling to feed their families. Knowing the locations of so many as yet uninvestigated or partially-investigated sites, it made sense that in their desperation they would turn to looting, to the possibility of unearthing items beneath the sands to sell on the black market. Perhaps it was even a part of the Illuminati master plan, who knows?

It made me think of the old saying:

'Better, the devil you know, hey, Bill. You know, in a bizarrely twisted way, even though the previous system under Zahi Hawass was totally corrupt, at least it was organized crime and not the disorganized chaos that exists now.'

'Either way, Alex, it's the people who are still suffering.'

'True.'

'And the stark reality is that if something isn't done soon to fix the political mess in Egypt, these sites, which belong to the world and which are only in the caretakership of the Egyptians, could be irreparably damaged and irretrievable knowledge and evidence could be destroyed or lost forever.'

As we reached the north face of the pyramid, and all stood before the entrance, Saeed took over.

'Haakim he say we go in two at a time as it is very small.'

Ever the gentleman, Bill gestured to the entrance, just above ground level.

'Ladies first.'

Pernille was hesitant.

'How far in does it go?'

I read from my notes.

'At first there is a short, eight-metre descending passageway, lined on the walls and ceiling with red and black granite. It leads to a small, level vestibule with a pink-granite portcullis at the far end. After this, the next corridor travels for 25 metres with a gradual incline, becoming level near the antechamber, which is at the same level as the base of the pyramid. The antechamber and burial chamber are so ruined that their exact plan cannot be determined, though the antechamber lies directly beneath the pyramid's vertical axis.

The burial chamber has a gabled roof which consists of three layers of huge limestone blocks, the first smaller than second, the second smaller than the third. . Only small fragments of a sarcophagus were found when the badly damaged burial chamber was entered in the early 19th Century.'

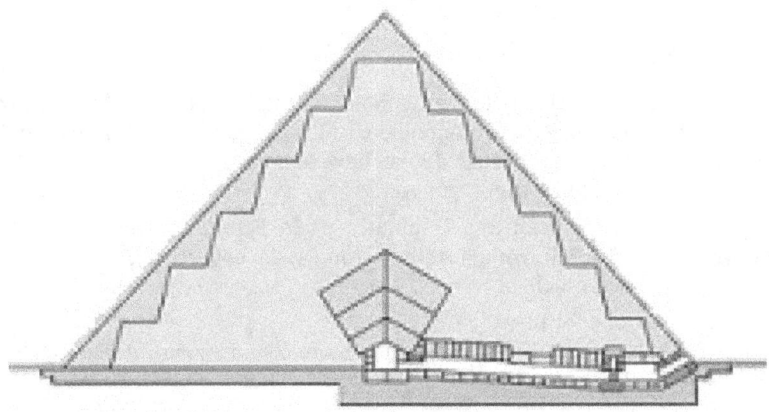

Pernille was still anxious.

'So, about forty metres?'

'Less, maybe thirty-five.'

'I'm nervous, this will be my first pyramid; will you come with me?'

She'd looked to her knight in shining armour, and how could he refuse.

'Of course.'

In preparation to enter, Haakim handed a torch to Pernille and Bill, but I was still curious.

'You didn't go into the one at Meidum, or one of the ones at Dahshur?'

'We were able to go a few feet into the pyramid at Hawarra, but it was flooded, and after lunch with Mohammed and his family, we came straight here.'

'OK, well enjoy it.'

Haakim led them into the pyramid, leaving Crystal, Saeed and I outside. Bill's mention of Mohammed reminded me I owed him quite a bit, so I took a wad of cash out of my pocket and gave almost all of it, a thousand Egyptian pounds, to Saeed.

'Here, this is for Mohammed and his family.'

Saeed was most appreciative.

'Shukran, Indy, Mohammed he will be most grateful.'

I noticed Crystal looking at me, smiling, not grinning, but smiling like a mother who had just seen her child do a good deed to a stranger, so I took the opportunity to try and get back in her good books.

'So, your trip to Hawarra, was that something to do with remembering who you are?'

'Yes.

'Did it have something to do with the Labyrinth?'

'You know it did, why do you ask?'

'But the Labyrinth is at least twenty, thirty feet below the sand, how did you get in? Do you know about the secret tunnel Mohammed's grandfather talked about?'

'No.'

'Then how did you get in?'

'I didn't say I did.'

'Did you?'

'Did I what, *say* I didn't get in, or did I *get* in?'

'Did you *get* in?'

'No.'

'So what did you do?'

'I got in.'

'What?'

Crystal was clearly toying with me. Thankfully she gave me a break.

'I found a piece of red granite by the canal and held it in my hand. All things are one, all things are connected, all you have to do is ...'

'Feel the stone. Right, got you.'

It had only been a few minutes when Pernille emerged from the pyramid, followed closely by Bill, with Haakim waiting at the entrance.

'That was quick.'

Bill spoke for them.

'It's cramped in there, tiny; it's more like a miner's tunnel and Pernille was getting a little claustrophobic.'

They handed us the torches and Crystal and I followed Haakim as he returned into the descending passage; after crawling through the Bent Pyramid with a torch in my mouth, this would be easy. Suddenly I remembered Nemo and running down a dark corridor lined with red granite, and here I was about to enter another dark corridor lined with red granite. Was this it? Was this where I would meet my fate? I paused before entering, looked around half expecting the Secret Police to jump out from behind piles of dirt and broken columns, then, realizing it was all clear, followed Crystal's hot ass into the darkness.

I reluctantly turned my attention to the subterranean structure, that clearly showed signs of the incomplete 'repair' and 'reconstruction' work done by Zahi Hawass twenty years ago, bags of cement stacked up along the walls. Remnants of the portcullis protruded from either side of the wall as we entered the ascending corridor, the ceiling propped up with wooden beams; I could see why Bill had described it as a miners' tunnel.

Squeezing my way past Haakim and through the small antechamber, I joined Crystal in the main chamber, the three moving torch lights creating an eerie atmosphere.
'Shit, that doesn't fill you with confidence....'

I could see why Pernille felt so claustrophobic; the room was filled with piles of stone indicative of a considerable internal collapse, parts of the gabled ceiling visible above the rubble.
'...I wonder why they built these the way they did, surely it would have been easier to dig the chamber into the pyramid's base, then rest the ceiling blocks on the pyramid's base?'

'If they had done that, they would not have been able to isolate the ceiling stones from the base. Why would you build your future on shaky ground, surely you understand that?'

'Of course, but it makes you think that it may have compromised the integrity of the structure.'

'The integrity of any structure is most tested by unexpected external forces.'

'Yeah, but you don't want to be inside when the walls come crashing down.'

'It has been this way for at least twenty years, possibly centuries; I do not think it is likely to collapse any more, not unless an earthquake were suddenly to befall us, and, if it did, we would have limited time and opportunity to escape; only one of us could exit the chamber at a time. I wonder, would you rush for the exit, or insist I go first?'

'What?...'

She'd caught me totally off guard.
'...Well, I'd make sure you got out first.'

'How noble of you, even though I am furthest from the entrance. And what if I insisted you should go, because you are closer to the exit and you have more chance of survival, or that your life was of more importance?'

Was she testing me?
'I'd still insist you go first.'

'Self-sacrifice, how illogical, and how egotistical.'

'Egotistical?'

'Most definitely; and, in the process of debating the point, would we both be trapped and die.'

I couldn't believe that not only were we here in the heart of a collapsed pyramid having the conversation we were having, put that is was not going well for me. And then an idea hit me; Crystal was talking in metaphors. What did she say, "The integrity of any structure is most tested by unexpected external forces."

'What you're really saying is that someone's ego can trap them in a situation, where, to defend their position, they will not only compromise their existence, but that of those around them. That when an unexpected external force comes along it can compromise their integrity and bring their world crashing down upon them.'

Crystal smiled.

'Very good, now we can go.'

That said, she walked straight past Haakim and out the door. I stood there stunned for about ten seconds wondering what the hell had just happened. Haakim was even more mystified than me, just shrugging his shoulders then indicating for me to follow, which I dutifully did.

Trailing the silhouetted goddess that preceded me, I pondered over what had just transpired, rapidly coming to the conclusion that I had absolutely no idea, but that, whatever it was, I'd passed.

All safely outside, we made our way back towards the temple, Haakim resuming his role as tour guide.

'Now we go Pyramid of Niuserre.'

Crystal had other thoughts.

'You go, I will wait back at the minivan.'

I was hoping to continue our discussion, but Crystal clearly knew the places she needed to be, and those she didn't. So, it seemed, did Pernille.

'I think I'll come with you...'

She turned to Bill.

'... You don't mind do you, I'm a bit hot and bothered."

Obliging as always, Bill acceded to her request.

Saeed spoke to Haakim, who nodded, and, once back at the middle of the central corridor between the outer and inner temples, we parted ways, Saeed and the two ladies exiting through the courtyard and causeway, and Haakim, Bill and I via the southern exit to further explore the lay of the land.

The southern end of the central corridor led through two small side chambers, past a portico with the bottom parts of two pink-granite columns, and out into the desert. Haakim pointed to a small rounded mound of sand and small stone fragments.

'Cult pyramid of Sahure.'

There was nothing really to see, other than that the mound contained shards of basalt, granite, limestone and quartzite. I wondered if there was a subterranean chamber and if it had ever been investigated.

"The cult pyramid, though small in comparison to the main pyramid, and greatly damaged by stone thieves, had an entrance corridor that first descended before rising into the inner chamber, though nothing was found inside."

There was, and it had, but there was no statement as to what the inner chambers were made of, or if there was a portcullis. Still, I was convinced that there was granite down there; the shards on the mound pretty much confirmed it.

As we left the mound and headed across the sand towards the Pyramid of Niuserre, I explained my binary star theory to Bill, who seemed most receptive.

'It makes more sense than the cult pyramid theory, or the queens pyramid theory.

As we passed the mastaba of Ptahshepses, I thought I'd push my luck.
'Haakim, this is mastaba?'
'Yes, mastaba of Ptahshepses, vizier of king Niuserre, five dynasty.'
'Can we have a quick look? I mean, is it open; do we have time?'
'Yes, but five minute only.'

Momentarily I wondered if that was Egyptian time, or western time, but then realized I wanted to be as quick as possible to get back to spend as much time with Crystal as possible.

As Haakim led us around to the eastern side, Bill popped a question.
'Ptahshepses; anything special about him, or particularly worth seeing?'
'No idea, but, never go, you never know.'

I dived into my notes.
'*"Originally a royal manicurist and hairdresser, meaning he was also a high priest as to groom the king meant to touch the body of a living god, Ptahshepses was vizier and married Niuserre's daughter, Khamerernebty."* Smart move, he married the *sang réal*, just like Ti married Neferhetepes, who was the mother of Sahure and the wife of the deceased king, Usekaf.'
'A person of some interest!'
'It would appear so.'
'*"The location of the mastaba, almost equidistant from and in front of Sahure's and Niuserre's pyramid complexes, suggests a deliberate attempt at associating him with royalty."* Or, simply because he was vizier, it meant his office was close to the action.'
'His office?'
'Yeah, I don't think the mastabas were tombs, they may have been built on the sites of previous subterranean chambers, but I'm not convinced the superstructures were built as tombs, I think they were admin buildings.'
'An interesting theory.'
'*"Constructed from mud-brick and stone, at eighty by a hundred-and-seven metres, and second in size only to that of Mereruka at Saqqara, the Mastaba of Ptahshepses is the most extensive and architecturally most complex non-royal tomb known from the period of the Old Kingdom. However, before its modern excavation, the ruins sat under six to eight metres of sand and rubble that took seven seasons to remove."*
'Ah ha! There's more evidence supporting your tsunami theory. Take away the twenty-odd feet of sand and rubble and that puts the ground level in 2500 BC and the floor level of the mastaba at about one and the same place.'
'It sure does.'
'I really think you're on to something there, Alex.'

Turning the corner we arrived at the entrance to the mastaba, located in the northeast corner of the complex. It had been recently reconstructed and consisted of a portico, eight metres high, flanked by two six-metre-high eight-stemmed fine white limestone columns, shaped as lotuses with closed buds. Each column was made from a single piece of the fine white limestone, and, together, they supported a massive architrave of fine limestone, on which rested large slabs of limestone that formed the roof terrace.

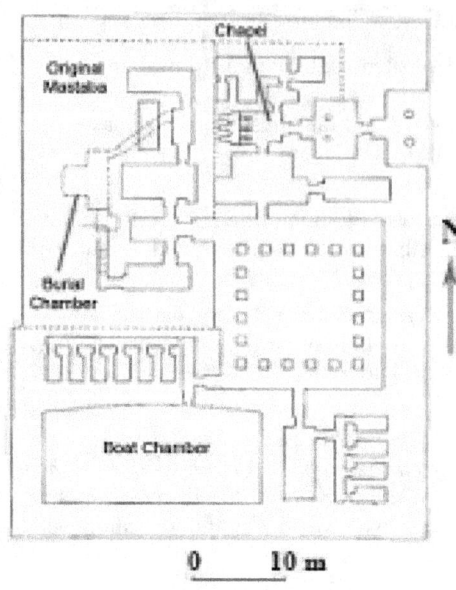

Original
Mastaba

Chapel

Burial
Chamber

Boat Chamber

0   10 m

N

The entrance led through a small door to a small vestibule, a room with two smaller six-stemmed lotus columns; it looked like another entrance, and was probably the entrance before the 'Niuserre' extensions were added, and was simply enclosed when those additions were made. The walls were decorated with scenes of boats and bearers bringing funerary equipment and other items including furniture, jewellery, cloth, grain, and fruit.

From the vestibule, a narrow passageway, containing images of Ptahshepses and depicting the slaughter of sacrificial animals, led to a raised chapel that contained three niches that would have once housed slightly larger-than-life statues of Ptahshepses.

The chapel also contained numerous different multicoloured scenes representing Ptahshepses in three different functions; as an official, as a priest, and as a private individual. The reliefs included Ptahshepses overseeing agricultural work, servants bearing offerings of fruit, fisherman, herdsman milking cows, someone driving flocks of duck, geese and cranes towards capture, sculptors, metal-workers, carpenters, Ptahshepses receiving offerings at his feet, and Ptahshepses' six sons walking. Finally, there were scribes recording everything.

'All these images; they're all of daily life. They just make me think this wasn't a tomb, rather a place were people came to pay their taxes or plead their case to Ptahshepses.'

'You could be right.'

North of the chapel were four storage rooms, to the south, two annexes, now with the roofs missing and open to the air, that led to a large porticoed open-air courtyard that would have been added in the third and final stage of the extensions, most likely when Ptahshepses became vizier.

Evenly spaced around the perimeter of the courtyard were twenty square-cut limestone pillars, each one bearing a life-size image of Ptahshepses in sunken relief on its interior side. The images were arranged in such a way to direct a visitor's attention to the northwest corner, to the original mastaba. I went to my notes for more details.

' *"Above each figure, in sunk relief, were carved the titles of the tomb owner. Though none of the pillar crowns have survived intact, it is clear from fragments that his titles began with "King's Son." Hence, by the time of the final construction, Ptahshepses had already attained the status of prince, undoubtedly as a result of his marriage to Khamerernebty, the daughter of King Niuserre."* That confirms my thinking that the courtyard and entrance must have been added after Ptahshepses became Vizier.'

'Perhaps *because* he was made Vizier, because of his newly acquired status?'

'I think you're on to something there, Bill.'

"In addition to his titles of 'Barber of the Great House' and 'Manicure of the Great House', other reliefs throughout the complex give Ptahshepses other titles

including: 'Prince', 'Servant of the Throne', 'Councillor of Nekhen', 'Guardian of Nekhen', 'Highest Lector Priest of Nekhbet', 'Chief Justice', 'Vizier', 'Overseer of all the Royal Works', 'Beloved One of his Lord', 'Privy to the Secret Sacred Writings of the God's Words'."

Bill chuckled away.

'It's 'The Mikado' revisited; where Poo Bah has all the titled positions, and the salaries to go with them.'

The walls of the courtyard would once have been richly decorated with reliefs, although now only a tiny fraction of those decorations remained in situ. On the northern wall, Ptahshepses was being carried on a litter by servants, and, to the southwest, there was an interesting scene that showed colossal striding statues of Ptahshepses being dragged on wooden sleds.

Bill scoffed.

'Well, that doesn't make any sense at all. Firstly you'd think such massive statues would be reserved strictly for the pharaoh, and secondly you wouldn't transport such large statues standing up, they'd be way too unstable; you'd lay them down flat, on their backs.'

"The inscriptions describe statues of red granite measuring seven cubits, approximately three-and-a-half metres, however, though many statue fragments were discovered during excavations, none were part of colossal statues." What do you make of that?'

It bemused Bill.

'I didn't think colossal statues even appeared until the New Kingdom, starting with Amenhotep I.'

'There may have been one to one of the Amenemhats in the Middle Kingdom but I'm not sure; they certainly weren't the norm.'

'And yet here we are in the 5th Dynasty and they're making direct reference to them.'

'Which makes you think they must have been around then, perhaps even before?'

'So how is it that in the 5th Dynasty they supposedly have the technology to quarry and produce such massive statues, but are still so lacking in technology that they have to drag them on wooden sleds? It doesn't add up.'

'Maybe it was wishful thinking, or symbolic, maybe Ptahshepses was trying to emulate the status of some ancient deities? Or maybe the statues, like the temples were just usurped?'

'Who knows? But it just goes to show, don't believe everything you read.'

'Or rather, read between the lines.'

In the middle of the south wall was the entrance to another elongated chamber, that, in turn, had a corridor off it leading to a further four smaller chambers.

'You know, Bill, I think this is where the farmers would have come to plead their case; I think these are like little offices, not store rooms at all. I think the local farmer came into the building with a problem, made his offerings at the door, which were stored in the rooms to the north of the chapel, then he had to get past the secretary or PA in the rooms just south of the chapel. If he was worthy, he was allowed to wait in the courtyard until called. Having waited in the courtyard, he gets called forward and directed into the relevant office or department, to be heard.'

'Makes total sense to me; Ptahshepses would need lots of scribes and assistants to handle the day to day administration given all the titles he held.'

Moving along, in the southwest of the courtyard a short corridor led to six smaller chambers to the north and, to the south, a large chamber, the largest in the complex, with a long curved wall and supposedly for boats.

'According to the Egyptologists, this room was for boats.'

'Boats? Did they find any here?'

'No.'

'That would be right, vivid imaginations. Don't let the truth get in the way of a good story.'

'So why the curved wall?'

'Simple acoustics, a rectangular room would be very echoing, but the curved wall disperses the sound. It may even have functioned like a whispering wall, like the wall at the Philosophers' Circle, enabling someone at one end of the hall to hear someone at the other end over the top of the general hubbub without having to shout.'

'So this was a meeting room.'

'Possibly, more likely another waiting room for people waiting to see officials in one of the six offices to the north.'

'So you agree, it wasn't a tomb.'

'Nothing I've seen so far indicates it was a tomb, and everything I *have* seen supports your thinking it was an admin building.'

'That just leaves the original mastaba itself.'

In the northwest corner of the court, a short corridor led to the original mastaba, its roof gone and now open to the elements. To the right were the remains of a serdab, on its eastern wall a fragment of a relief showing the lower part of a well-carved, multicoloured false door in the form of a palace façade. There were also the remains of an actual false door, and, in the floor just beneath the false door, a shaft that communicated with the subterranean chamber.

Heading back to the south, then to the right, a sloping corridor led down to a partly rock-cut subterranean chamber lined with walls made of white limestone slabs.

"The burial chamber was constructed with a gabled ceiling built of huge monolithic limestone blocks."

'Well, they're gone now.'

'The sarcophagi aren't though.'

A huge well-preserved and well-carved red-granite sarcophagus, supposedly belonging to Ptahshepses, still remained in the chamber, along with a smaller one, its lid broken, along side.

'Two sarcophagi?'

I looked for answers in the notes

' *"Despite the fact Khamerernebty's own mastaba was found near Niuserre's pyramid complex, it is still significant that the name of Princess Khamerernebty has been found among the inscriptions recorded in red directly on the rough limestone blocks that were used to construct the core of the original mastaba."* I guess the smaller one supposedly belongs to Khamerernebty, Ptahshespses' wife.'

'Then she must have died at the same time because there's no way her sarcophagus could have been carried through that narrow descending passage. But even that doesn't make sense, there's been no planning of the chamber to incorporate her sarcophagus, it's like it's just been put alongside his as an after thought.'

'Maybe the small sarcophagus is Ptahshepses', maybe they couldn't open the large one?'

'But that would mean it had to be lowered in place when the chambers had no ceiling, when the original mastaba was half finished, and that doesn't make sense either as it would mean the extensions to the mastaba through the second and especially the third stages would have been done *after* Ptahshepses died.'

'Good point.'

'Come, we go, time, yes.'

Haakim was right, we'd already spent at least twice our time allotment. As we made our way back to the courtyard and out of the mastaba, I had a thought.

'OK, how about this for a scenario; the subterranean chamber, lined with limestone, containing one large red resonance box, and covered with a vaulted ceiling of three layers of monolithic limestone blocks, was built before the last pole shift, maybe ten to twelve thousand years ago. The whole structure is some sort of resonance chamber and the vaulted ceiling some sort of pressure valve. Then the pole shift hits and not only is most of the civilization that built it wiped out, but the whole thing short circuits and the vaulted ceiling collapses.'

'Before the last pole shift,…a resonance chamber? Go on.'

'Then, thousands of years later, when civilization is being rebuilt, this time without the knowledge that built the chamber, someone in the first, second, or even third dynasty claims it as their burial site and builds a small mastaba over it. Even later, perhaps in the 5th Dynasty, someone else, lets say a High Priest by the name of Ptahshepses, claims the site as a sacred site of worship and extends it.'

Bill picked up on my thinking.

'First into a simple shrine, then, when he assumes the rank of Vizier, he turns it into a larger structure for the administration of all the daily goings-on of the people in the region.'

'Exactly! Then, when he dies, as a sign of respect, the tomb part of the original mastaba is uncovered, Ptahshepses interred in the smaller granite box, or into the larger box and his wife added later, beside him, when she dies.'

'It sounds more feasible than the official story.'

But Bill had not only understood the explanation for the mastaba, he was quickly off on another tangent.

'A resonance chamber you think?'

I brought Bill up to speed on my thoughts about the red-granite in the subterranean chambers and how I believed it was indicative of a much older civilization and how the pyramids and temples were either usurped or later additions.

'You don't have to convince me, Alex.'

'But I can't figure out how, where, and why, the basalt fits in.'

'Maybe we'll find some answers up ahead in the temple of Niuserre. Do you have any notes on it?'

'Sure do.'

As I searched for the file, I filled Bill in on what I already knew.

'I'm convinced that Niuserre usurped the valley temple from his father, Neferirkare Kakai.

'How do you know that?'

'Here, have a look at the map; see how the causeway clearly once ran from Neferirkare's pyramid straight down to the Nile.

'Yes, it's an obvious straight line. Although it could have run from the Nile *up* to the pyramid.'

'Or both up and down.'

'Precisely.'

'And as you can see, now the causeway cuts across the slope to meet with Niuserre's mortuary temple.'

'Got any notes on the temple before we get there?'
'Yep.'

As we passed between the ruins of two structures, possibly a queens pyramid and temple, I took back the iphone, flicked a few pages, and, having found the file, read it out loud.

'Located on the eastern side of the pyramid, the Mortuary Temple of Niuserre is rather small and shaped in the form of an 'L'. Now, to my reckoning, the size and position of the mortuary temple was restricted because of the structures we just walked past; they must have pre-dated the temple, otherwise the temple would've been built directly eastward in keeping with the one at Sahure and Neferirkare. But it wasn't, and that makes me think those structures may well have been "queens' pyramids", and if a star map shows significant stars there then that would be a slam dunk.'

'Star maps?'

I realized Bill wasn't privy to my discussions with Frank and Mark.

'Yeah, the whole positioning of the pyramids along the lower part of the Nile directly correlates with a map of the stars along the Milky Way on the galactic equator.'

'Wow!'

Just as he said it, Haakim announced we'd arrived at our destination.

'This, Temple of Niuserre. Here is much basalt. Very good.'

The Pyramid Complex of Niuserre

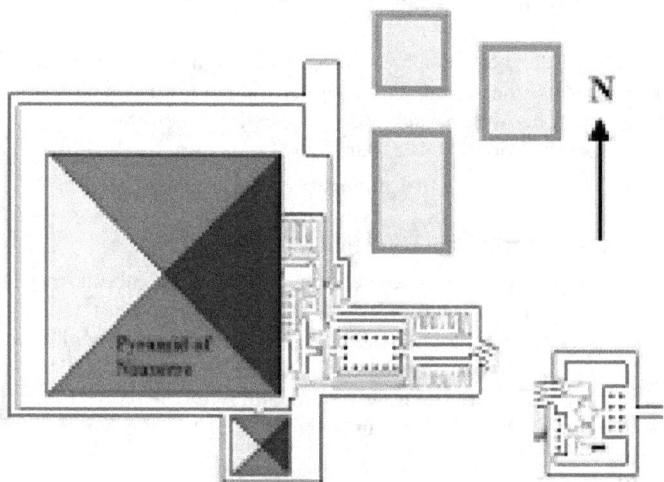

He wasn't kidding; inside the entrance was a long, entrance corridor, paved in irregular slabs of basalt. Bill scratched his head.

'Even more basalt, there must be a reason for it, because, although it's a pretty common extrusive igneous rock, it's quite rare in Egypt,.'

'Extrusive igneous rock, what does that mean?'

'It just means it's formed from the rapid cooling of basaltic lava exposed at or very near the surface during a volcanic eruption.'

'So why use it, and so much of it?'

'That's the million dollar question.'

We wandered through the entrance hall 'tire-kicking', looking for clues. Though once decorated, only fragments of the walls remained. Maybe the notes could point us in the right direction.

"The entrance corridor once had a vaulted ceiling and a dado of pink granite on the side walls."

It gave me my granite evidence, but nothing about why basalt was used.

Up a head we could see large blocks of granite scattered all around, particularly in and to the side of the courtyard that followed, which was also paved in basalt. As we moved into it, I kept reading.

"Paved in basalt, the courtyard once had sixteen papyrus-shaped columns made of pink granite, the middle inscribed with the Niuserre's names and titles along with symbolic representations of Upper and Lower Egypt."

Bill was scanning the courtyard.

'What do you make of it?'

'My thinking is that Niuserre usurped all the red-granite columns from his predecessors' temples, especially his brother and father, and replaced them all with wooden columns.'

'I meant the basalt, but surely the Egyptologists must have asked questions about the irregular use of materials; red granite, basalt, limestone, and wood, I'd never even heard of that? Surely they could examine the artefacts and work out how they were made and if they were contemporary with each other; different materials require different tooling techniques? I mean, anyone who had the technology to quarry and shape massive red-granite blocks would hardly make columns out of wood?'

'My thoughts exactly.'

'And the basalt?'

'Haven't got a clue. Is it something to do with its hardness, and that's why it's used as flooring?'

'Possibly, but I doubt it. Basalt gets its hardness from the tight interlocking of the minerals and microscopic crystals that form during its rapid cooling, too quickly for large mineral crystals to grow. It's what makes it considerably denser than granite; and what makes it hard to work, but also what produces such a finely detailed result and colour.'

'So basalt is denser than granite, that makes it heavier, right?'

'Yep.'

'Then it would be easier to make the floor out of granite than basalt, right?'

'Probably.'

'So why make the floor out of basalt, because of its density?

'No, more likely it's inorganic chemistry.'

'What does that mean?'

'Its molecular structure; the molecules that it's composed of, and how they interact.'

He might just as well have explained the physics of a flying saucer to me for all I understood about what he said. But before I could ask him for a layman's version, he wandered over to a neat line of massive basalt blocks that was clearly once part of the walls.

'It seems not only was the floor made of basalt, but so were the walls. Look at this. Just like at Sahure, the inner wall was made of limestone sandwiched between two thick walls, an inner wall and an outer wall, red granite at Sahure, and basalt here.'

'What did you mean, it's more likely it's inorganic chemistry?'

He was oblivious to my question, too absorbed in his observations, running his hand over the surface and edge of a square-cut block.

'Look at the surface of this stone, perfectly precision machined...'

It was, smooth as a baby's ass.

'…And here, the same thing as at Sahure.'

'What?'

'Look at the outside of the outer wall, almost pristine, virtually no signs of weathering at all. And yet the inside of the wall, which would never have been exposed to the elements until the temple was destroyed or dismantled, is crumbling.'

'So what caused it if it wasn't the weather; the sun, wind and rain?'

'It's been baked by extreme heat, the sort of heat created by electromagnetic radiation.'

'A nuclear explosion, a melt down?'

'Maybe, but maybe not a fission reactor, maybe some sort of fusion reactor.'

'Fusion reactor, that's like the nuclear reactions in the sun, right?'

'Yeah.'

Bill wandered off into the inner part of the temple, deep in thought, and naturally I was right behind him. Suddenly I had visions of my star map, and that each pyramid was literally a little sun, a nuclear fusion reactor; all the pieces dropped into place, except one.

'How did it work?'

Bill was so deep in thought he was almost in an altered state of consciousness.

'I don't know. The principal ingredient in basalt is plagioclase feldspar, usually labradorite or bytownite. Tholeiitic basalt generally has a composition of between forty-five to fifty-five percent Silicon Dioxide, five to twelve percent Magnesium Oxide, Calcium Oxide maybe ten percent, Aluminium Oxide fourteen percent, as well as five to fourteen percent iron oxides such as hematite, ilmenite and magnetite, and maybe a half to two percent Titanium Oxides.'

'Which means?'

No good, he was in another world, scanning the deepest wormholes of his memory, searching for the key to unlock the mystery.

'Chemical weathering of basalt releases readily water-soluble cations such as Calcium, Sodium, and Magnesium, which give basaltic areas a strong buffer capacity against acidification. No, that's not it. Calcium released by basalts binds up Carbon Dioxide from the atmosphere forming $CaCO_3$ which means they may well have created their own limestone blocks, a cement factory; no, it might have been a by-product, but not the primary function.'

Given I had no idea what Bill was mumbling about, rather than disturb his thinking I left him to his cogitations and turned my thoughts back to the temple, indicating for Haakim to stick with me and leave Bill to his musings. Poor Haakim he didn't have a clue what was happening. To tell the truth, I wasn't that far behind him.

Bill had wandered ahead but I was still in the ruins of the chapel, which once housed five niches. Now I started doing some thinking of my own; what if the niches once served some sort of regulatory function and were only used as niches for statues once the temple was usurped?

"Within the inner part of the temple was a chapel with five niches, the northwest one of which once housed a unique, pink-granite statue of a lion. Unfortunately only fragments of the statue survive, now located in the Egyptian Antiquities Museum."

The old Sumerian lion was taking on more significance, what that was I wasn't sure, but it had to mean something!

From the chapel, a small, square, decorated chamber, with a single central column and raised floor, led to the remains of the offering hall, directly on the east-west axis, the walls of which were once decorated and which clearly once had an altar and false door.

"The walls of the inner temple were decorated with ritual scenes related to Niuserre's death including images of Niuserre fighting enemies, the founding of the temple, offerings being delivered, and the sacrificing of animals, but it is impossible to tell if they were from the offering hall or from which room they originated."

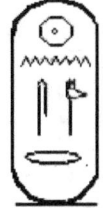

It was hard to tell, and maybe I was looking for evidence to support my theories, but from the reliefs it appeared that not only was the stone considerably weathered, but that the reliefs were made with more 'primitive' instruments than those used to craft the column itself.

'Here, basin.'

Haakim was pointing to a stone basin; it was the only one left in situ and would have been similar if not identical to those that would have been in the mortuary temple of Sahure.

'It once line with copper.'

I couldn't see how Haakim could come to that deduction from what was before me, but I could see where the piping would have entered at the top, which was a clear indication the water came *to* the basins, although it was hard to see where it was taken away, if it was at all.

I tried to figure out if the basins were part of the original building, or whether they had been added later when the structure was usurped and turned into a mortuary temple, but there was no evidence to make a determination either way.

'By George, I think I've got it.'

Up ahead, Bill had made his way over the ruined north wall of the inner temple and was now between the mud-brick enclosure wall and the temple on the paved limestone of the pyramid's outer courtyard. He was like a dead pharaoh having journeyed through the Underworld and been reborn, rejoining the land of the living. I quickly joined him.

'Spill the beans, Einstein.'

He kept walking, clearly still digging into the far recesses of his mind and meticulously putting the pieces together.

'Well, because of the presence of its oxide minerals, like magnetite, basalt can acquire strong magnetic signatures as it cools; it's how palaeomagnetic studies have been able to determine magnetic pole shifts, because of the alignment of the magnetic field which is locked and recorded into the stone as it rapidly cools.'

'It's about pole shifts?'

'No, but a pole shift might explain why the complexes short circuited.'

'Then what was it, did it have to do with the weathering?'

'The weathering isn't weathering, it's not even chemical weathering; the deterioration of the stone is as a result of huge, probably consistent or regular, bursts of high-level electro-magnetic radiation.'

'How do you figure that out?'

'At first I thought it was something to do with the basalt, granite, limestone, and alabaster, all having different resonances; meaning they all vibrate at different frequencies, thus making the whole structure more stable. But that was only a small aspect if it; the walls were the key, there had to be a reason for the triple layer.'

'And that reason was?'

'Pyramid of Niuserre...'

Despite now being more of a passenger and silent observer, Haakim was still trying to fulfil his obligations as tour guide.

"...Base eighty metre, angle fifty-one degree, high fifty-two metre. Build of seven-step, core limestone. Cover in white limestone.'

Haakim was doing his best, but there was nothing extraordinary; it was fairly typical of most of the other pyramids here and at Saqqara, little more than a pile of rubble. And how was Haakim to know that we were on the brink of the greatest archaeological discovery in the history of the world, well, the modern world. Still, he pointed to the base of the middle of the north face.

'Entrance here, lead to burial chamber of king Niuserre, five Dynasty.'

Though the entrance was at ground level, it was clearly blocked with rubble, so entry was not an option. I was eager to get back to Bill, who had wandered off westward and around the pyramid courtyard, but, just to be sure, I double-checked my notes.

"The entrance leads to a corridor lined with fine white limestone and reinforced with pink granite at each end. The corridor is divided by a barrier with two granite blocks, after which, the corridor ascends to the vestibule. Following the vestibule, the next corridor is larger than the first and turns east before arriving at the antechamber, and then the burial chamber, located slightly beneath ground level and under the foundation stones.

Both the antechamber and the burial chamber have a saddle ceiling consisting of three layers of huge limestone blocks set in place from above. Though there were no remains found of the king in his pyramid, it is believed that fragmentary scenes found within the burial chamber describe military campaigns against Libyans."

Apart from the military reliefs, which could easily have been added when the pyramid was usurped by Niuserre, it was exactly as I expected. I nodded to Haakim in gratitude and hustled after Bill, who by now was half way along the western face of the pyramid.

'Hey, Bill, what was that you were saying about the walls being the key to the function of the temple.'

'Not just to the temple, but to the pyramid as well. A few years back, there was a study done by several physicists from the Physics Department of Assiut University who showed that, between the range of four-hundred to a thousand Kelvin, the electrical resistivity of basalt and granite exhibited a rapid decrease with the increase of temperature, and that correspondingly conductivity was up to 5 orders of magnitude higher for basalt. I can only assume that extreme temperatures would possibly turn basalt into some sort of superconductor.'

'You're losing me, Bill; high school chemistry, remember?'

'OK, everything in the universe is tied in to vibration and electro-magnetism. All of these pyramids are positioned on one of the major magnetic Ley lines of the earth.'

Rounding the southwest corner of the pyramid, the south side of the paved limestone courtyard was narrower, due to the encroachment of Neferirkare's mortuary temple, but in the southeast corner was a binary-star pyramid. Despite all Bill's explanations, I was still in the dark.

'All very interesting I'm sure, but how did it work?'

'I'm not sure exactly, but the inner basalt wall must have enclosed an electro-magnetic field, the limestone then acted as some type of insulator, and the outer layer must have formed a counter magnetic field to maintain neutrality and create the electrical polarity of differential.'

'OK you've got a magnet sandwich, but where did the energy come from?'

'The main chamber of the pyramid; it must have used some sort of rotational energy of the earth, or vibrational energy, amplified it and directed it into the temple. But it would have needed an anode connected to the ground to complete the circuit.'

'An anode?'

'An opposite pole, like positive and negative on a battery.'

We were right before the cult pyramid and almost subconsciously I pointed to it.

'You mean like another pyramid?'

Bill stopped dead in his tracks and went into another altered state.

'Brilliant. Alex, that's it, you're a genius; that explains the purpose and function of the cult pyramids. Your binary pyramids are the alternating current; they created an opposing energy, which was supplied to the outer wall of the temple. I can see it so clearly, it's all symbolic, just like the proton and electron in a hydrogen atom, and so so simple.'

Somewhere the sun sets, somewhere it rises

The problem seemingly solved, and the sun starting to set in the west, Bill set off like the clappers back through the temple courtyard towards the minivan. With a bemused look, Haakim gestured in Bill's direction.

'All is good?'

'Brilliant, more than you can possibly imagine.'

'Very good. We go; eat?'

'After you, Haakim.'

By the time we were exiting the temple, we'd caught up.

'Hey, Bill, do you really think it's possible the pyramids were nuclear reactors?'

'Possibly, they were certainly some sort of advanced machine; definitely not tombs. They may have been used thousands of years later as tombs, and the temples turned into, well, turned into temples, but it's pretty obvious that's not what they were originally designed to be.'

'So you don't think they were built by the ancient Egyptians?'

'No way; not the dynastic ones, that's for sure. From what I've seen, whoever built the pyramids and original temple complexes had an advanced knowledge of all sorts of sciences; vibrational acoustics, geology and inorganic chemistry, and electro-magnetic physics just for starters.'

'Add to the list astronomy, architecture, and sacred geometry, and I don't think we're talking about modern man here, I think we're talking about the Annunaki.'

'It would seem the most logical explanation.'

'You know the Egyptologists would laugh at us, just ridicule our theories.'

'This coming from so-called educated men and women who, despite vast examples of evidence to the contrary, and plain old common sense, still believe these massive blocks of granite and basalt were quarried and shaped with copper chisels and fist-sized blocks of diorite, then transported hundreds of miles on boats made of papyrus and wood, before being dragged on wooden sleds and rollers and lifted hundreds of feet into the air by massive armies of slaves. Most University educated Egyptologists don't deal in fact, they deal in romantic fantasy and the dream of discovering buried treasure.'

'So how do you get them to accept a theory that the ancient Egyptians had nuclear fusion reactors?'

'You'd need irrefutable proof.'

'Such as?'

We walked back between the unknown structures northeast of Niuserre's pyramid.

'I don't know, maybe twenty or thirty actual structures.'

'But there is, the pyramids and temples, they're all still there.'

'Exactly. Sometimes you can't see the forest for the trees.'

'But if they took samples of the stone and studied them, took radioactive measurements, surely they'd have the proof.'

'Alex, that's not proof, that's just evidence, and you can come up with any cock-and-bull theory to interpret the evidence any way you want.'

'How would they explain all the crumbling basalt in the inner walls of the Temple of Niuserre?

'Weathering.'

'But that's bullshit.'

'Sure it is, but they'll stick to their story, publish it in their journals, and regurgitate it ad-nauseum in documentaries until the cows come home. If you tell the people a lie enough times, eventually they'll believe it. I think my personal favourite is the good old mysterious and unidentifiable tomb robber, who personally seems responsible for destroying or concealing much of ancient Egypt's history.'

'Like Zahi Hawass.'

'Greatest of them all.'

'And religions.'

'Exactly.'

'And Bill Clinton saying "I did not have sexual relations with that woman".'

'Everyone knows he banged her senseless.'

'But, nuclear fusion, surely that would be hard to refute.'

'If there was evidence, perhaps, I don't really know.'

Making our way past the Mastaba of Ptahshepses, like a dog chewing on a rag-doll, I was still looking for answers.

'Do you know much about Nuclear Physics, Bill, about Nuclear Fusion?'

'A little, you?'

'About as much as I know about quantum physics?'

'Which is?'

'How to spell it?'

He laughed.

'Well I know that it takes a considerable amount of energy to force two nuclei together and make them fuse, even the lightest element, hydrogen, which is probably what they used.'

'How would they get their hands on hydrogen?'

'Alex, you surprise me, hydrogen is the most plentiful substance in the universe, they most likely sourced it directly from water, from the Nile.'

'Up the drainage channels in the causeway.'

'It would be logical.'

'Good old H_2O. So, they split the hydrogen from the water, leaving the oxygen as a by-product; brilliant, clean fuel.'

'A simple charge can do that, but it's not until they combine the hydrogen atoms together again to form an alpha particle that fusion happens.'

'An Alpha particle?'

'It's where four protons fuse together, releasing two positrons, and two neutrinos, which changes two of the protons into neutrons, and the whole thing turns into a helium atom, releasing a small percentage of the mass as electro-magnetic energy.'

'Helium? Do you think all the helium in our atmosphere was caused by the ancient Egyptian fusion reactors?'

'Wow! Now *that's* a great question! I don't know, but it's possible.'

'Maybe that's what the vaulted ceilings were for, to release the helium through a series of simple pressure valves?'

'Alex, that's another great question. I wish I had the answers.'

It was really just a side thought; I was still back at step one.

'The question is, how would they force the hydrogen atoms together?'

'They'd need extremely high temperatures, or pressure actually, to create the extreme temperature necessary to form an electro-magnetic pool or cloud of ions and electrons called a plasma; it's just like a mini sun.'

'A mini sun, how do they stop it melting through everything?'

'With electro-magnetic confinement fields, like a super-conductive torus, a donut-shaped hollow tube, that would have hung suspended, or levitated, maybe in the courtyard. We've got scientists doing experiments to create just that now.'

'What would this torus have been made of?'

'I don't know, gold maybe, or copper lined with gold.'

An image rushed into my mind.

'A circle of gold! How would it have worked?'

' I'm sorry Alex, that's about all I know, I'm a rock man remember. Maybe you can jump online and find out more?'

'What a good idea.'

Reconnecting with the causeway of Sahure, I did just as Bill suggested, logged on, punched in Wikipedia, and pulled up an article on nuclear fusion. As I scanned through, I read out bits I thought may have been relevant.

'The Coulomb force?'

'I think that's just the name of the force needed to overcome the repulsive electromagnetic force of two protons from forming a nucleus. It wouldn't explain how to over*come* the force.'

'What about Pyroelectric Fusion, do you know what that is?'

'Never heard of it.'

'*In April 2005 a team of scientists at UCLA used a pyroelectric crystal heated from minus thirty-four to plus seven degrees Celsius, combined with a tungsten needle, to produce an electric field of about 25 gigavolts per metre to ionize and accelerate deuterium nuclei into an erbium deuteride target.*'

'That's a lot to comprehend; but it sounds like the sort of thing we're looking for. You know, the ancient Atlanteans were big on crystals, not so much the ancient Egyptians as far as I know, but maybe it has some relevance. Maybe there were crystals inside the burial chambers of the pyramids, inside the sarcophagi, but now they're long gone.'

'Stolen!'

It had hit me like a thunderbolt.

'Probably.'

'No, Frank figured it all out yesterday, Joseph, Moses, he stole the crystal that was inside the King's chamber of the Great Pyramid; that's the *real* reason why Kamose chased him, not just out of Egypt, he pursued him through the Red Sea and into Saudi Arabia to get the crystal back.'

Bill was straight on board, putting the pieces together.

'There was a crystal *inside* the sarcophagus of the king's chamber that amplified and directed the frequency of the chamber.'

'Yes, Frank mentioned a book called *"The Giza Powerplant"*, by an engineer called Christopher Dunne. In it, Dunne talks of a massive crystal sitting inside the sarcophagus of the King's Chamber. But the sarcophagus wasn't a sarcophagus, it never was, it was a resonating box, a chamber within a chamber, used to concentrate and amplify a specific frequency.'

'And the crystal was attuned to that frequency, wow! Yes, pyroelectric activation. That reminds me, there was a study done by Francis Hitching a few years back, who demonstrated that voltage can be generated by applying pressure to quartz, that a pressure of four-hundred-odd kilos applied to each surface of a small quartz crystal about ten to fifteen millimetres in diameter generated a voltage of around twenty-five-*thousand* volts, and granite is around sixty-two percent quartz, silicon dioxide.'

'So, if you create pressure in a granite chamber, you can create voltage?'

'Basically, yes.'

'And that pressure can cause a crystal to release a massive electrical charge.'

'In principal, yes.'

'And Moses, Joseph, used it; he knew it was in the king's chamber, he knew how to get inside the king's chamber, he knew the crystal's frequency, how to initiate it and operate it, and he used it to intimidate and control the people, and to carry before his armies.'

Bill still wasn't completely convinced.

'One problem, once the crystal was out of the king's chamber, how would they activate it?'

'Maybe just by humming into the Ark, it was the same ratio of dimensions as the sarcophagus, right?'

'Of course! Sympathetic vibration: chanting, toning, prayers; not the actual words, but the frequency! Amazing!'

'Besides, if it was part of a fusion reactor, it would've been radioactive for millennia.'

That snapped Bill momentarily out of his contemplative wormhole.

'Not necessarily, nuclear fusion reactions are not as dangerous as nuclear fission; the natural product of fusion is a small amount of helium, which is completely harmless. There's also no risk of runaway chain-reactions or a meltdown in a fusion reactor, because once the mechanism is interrupted the reactions stop, so no elaborate failsafe mechanisms are required....'

And that added another piece to the puzzle.

'...Which means the fusion reactor can be designed using materials that are selected specifically to be "low activation", materials that don't easily become radioactive.'

'Like granite, basalt, limestone?'

He went back into think mode.

'Yes, I suppose so; most natural stones have some degree of radioactivity. And granite is no exception, although there are some granites reported to have contained around ten to twenty parts per million of uranium, which raises some concerns about their safety. In contrast, limestone and other sedimentary rocks usually have equally low amounts of radiation. But as to whether they become more radioactive, I'd have to look into it to be sure. Anyway, I think you're on to something.'

'I think *we're* on to something.'

Bill smiled; I think he appreciated my including him in the discovery.

'Don't get too carried away, we might have cracked the code, but I think we're a long way from deciphering the message.'

'Then let's work it out. What's the deal with the radioactivity, is there any?'

'I think so, yes, but I know fusion reactors aren't like fission reactors, so I'm not sure. What does Wiki say?'

It took me a few seconds to find the relative paragraph.

'Here it is. "*In a fission reactor the waste remains radioactive for thousands of years, but in a fusion reactor most of the radioactive material would be the reactor core itself, which is far less damaging biologically, and would only be dangerous for maybe fifty years, and the low-level waste another hundred.*' Do you think that's why they built mastabas and pyramids over the top of them, just like the concrete sarcophagus lowered over the Chernobyl reactor? Do you think the original mastabas were built to seal in the radiation, and that the reason there's no trace of radiation now is because it only lasted maybe a hundred-and-fifty years?'

'Boy, are you asking some amazing questions. It all makes perfect sense, although it still doesn't solve the question of how they actually created the energy.'

I skipped through the paragraphs, searching for more clues.

'What about this?' "*Devices referred to as sealed-tube neutron generators are particularly relevant to this discussion. These small devices are miniature particle accelerators filled with deuterium and tritium gas in an arrangement that allows ions of these nuclei to be accelerated against hydride targets, also containing deuterium and tritium, where fusion takes place.*" Remember those strange reliefs in the crypts at Dendera, of the tubes with the snakes inside, do you think they could have been neutron generators?'

'Shit, Alex, you're on a roll. Wouldn't that be amazing, if the ancient Egyptians had particle accelerators, neutron guns? If they did, it would turn the history of Egypt and the whole scientific world on its head. The only problem is, you've still got to make the deuterium and tritium.'

'What about bubble fusion?'

'Sounds like a pop band from the 70s?'

'Listen to this. "*Sonofusion, or bubble fusion, is a controversial variation on the sonoluminescence theme, suggesting that acoustic shock waves create temporary bubbles, or cavitations, inside extraordinarily large gas bubbles, that expand and collapse shortly after creation, producing temperatures and pressures sufficient for nuclear fusion*".'

'If it actually works, that could be it, "Bubble Fusion" could be the answer. The rotational energy of the earth has a specific vibration, and if the size of the chamber and the very granite itself is in sympathetic resonance with that frequency, then the use of a crystal could amplify the signal creating bubble fusion via pressure waves and pyroelectric initiation.

I don't know how you'd be able to test it, maybe check it against the frequency emitted by the earth, all the different sub-atomic net spin resonance frequencies of the granite, limestone, the acoustic properties of the chamber shapes, of various pure crystals like clear quartz. Then, if you could, and it worked, they were harmonically in sync, well, image the building of free energy generators all over the earth, using natural materials, all based on the technology of pyramids built hundreds of thousands of years ago?

I wonder if there's anything about *that* in those papers on your back? Now *that* would be something.'

I'd become so engrossed in our discussion I'd forgotten all about Kareem's papers, and about my predicament. But, Bill was right; what if there were clues in them to the truth? I had to get the truth out of Egypt, not just Kareem's papers, but all the revelations I'd discovered on my journey.

We'd been away for just under an hour, clearly plenty of time for Abdo to have set up dinner and returned, as he was waiting with the Saeed and the girls by the vehicles, all sipping on bottles of water. I was excited, but also keen not to have pissed off Crystal.

'I hope we didn't keep you waiting too long?'

She handed me a bottle of water, as did Pernille to Bill.

'It was only too long if your time was wasted. Was it wasted?'

'Not a second, on the contrary, it was priceless, right, Bill?'

He almost choked on his water.

'Invaluable.'

Before we could get into it, Abdo was keen to get moving.

'Very good. Come then, we go Abu Ghurab.'

It seemed Pernille was also keen to get moving.

'Can we still visit the temples, will we have enough time, sunlight?'

'Niuserre, yes, there is not anything to see at sun temple of Userkaf. Then we will have it dinner beside sun temple of Niuserre.'

Like the grand ringmaster, Bill shuffled everyone along.

'Then let's go, I'll fill you in on what we found along the way.'

As before Bill, Pernille and Crystal got into the minivan, leaving Abdo, Haakim and I in Abdo's car to lead the way.

Abu Ghurab

Our destination was Abu Ghurab, about a kilometre north of where we were at Abusir, six miles southwest of Cairo, on the west bank of the Nile between Giza and Saqqara. To the west of the village, in the outskirts of the desert, was another unfinished pyramid, and two solar temples, one attributed to Userkaf, the other to Niuserre. I wanted to make sure I wasn't missing anything.

'Abdo, how long until we're there?'

'Five minute.'

Given that in Egyptian time five minutes could be anything up to ten or fifteen minutes, I ran through my notes, the first thing I wanted to check out being the Unfinished Pyramid northwest of the pyramid of Sahure.

"About halfway between the pyramid of Sahure and the Solar Temple of Userkaf, is an unfinished platform for a pyramid which, if finished, would have had a base length of approximately 100 metres, making it one of the largest pyramids at Abusir. It is impossible to estimate the height it would have had, since the building activity stopped probably a few weeks after it had been started."

The pyramid wasn't just unfinished; it looked as if it had barely been started.

"Given our current knowledge, the structure can only be attributed to one of two 5th Dynasty kings, Shepseskare or Menkauhor, the tombs of whom have not been positively identified. However, according to a number of contemporaneous documents, it seems probable that Menkauhor built a pyramid either in North Saqqara or Dahshur, therefore, by elimination, it would seem that Shepseskare is the more likely of the two to have started the unfinished pyramid in North Abusir."

So basically the unfinished pyramid was attributed to Shepseskare based on the assumption as all the other 5th Dynasty rulers had pyramids attributed to them, and he was the last one left, he was the logical 'owner'. Good science, not! Especially as I was of the opinion all the pyramids had been usurped, so having made the first mistake, the Egyptologists simply compounded it.

"Even though the Turin King list, a New Kingdom document from the reign of Ramses II, indicates that Shepseskare ruled for seven years, most of the evidence we have about him indicates he may have only ruled for a few weeks. However, a stela of the 5th Dynasty official, Khau-Ptah, which lists an uninterrupted sequence of kings whom he served under, consisting of Sahure, Neferirkare, Neferefre and Niuserre, has no mention of Shepseskare at all."

Is it possible Shepseskare was a son of Sahure to a lesser wife, a non *sang réal* wife? And, if he was, might it explain his contemporaneous omission from the list of kings of the period?

As for the 'pyramid' it was similar to the unfinished pyramid of Neferefre, which coincidently had once been erroneously attributed to Shepseskare based on the discovery of a small chapel abutting the eastern wall on the pyramid. So, why would Shepseskare start a pyramid here at Abu Ghurab, not complete it, then build a chapel in front of another unfinished pyramid several kilometres away? It doesn't make sense. All that said, I don't think there was any way I could realistically attribute its 'destruction' to the tsunami, I'd have to find another explanation.

"The desert land was levelled and the excavation of the pit that was to house the burial chamber, and perhaps also an antechamber, had already started as well."

Was it possible that a trench and descending passage had been finished, just like with the 'unfinished' pyramid at Zawiyet el-Aryan just up the road, and the one attributed to Neferefre back at Abusir, but that it was almost completely filled in with sand and silt? And had they discovered the base, or the top of the first layer, like Petrie did with the Labyrinth at Hawarra? There was a clue in the use of the word 'platform', as opposed to base or foundation, and that implied a raised structure like at Zawiyet el-Aryan, and with Neferefre's 'pyramid', but without seeing it for myself, or someone doing a specific excavation, it was more than likely I would never know. So, move on.

"Because their names have been found written in contemporary papyrus documents, there is believed to have originally been six pharaohs of the 5th Dynasty who built temples to the Heliopolitan sun-god Re, though only two have been discovered, the solar temples of Userkaf and Niuserre, This has prompted some Egyptologists to speculate that the other four "lost" temples may never have existed, rather, that Userkaf and Niuserre usurped them, adding and building on the two known temples."

Finally some common sense, but did the 'experts' take it any further, that if the pharaohs usurped the sun temples, they probably usurped the mortuary temples, and if they usurped the mortuary temples, they more than likely usurped the pyramids as well? No. Why not, it seems blatantly obvious that's what happened? It also raised the question of the two sun temples themselves.

"In some respects, the sun temples resemble pyramid complexes in that they have a valley temple on the edge of the desert, a causeway leading from it, and leading to, a temple erected on a hill. However, though both the sun temples and mortuary temples are oriented east-west, the design of the sun temple differs completely from the mortuary temples associated with the pyramids, and the exact purpose and function of the sun temples is not known."

So what was the function of the sun temples, their purpose, which was *so* different to the function of a mortuary temple, that it necessitated another 'temple'? Yes, I know, one worships the sun while the other worships the dead pharaoh, but I wasn't buying it, the pharaoh *was* a living god, a representative of the sun god, Re; there had to be more to it.

Besides, if you're a new pharaoh, why not just build a new sun temple somewhere else, rather than usurp your predecessors? Was it because there was some specific importance to the locations of the two temples? There had to be. So, was that importance directly related to the positions of the stars in the constellation of the Pleiades? If it was, then they too may have pre-dated dynastic Egypt. That, it seemed, was the next mystery.

The Sun Temple of Userkaf

"The first king of the 5th Dynasty, Userkaf was the first king to build a sun-temple, named 'Nekhen-Re', Stronghold of Re, on a twenty-metre-high promontory at the edge of the desert at Abu Ghurab."

Alternatively, Userkaf was the first to *usurp* a pre-existing structure and turn it *into* a sun temple.

"There were no inscriptions found giving clues as to its original purpose, or the choice of its location, and, today, the temple is in ruin, blocks of granite and limestone strewn all over the place, with only a few fragmentary architectural elements of the temple remaining, including parts of a short granite obelisk which would have been placed on a pedestal building in the centre of the temple. Despite this, the general outline of the temple is still discernable."

The valley temple would have been built on the shores of the Nile, what is now

Abusir Lake, but now was badly destroyed. However, a plan was reconstructed from fragments, suggesting it was quite an elaborate structure that appears to have served multiple purposes.

"It included an open courtyard surrounded by a sixteen-pillared portico, with at least five niches or chapels at the rear. There may have been an entrance hall with annexes, but the ruins were such that this part of the temple could not be determined."

All I could think of was if the columns were made of granite; if they were, to me, it dated the complex as pre-dynastic. Alas there was no further information forthcoming.

"The temple was surrounded on the sides and back by an enclosure wall that opened on its southwest corner into the causeway, aligned south-west and divided into three lanes along its length by low mud-brick walls, the widest lane in the centre while the two outside lanes were narrow."

That was a different arrangement to the central groove at Sahure, but I quickly figured it out; one side channel took water up, the other waste down, and the central corridor was for commuting between the two temples.

"Archaeologists believe the upper temple was probably built in four stages, with additions by later kings, Neferirkare and Niuserre. Originally it was probably just a low mound of mud-brick, resembling a mastaba, built within an enclosure wall, the mound possibly supporting a wooden column with an image of the sun disc."

Possible, but what if the mound was put there to cover a radioactive chamber, and the pole was a sign saying "warning".

"In the second phase of construction, Neferirkare replaced the temple's original central mound with a seventy-metre granite obelisk, called a benben, on a pedestal clad in quartzite and granite. The pedestal had a winding staircase that led to its roof, and to a sacristy, and, rather than be in one piece, the obelisk consisted of a small pyramidion on a long shaft. Two stall-like shrines of diorite, which probably contained statues of Re and Hathor, the deities venerated in the sun temple, were also placed in front of the eastern face of the pedestal."

The use of the granite didn't add up, not during the reign of Neferirkare, not even in the 5th Dynasty. The Egyptologists were just guessing, so why couldn't I? The granite must have either been part of the original structure, which included a foundation 'mound', or been used to reconstruct the structure, and my thinking was that it was part of an original pre-dynastic structure on the site. The shrines were added when it was usurped and turned into a sun temple.

"In phase three, dating to the reign of Niuserre, the enclosure and the area around the obelisk were completely rebuilt, with the addition of an inner enclosure wall and several new chambers of limestone. Phase four consisted of the exterior surfaces covered in plastered mud-brick and the addition of some annex buildings against the southeast corner, thus giving the temple its final shape. The final phase involved the addition of a mud-brick altar to the east side of the pedestal, surrounded by a curiously diminutive enclosure wall, and, further east, five benches, or low tables made of mud and broken stone, for priests."

At first I thought all this work was clearly 5th Dynastic, but then I realized the mud-brick rebuilding could just as well have been done in the 19th Dynasty by Khaemweset following the destruction caused by the Thera tsunami; just because they hadn't found his cartouche on any of the fragments of stone didn't mean he hadn't had a hand here. It was all guess work, and my guesses were just as valid as anyone else's, irrespective of the letters after their name.

Just as we pulled up in Abu Ghurab, one last sentence grabbed my attention.

"During excavations, a beautiful schist head, belonging to a statue of Userkaf and wearing the red crown, was found here."

Was this one piece of evidence why they'd ascribed the temple to Userkaf, because they found a bust in the rubble? It accentuated the Egyptologists' predisposition and conditioning to ascribe the 'ownership' of a site to the earliest cataloguable evidence they find, totally discounting it could have been built before then, and the statue was a later addition. Did they ever consider the advanced civilization that built these granite structures had no need to 'claim' them by scratching their names into the rock like primitive cavemen?

Time of the essence, we skipped the chit-chat and immediately followed Haakim and Abdo down a path, a grove, that led towards the setting sun, and out into the desert. Pernille was quite excited at Bill and my discoveries and was eager to get to our destination, Crystal on the other hand was as relaxed and centred as always. I took the opportunity to reconnect.

'It's been quite a trip.'

'Yes, one more day; just here, the king's chamber and the valley temple tomorrow, and that's it.'

She was clearly talking about her own trip; her awakening and remembering.

'Bill was telling me that you're joining Diane's group in the king's chamber tomorrow morning. I wish I could join you.'

'Is there a reason why you cannot?'

'Well, there *is* the little issue of the Secret Police chasing me.'

'They will be chasing you no matter where you are.'

'True.'

'So what is it that is preventing you from coming?'

'Well, I could get caught.'

'You *could* get hit by a rogue asteroid, you *could* be bitten by a cobra, you *could* ...'

'I get it, OK, there's nothing preventing me from coming.'

'On the contrary, there is most definitely something preventing you from coming.'

'There is? What?'

'Fear. Your fear of being caught, and your fear of what they will do to you once they catch you.'

'I suppose so.'

'Did Kareem listen to that fear when he gathered together all those papers you carry on your back?'

'I guess not.'

'Did he listen to that fear when he handed you the papers, knowing that it would probably mean his certain death?'

'I guess not.'

'Of course he did! How could he not? He listened to it, it is a powerful and convincing voice, but he was not a slave to it; the importance of bringing the truth to the world overcame that fear.'

'But it got him killed.'

'His body was going to expire anyway, we are all aware of that. But it is not when or how we 'die' that matters, it is how we live our life that matters. Do we live it in perpetual fear, of anything and everything, or do we live our life free from fear, free to *embrace* anything or everything if we so desire? Kareem lived his life in freedom and he left his body the same way. This is what he takes with him, the detachment and freedom from fear.'

'You can take your fears with you when you die?'

'Of course, and you bring them back when you return. All emotional attachments hold you in the fourth dimension, this is where so-called ghosts live, and where the reptilians rule supreme, it is where you are free from your body to create and manifest at will, but where your emotional attachments and conditioning from the third dimension, including your fears, determine your choices. *This* is your heaven *and* your hell.'

I'd barely been able to take it all on board when, emerging from the avenue of trees, Haakim pointed south to what looked like the remains of a pyramid at the peak of a rise of sand about a hundred metres away.

'Sun Temple of Niuserre.'

Romantically silhouetted in the pre-twilight, it had both a majestic and mysterious air of foreboding about it.

'After this, we have dinner, yes? Twenty minute, yes?'

Abdo pointed to an area off to the right where they had set up a campfire, someone cooking our meal. Alongside was a makeshift low table, surrounded by cushions and blankets; it looked great silhouetted against the sand dunes and the setting sun, very 'Lawrence of Arabia'. Haakim stayed with us, leaving Abdo and Saeed to join their compatriot at the campfire.

If I didn't go to Giza the next day, this was probably going to be my last chance to be with Crystal, so, as we trekked up the slope to the temple, I reconsidered my options.

'I'd like to come with you tomorrow, to Giza.'

'You'd *like to*, or you *are*?'

'I am. I'm going to join you in the King's Chamber.'

'That is not up to me, that is up to Diane, it is her group, you would have to ask her.'

'How can I do that?'

'We are having one last circle with them tonight, in preparation for our time in the King's Chamber tomorrow morning. I am sure you would have to attend the circle if you wished to join us in the pyramid.'

'Then I'll come with you back to Cairo, if that's OK?'

'It sounds perfect.'

Why did I get the feeling Crystal knew more than I did about what lay in store the next day? It was probably because all along she *had* known more than me; she was the most switched on, aware person I had ever met. Somehow, as we reached the foot of the temple, knowing Crystal was going to be there tomorrow made me feel everything was going to be fine.

The Solar Temple of Niuserre

Niuserre's complex also sat atop a promontory on the desert's edge, and, like its counterpart five-hundred metres to the southeast, once had three primary components; a valley temple, an upper temple, and a causeway connecting the two. Following the easiest path we scaled the sand dunes and approached the temple from the northern part of its western side. It was unlikely I was going to find anything new here. Still, you never know, so, just to be sure, I did a quick check of my notes.

According to the Egyptologists, Niuserre was one of the most productive builders of the Old Kingdom. Not only did he supposedly complete the funerary monuments of his father, Neferirkare, his mother Khentkaus II, and his brother Neferefre, but he also rebuilt Userkaf's Solar Temple as well as finding the time and money to build his own pyramid, mortuary temple, and his own Solar Temple to boot. But wasn't it more likely, that like all the other pharaohs, he simple usurped most of them, extending them as part of his claim? It seemed more logical, and if that was the case, then did he really build the sun temple here at Abu Ghurab, or just make renovations?

As usual, like we had with the pyramid of Sahure, I decided to start with a lightning visit to the valley temple, pointing towards the river.

'Haakim, valley temple?'

He shook his head.

'No visit valley temple, all gone. Under water.'

That put the kibosh on that idea. It seemed I would have to rely on my iphone.

"Very little of the valley temple remains, and what does stands in shallow boggy swamp water. "

A wise decision, I hadn't seen any cobras yet in my travels here in Egypt, apart from the images on the walls, but if there was ever a likely spot to encounter one, it was on the edges of a boggy rat-infested swamp next to a village. It's not that I was scared of snakes, it was just a matter of priorities; mainly the inconvenience of dying an agonizing death before getting Kareem's papers safely out of Egypt that held me back.

"Built with thick walls, the entrance was a pillared portico with four palm columns built into a pylon-like facade of fine white limestone. In addition, to either side of the building, were two-columned porticos that accessed narrow corridors and rooms that led into the centre and to the causeway."

Again the main issue was of substance, granite columns or limestone? I guess, with time against us, I wasn't going to be able to find out.

While the others headed straight over the ruins of the enclosure wall and into the sun temple from the rear, I wanted to come in via the entrance, so circumnavigated clockwise until I hit the remains of the causeway, which, like those of others sites, would have once been covered. It steeply ascended to an impressive upper terrace, formed by extending and leveling a natural platform of rock using mud-brick encased with limestone blocks, upon which the actual sun temple was built. But why was the causeway built at such an acute angle to the temple?

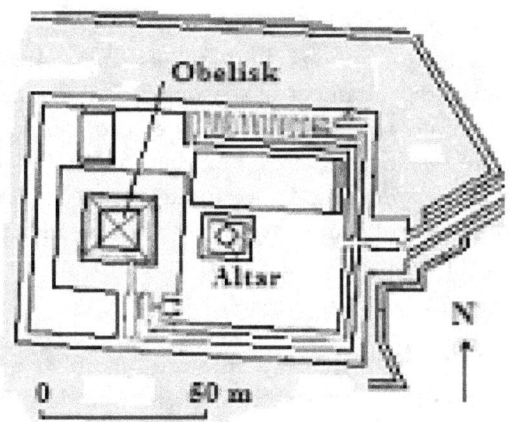

"Although the sun-temple is oriented east to west, the causeway was offset towards the north-east and the valley temple. Some archaeologists suggest that the causeway was pointing in the general direction of Heliopolis and may indicate a solar or astronomical purpose."

The "general direction"? That was too obscure, and too complicated; I needed something more rational.

Clearly the location was important, important enough to build up and level the ground rather than build it fifty metres further west, and, assuming it *was* the position of the upper sun temple that was paramount, as well as its orientation, then the causeway simply took the shortest path to the river.

And could the earlier tsunami, the one that buried the Osireion at Abydos, also have washed away part of the bank of the river? Then in dynastic times, the promontory was reinforced with simple mud-brick, and later, perhaps in the 19th Dynasty, after more damage by the Thera tsunami, been rebuilt by Khaemweset with limestone plaster? Or vica versa? It all seemed highly plausible.

The upper temple complex itself was rectangular in shape and oriented east-west; its walls constructed in mud-brick and later encased in yellow limestone. The entrance was from the east, through an entrance hall that extended from the temple's enclosure wall, and consisted of a long corridor that led to a second, traverse corridor, which opened onto the temple's open court. Within the T-shaped entrance were the remains of several granite-lined doorways, including those to the left, right, and straight ahead, clear evidence to me elements of this structure were much older than the 5th Dynasty.

The others were ahead in the courtyard, and, given I could scramble over virtually any wall foundation at any time to join them, I decided to do a lap and took the corridor to the left that skirted around the southern edge of the courtyard.

"The corridor was once decorated with scenes of the Heb-Sed festival, indicating that not only did Niuserre rule for at least 30 years, but that this part of the temple was probably built and decorated at quite a late stage in his reign."

It led completely around the courtyard to the southern side of the obelisk, to a small, independent structure called the "chamber of the seasons".

173

"The Niuserre temple contained a large number of invaluable inscriptions and reliefs from the king's reign In particular, the 'chamber of seasons' was decorated with numerous finely carved scenes depicting the three seasons of the Ancient Egyptian year, harvest, inundation, and sowing, which is unfortunately missing. Unfortunately, many of the reliefs from this, and the adjacent chapel, were sent to museums in Germany, where alas a number were destroyed during World War II."

The adjacent chapel, to the east, was little more than a shadow of its former self.

"The small chapel before the "chamber of the seasons" was once decorated with scenes of the dedication of the temple. Unfortunately, these reliefs were applied to poor stone enhanced with a coating of lime plaster, and were either in poor condition or had been removed to museums in Germany, and destroyed during World War II."

Given the chapel was most definitely a later addition by a 5th Dynasty ruler, probably Niuserre, it wasn't really within my field of interest; I was after evidence from a much earlier period, not only pre-dynastic, but pre pole-shift.

Running parallel to the "chamber of seasons" was another narrow corridor, this one leading towards and inside the main mound, or "pedestal" as the Egyptologists referred to it. The pedestal formed the base of the sun temple's main edifice, and took up most of the western half of the open court. Because of its square base and sloping sides the pedestal looked to me more like a mastaba, a truncated pyramid, or the first step or two of a Step Pyramid. Was that because it originally was one?

The entrance corridor looked as if it intersected with an inner corridor that once ran around part of the inner perimeter of the pedestal, sloping gently up until it reached the top of the base and providing access to the roof of the pedestal, most likely for rituals. Unfortunately I couldn't explore it as it appeared as if the pedestal had collapsed in and buried the corridor.

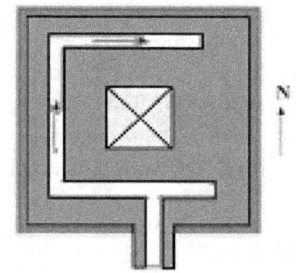

I could only imagine what treasures may have been buried within, on the walls, on the ceiling, there may even have been other corridors or chambers that ran off it, perhaps leading to a central chamber, or even to a subterranean shaft that led to subterranean chambers lined with red granite.

The pedestal itself once rose to a height of twenty metres and was primarily built of limestone, however, moving on and around, I discovered that more importantly it had colossal, precision-cut and polished, red-granite casing blocks, that must have weighed several ton each, positioned with incredible accuracy around the base.

There was clearly much more here than originally met the eye and I was extremely keen in the limited time left to dig deep to discover it.

"Then, some unknown force caused these massive granite casing stones to be scattered around the site like Lego blocks, as if a massive hand had swatted it like a sand castle."

It wasn't unknown at all, it was a number of tsunamis, the most drastic probably being the one during the pole shift that resulted in the burying of the Osireion.

Although it was most probably usurped and rebuilt during the 5th Dynasty, it is uncertain what it may have been before that. It could have been a pyramid, a mastaba, and that raised the question of whether there was an as yet undiscovered subterranean chamber accessed by a descending passage from the north. That in mind, I continued my circle around the west face and to the northern side.

Of course, much of the damage visible today was more likely due to the Thera tsunami, although there may have been restoration work done by Khaemweset in the 19th Dynasty and that could have been undone by the tsunamis three-hundred-or-so years either side of the time of 'Jesus', for surely they must have had some impact as well.

According to my notes:

"Atop the pedestal once stood a 36-metre high limestone obelisk that probably symbolized the 'ben-ben' stone, on which the sun's rays first shone in the Heliopolitan creation myth. Pieces of it are scattered all over the place. In fact, the entire site is one giant debris field with pieces of limestone scattered everywhere that appear to have come from structures that once existed here."

It was highly unlikely, the obelisk had been carved from one solid massive piece of limestone, more likely it was constructed from numerous large blocks, which would not only be consistent with the technology of the 5th Dynasty, but also with the evidence remaining.

If it had been made of one massive piece, it would most likely have broken into a few pieces when it 'fell'. So, it must have been made of numerous blocks for them to have been scattered everywhere, unless of course it somehow exploded from numerous well placed sticks of dynamite, which I highly doubted. It all reinforced the Thera tsunami scenario; if the tsunami knocked over a massive piece of limestone thirty-six metres long, it would fractured when it hit the ground but the major pieces would still be fairly close together. However, if it was made of numerous smaller blocks, then the effect of the tsunami would be to knock the obelisk over, break it into individual elements and tumble them across the south and southeast of the temple courtyard, and that's what the evidence suggested.

As for it being a 'ben-ben' stone, I had my doubts; it was possible, but it was also possible the Egyptologists were just trying to put square pegs in round holes. In the end, who knows what it was really used for, but clearly, as it was limestone, the "obelisk" was a 5th Dynasty addition, why, because if it'd been contemporary with the base it surely would have been of granite. That in itself again raised the probability that the original superstructure was most likely a mastaba or pyramid, and before that a simple subterranean chamber, like at Mazghuna. The plot was thickening.

My interest in the north side of the structure had suddenly turned to the search for a hidden entrance to the substructure somewhere near what I believe would have been the middle of the original mastaba. Kicking and scuffing around in the sand, what I discovered was a limestone pavement, about six inches above the surrounding court, with carved channels in the upper surface. Like at other pyramids, was this the foundations and courtyard of a previous north chapel? If so, the entrance to the descending passage, if it were there, would surely be somewhere beneath one or more of the pavement stones.

"North of the obelisk is a small area for cattle to be slaughtered as offerings to the sun god, Re. The limestone pavement had been raised about 13 cm above the level of the surrounding court, with channels carved into the surface that probably drained down to a row of large alabaster basins about 1.18 m (3 ft, 8 in) in diameter, each of which having three drainage holes."

As I looked around, in the shadow of the pedestal, against the northern wall, were a number of large basins, well over a metre in diameter, made of limestone. I ran my hand across the inner surface of the basins; incredibly they were still smooth to the touch. I wondered if alabaster was usually this smooth? I was sure it could be, but my thoughts were there had to be more to it.

Several marks inside the basin caught my attention, they looked like machining marks made by some type of circular cutting tool, which instantly told me that whoever created these basins possessed the sort of technology we'd appreciate today.

In addition, each basin contained three holes just below the rim; three perfect circles drilled through the alabaster. Were they there to hold the copper piping that had been evident in the mortuary temple of Niuserre back at Abusir? If they were, what was it that ran through the pipes? I speculated that one would have been for hot water, one for cold, and the third for drainage perhaps? No, that didn't cut it, if it was drainage it would be like our modern sinks and have been at the bottom of the basin, not equally at the top. No, the three holes had to be the inlets for three different liquids. As to what those liquids were, apart from one most probably being water, I had absolutely no idea.'

"Some Egyptologists believe that this area was not for slaughter, because there were no tethering stones, flint knives or bones found; the sort of evidence that has been present at other sites where animals were slaughtered."

I didn't think it was a slaughter area either; it was too close to the main structure. The Sanctuary of the Knife, the slaughterhouse at the mortuary temple of Neferefre, was outside the temple and to the south-east. A certain consistency of 'building codes' of the ancient Egyptians had me believing that if there *was* a slaughterhouse here, then it would have been there, outside the temple and to the southeast. Anyway, why the need for another slaughterhouse when there was already a perfectly good one a kilometre or so south? No, it wasn't slaughterhouse, but what *were* the basins and drainage for?

Leaving the basins behind, I headed towards the northeast corner of the courtyard, to where Bill, who had split from the girls, was similarly examining a number of basins that had been lined up along the inner eastern wall; I was keen to get his thoughts on what they may have originally been used for.

Along the way I passed numerous 'pieces' of the temple, scattered across the courtyard. In particular, I took notice of a heavily weathered piece of red granite, possibly part of a doorjamb, that had been inscribed with Niuserre's cartouche and stood in part of the courtyard.

Though the granite was much harder than the alabaster basins, and it should have resisted weathering much more than the alabaster, it looked significantly more weathered, which could only mean one thing, it was hundreds if not thousands of years older than the basins; the proof of the pudding, as they say!

Nearby were several sections of limestone with shallow grooves carved into them. At first, because of the pattern, and because they looked to me pretty much like part of the traditional palace façade style decoration typical of the Old Kingdom, I thought they were sections of the limestone wall fascia.

However, the standard of the finishing was pretty crap, even for the Old Kingdom, and I quickly realized the slabs weren't part of the walls, they were part of the grooved flooring from the area the Egyptologists had called the slaughterhouse or offering area.

As the floor slabs were made of limestone, not basalt, I doubted they were part of the original temple, thus not part of a nuclear fusion reactor, rather they were most likely a 5th Dynasty addition to the temple. I also realized that the grooves were not just there for drainage, or some sort of channelling of the liquid, but that they therefore must have been directly related to the function of the basins, whatever that function was.

And, as he was inspecting a row of alabaster basins that clearly had been placed at the eastern end of the courtyard at some recent point in time, possibly enroute to another location, my reckoning was that Bill probably had a few good ideas to fill in the gaps.

As I made a bee-line straight for him, I past through an area similar to the paved area to the north of the mastaba, but much bigger, and on past what would probably have been storage rooms on the left,
'What do make of them, Bill?"

He was deep in thought.
"Ink wells for giants?…"

At first I wasn't sure if he was serious or kidding.
'…Or contact lens holders for the gods?'

No, he was kidding.
'Do you think they had the same function as those at the mortuary temples of Niuserre and Sahure back down the road at Abusir?'
'No, I don't.'
'Why not?'
'A few reasons. Firstly, look at these decorations on the top.'

There were strange gear-like shapes running around the circumference of the basin.
'What do you make of them?'
'I don't know, but what ever they are, they aren't purely decorative; perhaps something attached to them for some reason.'
'How can you be so sure?'

He pointed across the courtyard back to the other basins.
'Because those over there don't have the same design.'

He was right, the ones I'd looked at earlier had a smooth rim and no gear shapes around the circumference; they *must* have had a different purpose. I checked what my notes had to say.

'Although their function may have been purely symbolic, the presence of nine alabaster basins, each one-point-one-eight metres in diameter, may have been related to rituals of offering, each one used to hold sacrificial animal blood that ran through

perfectly round channels cut into the paving.'

Once again Bill ran his hand across the inner surface of one of the 'geared' basins.

'Rituals, hey? I'm sure if there was any blood in here in the past it would have stained the stone, but there's nothing, not a drop.'

'I've already ruled that one out, Bill. If they'd slaughtered any animals here they would have done it outside the temple in a special abattoirs; besides, there's one about a kilometre back upriver outside the mortuary temple of Neferefre. So I'm pretty sure they weren't for animal blood...'

I directed his attention to the radial marks in the basins.

'...But what do you make of those marks?'

'I've been looking at those; they look like machining marks.'

'That's what I was thinking; freaky, hey.'

'And what about the holes?'

'They had to be drilled, they're perfectly circular.'

'Do you think they held copper piping?'

'It's possible. The question is, what ran through the pipes?'

'Well, I assume one would be for water, but as for the other two, I haven't got a clue.'

'I'll bet it has something to do with what's under the main mound of the temple, so maybe it's time to join the girls and see if we can't figure it out?'

We left the basins and headed towards the two girls and Haakim, who were at the far end of the courtyard, the girls with their hands on a large altar that sat before the eastern face of the mastaba.

We'd only taken a few steps when Bill stopped dead in his tracks.

'Shit, will you take a look at that!'

Once again Bill was down on his haunches running his hands through the sand and sweeping it to the side.

'What is it, Bill, more red granite, more sand?'

'No, mica.'

'What's that?'

He rubbed his hand over it, breaking away a few flakes.

'Mica's a silicate mineral compound that forms in thin layers, or sheets, basically potassium aluminium silicate; Muscovite being the most common type. But it's not so much what it *is*, but what it *does*.'

I looked around, it was clear there were huge slabs of it under the sand and in front of the pyramid.

'And what does it do?'

As he rubbed some of it in his fingers, Bill went 'memory digging' into another one of his detached altered states.

'Mica, mainly muscovite and phlogopite, has unique physical properties; the sheets are chemically inert, dielectric, hydrophilic, insulating, refractive, and resilient.'

'High School science, Bill.'

'Basically it's a good electrical and sound insulator, a dielectric, so it can support an electrostatic field while dissipating minimal energy in the form of heat, and it's a good thermal conductor, being stable up to around nine-hundred degrees Celsius. It's resistant to coronal discharge, and it's used in atomic force microscopy and as moderators in nuclear reactors as it has a high resistance to fast neutron penetration.'

'Nuclear reactors?'

'Yeah; it can be split very thin and is mechanically stable in micrometre-thin sheets which are relatively transparent to radiation such as alpha particles while being impervious to most gases.'

'Alpha particles, they're part of the fusion of hydrogen into helium, aren't they?'

'They are.'

'So this is pretty much slam-dunk proof these places were nuclear fusion reactors.'

Bill had a weird, distant look in his eye.

'Maybe, but I'm not so sure that's all there is to it.'

'OK, Bill, I'm all ears, what else could it be?'

He brushed away more sand, exposing even more of the mica.

'Mica wasn't just known to the ancient Egyptians you know, it was also known to the Mayans and Aztecs.'

'Context, Bill, relevance?'

'Patience, my friend; working on it. Apparently archaeologists discovered considerable amounts of mica, in layers up to thirty centimetres thick, underneath the Pyramid of the Sun at Teotihuacan, just north of Mexico City.'

'How thick is it here?'

'Hard to tell, but very possibly around the same. Anyway, about forty years ago a complex underground chamber system was discovered directly underneath the Pyramid of the Sun that included a lower passageway, seven feet high, that ran almost two hundred feet.'

'You mean, just like the causeways here in Egypt?'

'Yep. What's more, the floor of the tunnel contained drainage pipes and led to a strange hollowed out area shaped like a cloverleaf and supported by columns and basalt slabs.'

'Basalt hey; the plot thickens.'

'It does indeed.'

Getting to his feet, Bill continued to speak as he scanned the surrounds.

'The theory is that the whole complex was an enormous water processing plant, employing water from the adjacent river for a technological purpose.'

'That purpose being?'

'Initially they thought it was to create power, electricity...'

He started waving his arms around, like he was doing his tai chi, picturing how the temple may have originally looked.

'...Somehow the water would flow over the mica sheets and, through the piezoelectric effect produced by the mica, electricity was produced. But I think there's more...'

He turned back to face me.

'...I was talking to Pieter about these Annunaki beings, the ones that came to Earth over four-hundred-and-fifty thousand years ago in search of gold. He said that in addition to surface mining, the Annunaki used sophisticated water-mining techniques to 'filter' or to process gold directly from the water.'

'There's gold in water?'

'Some estimates are that the oceans contain up to seventy-five billion tons of it, however it's so diluted that its concentration is of the order of a few parts per *trillion*. But, still, it's there.'

'But that's seawater, the Nile is fresh water.'

'Not too "fresh" nowadays, and seawater is not the only source, the continental

179

rivers can carry huge quantities of gold to the sea; and not all of it is dissolved or in colloidal solution. Besides, who's to say that before the last pole shift, the Nile as we know it today wasn't part of a larger body of water that connected the Mediterranean Sea directly with the Indian Ocean?'

'So what you're saying is, that before the last pole shift, the sun temple was originally a gold refining facility?'

'It's a possibility....'

Bill turned back to face the main structure, again tracing his hands over imaginary elements.

'...Somehow the water was pumped up, or drawn up from the Nile, perhaps over or even under the mica, possibly flowed out and over the quartz crystal-laden red-granite face of the pedestal or pyramid structure, creating a piezoelectric effect. The water would then be piped into the basins, not so much hot and cold but perhaps one electrically charged stream, another uncharged, and would be spun around inside and flow up and out through the third of the round holes in the sides. That would mean that using centrifugal force and gravity the gold could filter down to the bottom and remain in the centre of the basins, without being drained away, and could easily be scooped out and retrieved at the end of each day.'

It all sounded plausible except for the fact that I'd pigeon-holed the limestone basins as being part of the Old Kingdom.

'So why were the basins made of limestone, and not granite or basalt?'

'Maybe because of their relative neutrality to electric charge?'

'So the basins were huge decanters?'

'Possibly.'

'Then why the two different types?'

Bill scratched his head.

'No idea, maybe one was for gold, the other for silver or some other substance. One thing I can be pretty sure about is they must have been connected in some way to the altar the girls are looking at. My guess is the basins weren't originally where they are now, but may have been placed in a circle either around the pyramid, or around the altar.'

'And what function did the altar have?'

'I don't know. Let's go find out.'

Situated directly before the pedestal, the altar sat in the centre of what appeared to be a raised square platform about twelve metres wide, although numerous large sections of the surrounding floor had been either removed or washed away. The altar itself was huge, six metres in diameter, built from five massive slabs of 'machined' calcite, exactly the same substance as the altar in the outer courtyard at Karnak Temple and the 'shrines' of Amenhotep I and II in the outdoor museum.

The difference here was that the altar was more than just a rectangular block, here it was constructed from five massive smooth blocks fitted together to create an eight-pointed star, with a central cylinder just under two metres wide.

"The central part of the altar was shaped to represent the sun, while the four slabs around it, formed from four 'hotep' signs representing the hieroglyphic sign for 'offering', 'peace' or 'satisfied', meant the whole altar was shaped to symbolize the words 'May Ra be satisfied'."

None of that meant that's what the altar actually meant or even what it was built to represent, it was just an attempt by the Egyptologists to make some sense of the altar based on their own conditioned beliefs. So what did it mean?

By the time Bill and I arrived at the altar, Pernille and Crystal had climbed on top and were sitting on the central 'sun' cylinder; cross-legged, facing each other, holding hands and toning. Probably to make sure they weren't disturbed, Haakim met us several metres before it.

'Altar is one of oldest sacred site of ceremony on whole planet; from before time of pharaohs.'

It seemed Haakim may also have been a mainstream dissenter, however, just in case I may have misunderstood him, I politely pressed him for more details.

'You mean before the 5th Dynasty?'

'Many year before 1st Dynasty. Abu Ghurab it build to create it the high spiritual awareness through the sound send out through alabaster of altar it connect with it sacred energy of universe call Neter that once appear here.'

I had a fair idea what Haakim meant, but, as Haakim's English wasn't so great, Bill paraphrased to be sure of his meaning.

'What you're saying is that the gods, the Neters, Osiris, Isis, etcetera, once came down to earth and made a physical appearance at this very spot, and that this altar was built to communicate with them when they left? That the alabaster platform and altar can be activated with specific sound frequencies so as to not only expand your own awareness, but to further open the senses so that you can "communicate with" and "be one with" the Neters?'

'Yes, this it is it.'

I turned to Bill.

'You know what Haakim just described?'

'What's that?'

'A sort of star-gate.'

'A star-gate to where?'

'Who knows?'

'Then maybe we should join the girls and find out?'

And with that he stepped forward onto the platform and laid his hands on the eastern point of the altar, perpendicular to the north-south line created by the two girls, and started toning.

The last time I'd lain my hands on a large altar of alabaster was in the outer courtyard at Karnak, and that was trippy to say the least; dark shadows of Amun Priests chased me all over the temple. I wasn't sure if I wanted to go through that again, and yet there were the visions, the myriad of colours and universal probabilities. What the hell!

ET, phone home

I stepped onto the platform and made my way around to the western side of the altar where I slowly placed my hands on the point, closed my eyes, and joined in with the toning. Maybe I was just projecting Haakim's thoughts, but almost instantaneously I felt the stone vibrating in sympathy with my voice, or was I simply tuning in and in sympathy with the already vibrating altar? In either case, the air seemed alive with an amazing harmonic cosmic musical chord that seemed to oscillate and undulate at will.

A few breaths later, Nemo appeared, surprising enough splashing around in a water-filled chamber about twenty feet immediately beneath the central cylinder. Was the altar also the cap of a well, a water well, maybe even a wishing well? As Nemo darted to and fro, he ducked in and out of numerous underground tunnels, canals, and ducts that ran into and from the central chamber; there was much more below the ground here than anyone was aware of. Suddenly he jumped up above the ground and swished back and forth between Crystal and Pernille.

I opened my eyes; there was a circular shaft of white light about two metres wide, encompassing both Crystal and Pernille, that shot straight up into the air like a search light to…I couldn't tell which star system, as the sun was just setting and the stars still weren't visible, but I had a hunch, a feeling where. Or was it shining down from there upon the two of them, *because* of the two of them? They looked just like they were in a Star Trek movie, when a person is in the initial stage of being transported; they were there, but they weren't, they were transparent, but they were shimmering like a billion fireflies. They were pure energy. And so was Nemo.

After briefly dancing around between Crystal and Pernille, Nemo shot up into the air and disappeared into the ether. If this *was* a star gate, then Nemo had just passed through it. For a moment I wondered if I would ever see him again.

Moments later, a tall 'being', dressed in a full-length white gown, materialized on the central disc between Crystal and Pernille. I couldn't tell if it was male or female, as it was facing Bill and had it's back to me. I didn't know who, or what it was. I wondered if it was Nemo reappearing in another form, or maybe one of the Annunaki gods. If I didn't know better I could easily have been misled into believing 'he' was the Christian-conditioned persona of 'Jesus'. One thing was for sure, its arrival triggered Bill into another of his impromptu channelling session.

'Itanaa, öveqatsit ep qátuhqa, nam uhnatngwani pas kyaptsi'tiwaa…'.

Having set Bill off into a mumbling state of adoration, slowly the radiant 'being' half-turned, towards Crystal, enough for me to see it had no beard, so that ruled out the 'Jesus' scenario, and the head was slightly elongated, but nothing like the images of the Annunaki like Akhenaten, so that ruled them out.

Like an adoring parent, it placed a hand on Crystal's shoulder and communicated something to her. I couldn't make it out, but whatever it was brought a beaming sparkle to her face.

Next the 'being' turned to Pernille, it was her turn to receive a 'blessing', because that's what it looked like. Whatever it was left her somewhat stunned in awe. Finally, the being turned to face me, giving me a clearer look.

Maybe seven to eight foot in height, fair, with elongated elfish features, much like that arrow-shooting elf in "Lord of the Rings", but taller, it appeared as if the 'being' could have been either male or female, or both. It reached out to me, somehow managing to cover the three metres with its reach and similarly placed a hand on my shoulder; its eyes fixed on mine, both drawing me into them and simultaneously flooding into mine.

'The time has come, my brother, for you to set aside your human persona, your human ego, and remember who you really are, and why you have chosen to come here.'

The thin lips didn't move for even a mutter, and yet I 'heard' ever word as clear as day in my mind.

'Your path may not always appear to be easy, but this is the path you have chosen, so walk tall.'

A thousand questions flashed through my mind, however, before I could latch onto one and put the words into action, the 'being' dematerialised, the shaft of light disappeared, and the angelic resonance that had filled the air drifted away like the fading rays of the setting sun. Was what happened just real, or part of my imagination?

I shook some sense back into my head as Crystal and Pernille hugged, then moved to assist Bill, who was vaguely back in the here and now.

'Dinner, yes?'

Haakim was right, it was time to eat; I could digest what had just happened over dinner.

Nothing was said on the way back to the campfire, everyone was either still stunned, or in awe of the amazing sunset; Crystal seemed totally unaffected. Had they seen and heard what I'd seen and heard, or was I totally losing the plot?

We arrived back at the campfire, where Abdo had organized a fantastic spread of barbequed chicken, breads, rice, and vegetables, and, amid the most amazing setting of the silhouette of the pyramid against the setting sun, all sat down on the sand to enjoy it. A few mouthfuls into dinner, I broached the subject of what had just happened.

'Did anyone notice or experience anything *unusual* when we were at the altar?'

'Unusual for you, or unusual for us?'

'Well, both, either, anything out of the ordinary?'

'"Out of the ordinary", what do you mean by "out of the ordinary"?'

Crystal was putting me on the spot and I could either back off or spill my guts and risk the ridicule of the others. I decided to do it in instalments.

'Well, a sort of humming, a musical chord?'

'Pernille and I were toning, do you mean that?

She was challenging me.

'Not just that, it was like the whole altar and everything around it was humming.'

'Everything in this universe is vibrating, in a constant state of humming. Is what you are saying that you heard it, that you tuned in?'

'Well, yes, I guess so.'

'And haven't you experienced that before, at other places here in Egypt?'

'Well, yes, I guess so.'

'Then that would not qualify as being unusual.'

This was excruciating, like pulling off a sticking plaster one hair at a time. I decided to pull the plaster off in one fell swoop.

'Did anyone else see a tall being in a shimmering white gown standing in the middle of the altar?'

'You mean the Pleiadean Emissary from the Galactic Federation?'

'Is that who it was?'

'Yes?'

'You saw it?'

'Of course.'

Pernille chipped in.

'We all did?'

'And that's not unusual?'

'After I found the crystal ball at P'aaleq, I had a dream that night; it was the same being. It held up the crystal skulls to me and told me that combined they held the collective history and knowledge of the human existence on earth. That I was a keeper of the crystals.'

'Bill?'

'Actually, I got a first glimpse at Karnak, in the Temple of Ptah, so it came as no surprise to be visited again. Somehow, after that first visit, I just knew of an old Indian story that formless "thought beings", beings of light, had arrived here on a sound wave, a transmission, from the Pleiades star system, through a hole in space, a wormhole, and created many of the Indian tribes, the Cherokee, the Sioux, the Hopi.'

'But that's North America, how does that relate to Egypt?'

Crystal knew how it connected.

'The ancient Egyptian Building Texts from Edfu tell of formless beings, called Sages, who came from the stars to Egypt and created an original mound, surrounded by the primeval water, called the Island of the Egg, where the creation of human kind took place.'

'How do you know that?'

'Did I not tell you to *feel* the stone?'

'Yes, but I didn't get that.'

'Oh, yes you did. Once you tune in, it is all downloaded, you just have to locate it, like locating a file on your computer, punch in the topic and hit the search button. Or perhaps you should read the little-known book 'The Mythical Origin of the Egyptian Temple' by Doctor Eve Reymond, it may jog your memory.'

Bill jumped back in.

'As Crystal explained it to me, the Edfu story of a civilization founded by the gods who created a hybrid race of humans, exactly matches the Atlantis story as told by Plato of a high civilization founded by *the gods*, and populated by hybrid god-men. I think Plato got the story from ancient Egypt, from the Edfu Building Texts.'

I suddenly remembered what Frank had told me.

'You're right, he did get it from ancient Egypt, but not from Edfu, that was probably just a copy, I think he got it directly from the Books of Isis and Horus, from the original metal disks and books in the sacred chambers beneath the Great Pyramid.'

'What sacred chambers beneath the Great Pyramid?'

'They were discovered in 1976 by several 'seekers' from a California University who were following the directions written on an ancient Greek scroll.'

'What?'

'Man, I've got so much to tell you, I don't know where to start.'

'Well, one thing at a time, let's stick with Plato and these chambers.'

'Basically, Plato was an initiate of the Tat Brotherhood who, like Pythagoras before him, and Alexander after him, was invited to Egypt to "make the acquaintance of the prophets of wisdom", and to take part in "the great learnings of the Mysteries along the Nile". Plato spent thirteen years in Egypt, supposedly "consulting the scribes and records in the Library of Alexandria", even though the library was supposedly built in the Ptolemaic era and didn't exist for another hundred years. Which means Plato must have learned directly from the "Books of Isis and Horus" which are metal disks and books in the sacred underground chambers.'

'Jesus!'

'Plato was then initiated in the underground halls of the Pyramid and the Sphinx by the Hierophant of the Pyramids, who gave Plato the highest esoteric teachings and sent him out into the world to do the work of the "Great Order".' Naturally he related the story of Atlantis as he had learned it from the "Books of Isis and Horus".

We could have talked for hours, however Saeed interjected.

'Miss Crystal, it is time, we must go.'

Immediately she got to her feet, Pernille following suit. I checked my iphone; it was 7:15.

'Where are you going?'

'Back to Cairo, to Diane's circle.'

I stood to join them.

'I have to come with you.'

Saeed was not so sure.

'Indy, the Secret Police could catch you.'

As Bill handed a wad of baksheesh to Abdo, I took a leaf straight out of Crystal's book.

'Ahoya, they could catch me anywhere, no matter where I am. Besides, they've probably figured out by now that Cairo is the last place I would be.'

'It is too dangerous.'

I held up the backpack that had been sitting on the sand beside me.

'Did your uncle think it was too dangerous when he gathered all these papers together?'

'I guess he did not.'

'Did he listen to his fears when he handed me the papers, knowing that it would probably mean his certain death?'

'No.'

'Of course he did! He listened to his fears, but he was not a slave to them; the importance of bringing the truth to the world overcame those fears.'

'But, Indy, my brother, Kareem he was killed.'

'Saeed, it's not how we 'die' that matters, it's how we *live* that matters. Do we live in fear, ruled by fear, or do we live our life free to *embrace* anything we desire? Kareem lived his life in freedom and he left his body the same way. Besides, it's not fair to put Abdo and his family in further unnecessary danger; he has already risked his life for me.'

Abdo spoke up.

'Mister Alex, it is my pleasure, I do not mind to do this.'

'And I am most grateful, for what you have done, and for what you offer, however I have to do what I have to do, I have to follow my intuition, and my intuition tells me to go back to Cairo.'

Before any further discussion could ensue, Crystal spoke strongly and clearly.

'We must all follow our path, sometimes that path may not always appear to be easy, but when it is the path we have chosen, we must walk tall and without hesitation.'

Had she heard what the Emissary had said to me, was she reinforcing the message? Was there a reason I had to go back to Cairo? Did it mean I had to return, to face my fears? In any case, it put an immediate end to any further debate about me going, except for one little obstacle Abdo pointed out.

'Where will you stay? It would not be wise to come back to the Cairo Palace.'

Bill had a solution.

'You can stay at our hotel.'

'They will want a passport.'

'Ah, yes, that could be a problem.'

Once again Crystal took charge.

'Only if you wish a separate room; you can sleep in my room.'

I certainly had no qualms about that option.

The problem solved, we all hugged Abdo and Haakim, thanked them for the amazing meal and experience, and headed for the minivan, reluctantly leaving the stunning Egyptian twilight of the desert behind us. As we strolled purposefully through the treed grove I revived the conversation.

'You heard what the Pleiadean Emissary said to me?'

'I did, but it is more important that *you* heard what was said.'

'I did. I'm just not sure what it means. *"Your path may not always appear to be easy, but this is the path you have chosen, so walk tall".'*

'If you cannot see the view of the valley from the top of the mountain while you are still climbing then you must...'

'Keep climbing until you reach the top.'

'Exactly! And this is when you are most fatigued, most challenged, most ready to give up. Was this all you remember?'

'No. *"The time has come, my brother, for you to set aside your human persona, your human ego, and remember who you really are, and why you have chosen to come here".'*

'And what does this tell you?'

'That my human ego is still blocking me.'

'From what?'

'From remembering who I am and why I came here?'

'And what does that tell you?'

I wasn't sure what she was getting at.

'I don't know, I don't remember anything.'

She wasn't impressed.

'You have a brain; use it! If it is your *human* ego that is blocking you, and the Light Being was a...'

'Pleiadean Emissary.'

'Yes, and the Emissary called you...'

'"My brother", *his* brother, which means that I'm..a...I'm a Pleiadean Emissary?'

Crystal seemed a little frustrated with me.

'Or something akin to it; an emissary from the Galactic Federation.'

'What is the Galactic Federation, is it something like the Federation in Star Trek?'

'It is exactly like the Federation in Star trek, except for one thing.'

'And what's that?'

'The humans are not currently a part of it, and they are a long way from being admitted into it.'

I doubted the "Trekkies" or New Age gurus would be happy to hear that.

'So who is this Galactic Federation, and why their special interest in the human race?'

'For billions of years, most of the physical 3rd Dimensional universe has been conquered by the reptilians, mainly the Dracos, but also the crocodile hominids, lizard hominids, snake homipnids and other various reptilian beings, all created by bird beings in the constellation of Draco. You will see representations of these beings on many of the walls of temples and in tombs from the New Kingdom. However, eventually the mammalian life forms "evolved', primarily the lion people, and they resisted and rebelled against the reptilians, resulting in an intergalactic war.

Whereas the bird beings, who created the reptilian beings, created the reptilians to be lower-chakra, masculine beings of logic, the Lion people, a benevolent and fearless race, created "humans", in the constellation of Lyra on a planet that orbited Vega, to be upper-chakra, feminine beings of the light. And when I use the term "human" I am not referring to the human form on this planet, rather the original homanid form from which earthly humans were ultimately engineered.

Believing that the only way order could be imposed in the universe was for beings to adhere to a rigid, tyrannical regime, the Draconian beings attacked the "humans'" in the Lyra system, forcing them to flee to other parts of the universe, most notably to Andromeda, Sirius, and the Pleiades. Of these refugees, it was the humans who migrated to Andromeda who were the most successful, avoiding many of the hardships that the humans who migrated elsewhere endured.

Having experienced what too much lower-chakra energy can do, those humans who fled to the Pleiades decided to completely exclude usage of their lower charkas and polarize themselves to light and love. Similarly, the Sirian refugees eliminated all but logic, as they believed this was the best way to deal with the Draconian threat.

But the Draconians were unrelenting and, about four-and-a-half-million years ago, the Star League of the Pleiades, the Andromedan Confederation, the Lyra Light League, and the Sirian star-nation banded together with their Lion people elders to form the Galactic Federation of Light, an opposition force to combat the Draconian Empire.'

'You're basically describing the plot to Star Wars.'

'You think George Lucas just "came up' with the idea?'

'It was seeded?'

'Of course; to prepare earth humans for the truth.'

It all seemed way too absurd.

'Phft! OK, but me, a Pleiadean Emissary from the Galactic Federation? No way!'

Crystal seemed disappointed with my lack of awareness, but persisted.

'I did not say you were a *Pleiadean* Emissary, but until you can let go of the limiting belief that you are *not* an emissary from the Galactic Federation, and accept there is a possibility that you are *not* human, simply a star-seeded consciousness in a human body, then you cannot re-member, because your very human thinking blocks all further re-membering and awakening.

Answer this; is it possible you *could* be a Galactic Emissary, a Light Being, in a human form, but that you have lived so many lives in human form that you have forgotten, that you now identify with your clothes and have forgotten who it is that wears the clothes?'

'I suppose so.'

'Is it a possibility, yes or no?'

'Yes, it's a possibility.'

'Now answer simply yes or no; have you had other incarnations on this planet, other lives?

'Yes.'

'Was one of those incarnations as the being known as Akhenaten?'

'Yes.'

'Was Akhenaten, Annunaki?'

'Yes?'

'Did the Annunaki come from another planet?'

'Yes.'

'Were the Annunaki human?'

'Well, yes and no, they used their DNA to create the human form.'

'So they are not human, they are extra terrestrial beings?'

'Yes.'

"If you can trace your consciousness back to lives in Annunaki bodies, is it possible you incarnated in other species before then?'

'Yes, I suppose so.'

'This is what re-membering is about, reconnecting to *all* your other selves, and to the Higher Self that created each and every one of these lives, and ultimately to the Oneness that creates and is all things. And once you remember who you really are, then you will remember why it is you have chosen to come to this planet, your purpose, your role, and what it is you have to do next.'

As we got into the back of the minivan a strong urge was compelling me.

'I feel the next thing I need to do is to go to the circle.'

'Very good.'

Bottom of the ninth

We were quickly underway, and I felt as if I was walking tall, but I was still curious.

'Crystal, what did the Pleiadean Emissary say to you?'

'It was the Pleiadean Emissary who directed me to come to Egypt, to remember.'

'So you'd met before?'

'Many times.'

I sat back, somewhat disappointed in myself.

'I guess I was just slow on the uptake.'

'You *did* have a lot of resistance to overcome.'

Despite what I had witnessed with my own eyes, parts of that resistance were clearly still running.

'A "star being", a Pleiadean Emissary; I knew Abusir was somehow connected to the Pleiades.'

'That visitors from the stars, from the Pleiades, came to earth, and still do, is not just an Egyptian fascination, it is the obsession of virtually every ancient civilization and parts of every modern civilization in the world.'

'So was the temple built as some sort of homage to them, or as a gold mine, or a nuclear fusion reactor, or is it a star-gate?'

Bill chimed in.

'Maybe at various points it was all of the above?'

'More than just a sun temple, a place to worship Re, that's for sure.'

Crystal had even more information.

'It was a sun temple, yes, but not to *our* sun, to a sun in the Pleiadean star system.'

'You've read Wayne Herschel?'

'No. Who is he?'

'A South African guy who Mark told me about. He's figured out that every pyramid along the Nile corresponded to a main star and constellation along the galactic equator of the Milky Way, and Abusir corresponds to the Pleiades.'

'Then he is very aware.'

'But if you haven't read any of Herschel's work, how do you know, did someone tell you?'

Pernille joined the conversation.

'Didn't you see the evidence when we were at Dendera?'

'At Dendera? Where?'

'Everywhere, on the ceilings.'

'The ceilings of the hypostyle hall, or the zodiac on the ceiling in the Osiris suit on the roof?'

'Both.'

'Where was it in the zodiac?'

'In the centre.'

'Right in the centre?'

'You can't miss it, it's the most important part; always look at the centre of the mural to see what is most important.'

Thankfully Bill chipped in.

'Don't feel so bad, Alex, I didn't see it either, and neither have all the so-called experts, even though it's as obvious as the nose on your face.'

'What is it?'

Bill handed the reigns back to Pernille who graciously continued.

'Taweret, the hippo deity, the goddess of childbirth and Genesis symbol of Egypt, and what is at the centre of the circle is what the focus of the whole circle is there to represent....'

As Pernille continued, I dived into my iphone to bring up Wayne Herschel's site, thehiddenrecords.com, quickly finding the relevant image.

'...Taweret is the constellation of Bootes and includes the star Arcturus as her womb. From there are two strange lines leading from Taweret's hands or belly that attach to the leg of the bull, a symbol of the bull of the heavens, Taurus. Standing on the lines is a dog, which some think refers to Anubis and the underworld, but it really represents the journey of Taweret through the constellation of Canis Major, through Sirius.

And there's absolutely no doubt the leg symbol represents a cluster of seven stars, the Pleiades, and that the Pleiades is the origin of the gods and thus the star ancestry of the human race, which is exactly what all the ancient civilizations and modern New Age visitations and channellings seem to indicate and confirm.'

'And there's more evidence on the ceiling?'

'At Dendera?'

'Yes, on the ceiling of the hypostyle hall, right?'

'Yes.'

I found an image from Dendera on Herschel's website and handed my iphone to Pernille.

'Is this part of it?'

'Yes, look at the way the leg of the bull is also jointly represented as the bull itself, and at the seven stars around it; that confirms the leg symbol is the Pleiades. If that isn't enough, look to the right at how Horus, son of Osiris, is using an arrow to point straight at the bull.'

'Isn't that a spear?'

'No, it's a pointer, and it points specifically between the horns of the bull. And to the left is Taweret, holding on to the leg with a length of rope.'

She handed it back and I had a closer look.

'That's not rope, that's a double helix, DNA; it confirms there's a DNA connection between Bootes, Arcturus, the Pleiadeans, and humans, and why Taweret was known not only as the goddess of childbirth, but also as the Genesis symbol of Egypt.'

And then I saw something else.

'And look above the bull, not one, but two red suns. Could that be a reference to Nibiru?'

Crystal was definite.

'It could, but it's not, it is merely a representation that Taurus is a binary star system.'

It was like a giant jigsaw puzzle where all the pieces were magically falling into place.

'So what you're both saying is that not only is the sun temple at Abu Ghurab directly linked to the Pleiades, but so is Dendera?'

'Exactly!'

Pernille added another.

'And Esna as well.'

'And if those three are, then in some way the location of all the pyramids and temples along the Nile are as well?'

'Precisely!'

'Well, thanks to Herschel I now know the whole Milky Way follows the Galactic Equator and the ancient Egyptians built their pyramids as a direct copy of what was in the sky.'

Crystal laughed.

'You *knew* that before, you always have known it, it has just taken this man Herschel to re-mind you.'

'That's one way of looking at it.'

Pernille had even more to contribute.

'You know you can draw a straight line along the Galactic Equator from Sirius through Orion's belt, that goes through Taurus to the Pleiades, and on to Andromeda.'

I turned to Crystal.

'Doesn't that include all the places you said formed the Galactic Federation, Andromeda, the Pleiades, Sirius, and isn't Lyra something to do with Orion?'

She smiled.

'Very astute; in many ways the line is a lineage of the pre-history of the development of the human form from the various original humanoid life forms, and therefore it represents the many influences on the past present and future development of human consciousness.'

Bill threw his post-religious two cents in.

'"Our father, which art in heaven, hallowed be thy name, thy kingdom come, thy will be done on earth as it is in heaven"; now let's reinterpret that. "Our creator, who comes from and lives amongst the stars, your name is sacred, or rather, it is a secret who you really are, your dominion and rules envelope us, protect us from the Dracos, your rules, regulations and beliefs must be adhered to on earth as they are in the stars and higher dimensions."'

'I remember Pieter and I discussing that the ceilings at Dendera and Esna were retellings of the gods' journeys through the stars, that the solar barques must have been spacecraft, possibly Light Ships, and that the gods were travelling through space, and possibly time. Of course that raised the questions of who "the gods" actually were, where they came from, why they came to earth in the first place, where they are now, and why they aren't communicating with us?

Pieter thought that all the different-looking gods, Osiris with his green skin, the ibis-headed Thoth, the Lion Goddess Sehkmet, the falcon-headed Horus, even the crocodile god Sobek, Anubis the jackal, they might all have been a representation of the arrival of the different members of the Galactic Federation. Turns out he was probably spot on; I bet he wishes he was here now.'

I found a quote about Abusir on Herschel's website and read it out to the others.

'Listen to this. *"The Sun Temple of Ra at Abusir forms the epicentre of the entire pyramid field along the River Nile, dividing it proportionately into two distinct halves to either side, and correlates with one of three Sun-like "G" classification stars in the Pleiades star field as they appeared 17,250 years ago. Gauging by what many Egyptian texts say, and from an apparent global obsession with this particular cosmic area, the star represented by this unusual pyramid undoubtedly qualifies as the 'x' that marks the spot on the star map".'*

Bill laughed.

'And so the treasure hunt is on again! Randy would love it.'

Then I discovered another image on Herschel's website that blew me away.

'Look at this!'

It was an image from the New Kingdom tomb of Senenmut, consort and first cousin of Hatshepsut, and most likely a High Priest. Even though the mural was completely surrounded by stars, which meant the mural related to astronomical events, I took Pernille's advice and looked immediately at the centre of the image.

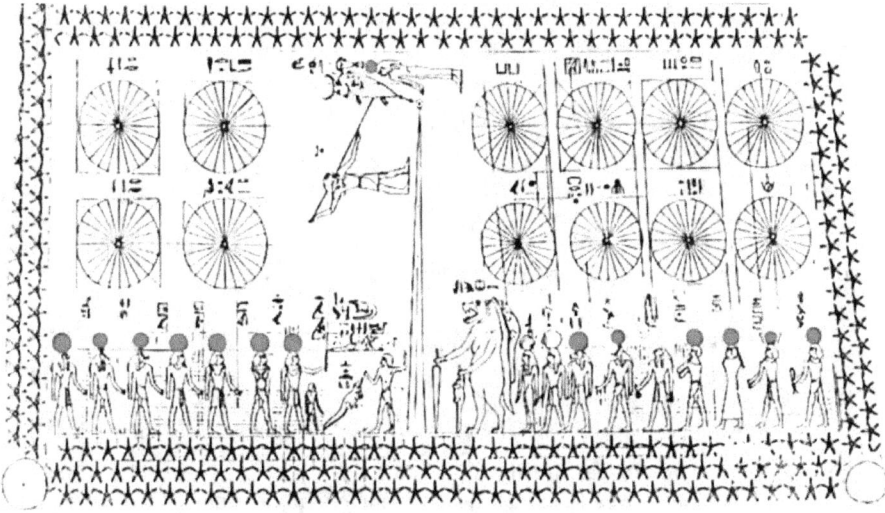

There was Horus again, the god of truth, at centre, this time with a spear, signifying Orion's belt, pointed directly at the leg of the bull in the heavens. Beside the bull's leg, as clear as day, and aligned with the bull's leg, was a figure that could only have been Isis, the throne upon a red sun disc upon her head. And, amazingly, there was a beam that shone from a star at the foot of the bull's leg directly down to earth.

Was this the very same beam that I had witnessed about an hour ago, shining down onto Crystal and Pernille in the centre of the altar, the very beam that the Pleiadean Emissary had arrived on/in? As I handed it to Pernille, she was quick to spot Taweret.

'There is Taweret, at the bottom, on earth, with the bull's leg in one hand, and I don't know what that is in the other.'

I didn't quite see it that way.

'I don't think that's a bull's leg in her hand, I think it's a crocodile, just like the one on her back and the one on the other side of the beam. And I bet that's the exact same beam that the Pleiadean Emissary arrived on.'

Then something Frank said about the 1976 expedition who found the secret entrance into the Great Pyramid sprang to mind.

'You know, Frank said the secret door in the south face of the Great Pyramid only opened at certain specific times of the day.'

Bill did a double-take.

'There's a secret door in the south face of the Great Pyramid?'

'Yeah, about four-hundred feet up; it leads down beneath the ground to the sacred chambers and the Books of Isis and Horus, and to all sorts of other goodies I'll tell you about later. I wonder if the door only opened at certain times because once the pyramid had short-circuited due to a pole-shift, it was only activated, powered-up, when it was directly in the beam from one or more of the distant star systems?'

'Jesus!'

Pernille had handed the iphone to Bill, and he suddenly sat glued to his seat, transfixed by the mural.

'What is it, Bill?'

'I've seen this before.'

Crystal was quick to re-mind him.

'Of course you have, you commissioned it for the wall of your tomb three-and-a-half-thousand years ago; you were...?'

'Senenmut!'

Bill laughed and he handed it back to me.

'I thought it looked familiar.'

Crystal smiled, then prodded me.

'What else do you see?'

'Well, all the other figures are clearly on the earth, but they have the same red disk on their heads indicating they come from the same place as Isis.'

Bill corrected me.

'Some don't, two have white disks, which means they come from another sun system.'

Crystal gave me another prod.

'Anything else?'

Clearly there was, I just had to find it.

'Well, they're all facing Taweret, with a hand or hands out, holding something, bringing something to her...'

And then I saw it.

'...and the last one on the right is carrying the twisted double helix of DNA, which means that each of these 'beings' must have contributed genetic material. And just to the left of the beam is a man, the product of Taweret's efforts.'

I thought I'd cracked the code, but Bill was either still trying to decipher the message, to solve the last piece of the puzzle, or to lead me to discovering it.

'So, what do you think all those circles are, they're clearly not stars or planets?'

'Maybe they're Galactic co-ordinates that relate to the beings at the bottom?'

'No.'

'Maybe they used the sun temple at Abu Ghurab as some sort of star-gate or navigation beacon?...'

And then I remembered something Pieter had said.

'...No, if that was the case they'd be related to the decans.'

'Decans?'

'The thirty-six small constellations that rise consecutively on the horizon throughout each rotation of the earth. If the circles related to them, then each circle would surely be divided into thirty-six, whereas these circles are divided into twenty-four equal segments.'

'Well the only thing I know that is divided into twenty-four is the hours in a day.'

Though she wasn't aware of it, Pernille was the one who solved the mystery.

'They remind me of the world clocks, with the major cities all having different time zones.'

'That's it, that's exactly what they are, but the other way round.'

'Sorry, Alex, I don't understand.'

'As the earth rotates, the star system directly in line with Egypt, in line with the altar at Abu Ghurab, changes, the alignment changes. And that's fine at night, because you can see the alignment, so you know which star system aligns with the altar and when the two locations are in sync, but during the day you can't see the stars, so you wouldn't know which system aligned when. These are clocks, timetables, each one indicating when each separate star system is in direct alignment with Egypt.'

Bill got it.

'Like a window of opportunity once every twenty-four hours for ET to phone home?'

'That's it! Although it still doesn't explain *why* they're here in the first place.'

Crystal knew.

'To assist the human race expand its conscious awareness.'

'So why come to *us* personally, why wouldn't they appear to the whole planet?'

'Under Federation law, they are not permitted to interfere directly with the development of conscious life forms unless invited; conscious life forms must be free to develop of their own will and intention.'

'Then how can they be here, talking to us, they're breaking the rules.'

'Because they are not communicating with human consciousness.'

'Huh?'

'Remember, while you may be in a human body, your consciousness is not human. Star Beings are not allowed to directly interfere, however, they are permitted to incarnate into a life form that contains their DNA and thus influence the development of human consciousness by being 'born' human. The difficulty is, the more lives you lead as a human, the more you run their behaviour patterns, the more you believe you are one.'

'All that's fine, but why would the gods have such a big interest in a species that has proven over and over again to be unpredictable, racist, bigoted, sexist, fearful, greedy, homicidal, and genocidal?'

As usual Crystal put it all into perspective.

'All children go through stages of being unpredictable, single-minded, self-centred, intolerant, demanding, greedy, and violent, but do we abandon our children when they act that way? No, we try to enlighten and educate them.'

We arrived at the hotel a few minutes after 7:30, 7:33 to be precise.
'What time's the circle?'
'7;30, we're late.'

Making a hasty exit from the minivan, we thanked Saeed and bid him goodnight.
'I will pick you up tomorrow morning at 4:30.'
'4:30!'
'Yes, we will have it the breakfast with the camel owner.'

Bases loaded

It didn't take us long to make our way to Diane's room.
'Sorry we're late.'
'All in divine time, come in and make yourself comfortable. Alex, it's good to see you again, how has your trip been?'

I laughed.
'Eventful, but somehow I think the best is yet to come.'

After we'd taken a few minutes to quickly renew our acquaintances with everyone, Diane got down to business.
'Right then, let's get started.'

As she had at all the other circles, she held out a large clear quartz crystal in both hands.

'Divine Aset, Highest Goddess, we gather here in your name that we may fully re-member our Highest Self and fulfil our true purpose here on this planet at this time…'

Purpose? What was my purpose? What *is* my purpose?

'…We meet in the eternity of this moment to fully embrace and embody the creative Goddess, Source, that is at the heart of each and every one of us. Once again we welcome to our circle, our goddess sisters Pernille and Crystal, and extend a warm and loving special welcome to our brothers and protectors, William, and especially Alexander; we most gratefully thank you both, from the depths of our hearts, for your presence, your spiritual support, and your physical intervention and protection when needed.'

She changed the music on her ipod from background meditation music to the choir of women's voices she had used previously.

'Make sure you're completely comfortable, lie down if you want, close your eyes, and tone along with the sacred recording if you so desire. Once again, gentlemen I would ask that you refrain from toning, that instead you hold and protect the space for the divine feminine.'

As the ladies assumed various poses and positions, Bill and I simply smiled and nodded, leaving Diane free to do her stuff.

'Let us all go within our hearts; fully within. Picture your heart opening like a vibrant blossoming flower; each petal unfolding in grateful receiving of the sunlight, water, and caressing breezes so as to offer its sweet fragrances, pollen and nectar to the birds and insects that will in turn spread the seeds of your intent, of your love, truth and wisdom, around the globe.

In the centre of your flower, the centre of your heart, visualize the eternal flame of creation burning within you. See it flickering as it rises from the deepest red, through orange, yellow, green, blue and to the highest violet light of knowingness and awareness. See it extend out through your feet and out of the top of your head, connecting you completely with, the Source of All That Is.

Now relax your mind, release your mind, for there is nothing to learn, nothing to acquire, your responsibility is to yourself, to *be*, nothing more, nothing less, nothing else.'

She paused for a few breaths, to allow for everyone to fully let go, before continuing.

'Over the passed ten days we have journey to many temples and sacred sites along the Nile, to re-member, to re-awaken to who we were then, and to who we are now, and to who we have *always* been. This has been an often-challenging journey of both re-membering and initiation, through which we have cast aside our disguises so as to embrace the true goddesses within each and every one of us. Without judgment, without fear, we have supported and nurtured one another until such time as we each remembered how to stand alone, not lonely, but without the need to lean on anyone else as a crutch.

Tomorrow, this journey reaches its destination when we enter the Great Pyramid, to face our greatest tests and to receive our final initiation as daughters of Aset. And this we must do, this is a step on our great earthly journey, for Gaia, Mother Earth, will soon be given the opportunity to move to a new level of awareness, and the human race, whom we have loved and nurtured for so long, but which has been preoccupied with power, greed, and selfishness for thousands of years, will collectively be given the opportunity to take a step with her, a step that will take human consciousness from the turmoil of the level of solar plexus consciousness, to which it has become addicted, into the full embrace of heart or life-force chakra energy.

It is time for the energy of the Goddess, the pure creative energy of Source, to reclaim this planet, and this it must do through the feminine, through the women, through goddesses such as yourselves, who must first fully awaken and embrace your *own* Goddess energy before the men of this planet can see it and fully awaken it within themselves; this is why we have all come here, to assist human consciousness on its journey into the heart of the life-force chakra, however not at the expense of all the other lower chakras, but as a new master.

I invite you to cast off any remaining masks you are wearing and regurgitate all that you have absorbed in the past; use it all to wrap around yourself to form a cocoon, around and around until if fully surrounds you. It is here in the darkness you will make your final transformation, for as the caterpillar undergoes metamorphosis into the butterfly, so must the human consciousness endure the gut-wrenching darkness and transition that accompanies transmutation. In this, their time of greatest turmoil, each of you will be called upon to be fearless lanterns that light the way through the darkness.'

And that's where Diane's voice drifted totally into the background, leaving me in the darkness.

It wasn't more than breath later when, out of the void, appeared a now very-familiar star system, the constellation of the Pleiades. From there I was rapidly drawn face to face with the Pleiadean Emissary.

'My brother, unfetter yourself from your human persona, remember who you really are, and your purpose.'

Easier said than done.

'Who am I? What *is* my purpose?'

The Emissary gestured for me to pass.

'This is the path you have chosen, walk tall.'

Suddenly I was again hurtling through space at maximum warp speed, like I was surging through a wormhole, this time towards Andromeda. From there I knew where I was headed, and it wasn't long before I reached my ultimate destination, the Source of All That Is.

'Who am I?'

'This was the first thought that ever came to my being, and it has been the seed of every thought since.'

'OK, but who am *"I"*?'

'You are my eyes, as I am your eyes, you are my ears, as I am your ears, you are my thoughts, as I am your thoughts, you are my heart, as I am your heart, you are my breath, as I am your breath, you are my being, as I am your being, for All is One as One is All.'

'Yes, but *"who"* am I?'

'It is not *who* you are that matters, what "matters" is who you *are*.'

I knew Source was being clear as crystal, and I knew I knew the answers, but, right at that nanosecond, it felt like Source was talking in riddles and I couldn't think of the answers. I decided to shift tack.

'OK, what is my purpose? Is it your purpose?'

'Your purpose relates my purpose, your purpose reveals my purpose, your purpose defines my purpose, your purpose fulfils my purpose, for All is One as One is All.'

'And what *is* your purpose?'

'To be, to create, to experience.'

'And that is *my* purpose?'

'No. Your purpose is to experience, to create, to be, for you are my eyes, my ears, my thoughts, my heart, my breath, my being, for All is One as One is All.'

'Alex?'

Someone was behind me, grabbing hold of me, attaching, pulling me back.

'Alex?

It was Diane. Damn it, I'd started thinking; it pulled my awareness back from the infinite time and space of All That Is into a finite room surrounded by walls at a definable time in definable space; talk about the ultimate come-down.

I opened my eyes and rejoined the circle, which, it seemed, had concluded, as Diane was kneeling before me.

'We have finished the first part of our circle; it looks like you got what you needed…'

Had I? I mean, I <u>had</u>, but had I, had I fully understood what I had received?

'…However, we have some final sacred goddess work to do so that the divine feminine can truly reawaken, rediscover and know itself, and this work can only be done in the absence of the subliminal energetic influence of the masculine.'

Pernille had taken out her newly acquired crystal ball and was placing it on a scrunched up scarf in the centre of the circle.

'Secret women's business, hey? That's OK, I get it.'

Bill and I gave each of the women a hug and thanked them for allowing us to be present, I retrieved my backpack from inside the door, and we left the Daughters of Aset to do their stuff. Heading down the corridor, Bill had a little chuckle.

'I guess they're all going to dance naked around the campfire, around the crystal ball.'

'I suppose so, it's what witches do; the good ones that is, the white witches, not the ones who ride broomsticks and threaten Toto just so that they can get the ruby slippers from Dorothy.'

'And what is it we wizards do?'

'A beer?'

'A beer it is! My shout.'

We made our way up in the lift and back to Bill's room, or should I say Bill's penthouse "suite"; Christ, how the other half live, king-sized bed, lounge chairs with coffee table, dining suite, fully-stocked bar fridge! Outside the window, a balcony with table and chairs, *and*, illuminated by lights, were the pyramids of Giza, seemingly so close you could almost reach out and touch them.

'Sit down, make yourself at home.'

As Bill knocked the top off a couple of beers I put my backpack on the table, collapsed into a chair, and took in the view.

'What a day!'

'You can say that again.'

He handed me a beer…

'Cheers!'

'Cheers!'

…and likewise collapsed into a chair.

That first mouthful after a hot day out in the desert is amazing, the way it has the effect of making your whole body let go. I thought I was already completely relaxed from the circle, but that put the icing on the cake.

'Well, that was interesting.'

'Tell me about it!'

It was just a figure of speech, but Bill took it literally.

'I started drifting off during the circle.'

'Me too, where did you go?'

'England, Stonehenge to be precise, some time just before the time of King Arthur.'

'It must have been on your mind from earlier today; Percival and the search for the Holy Grail, the royal bloodline.'

'It has been.'

'What happened in your dream?'

'There was a meeting of priests, wise men, prophets,…'

'Druids?'

'Possibly, they wore long white gowns like the druids. Of course they could have been Culdees.'

'Is that the Pythagorean Druids you talked about at Dendera, the ones we figured out were part of the Tat Brotherhood?'

'That's them. Of course they could just as easily have been a gathering of Pleiadean Emissary's.'

I almost choked on my beer.

'So you saw him too?'

'Hard to miss him; initially I thought it was the second coming of Jesus and I was getting a personal preview, but that was just my earlier conditioning clicking in. Thank god it was just an advanced alien from a far distant galaxy.'

That made me laugh.

'So, you think your gathering of the Tat Brotherhood was also a meeting of star-seeded beings?'

'Both, one or two were seeded, but most were human.'

'Was Merlin there?'

'Myrrdyn, yes.'

'Myrrdyn?'

'That was his real name; Merlin is just a 12th Century invention by Geoffrey of Monnmouth.'

'I take it you know a bit about Camelot, Arthur and the Knights of the Round Table?'

'You could say that; I'm a bit of an "Arthurphile". Don't really know why, but I've always been interested, since I was a kid; I think I've read every mediaeval text on the subject.'

I took a big swig of my beer.

'You were probably there.'

I could see him running through a list of contenders and weighing up the options.

'Possibly.'

'So, is it true or myth?'

'Both; all myth is based in some truth. The story comes from the *Annales Cambriae*, or *Welsh Annals*, that date to the 10th Century, which themselves were based on a chronicle begun in the late 8th Century that details Arthur's battles from around 516–518 AD, and the Battle of Camlann around 537–539, in which Arthur and his son, Medraut, or Mordred as he is know known, were both killed.

And the notion of "Camelot", as we now know it, didn't exist; there was no gleaming castle of white, or knights in shining armour. The dwellings were made of basic wood and thatch, with a central hall that was the social centre of the community, and the typical dress of native Britons was a simple tunic and trousers.

"Camelot" is just a romanticized invention based on the fact Guinevere, whose correct name was Gwenhwyfar, or as we would call her today, Jennifer, was the daughter of King Leodegrance of Cameliard.'

'And who was Arthur, was he really the rightful king?'

'That's a good question! According to the earliest texts, Arthur was a great warrior who, during the early 6th Century, defended Britain in at least twelve battles from human threats, such as the Picts, Scots and Saxons, and eventually established an empire over Britain, Ireland, Iceland, Norway, the Orkney Islands and Gaul, or France, which, at the time, was still held by the Romans, but mostly his battles were against supernatural enemies, including giant cat-monsters, destructive divine boars, dragons, dogheads, giants and witches.'

'Cat-monsters, dogheads, giants; do you think they could be the ancient Egyptian gods? Is it possible Arthur, as a human, took a stand against "the gods"?'

'I'd never thought about it before this trip, however, given the discussions we've had, it could well be a possibility. You know the origins of the name "Arthur" varies from the Old Irish, "Art-ri" meaning "bear king", and the Welsh, "Arthwr", meaning "bear man"...'

'So it's connected to bears.'

'Except there were no bears in Southwest England in the 6th Century.'

'A good point.'

'Yes, so it didn't refer to the bears on earth.'

'You've lost me.'

'Well, there's also a school of thought that the name "Arthur", meaning "guardian of the bear", derives from "Arcturus", the brightest star in the constellation of Boötes, near Ursa Major, the Great Bear.'

'You mean the same Arcturus that represents the hippo god, Taweret, on the ceiling at Dendera?'

'One and the same.'

'Hell of a coincidence if you ask me.'

'Too much of a coincidence to be a coincidence.'

'So, what's the significance, what's the connection?'

'I'm not sure, yet, but I'm sure there is one.'

Then, as if to revive his memory, he took a mouthful of beer. I pressed him for more.

'OK, but was he the rightful king, was he of the bloodline?'

'Again, before this trip I'd never really questioned it, but now that the "rightful" aspect seems to relate more to the blood lineage of the women, the *sang réal* as you put it, it makes me think. What we *do* know is Arthur was the "illegitimate" son of Uther Pendragon and Igraine, who, at the time Arthur was conceived, was married to Gorlois, the Duke of Cornwall.'

'So, if we follow the *sang réal* line of thought, then Igraine must have been the *sang réal*, a direct descendant of Mary Magdalene, Cleopatra Selene II.'

I could see Bill's mind shifting into another gear.

'Which raises the question of whether Myyrdyn knew that, and whether he deliberately intervened, and if he did, why?'

The cerebral gear-shifting was contagious.

'And that raises the question of who this Myrrdyn really was?'

'According to the texts he was a prophet and the illegitimate son of Morfyn Frych, a minor Prince of the House of Coel, and a monastic Royal Princess of Dyfed, who was the daughter of King Meurig ap Maredydd ap Rhain.'

'So if he was a member of *two* royal families, and a prophet, then in ancient Egypt that was what we called a High Priest of Amun, or possibly a member of the Tat Brotherhood, which would account for him also being an alchemist, a wizard.'

Bill's mind starting ticking over at great speed.

'Yes, it would, wouldn't it…'

Before he drifted off again into another intelligible altered state, I focused back on his experience in the circle.

'What was the meeting of priests all about?'

Bill tuned back in.

'Wow, they were discussing just that, the lineage, the bloodline, who should be king, who should be the rightful ruler to lead them out of the dark ages after the events of Europe and the Roman conquests. But there was some sort of problem, a break in the lineage, and heated discussion as to not just who should be king, but how to *restore* the rightful lineage….'

And then it hit him.

'…Jesus, Alex, it was all about the women, the *sang réal*!'

He leapt to his feet, rushed inside, grabbed a sheet of blank writing paper and pen from the desk unit, sat back down and started drawing a family tree for King Arthur.

'Myrrdyn's mother was the *sang réal*, she had to be, but there was no way Myrrdyn could assume the throne because he was illegitimate, he didn't have the double blessing because his father wasn't born of a women who was the *sang réal*. That said he would still definitely have been raised as a priest, probably a Culdee. It's also highly probable Myrrdyn's mother had other older sisters who were first choice, and my gut feeling is that one of these women was more than likely the mother of Igraine, Arthur's mother... '

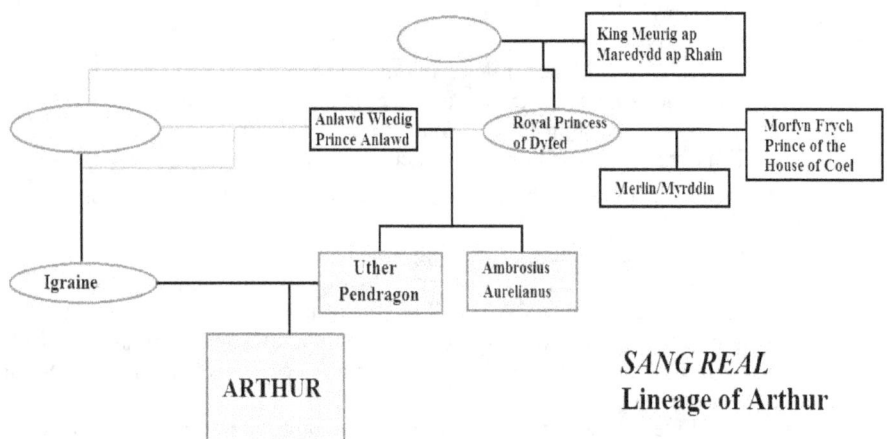

SANG REAL
Lineage of Arthur

'...On Arthur's paternal side, his grandfather was Prince Anlawd, who may well have married into the bloodline, and produced two sons, Ambrosius, who is often associated alongside Myrrdyn, and Uther Pendragon, Arthur's father. But how did Uther and Igraine get together, or rather, why?'

'Even I know that, Bill, Uther had the hots for Igraine, so he got Merlin to cast a spell on her, making her think Uther was really her husband. The spell worked and Igraine and Uther conceived Arthur, after which Uther killed Igraine's husband in battle and took his place.'

Bill was shaking his head vigorously as he expanded his drawing.

'No. No, I don't buy it. Igraine was married to Gorlois, the Duke of Cornwall, and they had three daughters, Elaine, Morgan le Fay, and Morgause, who would all have been the *sang réal*. I don't know what happened to Elaine, other than she married King Nentres of Garlot. Morgan le Fay was the wife of King Urien of Gorre, and supposedly studied under Myrrdyn, meaning she wasn't an evil sorceress, rather she was a priestess, and she became one of the nine maidens of Avalon who eventually took Arthur's body away after he died. And Morgause, who had a son, Mordred by her half-brother Arthur, was actually married to King Lot of Orkney, brother of Urien, and they had four sons, Gawaine, Gaheris, Agravaine, and Gareth.'

'All that inbreeding, they were just as bad as the ancient Egyptians.'

The sudden state of Bill's excitement showed he was clearly on to something.

'Yes, they were...When Ambrosius died and Uther assumed the throne, he could just as easily have "claimed" Igraine if he really wanted her, there was no need to involve Myrrdyn, or rather for Myrrdyn to get involved, there had to be another reason.

I think that was exactly what the circle of priests was planning, how to reunite the two streams of the bloodline, Uther with Igraine. I think Myrrdyn was appointed to make it happen. Then, Gorlois was eliminated before the child was born, so that Uther could marry Igraine before the birth so as to legitimise the child.'

'Wouldn't that make Arthur undisputed king according to both streams of the *sang réal*?'

'It would.'

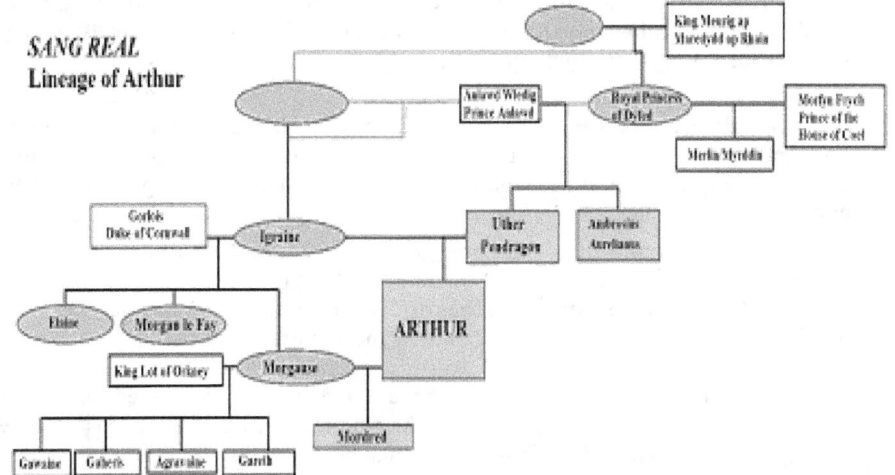

SANG REAL
Lineage of Arthur

'Then, if he was the rightful king, why did Myrrdyn whisk him away and hide his identity by placing him with another knight?'

'With Sir Ector, yes, clearly for his protection; exactly as Cleopatra sent Caesarion away to India in the care of Joseph and Mary.'

'History repeats itself, except that Myrrdyn kept Arthur close.'

'Where was he going to send him, the Roman empire, particularly the Roman Catholic Church, was everywhere, and they definitely didn't want a direct descendant of Caesarion, of Jesus, resurfacing, as Jesus had done in Jerusalem?'

'Do you think Arthur was a reincarnation of Caesarion, of Jesus?'

'It's possible. Maybe that's why Myrrdyn kept him close and tutored him in the ways of the wizards, the teachings of the Tat Brotherhood, of the Divine Feminine.'

'Until Arthur pulled the sword from the stone.'

Bill scrunched up his face.

'Yes…so the story goes, but it makes no sense. Firstly the idea of thrusting a sword into a stone and it getting stuck makes no sense, nor does a fifteen-year-old pulling it out when no one else can. I think that part of the story is all fiction.'

'But it must be based on some truth? Do you think Myyrdyn was able to shift matter, using vibration, to put the sword into the stone, and then only that vibration could remove the sword?'

'I guess it's possible, but, as there are no other records of any such feats around that time, I think it's highly unlikely.'

'So?'

A light-bulb slowly started to glimmer above Bill's head; firstly just a flicker, then more and more.

'What if, just like the Essenes, and the Dead Sea Scrolls, the texts were all in pesher, or some other similar metaphoric code?'

'That makes sense, but what's the real message; what does the sword represent?'

'Excalibur, "he who draws it from the stone, he who holds it, is the rightful king", meaning he has the rightful bloodline….'

And then the light-bulb flashed full strength and Bill burst out laughing.

'…It's about genetics; of course, Excalibur is a phallic symbol! Excalibur represents Arthur's coming of age, of sexual maturity. Arthur succeeds Uther at the age of fifteen, upon Uther's death, but not before a period of challenge and turmoil. He doesn't just walk into the position, there's a time lapse when many others put claim to the throne. The challenge is to draw the sword out of the stone, basically to flop your dick out and prove your genetic lineage.'

I laughed my head off.

'It's crazy, I love it! I can just imagine them all sitting around the campfire like boy scouts, with Merlin the scout master suggesting they all play soggy biscuit to decide who's going to be king, then some fifteen-year-old kid comes along, flops his dick out and says, "hey my dick's bigger than your dick, so I get the crown".'

We burst into fits of hysterics, Bill grabbing another round from the fridge. Settling down, I picked up the story where we had left it.

'So, Arthur becomes king, marries Guinevere and they live happily ever after, that is until Lancelot comes along and upsets the applecart.'

'Forget about Lancelot, he was just a monogamistically-inspired invention of Chretien de Troyes, a romantic 12th Century French author, created as a deliberate distraction to undermine the divine feminine. Besides, Arthur had at least three wives. Lisanor, Gwenhwyfar, and Eleirch, all of which bore him sons, but…'

And he rechecked and expanded on his drawing.

'… come to think of it, interestingly enough, no daughters.'

'So why was Guinevere singled out, what was so special about her?'

'Gwenhwyfar was the daughter of King Leodegrance of Cameliard, and Arthur's second wife, so it may well have been a simply political marriage to keep the peace. Remember, all the written texts at the time were written by scholars, the priests, the very people who would have written what they wanted people to know, not necessarily what actually happened, and they may well have written it all in code.

What's more important is Arthur's relationship with his half-sister Morgause, or Morgana as she has been called in later tellings of the tale.'

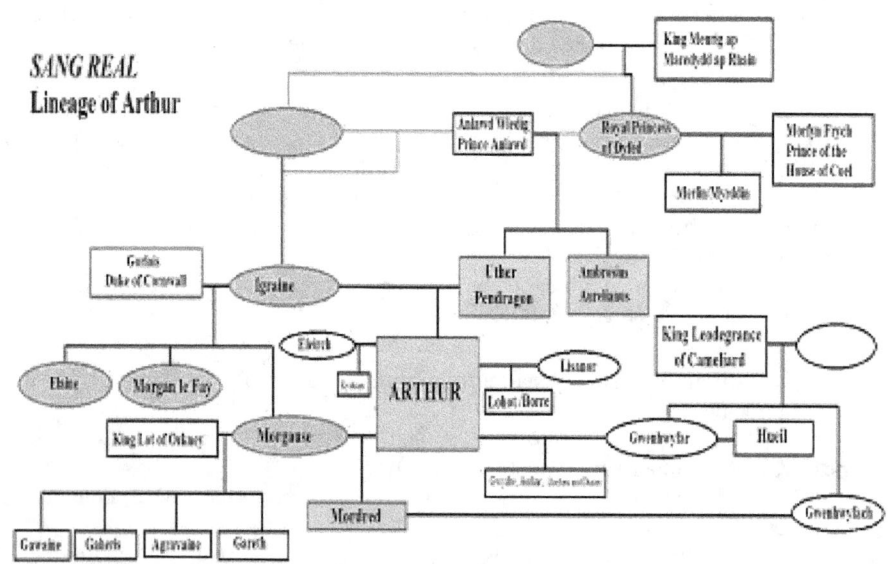

SANG REAL
Lineage of Arthur

202

A thought suddenly jumped into my head.

'Morgana! Bill, I just remembered something. Did you know Morgan is the mother of the fairy king, Oberon, by none other than Julius Caesar?'

'Really?'

'Yep. Maybe Morgan is a code for Cleopatra and Oberon for Caesarion, so Morgana, or Morgause, is a coded reference to the *sang réal*.'

'And over the years the Church, just like they'd done with Mary Magdalene in turning her into a prostitute, ruled that incest was a no go zone and changed the Arthur story to make Morgana out to be the instigator, to be a witch.'

'Like they did with all the divine feminine links and *sang réals*.'

That sparked Bill again.

'Yes…If Myrrdyn arranged for Uther to sleep with Igraine, who was possibly his half-sister, then the absence of female offspring from Arthur's three wives may have compelled Myrrdyn to do the same with Arthur and Morgause, even though she already had four sons. What he didn't plan on was another male child, Mordred, who eventually married Gwenhwyfach, Gwenhwyfar's sister, also *not* of the *sang réal*.

And by the time Arthur and Mordred died, all Arthur's other sons must have died, or not been recognized by the Tat Brotherhood, the round table, as legitimate bloodline heirs, as their mothers were not of the *sang réal* bloodline, so the crown was passed to Arthur's "kinsman", Constantine.'

I examined Bill's drawing.

'And Constantine was probably a younger half-brother of Arthur, a son of Uther but to a non-*sang réal* wife, or possibly a first or second cousin via Ambrosius.'

'The problem for Constantine was, there were no *sang réal* females for him to marry to secure his right to the throne and procreate.'

'Which is why Myyrdyn sent Percival on the quest for the Holy Grail, on a search to find the *sang réal*.'

'Exactly…'

Bill traced it back through his drawing.

'…but it would have been back through Elaine or Morgan le Fay, or if they had no daughters, back to any sisters of Igraine, or even an earlier generation. No wonder it took Percival so long, he wasn't looking for a cup, or a platter, he was trying to find a direct female descendant.'

'And when he finally found her, sometime around the late 6th Century, he took her to the real Holy Land, Egypt, where the Coptic Church was still strong, probably married her, and continued the bloodline in Egypt.'

'Possibly, I'm sure he took her to Egypt, but they may not have stayed there, they could have gone anywhere. The bloodline certainly wouldn't have hung around in Egypt after the Islamic invasion in 639; it could have gone underground, but my logic tells me they would have sought more hospitable territories such as those just across the Mediterranean, in the south of France, with the Gnostics and Cathars. From there it's a simple path to the founders of the Templar knights around 1100 AD, overall a gap of maybe four-to-five-hundred years.'

'So, after Arthur, the bloodline continued in south France, with the Gnostics, then through the Cathars, into the Templars and ultimately the European royal families.'

'It looks that way, and it makes perfect sense.'

'So Princess Diane may well have been the reincarnation of Cleopatra Selene II?'

'I'm not sure; it's possible. What's highly likely is that she was of the *sang réal*.'

Then, an earth-shattering thought flashed into my mind.

'Bill, what if the interbreeding of the *sang réal* had an even bigger hidden secret message?'

'Such as?'

'Well, I was thinking of the images on the ceiling at Dendera, of Taweret and the bull, what if the mixing of genetic material was between the star systems of Arcturus and the Pleiades to create the human form?'

'Wow! All the pieces fit.'

As I contemplated the complete implications of the extended lineage of the bloodline through the bottom of my empty bottle, Bill finished his and, in true Aussie fashion, decided it was an apt moment to grab another round of beers from the fridge. Upon his return he handed me a fresh coldie and flopped into the chair.

'It's thirsty work all this historical detective stuff.'

'Sure is, but, Bill, I've gotta tell you, this has been the most amazing two weeks of my life.'

'I'm with you on that, cheers!'

'Cheers.'

'I do have to say though, I wasn't sure we'd see you again after you took off with Saeed and then he returned to tell us about how the Secret Police were after you.'

'That's nothing compared to what else has been happening.'

'Well, unless we run out of beer in the next hour, and room service goes on strike, I'm not going anywhere, so I'm all ears.'

In between sips of beer, as we gazed out over the pyramids, I told Bill all about Amarna, about the Labyrinth, Frank and Mark, the precision-machined red-granite chambers, portcullises, and pressure-valve vaulted ceilings all over the place, at Meidum, Dahshur, Mazghuna, Zawiyet el-Aryan, Abu Raoush and Saqqara. I shared my initial thoughts about them being part of a sonic resonance chamber. Bill agreed that the internal structures of the pyramids showed a progression of engineering, or different purpose, and that any mud-brick in the structures was most likely repair work done during the New Kingdom. Then he asked a profound question.

'Hey, Alex, I was just thinking, given the complexity and advanced technology needed to build the pyramids, have you ever wondered why they have different slope angles; clearly it was deliberate and not a random outcome?'

I looked at the Great Pyramid and the Pyramid of Khafre alongside, the difference discernibly visible.

'Well, given it's all about vibration and frequencies, my guess is that each pyramid has it's own specific pitch determined by it's structure, the angle of its sides and it's volume, and that that pitch somehow relates directly to its function and purpose; maybe the pyramids are a series of radio stations all broadcasting on separate frequencies.'

As I said it a shiver went up my spine, the hairs on the back of my neck stood on end, and I got goose-bumps all over. Bill reacted as well.

'Radio stations broadcasting to all parts of the galaxy: I like it. Question is; what are they broadcasting?'

'If they *are* broadcasting; maybe they're inactive, offline, deactivated, damaged or short-circuited by the effects of a pole-shift?'

'Or, maybe without their own power source, they only become active when they're in alignment with, and drawing power from, their target constellation?'

'Like with the altar at Abu Ghurab?'

'Yes.'

'And with the Great Pyramid, especially with opening the secret entrance high up in the south face.'

'It explains a lot. I wonder if there's anything about *that* in those papers of yours.'

I looked at the backpack, the elephant in the room.

'I doubt it.'

'You never know.'

We went on to chat about how the star alignments corresponded to the positions of the pyramids, about how the size of each pyramid may have been related to the brightness of the relative star as seen from earth, and that the cult or satellite pyramids were probably indications the star was a binary star. I briefly explained how I believed Abu Raoush was probably built first, as it represented Sirius, and that the pyramids were built when Egypt was once in the southern hemisphere, before the last pole shift.

As we progressed on to our fourth beer, I went on to tell Bill about my ambush at the Australian Embassy, my hasty retreat to the Cairo Palace and timely rescue by Abdo, and how he whisked me away to Saqqara to meet up with Saeed. At that moment the room phone rang and Bill looked at his watch.

'Nine o'clock: I forgot, I've got a business call, might be fifteen minutes or so, if you'll excuse me. Have another beer, I'll be as quick as I can.'

'Sure, take your time.'

With the events of the past few days fresh in my mind, I decided that, before the beers clouded my thinking too much, it was a good time to catch up on my notes, so I fired up the laptop. Fortunately I only had to bring them up to date from the morning, because I'd covered quite a bit of territory through the day, from Zawiyet el-Aryan, to Abu Raoush, the Embassy and Cairo Palace, then Saqqara and Abusir, and finally the experience in the circle.

That done, and seeing I had wifi reception, I downloaded my notes and photos again into an email, and sent a copy to myself, copying Mark in as well. Just as I hit send, Bill wound up his phone call.

'Sorry about that. Now, where were we?'

'I think I got up to Saqqara.'

He picked up his beer and nestled back into his chair.

'Yes, very interested to hear your thoughts on the Serapeum.'

To start with, I filled Bill in on my thoughts about all the pyramids being usurped, how the step pyramid of Djoser really belonged to Narmer, that the supposed mastabas were probably originally office buildings, the basalt at the mortuary temple of Userkaf, the sound of moving rock when I toned in the passage of the pyramid of Teti, and finally my thoughts on the Serapeum, on the massive precision-machined sarcophagi and the chicken-scratches on the sides.

'Apis bulls,…'

Bill laughed.

'…I think the Egyptologists are believing their own bullshit.'

'What do you think they were?'

Bill went into another of his characteristic chin scratching poses.

'I'm not sure; they certainly weren't designed to be sarcophagi. So, my guess is, given they're all made of granite, and so are the chambers beneath the pyramids, that it's something to do with resonance frequencies. You?'

'Resonating chambers the Annunaki used to regenerate their physical bodies.'

'Get out of here! Wow! Makes sense.'

I told him about my experience with Nemo, although I admit I left out the Nemo part, and about Crystal lying inside one and toning.

'Well she sure looks amazing for someone who's really four-hundred years old.'

'What?'

'Just kidding, but, hey, age is just a state of mind, right?'

As if on cue at the mention of her name, the door opened and Pernille entered, Crystal right behind her. Ever the gentleman, Bill got up to greet them.

'Hello ladies, how was the rest of the circle?'

Pernille and Crystal looked at each other, then spoke together as one.

'Perfect.'

'Would you like to join us for a drink?'

Crystal was polite but to the point.

'No thank you, it's an early start tomorrow, I just stopped by to get Alex.'

There was no stuffing around where Crystal was concerned; once she had stated her intention, she followed through. She hugged Pernille, bid her, then Bill, goodnight and turned to exit, pausing briefly at the door to address me.

'Are you coming?'

'Right behind you.'

I took one last mouthful of "Dutch courage", scrambled to my feet, and stuffed my laptop in my backpack.

'Thanks for the beers, Bill; next time it's my shout. Fascinating discussion, as always, let's chat more in the morning.'

'I look forward to it.'

'Goodnight, Pernille.'

'Sleep well.'

And I bustled out the door.

Here's the pitch

Crystal was halfway down the corridor by the time I caught up with her.

'Did you have a good discussion with Bill?'

'Amazing, as always.'

'Very good; then you are ready for tomorrow?'

As we got in the lift and headed down to her floor, I wasn't sure what to say, mainly because I wasn't sure what she meant. Did she mean the escape to Greece, the trip to the Giza Plateau, or something else all together? I took the easy option.

'As ready as I'll ever be.'

The reality was, as we exited the lift and entered Crystal's room, tomorrow was the last thing on my mind; all I could think about was tonight. No sooner was Crystal in the room than she was in the bathroom, had turned on the shower and was undressing. It was at that moment I realized that if I didn't make a move tonight, or at the very least tell her how I felt, that tomorrow was probably the last time I would see her as I'd be escaping Egypt on Bill's yacht and Crystal would be flying back to Germany, there would be no time or privacy to say what I wanted. Tonight was my last chance.

Putting the backpack on the floor, I sat down on the bed and took off my shoes and socks, contemplating my next move; Crystal had left the bathroom door wide open and I weighed up whether it was an open invitation or just a reflection of her open attitude?

I remembered when she first walked on the boat and totally transfixed everyone with her sapphire blue eyes, when she said we'd *"met many times before"*. And then, on the felucca, when she first went for a swim in her lacy dark-crimson underwear, emerging from the Nile with her dark hair curving back over her head and the wet fabric clinging to her svelte body. What a set of buns!

From there, how she taunted and teased me on numerous occasions; watching silently while Candy straddled me then gave me a blowjob. How she frolicked naked in the Nile with Pernille and Yuko, running her hands over her breasts and nipples, and down past her pubic hair to flick the water from her legs.

"I believe it's important to always recall things you have seen", she said.

How could I ever forget those eyes, her perfect breasts, her slender curved hips and neatly-trimmed pubic hair.

As I slowly took of my shirt I recalled something else she had said?

"I am all that I express in any given moment of all that I am", and *"You can wait as long as you want, if that's what you desire, I live the now, and right now I am hungry, very hungry"*.

Finally, there was the time in her room at Luxor, when she caught me masturbating in the shower and *"sized up her options"*, suggesting she *"might be tempted never to get out of bed again"*.

Hell, it was obvious! Not only that, she'd said we'd been together in numerous lives; it was now or never. I dropped my strides, removed my Calvins, and walked into the bathroom. I stood there admiring her as the water from the shower flowed over her head, through her hair and down over her body. She caressed her hair, her breasts; she was truly a goddess.

'Now that's a sight I could get used to waking up to.'

She didn't bat an eyelid.

'Is there something you want?'

'No, not something I want, *everything* I have ever wanted.'

She stopped washing her body and looked me straight in the eye.

'Then what are you waiting for, a written invitation?'

This time it was my turn to do a little teasing.

'No, I'm merely "sizing up my options", after all, I might be tempted never to get out the shower.'

Wait a minute! What did she mean by me "wanting a written invitation"? There was something in what she'd said that stirred something deep inside me; she had a way of doing that, not just the surging blood in my groin, but something at the very depth of who I was, or rather who I *thought* I was. Had I spent my whole life waiting for written invitations? Shit, I had!

I'd been brought up by my parents, or rather conditioned by them, to be polite, patient, considerate, and I'd absorbed those patterns so 'successfully' that I sat back until I was invited, given permission by someone else to follow my own destiny, even more to forge my own destiny, forge my own path. I was often even too scared to ask for fear that I might be perceived as self-centred or even selfish. As a consequence I had not really taken control of my own life, I had just taken the path of least resistance, not stirred the pot or upset the applecart, just gone with the flow.

But was I even in the flow of life? *"I might be tempted to never get out of the shower."* That's what I'd said, but what did it *really* mean, because right at that moment,

I wasn't even *in* the shower; I was like the basketball player on the bench, eager to dribble, eager to shoot and score, but only when you're actually *in* the game can you influence the outcome. Even worse, I was just a spectator standing there with a raging hard on wanting to fuck the brains out of life, but, instead, jerking off; "life" was standing before me, luscious, sensual, exciting, and I was just convincing myself I was part of the game. And then I had an epiphany.

In the early periods of my life I'd tried swimming up river, tried to achieve all the goals everyone else was attached to, fame, fortune, love, but I quickly realized that was a fool's game and decided to follow my own path, as uncertain and unpredictable as that might be, and go with the flow. And, for much of my adult life, that's pretty much what I'd been doing, going with the flow, but with the flow of my emotions, and my emotions had led me downhill like a blind tour guide without a map.

In my previous relationships and marriages I had gone with the flow, believing I loved the women I was with, but now I realized that was all illusion, it had to be, because love is just a state of being, a state of being not determined by any other person.

And love is not the be-all-and-end-all of the universe, not the be-all-and-end-all of Source. Love is just one state of being of Source. Source is not all "Light and Love", it is also Dark and Hate, and everything in between; it is all valid. What colour is a rainbow, one of seven colours? No, there are infinite 'colours' and they extend beyond what the human eye can see in both directions of the spectrum.

So it is with Source; Love is just one state of being *created* by Source, and all of them are totally valid for when they are there; horses for courses.

For a short time, thanks to my false incarceration, I became a spectator of the river, and found out not only what it was to be a spectator, but also to see how others struggled to swim upstream, or how they gave up and drowned, or struggled to shore and themselves became spectators, or how they 'surrendered' and went with the flow. Now I could see it all so clearly, and now I could truly see the river as the river saw itself.

I had been going with the flow, but not actually *being* the river; I'd been carried along in the direction I believed I wanted go, but every now and then had hit the rapids and been tossed to and fro, or crashed into immovable objects. That's what happens when you go with the flow. Now it was time to actually BE the river, to have an intent, to know where you are going, and that it is part of a massive cyclic journey. It was time to carve out a path, not just follow it, and to persist through, or over, or find a way around, any obstacles that come between you are your destination, the Oneness of the sea.

It was like a light globe had been switched on, and it had illuminated the infinite vastness of the dark sea of possibility. Was this why the universe was filled with so much "Dark Matter", was this the as-yet unmanifest potential of 'The Void', was there still so much potential to create? Did all 'existence' start as Dark Matter, which was then illuminated and manifest by consciousness and ultimately, at the end of a long cycle of 'being', is absorbed and recorded in black holes, a cycle of physical manifestation that represents the cycle of consciousness? It was all downloaded and illuminated in an instant, and in that instant, I made a decision to no longer be affected by change but to BE the change, for in changing my Self, my Consciousness, the whole universe changed.

Life changes in microseconds, in decisions made, not decisions delayed or avoided. Without hesitation I stepped into the shower behind Crystal, wrapped my arms around her, cupping a breast in each hand and pressing my erect penis against the crease in her buttocks. In response, she wrapped one arm around mine, the other back around my ass, pulling it closer, grinding her butt into my groin, and throwing her head back, exposing her neck, which I naturally kissed, nuzzled, then started to gently nibble at her neck and ears.

Almost instantaneously her hand shifted from my butt to around between us, grabbing my erect penis and directing it down and between her legs, arching her pelvis so that my penis ran tantalizingly along the entrance to her vagina. I firmly kneaded her breasts, moving to her nipples, pinching and rolling them in my fingers. It was just a matter of minutes and she was on the point of orgasm. Taking a deep breath, Crystal pulled away and turned to face me, grabbing my head, pulling me fully under the showerhead and passionately kissing me. Grabbing hold of my ass, she pulled me even closer, wrapping a leg around my hip and grinding herself against my upper thigh. Within a minute, she again sounded like she was about to orgasm; it was amazing, and driving me insane.

Then, once again, she pulled back, this time slowly tracing her fingers and lips down my chest and stomach until she reached my raging erection. There was no holding her back; she was ravenous, voracious, insatiable. As my legs wobbled under the onslaught, I had to hold on to the wall and curtain rail just to keep my balance. There was no way I was going to last, and Crystal must have known it, because she stood back up, kissed me again, her hand still grasping my penis, and stepped from the shower, pulling me with her.

Grabbing a towel in her other hand, she led me from the bathroom into the main room. Once there, she laid the towel on the bed, then, without a word, pushed me down on to the bed and climbed on top, again grasping my penis, but this time straddling my face so we were in sixty-nine position. No, I didn't need a written invitation; I grasped a cheek in each hand and firmly kneaded her butt, pulling it wide apart and flicking my tongue in and around her labia, teasing her clitoris.

Crystal alternated between her lips and tongue and her hand and spit on my penis, working it like a pro; she made Candy look like a rank amateur. It was ecstasy, and it was all I could do not to explode. Momentarily she took her mouth from my penis.

'Eat me!'

It wasn't a polite request, it wasn't an offer, it was an order, a demand, and I was more than willing to comply. I squeezed her ass cheeks hard and spread her ass as wide as I could, opening her completely up, then wrapped my lips around her clitoris, my nose burying deep inside her. Slowly licking and sucking her clitoris I monitored exactly how she reacted to each flick or roll of my tongue, each change in suction.

'More!'

Increasing the focus and intensity on her clitoris, I also started gently rubbing her anus with the tips of my fingers.

'MMm, Yes!'

I could tell by her groans and reactions that she liked it, so I did more, gripping her cheeks even harder, slipping fingers both in her ass and in her pussy at the same time, licking and sucking her clitoris as I rubbed her G spot and glided my fingers in and out of her private orifices. She loved it, wanting more and more, faster and deeper.

Grinding away, all of a sudden she rammed her pelvis down on my face and climaxed, screaming out as she squirted numerous shots of exquisite juices of love all over my face. That had never happened to me before and, apart from it taking me completely by surprise and almost drowning me, it was amazing.

Now you might expect that after such a bodily fit of ecstasy like that, Crystal would collapse on the bed. Ou contraire mon ami; instead, she pivoted around, grabbed hold of my rampant hard on and mounted me, impaling herself, riding my stallion like Annie Oakley in the grand finale of Wild Bill Hickock's Wild West Show.

Unlike with Candy, I didn't have time to contemplate the possible consequences of any 'nasties', besides, by the time I did, it was too late and there was no way I was pulling out. I rationalized that Crystal didn't look or act like the sort of girl who would carry undesirable micro-organisms and knowingly inflict them on other people. In any case, I didn't think about it for long, because boy, did this girl know what she was doing; with each thrust she gripped my shaft like a boa constrictor, milking me rapidly towards climax.

'Squeeze my breasts! Hard!'

Naturally I obliged.

'Harder!'

I did as she asked and she rode me like a woman possessed. Within a few thrusts, Crystal had a second, and this time, massive orgasm, twitching and convulsing like an electrocuted squirrel. That was it for me, I couldn't hold back any longer, and I exploded, pumping several days of pent-up energy, frustration and anxiety deep within her. It seemed to prolong her orgasm and she flooded first me, and then the towel, with even more of her astonishing juices.

Both totally spent, she kissed me passionately, then rolled off and on to the other side of the bed. And that was it! Of course I would have loved to have gone another round or three, but the truth was, after several days on the run, most of it in the Egyptian desert, and one too many beers, that while Crystal was recovering, I fell asleep.

If that was heaven on earth, then I'd found it. Little did I know what the next day would bring!

Also in this series

RED GRANITE
The Grains of Truth Beneath the Sands of Egypt
I
Abu Simbel - Wadi Hillal

RED GRANITE
The Grains of Truth Beneath the Sands of Egypt
II
Luxor - Karnak

RED GRANITE
The Grains of Truth Beneath the Sands of Egypt
III
Dendera - Dahshur

RED GRANITE
The Grains of Truth Beneath the Sands of Egypt
V
Giza - Alexandria

Other books by this authior

PIAHNA'S GIFT

12 FOOT FENCES

211

www.ingramcontent.com/pod-product-compliance
Lightning Source LLC
Chambersburg PA
CBHW071433260626
47170CB00008B/2700